# THREE DAYS OF DARKNESS

## Peter Hess

# ACKNOWLEDGMENTS

Karen Fulwiler, Laura Cannon,
Robert Hess, Jerry Miss

# CONTENTS

Part Three: The Third Day

# PRONUNCIATION OF NAMES

| | |
|---|---|
| Aaron | AIR un |
| Abiasaph | uh BYE uh saff |
| Abdeel | ADD bee ell |
| Aphiah | uh FIE uh |
| Bezaleel | beh ZALE aa ell |
| Caath | KAY aath |
| Caleb | KAY lebb |
| Ebebieh | BAY bye |
| Eldad | ELL dadd |
| Elishamae | e LISH uh muh |
| Hor-em-heb | HORE emm hebb |
| Isusiss | OOSE |
| Libni | LIBB nye |
| Menna | MENN nuh |
| Mi-Sakhme | mee SOCK meh |
| Mishael | MISH ah ell |
| Mosheh (Moses) | MOE sheh |
| Mugolla-sekh-mugolla | moo GAH lah sek moo GAH lah |
| Neshushta | nee HUSH tah |
| Orusi | oh ROOSE sye |
| Oshea (Joshua) | oh SHEE uh |
| Petephis | PET ii fiss |

| | |
|---|---|
| Pharez | FAY reeze |
| Ramesses | RAM zeeze |
| Salma | SAW muh |
| Shelomi | shee LOME eye |
| Shimri | SHIM rye |
| Shobab | SHOW babb |
| Sinuhe | SIN yu hee |
| Seti | SET tye |
| Tebaliah | tee buh LYE uh |
| Tola | TOE luh |
| Vophsi | VAHF sye |
| Zichri | ZICK rye |

# INTRODUCTION

*T*hree Days of Darkness is an account of an actual historical event. The exact time is questionable, but it is estimated that these events took place around 3,500 years ago, or approximately 1,500 BC, in Egypt. At that time, Egypt was called *Two Lands* by its inhabitants. Though it seems contradictory, the northern part of Egypt was known as the *Lower Land,* while the area south of it was called the *Upper Land.* The inhabitants of the two lands referred to themselves as the *People.* Egypt's kings were given the name *Pharoah,* and the two titles were used interchangeably.

This story took place in the Lower Land, where the Biblical Garden of Eden was located. The people had two names for the Lower Land—the part surrounded by the Nile river was called Kemet, meaning *the Black Land,* so-called for the rich, black silt that annually overflowed the Nile and fertilized the soil. The Black Land was inhabited mostly by foreign slaves, both Hebrews and other exiles, who often referred to their Egyptian neighbors as *the people of Kemet.* The rest of the Lower Land, which was mostly desert, was called the Red Land.

Avaris, the capital city of the Lower Land, was located just off the Nile where the seven forks of the river led into the Mediterranean Sea. It lay on the eastern side of those forks, in the northern tip of the land of Goshen.

Ramesses, the king of Egypt, had recently been warring against nearly every nation that bordered his land, proudly displaying his power and might in battle. The renowned pharaoh was also in the process of rebuilding his country, a project undertaken as much to satisfy his monster ego as for any of the valid sociological reasons. Temples and monuments were erected in his honor, and entire cities were built through the Two Lands. King Ramesses was making a name for himself that he believed would last forever—and it did.

The construction of a huge temple at the gate of Avaris was his foremost project as well as his greatest concern. The work at the temple site was slowed considerably by the unnatural calamities that befell his land and his people.

# PROLOGUE

This brief preface has been taken from the books of Genesis and Exodus in the Old Testament of the Bible and paraphrased for clarity. These passages, which cover many years, have been pieced together to give the reader a better understanding of the story that follows.

Hundreds of years before the time of this story, Joseph, the son of Jacob and the great-grandson of Abraham, the patriarch, was sold by his jealous brothers to a traveling tribe of merchants who were journeying to Egypt. Some years later, Joseph found favor with the king of Egypt by interpreting the king's troublesome dreams that predicted famine for the land.

The famine came as promised. Joseph, who'd been put in command by the king, had enough food stored to feed not only Egypt but the surrounding lands, as well. When his brothers came to Egypt in search of food, Joseph forgave them for their earlier hatefulness. At the command of his friend, the king, Joseph gave his family the best area in Egypt in which to dwell—the land of Goshen. Jacob and his large company moved their families and herds to that new land.

Jacob's eleven sons and their tribes multiplied greatly in Egypt. They adjusted quickly to their new lives and worked the land of Goshen fruitfully.

Later, a new king came to power in Egypt, one who didn't have the same favorable attitude toward the Hebrews, and he forced them into slavery. They were forced to work under brutal taskmasters, and their lives became bitter.

Many years later, with the Hebrew nation still in bondage, a different king in Egypt issued a strange, cruel edict. His counselors predicted that a male son born to a Hebrew woman would grow up and create so much upheaval in the land, he would cause the destruction of Egypt. When the king heard the prognostication, he commanded all male Hebrew babies be put to death.

In Goshen, a woman placed a basket in the reeds along the Nile. Inside was the three-month-old son she hoped to hide from the pharaoh's mad scheme. The king's daughter found the child and decided to raise him as her own. She named him Moses, which meant, *I drew him out of the water.*

Moses grew up in Pharaoh's court, next in line to the throne of Egypt, but his heart was with his own people. When he was forty years old, he saw an Egyptian officer beating a Hebrew slave. In defense of his countryman, Moses killed the Egyptian, but that act of defiance forced him to flee the country in fear of his life.

He spent the next forty years as a shepherd in the land of Midian. There, God called to him from a burning bush and said, "Moses, Moses, I have seen the affliction of My people in Egypt. I have heard their cry because of the cruelty of their taskmasters. I know their sorrow, and I've come down to deliver them from the land of the Egyptians."

Following God's instructions, Moses and his brother, Aaron, went to the king of Egypt. They told him of God's command to allow the Israelites to journey into the wilderness to perform their rite of sacrifice. The king, outraged by such a request, laid an even greater workload and harsher punishment on the Hebrew people. The Egyptian taskmasters became merciless, and the Hebrew people blamed Moses for their increased persecution.

God used Moses and Aaron to deluge the Egyptians with a series of plagues that caused them great discomfort, illness, and death. There were ten plagues in all, and they occurred over a time span that encompassed less than a year and are described in the book of Exodus as follows:

\* \* \*

The Lord said to Moses, "Pharaoh's heart is hardened, he refuses to let the people go. I will strike the waters which are in the river and they shall be turned to blood."

\* \* \*

All the waters of the Nile changed to blood. The fish in the river died, and the river smelled so badly, the Egyptians couldn't drink from it. There was blood throughout the land of Egypt.

\* \* \*

Aaron stretched out his hand over the waters of Egypt, and the frogs came up and covered the land. When the frogs finally died in the houses, courtyards, and fields, they were piled into heaps; and the land reeked of them.

\* \* \*

Aaron stretched out his staff and struck the dust on the ground. It became lice, which covered the men and animals. All the dust throughout the land of Egypt became lice.

\* \* \*

Dense swarms of large flies poured into Pharaoh's palace and into the houses of his officials and into the land of Egypt. The land was ruined because of the swarm of flies, but God dealt differently with the land of Goshen. No swarms were found there.

* * *

Then the hand of the Lord brought forth a terrible plague or pestilence. All the cattle of Egypt died, along with the horses, donkeys, and camels. None of the livestock of the children of Israel died.

* * *

Moses and Aaron took ashes from a furnace and tossed them into the air in the presence of Pharaoh. It became fine dust that settled over the whole land of Egypt. Festering boils broke out upon the men, animals, and all the Egyptians.

* * *

The Lord sent thunder and hail onto the land; and lightning flashed down to the ground. There had been nothing like it in all the land of Egypt since it became a nation. The Lord struck both men and animals and everything that grew in the field. He broke every tree. Only in the land of Goshen, where the children of Israel were, was there no hail.

* * *

And the Lord made an east wind blow across the land all day and all night. When it was morning, the east wind brought locusts. They invaded all of Egypt and settled down in every area of the country in great numbers. They covered the ground until it was black. They devoured every herb of the land and all the fruit of the trees that the hail had left.

\* \* \*

Moses stretched out his hand toward heaven, and total darkness covered Egypt for three days. They couldn't see one another, and no one left his place for three days. The children of Israel had light in their dwellings.

\* \* \*

It came to pass that at midnight, the Lord killed all the firstborn of the land of Egypt, from the first-born of Pharaoh to the firstborn of the captive in the dungeon.

\* \* \*

The Lord gave His people favor in the sight of the Egyptians, so they gave the Hebrews gold and silver and whatever things they asked.

\* \* \*

All the people of the Lord went out from the land of Egypt as God promised.

# PART ONE
# THE FIRST DAY

# CHAPTER ONE

# SLAVE LABOR

The young man, obviously upset, slapped his forehead with his palm and gave a soft moan. *I'm so stupid,* he thought angrily.

He collapsed beside the long canal, throwing his arms up in disgust. Libni, his working companion, seeing the strange behavior, came toward him.

"Shelomi, are you all right, my friend?"

"Am I all right?" Shelomi asked in disgust. "No, I'm not all right. I've been foolish. I have surely brought harm to myself and possibly even to you, too. No, I'm *not* all right."

He sighed and gazed blankly into the red evening sky. Libni offered no response. Shelomi slowly raised his head until his eyes met those of his coworker and overseer.

"We're behind in our work, Libni," he said. "Let's work quickly, or we'll catch the ire of the guards. It's my fault. I was foolish and allowed my own problems to interfere with my ability to work. Now, look. We haven't even finished this canal."

Libni put his arm around Shelomi's broad shoulders and squeezed lightly. "This isn't an easy time for us. Don't expect yourself to think and act as if we were free men."

"Bah! Free men, you say? We are *not* free men. We can't be, but we *are* men. We must be strong for the sake of our families and others. I haven't been." His voice lowered. "Look at us. We sit here talking, and our work isn't done. You know what that means, don't you? It's my fault. I've been angry all day, because I fought last night and this morning with Naomi.

"Why is my marriage dying? I work hard under the threat of beatings all day, and I want compassion and understanding from Naomi in the evening. Instead, we fight, arguing about Mosheh. We can't agree regarding the proper way to teach our children.

"I'm tired when I reach home at night, Libni. I want to rest and enjoy my family, but that isn't to be. All day, my mind dwells on these things, not on my work. Here I sit, angry, wondering, complaining, bitter, and worrying, and I'm not doing my allotted work. Now it's too late. If Mi-Sakhme sees how little we have done...."

Shelomi ran his hands through his thick hair. "Where's Shobab? Is he working?"

"Yes. He's beyond the bend of the canal. We have some large stones to remove, which was why I came for you. It's more than we two can lift. Come, let's put our minds on our work, or, as you say, we may find ourselves at Mi-Sakhme's mercy."

The two Hebrews hurriedly walked to assist their fellow slave.

"What do you think Pharaoh Ramesses is doing now?" Libni asked.

"I hope he's choking to death. Whatever he's doing, you can be sure he's not as miserable as we are."

Libni tapped his friend's shoulder. "Don't be so sure. The plagues have been felt. I believe they've caused Ramesses great concern. He may not be in such a festive mood as we've been led to believe. Have you considered that?"

"Bah! If the plagues had a serious affect on him, he would have relented to Mosheh, and we'd be in the wilderness now, sacrificing. Look around. Where are we? Ha! We're in a muddy canal, deeper in Pharaoh's hate than ever before.

"I envy you, Libni. You believe strongly in the traditions and hopes of our elders. Maybe that's why you're less troubled than some of us. I can't hide the troubles I feel. I lie awake at night and cry, wondering what kind of life my son will have."

Libni saw the deep concern on Shelomi's face. He wanted to help, but he knew it wasn't the right time. They had much work to complete to escape their taskmasters' wrath.

The two Hebrews turned the bend in the canal where they saw Shobab sitting on the large rock, awaiting their help. The three men quietly returned to work.

\* \* \*

The man toyed with his food, which was no longer warm or fit to eat. He drummed his eating utensil against the brass plate. Eating, usually a highly enjoyable passion for the king, had no place in that day's schedule. His thoughts were elsewhere. The powerful road to fame and immortality, which he had so carefully planned and executed, was in jeopardy.

His greatest fear was rebellion. *Would they dare rise up against me? Has this Mosheh, this Hebrew magician, turned my own people so far from me that they would rebel against me?*

"No!" he shouted. "Never!"

Startled by the sound of his voice, Ramesses looked up from the table and out over the short fence separating his courtyard and what was left of his once-attractive gardens. He slouched in his chair, sighed, and clapped his hands once, summoning the cook's steward.

"Take this food away," he said irritably. "The weight of the world has crushed my ability to enjoy it. Send for Menna. Tell him to have wine brought to me. I'll be in my sitting chamber."

The great hero of the Two Lands rose and walked slowly to the room where he preferred to sit when he had much on his mind.

The sitting room wasn't large but was comfortable. Pharaoh liked to retreat there to think. When he did, he was usually alone.

The east wall of the sitting room had an open balcony, which, under normal circumstances, created a pleasurable view the king always enjoyed. He could stand at the luxuriously tiled balcony floor, look out over the short cedar rail surrounding it, and enjoy the magnificent view of his gardens and the beautifully landscaped terraces that spread as far as he could see.

The sitting room's inner walls were covered with blue and gold embroidered tapestries, many of which came from foreign lands. A large cedar mantel was secured against the wall, stretching from one side of the room to the other. Atop it sat trophies, ornaments, and plaques awarded to him for his many exploits and conquests. Curiously, he never remembered that most of the trophies were created at his own order.

He stopped inside the entranceway, letting his eyes move slowly across the front wall, taking deliberate notice of all the honors he had received.

*Were I someone else,* he thought, *I would greatly admire the man who acquired so many magnificent trophies.*

Affording himself a smile, Pharaoh Ramesses walked to the large, comfortable throne-like chair, a gift from an Eastern emperor to his father, and sat. He wouldn't walk to his balcony that day, as was his custom. There was no beauty to behold there. The hideous magic acts, plagues, wrath of the gods, or whatever had befallen him had seen to that. Instead, he would sit in the overstuffed throne and think.

He patiently waited for his wine. He'd spent many hours in that room in recent months, mostly due to the irritable intrusion of Mosheh, the Hebrew. Pharaoh Ramesses felt confident there, amid his many laurels, and he always believed that his better decisions were made in that room.

Had he not determined to attack the Hittites in this room, giving him one of the greatest victories in history? He relished that memory while looking at the mantel. There was the silver sword with Hittite markings on it.

*Cleverly done,* he thought. *Those poor shepherd warriors had no chance against the greatest in the land. Am I not the greatest warrior in all Egypt? Certainly. No one can deny it.*

Still, he was troubled by that cursed magician, Mosheh. Everything was going beautifully until that old Hebrew shepherd started interfering. How could Ramesses, the greatest in the land, allow an unimportant Hebrew to create such unease in his kingdom and within his thoughts?

Menna, his chief steward, arrived as ordered and announced that the cupbearer had the king's wine. Pharaoh took a long drink of the strong, bluish liquid, wiped his mouth on the silk napkin that habitually rested on the chair's armrest, and watched Menna refill the golden vessel. He motioned the man to sit.

"Menna, what has happened to my countenance? Why do I show the strain of our misfortunes? I am Ramesses the Great. I, more than anyone, know that the storm that has come against us is ready to turn and drown our enemies at my command. Why am I not full of life and happy as before? What are the gods doing to me? The priests have no answers. Tell me. You've been a faithful servant for a long time, and you know me better than anyone."

"Oh, Great Pharaoh, let not the things that have happened cause you to forget your great conquests and abilities. The gods will surely turn things your way. Your wisdom and might shall overcome any weapon of the enemy. Come, my Lord, let us drive to the site of the great temple at Avaris so you may enjoy what the world will see forever—your immortality. That will lift your spirits, my king, and you'll rule as you always have, with power, wisdom, and success."

Ramesses smiled. Menna was right. He was on the verge of everlasting greatness. He had overcome more adversity in his reign than any pharaoh before him, conquering more nations than all those pharaohs combined. Why had he allowed that old Hebrew shepherd to steal his joy?

He rose and slowly walked through the sitting room, making sure each trophy was in its place. His confidence increased with each step. What better way to regain his joy than to watch his own great achievements being produced?

*Menna has more wisdom than my counselors,* he thought.

Menna called for the pharaoh's favorite scribe to accompany them. Ramesses liked to have his important thoughts, decisions, and sayings recorded, so his legacy would be more complete.

The men walked to the large circular pavement and awaited the team of golden chariots that would transport them to the city gate.

\* \* \*

Shelomi was a proud Asherite. Unlike many of his countrymen, who, because of their circumstances, thought it a curse to be a

Hebrew, Shelomi considered his heritage a blessing. He believed that the stories passed down to him by his fathers had merit, and at some point in the future, the Hebrew nation would again flourish in another land. Whether this was the time was difficult to determine, though. It was hard to believe they were in the process of being rescued by the Almighty One when they were so mercilessly tortured, persecuted, and indoctrinated into a different lifestyle.

Shelomi married Naomi, the daughter of Admus, due to a pact made by the two fathers. Though many of his compatriots were breaking from that tradition, he was willing to accept their parents' bidding. Naomi wasn't beautiful, but she wasn't ugly, either. She had a *come hither* way of looking at him that reminded him of the stories of prostitutes from older, more different societies. She didn't disappoint him. She was passionate when they were alone, just as her impression gave when they weren't. In earlier years, she'd never been a disappointment.

That was long ago, though. The hours of slave labor they both endured took its toll on their relationship. Naomi worked in the fields only to give up most of her harvest in tax to the pharaoh. Like her husband, she was tired in the evenings and didn't act like a wife to him when he returned from his day as a work slave. Maybe it wasn't her fault. Her life was difficult, too. Did he have compassion for her?

It was too late for that. They no longer even liked each other. They just hadn't done anything about it.

They argued constantly about what should be taught to their son and daughter. Naomi thought the Hebrew teacher at the Goshen school poisoned their minds with too much religious information and not enough common sense. It was, therefore, her responsibility to balance the children's education by teaching them the ways of the world. She took them to every event the Egyptians put on—much to Shelomi's dismay. She drank the free beer available at the festivals, and his children watched her make a fool of herself as she drank.

Over the last year, that had changed. With the plagues creating a major disturbance in the Black Land, there were few festivals. It wasn't wise for Hebrews to attend because of the increased animosity. At least his children were still being taught in school. So many of his Hebrew brothers no longer saw the need to school their children. Slavery had changed many of them and destroyed their way of thinking. Now it was taking its toll on his family, too.

Foolishly, he allowed his personal problems to interfere with his work. As the overseer, he'd been given the responsibility to carry out the workload assigned to him each day. He and his crew were cleaning and making the banks secure for a long section of the canal that was used to move water from the Nile. The section they'd been told to finish was, as usual, a nearly impossible task, but the Hebrews had long since learned that their overseers never actually expected them to complete the tasks they were given. If the job was mostly done, the taskmasters were satisfied, although they never admitted it.

Shelomi and his partners, Shobab and Libni, weren't very big or strong. Even at their best, it was all they could do to come near to the quota they were given. That day, they weren't at their best and were falling far short of completing their work. Their taskmasters weren't going to be happy with that.

* * *

The king stood proudly in his chariot, his head cocked in the air, as he surveyed the work site. "What a magnificent construction," he muttered. "Menna, how does it compare?"

That was a fair question. Ramesses had constructed more temples, tombs, pyramids, and sphinxes than any ruler before him.

"Only a king as great as I could have undertaken such a project," he said. "It will be a memorial to me for all time. The people of the world in years to come will marvel at this structure and shake their heads in disbelief, wondering how such a temple could have been built by men."

"Well said, oh king," Menna replied.

For more than an hour, the pharaoh stood comfortably in his chariot, watching the workers. Still, he couldn't erase the thoughts of Mosheh. *What will the Hebrew do next?* he wondered. *How can I have fallen so badly to such a miserable old soldier? My father would laugh if he knew it. Am I not Ramesses, the greatest pharaoh of all?*

"Menna, who's the greatest pharaoh in our history?" he asked.

"My lord, everyone knows you've done more than any pharaoh before you. You'll be known as Ramesses the Great. Indeed, my lord, you're worthy of even a greater name if one could be found. May our king live forever."

"Why haven't I killed them?"

"I'm sorry, my king. Of whom do you speak?"

"Mosheh and the old one who talks for him. They've been a bother to me, causing much distress in the land. I never allowed anyone to trouble me like this before. Why have I allowed them to live?"

"Great Pharaoh, your father before you thought highly of Mosheh, as you know. He spoke of him often. It's out of respect to Seti, your father, that you've been lenient with the Hebrew."

*Yes,* Ramesses thought, *and I need these Hebrews to finish my work. Killing Mosheh might cause them to rise up against me. They're weak, but there are many of them.*

The proud king didn't fear the Hebrews, but he feared a war against them, because of the loss of their lives. That would greatly reduce the number of slaves for his work force. If only there was some way to rid himself of Mosheh without stirring up the Hebrew slaves. The man had caused a lot of trouble. The king's land had nearly been destroyed because of his magic, but Ramesses wasn't fooled.

"I'm the most powerful ruler in the world! I won't allow those two old, bearded, sand-crossers to take my kingdom from me!" He turned to Menna. "If I allow them to go off into the desert to sacrifice, as they request, they probably won't return. No, I have decided. I won't give in."

Angrily, he ordered Menna to drive on. They moved closer to the temple project. Three armed chariots accompanied the king and followed behind. When they were within fifty feet of the great temple, Ramesses ordered his steward to stop. He leaned against the carriage wall and stared quietly at the temple being raised in his honor.

The great granite pillars were finally taking shape. The men at the top of the scaffolding were working with the facial features, which were finally becoming recognizable after long months of hammering and cutting. The huge structure, which stretched menacingly into the evening sky, dwarfed the thousands of men around it who were responsible for its creation. Blocks of black granite, which would, in time, become human heads, sat atop the two carved, crouching, granite lions who would keep watch over the great temple's gates.

Ramesses was pleased with the progress, although he'd never let the slaves know. He wanted the work completed while everything was still going as planned. The future was too uncertain.

*What next will this Mosheh threaten me with?* he wondered. *The power the old man has shown is frightening, but he's warring against Ramesses the Great. I'll never give in to such an old magician. Never!* He felt comforted by his renewed confidence.

Smiling, he leaned over and issued an order. "Take me back to the palace, Menna, but drive slowly past the slaves. Get close enough to frighten them properly."

Menna passed the order to the head chariot driver. The team of chariots moved forward, driving directly into a large group of slaves and officers who were slowly maneuvering a huge boulder toward the main temple.

"Move! Move!" someone yelled.

Men dived in all directions, sprawling in the sand. Fearful and frustrated, they looked up and saw the golden chariot and gleaming golden crown, which belonged only to Pharaoh Ramesses. His chariot came to a screeching halt in their midst.

"I'll have your heads for this!" he shouted. "The work must be completed soon. Officers, use your whips! Now!"

The Hebrew overseers immediately jumped up. In frightened obedience, they slashed with their whips, tearing into the backs and legs of friends, brothers, and neighbors.

The team of chariots moved on, while the Hebrews and foreign slaves resumed work under the watchful eye of the Kemet soldiers and taskmasters.

\* \* \*

In late evening, south of Avaris, the slowly setting sun cast a beautiful orange glaze over the grayish-red desert sand. As the sun put its finishing touches on the day, the long river behind the slaves seemed to draw all the remaining golden rays toward itself until it danced with flashes of color. Red, blue, orange, green, and yellow lights played joyfully on its mirror-like surface.

But all was not so beautiful in Kemet. The sycamore, almond, mulberry, and apricot trees, and the tall, graceful palms dotting the land, were all either eaten or dried up. The awesome plagues of hail and locust saw to that.

The remaining beauty went unnoticed. Thousands of men, working in the scorching desert, were Hebrew slaves who didn't see any beauty in the setting sun. Rather, it was just another hard day ending, leaving them tired and bitter.

Farther south of the temple site, another group of slaves assembled — quarry slaves, the men who supplied the materials for the workers at the large shrine being made for King Ramesses. They loosened and dragged huge rocks, weighing thousands of pounds each, to the river, and floated them on wooden rafts to the building sites.

The quarry work was done for the day. The slaves were ready for a welcome walk back to the building site at the gate of Avaris, where they would work until dark in the brickyards.

"Move on, there! Hurry along! Stay in line! Move!"

It seemed all the guards shouted simultaneously. The methodical march began.

Among the quarry workers, three Hebrew slaves walked together slowly, enjoying the pause in their long day's work. Abiasaph, a thirty-year-old Levite, walked with Isus on his left, who was shorter than most Hebrews. The two men were dwarfed, however, by Shimri, the large man who walked beside them. Abiasaph and Isus both lived in the community of Benjamin in the land of Goshen. Isus, a Benjaminite, was Abiasaph's neighbor.

The other member of the trio, the large, loud Shimri, was from the tribe of Simeon. Shimri had always been popular among his brethren for his sharp wit. Lately, however, to everyone's chagrin, he'd become more abusive.

The three men talked in whispers so the guards wouldn't overhear them, but for Shimri, talking in whispers wasn't easy.

"Another two hours," Abiasaph muttered.

"No, it's only an hour and a half," Isus replied. "Then we go home to eat and rest. It's good they allow us time to rest. It never comes soon enough for me."

Abiasaph looked at him in disgust. "You're so grateful to them, Isus. They work you until you're almost dead, and you speak highly of them for the rest they give you. Its barely enough rest to allow you to work another day until you nearly die again. Don't thank them that we go home at night. Hate them, because we can't go home *until* night."

Abiasaph spoke quietly but deliberately. "I'd rather they didn't give us any sleep. In a few days, we'd all be dead. Then they could raise their cursed monuments by themselves."

Shimri laughed loudly. "Maybe they'd even bury us in the great tomb we've built. Then we, too, would live forever. Ha!"

"Move on, you filthy sheep!" a guard shouted. "Stop that idle talk."

The muscular black Nubian soldier lashed out with his whip and caught the back of Shimri's ankle. A welt grew quickly, and blood ran into his sandals. Shimri hobbled along quietly with the others. Abiasaph said no more. He didn't want to give vent to his friend's anger, but he couldn't help thinking that Shimri was correctly called the Behemoth. Even in a whisper, his snort could be heard for miles.

They walked on in silence. Abiasaph glanced at the slightly built Isus. He'd never liked his neighbor and had little respect for him. As far as he knew, Isus never made a major decision on his own. Whenever someone said anything to him, he later related it as if it were his own thought. Abiasaph liked being alone, yet it seemed whenever he turned around, Isus was with him, wanting to talk, even though he never had anything meaningful to say.

The Levite wasn't disrespectful. He wouldn't call anyone an unpopular name to his face, but in his thoughts, he invented names for many of the Hebrews and Egyptians he knew. Isus was the *Gnat*. He looked at his neighbor and smiled at how apt that name was. Then he turned and glanced at Shimri, who still hobbled a bit. Abiasaph had given him the name the *Behemoth*, too.

After some time, the men approached the brickyard. Abiasaph wanted to get right to work before a guard caught him. They enjoyed using their whips on the slaves.

Abiasaph walked quickly to a row of newly dried bricks where, luckily, he saw a smoothing stone and chipper. He nestled the tools in his arms, turned, and found a place to begin working.

He signaled to Soft Eye, the old, red, brickyard guard. When he had the man's attention, Abiasaph pointed at the goatskin that hung limply at his side. Soft Eye nodded. Abiasaph appreciated having Soft Eye at the brickyards. He was one of the few Black Land soldiers and guards who seemed to understand the plight of the Hebrews and foreigners. Abiasaph never saw Soft Eye beat anyone with his whip or club, and he seldom spoke harshly.

Someone once said he'd been a soldier in Mosheh's army in the past, and his fondness for Mosheh allowed him to be lenient to the slaves. Abiasaph didn't know if that were true, but he was glad the elderly Kemet guard was there. He was a welcome sight each evening.

Abiasaph quickly knelt on the ground, untied his goatskin jug, and took a long, slow drink of warm water. He had enough left for one more drink. He always rationed his water so it lasted all day. He felt refreshed from the respite, although it lasted only a few seconds.

He immediately set to work, finishing the pile of bricks in front of him.

\* \* \*

A few hundred yards away, Shelomi, Libni, and Shobab were busy repairing the canal, one of the many manmade waterways that branched off the river. It was only a short time until the *akhit*, the flood season, and the irrigation canals would have to be cleaned and strongly banked. Shelomi, of the tribe of Asher, was a very young overseer for such a project. He'd been given the task of having the canals cleaned and fortified by the end of the day.

It was obvious he wouldn't be able to finish, and the consequences troubled him. In the last few months, guards and masters had been exceptionally brutal in carrying out punishments for tasks that weren't finished. As the sun would set soon, Shelomi was frightened of the physical abuse he might soon face.

*It's my own fault,* he thought, becoming more depressed with each minute. *How could I be so foolish? What good will I be to my son if I'm injured? They'll certainly beat me.*

He prayed silently to the Almighty One of his fathers, about whom he knew but didn't really know. *Does the Almighty One listen to someone like me?* he wondered.

He tried to imagine a giant, bearded, old man as large as the sky looking down at him. *Is he angry or smiling? Where does justice come into the picture?*

He'd brought it on himself with his lack of discipline. Had he done things differently and been in a different frame of mind, he would have finished that canal—or nearly so—and would have appeased his taskmasters. They always demanded more than could be physically accomplished, and they didn't expect anyone to comply with such unreasonable demands, but he'd fallen too short of the task. He'd spent too much time thinking and feeling depressed.

It was too late to do anything about it now. His prayer to the Almighty One was more of a wish than a prayer. And he wondered if anyone even heard it.

A pair of storks played at fighting farther up the canal. He wondered how long it had been since he enjoyed himself as much as they seemed to be.

Seeing his co-workers filling a cave-in, he moved closer to help. Libni looked up and saw the concern on his face. "Don't be frightened, Shelomi. Even getting the work done wouldn't save us. Despite what you think, nothing will change the hearts of the evil-doers who lord over us. Let them do what they will. It can't be much longer until we're gone. The Almighty one sees us, and He remembers us. All that has happened in the past year attests to that. Be strong and courageous, friend. Let's do for this canal what we can and be satisfied."

Shelomi nodded. He liked hearing Libni talk. The man's confidence soothed him. The three men worked, their hard, stubby hands racing against the slowly falling sun. Despite Shelomi's wishes, it wouldn't stop its descent.

He looked at Shobab, whose life was also difficult. His father, Zichri, lay dying in misery, and his large brother, Shimri, whom they called the *Behemoth,* was no help. Their eyes met as they worked on the ditch.

Shelomi had been so engrossed in his own troubles, he'd nearly forgotten about Shobab's problems.

"Has the physician said anything new concerning your father, Shobab?"

"No. He says there's nothing to be done. As Shimri, my brother, says, 'The gods of Kemet look after their own, but where are our gods? We die without ever having smiled.'"

Libni looked into Shobab's sad eyes and touched his shoulder. "You're young, and you are understandably impressed by what your father and eldest brother say, but it's not wise to think that way. Shimri's one of us, and we're all together. He's mistaken in his way of thinking, though. We haven't been forgotten, not for a moment. Look at what's been happening. Can't you see something great is taking place in this land? We must take our minds away from our torture and look ahead with hope at the promises that are unfolding."

"I've been trying to believe as you do," Shobab answered. "My brother, Tebaliah, also believes very strongly in the Almighty One and Mosheh's promises, but I'm afraid to. It's easy to hope that we'll soon be taken from this slavery, but hope has no effect. Believing in it and then seeing it doesn't happen isn't something I want to face. I've seen what that does to people."

Libni, along with many others, knew that Shimri was mean and cynical, but he was also Shobab's brother.

"Yes," Shobab continued, "I listen to my Tebaliah and my brother Shimri, and it makes it difficult to form my own opinion. I become confused. I don't express much hope, do I?"

"No, my friend," Libni replied, "but that can change. Don't you see that every day the promise becomes more possible? Every day it becomes more true? Every report we hear, every sign we see, cries out, 'Yes, sons and daughters of Abraham, it's true. Your deliverance is nigh.'"

He balled his hand into a fist. "Shobab, I can believe. Who am I that I should be so different from you?"

Shelomi smiled slightly at his exuberant friend as they moved farther up the canal. They were working better than they had all day, but they knew it was too little, too late. The evening was stealing the light quickly. The cool night air was a welcome change for the sweaty men but didn't help relieve the tension in the well-liked overseer. His dolorous countenance wasn't lost on his friends.

Climbing out of the ditch, Shelomi saw a group of men approaching. He slowly stood and saw there were five of them. He immediately recognized Mi-Sakhme, the captain of the soldiers. Shelomi felt a lump in his throat and knew why they came. He felt himself weakening.

The five men stopped in front of him. Libni and Shobab remained in the canal and watched, fearing the worst.

Mi-Sakhme motioned to the taskmaster, who walked to within inches of Shelomi's face. "You have been made an overseer because of your ability to get work done in a fashion that has almost been acceptable. Today, we looked at your work, and you aren't even close to finishing this canal as instructed. You obviously don't have a reasonable fear of Mi-Sakhme, the captain of the guard force. After today," he said, smiling cruelly, "you'll have a very reasonable fear. Do you have anything to say, Hebrew?"

Shelomi knew his words would have no effect, but he was willing to try anything, hoping against hope that it might soothe Mi-Sakhme's ire. "This canal, Master, has been far more difficult than originally expected. There were many large rocks that took all three of us to move, and it took much time away from other work we should have been doing. We also were...."

The guard held up his hand and shoved Shelomi backward. "Enough! Those are just excuses. You haven't performed and must pay the price."

He called to a tall, Asian soldier, who walked to within a few feet of Shelomi and smiled with pleasure at being given the task. He lashed out with his whip and caught Shelomi squarely in the face.

The young Hebrew screamed then moaned horribly, clutching his face. The whip shrieked again, leaving a large gash across Shelomi's arm and on top of his head. He screamed in pain and terror. Again the soldier snapped his whip across Shelomi's chest and middle, creating deep cuts in his flesh.

Shelomi lowered his hands to clutch his bleeding stomach. The whip struck his face again, almost cutting off his nose.

He heard Mi-Sakhme yelling and cursing him, but he couldn't make out the words. All he heard was his own screaming and crying. Pain absorbed all his thoughts.

Shobab, his mouth open, watched in shock and almost couldn't comprehend what he saw. Though there had been many horrible beatings, that was the first one he had actually witnessed that was so serious. Libni, however, sank to his knees, covered his face, and prayed to the Almighty One in whom he had just expressed his belief.

Only a few minutes passed. Shelomi moved his head slightly and wondered if he were lying down flat or were still on his knees. His eyes hurt horribly, and he couldn't open them. He had to think.

*My face*, he cried inwardly. *Oh, my face.* He realized he was sobbing uncontrollably and bleeding very badly.

Had they finally stopped beating him? He heard someone call his name faintly. Then it slowly became louder. Someone was shouting his name.

He moved his hands away from his face and looked up in time to see a large wooden club crash down on his head.

\* \* \*

Abiasaph heard the screaming and knew what it meant. His first reaction was fear, and he looked around desperately for Caath, his son.

"Get hold of yourself," he scolded himself, aloud. "That wasn't Caath. It didn't sound like him. He wouldn't have screamed like that."

He was certain, because he'd taught him not to. Slowly, he relaxed. It was time to quit. The sun was completely down, leaving the faces of the men around him unrecognizable. He stood and motioned Soft Eye, who again quietly acknowledged his request.

He took his last drink of water, draining the goatskin, and saw the slaves moving together. The day was finished. The guards were preparing to march them back to the camp at Goshen.

As he closed in on the group, he looked for Caath and finally saw his son, who came over to stand beside him.

"Hi, Papa," he said softly. "Who was hurt?"

"I don't know. Be quiet. The masters might be angry tonight."

The men formed their usual rows of six, an arm's length apart, each row an arm's length from the next, and then they marched back to camp. The captains and taskmasters usually didn't accompany them, and that night was the same.

The guards and chariot drivers were unusually quiet, seeming to sense the slaves' solemn mood. As they walked, it appeared they'd have an uneventful march home. The whips were appreciatively silent.

"Nethaneel?" Abiasaph whispered to his neighbor in the rank. "Do you know who it was?"

"Yes. It was Shelomi, the Asherite. They say he's badly hurt, and his face has been destroyed. Libni and Shobab are carrying him. They wouldn't let me go back there. I'm afraid for him."

"I'm sorry." He knew Nethaneel and Shelomi were of the same age and knew each other well. He gritted his teeth and balled his hands into fists, trying to control his rage. *How many more?* he wondered. *Will you kill us off one at a time, Ramesses, you pig?*

Libni wrapped his sweaty garment around Shelomi's head to stop the bleeding. Pharez, the physician, walked with them and tended the badly injured young man. Even those who were farther away in the ranks sensed the seriousness of the injuries and times. Everything had changed drastically in the last few months. There had been many more beatings than usual, and much more bitterness.

Libni was near exhaustion. Two men quietly moved in, the larger one placing his hand on Libni's shoulder.

"We're of our forefather, Asher, as is Shelomi," he said. "Let us carry our brother now."

Libni and Shobab gently placed Shelomi's limp body into the arms of the two Asherites.

Shobab had been silent since the beating. When he tried to speak, his voice cracked. "Where is your Almighty One, Libni? I want to believe, but ...." He began shaking, losing control. "You say Shimri's wrong, but where is your Almighty One now? How could he ...?"

He couldn't finish. His broken voice trailed off into silence. Shobab had never experienced anything as brutal or ungodly as Shelomi's beating. He probably should have looked away, but he couldn't. He saw every lash of the whip, every slice of flesh stripped from his coworker's face, and every drop of blood that ran down his chin to his chest. Massive amounts of blood shot from Shelomi's face and head. Mesmerized by it, Shobab would always remember it.

Libni laid his hand on the young man's shoulder. "I can't explain everything about the Almighty One, but we must hope for His deliverance. We have nothing else to believe in or hope for.

"I'm sorry I'm not offering much help. This is a sad day for all Israel, but the Almighty One sees all these things. He hasn't forgotten us. Maybe tomorrow, if we work together, we'll talk again. Don't lose hope, Shobab. It's our only weapon."

Libni knew Shobab was greatly influenced by his brother, Shimri. He also knew that Shimri wouldn't be able to help. Libni hurt inside, thinking of what Shelomi's beating might do to Shobab, and what it had already done to Shelomi.

He closed his eyes and heard again the terrible sound of Shelomi's screams and the horrible thudding of the powerful weapon crashing down on his head. He licked away salty tears streaming down his cheeks to his lips. Slowly, he opened his eyes and marched on quietly and prayerfully.

"Don't lose hope," he muttered softly to himself. "It's our only weapon."

# CHAPTER TWO

# GOOD MORNING, AVARIS

The northern boundary of Goshen was the Great Sea. Along that borderland, centuries earlier, the Hebrew tribes of Rueben, Gad, and Manasseh set up their camps. They used the rich, plentiful pasture to graze cattle, goats, and sheep. Over the years, many tribal elders became wealthy through their great herds.

The rest of the Hebrew tribes set up communities along the banks of the Nile. The Black Land was dependent on the Nile's annual flood. Each year in the Upper Land, near the middle of the sixth month, the Nile swelled from heavy rain. The next few months, that swell moved northward until its reddish-black silt settled over the land, readying it for another growing season.

The Hebrew tribes who set up their communities learned the art of agriculture from their neighbors, the people of Kemet, early on. They planted and harvested large fields of wheat, barley, and flax and grew vegetable gardens filled with melons, leeks, cucumbers, lentils, carrots, lettuce, onions, and garlic.

Centuries later, there had been only a few changes in the life-style of those Hebrew tribes. They still engaged in the agricultural trade, but being enslaved by the Egyptians, they paid a stiff tax on the fruits of their labors.

Though each tribe continued to divide into clans and families, there wasn't the same degree of closeness as before. Many foreigners moved into the communities. Goshen became a refuge for criminals and exiles. Many Hebrews intermarried with the people of Kemet and other foreigners. Some were cut off from their tribes because of that. Others left their tribes and traditions to live on their own, thus becoming families unto themselves.

Abiasaph, a Levite, who chose that way of life, built a small mud hut where the communities of Benjamin and Simeon joined. There, on a woven mat laid on the floor of his hut, he slept restlessly.

"Papa! Papa!" his young son cried.

Abiasaph rolled off the mat onto the cold, hard, clay floor. His mind reeled under the thought of what had happened during the past few days. The soldiers, always hard and cruel, had become vicious lately. He thought of Shelomi, having glimpsed him when the slaves reached camp the previous night. The sight was sickening. Every day, more and more Hebrews were being cruelly and mercilessly beaten. Many died.

He thought of Nehushta, his wife, and wondered if he was better off with her dead. Would she have been able to handle things? Everything was more difficult than when she lived. Perhaps she could have. She'd been strong in her own way.

Often when he thought of her, he remembered her as radiant and full of life, healthy, lively, jumping and running. Of course, she hadn't been that way at all, but that was how he imagined her.

He thought of their marriage and their early months, filled with happiness despite their slavery and misery. For a few years, Nehushta gave him the ability to rise above the loneliness and sadness that enveloped his youth.

*Youth?* he wondered. *What youth?*

Along with everyone else, he'd lost his early years and had nothing pleasant to remember. He tried unsuccessfully to forget those years, but he also wanted to remember them.

*After all, I can't hate if I don't remember,* he thought.

"Papa! Papa!" Caath called.

He didn't respond or open his eyes. It wasn't time to march to work yet. Caath always took care of the morning chores. When he saw his father asleep, he baked the day's bread, prepared their skins, and awakened him in time to eat a little before leaving for the brickyards. Abiasaph was more tired than usual that morning, so he took advantage of his son's energy. He rolled over onto his bed and lapsed into reverie, but it was short-lived.

"Papa! Papa! Come see! The city is covered in black! Hurry!"

Abiasaph rose from his straw mat and realized there was a loud commotion outside. Before he could get to the open doorway, Caath reached him, tugging at his father's arm to drag him outside. Abiasaph blinked and looked toward Avaris. The sight was magnificent.

Every morning before dawn, the Hebrews awoke and moved about quickly, taking care of their chores in the vital early hours before the guards arrived. Women gathered fuel cakes, made of sun-dried crushed straw mixed with dung, to fuel the crude ovens used to bake the day's bread. Men drew jugs and skins of water and tended their small herds of sheep and goats.

*Prepare the day early, while the back and the whip are friends,* was the proverb they lived by. Soon, guards would arrive to march most of them to work sites and extract another day's labor from them. Once again the whip would be their enemy.

That morning, however, no one gathered or hurried about. All stared toward the great city of Avaris, or Ramesses, as the hated pharaoh named it, in honor of himself.

It wasn't a city that day. Although light dawned in Goshen, the great city was steeped in darkness. It was as if a large, black curtain had dropped from the sky, covering the city entirely. Behind the encampment, the rest of the land was equally dark. Only where the Hebrews lived was there any light.

Voices in the camp discussed the strange sight.

"It's a dust storm, the most powerful I've ever seen."

"No, no! Where's your faith? It's another plague."

"Could it be a trick? What are the soldiers of Kemet planning for us now?"

"It's another plague, worse than any so far. Maybe all the Egyptians are dead, and we're free!"

Abiasaph was suddenly awake. The land around them responded normally to the rising sun. Night fled into the heavens. As usual, the animals bleated and brayed, but the rest of the land outside of Goshen was dead.

People moved around excitedly. Everyone talked. Abiasaph noticed the Gnat gesturing in conversation with Tebaliah, the second son of old Zichri. He was glad to see some of the men had wisely continued with their morning chores.

*The guards and chariots are late,* he thought, *but they'll come soon enough.*

It was the latest in a series of strange happenings over the past year - disease, hailstorms, a plague of locusts, and this. Some time ago, someone gave these events the name plagues, and it stuck. Now it seemed that every time something unusual happened, it was called another plague.

Many Hebrews believed that the Almighty One was sending the plagues to punish the pharaoh and the people of Kemet for keeping the Hebrews in slavery for so long. Abiasaph wasn't among them. He didn't totally disregard the possibility, but he was convinced that practical thinking and wise decisions, based on the circumstances in which one lived, were the only sensible way to behave. When he looked at his world, he saw slavery, beatings, murder, bitterness, and much sorrow. That gave him no reason to rejoice, regardless of what the others thought.

*Well,* he thought, glancing at Caath, *nothing can be accomplished standing around like this.*

"Caath, I understand your excitement, but you haven't taken care of the animals. Where is our milk and fuel?"

"Sorry, Papa. I'll do that now."

"And I'll help you today."

They walked out to the community sheepfold, where they kept their animals. Abiasaph milked while Caath watered the flock. Then the boy filled his water jug, balanced it on his head, and carried it back to the hut. Abiasaph gathered dry twigs and dung cakes for the fire and went to meet his son.

He glanced at the strange sight in the distance. It seemed that the rest of the community wasn't being very practical. Most of the Hebrews were yelling and dancing, celebrating and making loud exclamations.

"The Almighty One is sure to come now. Look! He blackened the sky with darkness. The pharaoh can't get to us any longer."

"Where's Mosheh? Maybe we should prepare to leave."

"There are no soldiers. Surely, at the least, we'll have a free day. We can rest and celebrate. A free day! Praise to the Almighty One, the God of our father, Jacob!"

Abiasaph knew that many of the Hebrews singing such ridiculous praises were also cursing the Almighty One just as loudly the previous day when they sweated under the whip of the pharaoh. He paid them little attention. Sometime later in the day, or perhaps the next day, they'd be back at the work sites, slaving, thirsting, and hungering for freedom again.

As he approached his hut, he saw his neighbor, Isus, coming toward him and dreaded the intrusion.

"Abiasaph, isn't this a wonderful thing?"

All Abiasaph wanted was to go to his hut to rest. He didn't want to speak with the Gnat.

"Abiasaph, you know what most of the men are saying, and they're right. These happenings have been too strange to be normal, despite what some say. Now this. Who can explain it? How can you close your eyes to such things, my friend?"

Abiasaph slowly raised his head until his eyes bored into Isus'. "I haven't closed my eyes, Isus. I see with much caution and discernment, and I remember what I see. My eyes realize that everything they see isn't always what it appears to be. Don't preach to me."

Turning away from the Gnat, he glanced at the black city of Avaris. The brighter the day became in Goshen, the more awesome was the sight of the plague. Abiasaph wanted to think. He knew how precious each moment was, and he didn't want to listen to the Gnat anymore.

"Caath!" he called.

His son appeared at his doorway.

"It appears the guards will be late today. Prepare a good meal. We'll sit and eat well before we go to work."

Caath moved back through the narrow opening into their crude home where he had already started a fire in the center of the floor in anticipation of his father's command.

The Gnat, oblivious to Abiasaph's antagonism, resumed speaking. "I, too, once didn't believe what they say, but how can we deny these things? Isn't it possible that Mosheh could be sent to us as some say? How do you account for what he's done? Think of the frogs! I become sick when I remember them. Even you can remember that smell. No, I'm convinced, that this is ...."

Abiasaph angrily cut off the flow of words. "You're convinced of nothing, Isus. What will you say in a few hours when you're back under the eyes of the masters, and sweat drips into your eyes until it blinds you? When you sag under the load of another piece of rock that's impossible to move, what will you say? When the whip takes another layer of skin off the soles of your feet, and curses fight to break free of your lips, what will you say then of Mosheh and the stories? Don't be like the wind, Isus, swaying with every breeze that comes. Be like the tree that stands firm in the wind."

He turned and angrily entered his hut. He rolled up his mat and placed it against the wall, stood quietly for a moment, glancing through the opening, and soon, his wish was answered, and the Gnat left.

Caath watched his father intently. He'd overheard the conversation with Isus, but he had always liked the man. He was kind, although simple, and it seemed that he liked Caath in return.

As young as he was, Caath realized that Isus often spoke without being certain. By comparison, his father thought a long time before speaking and was respected for his hard work and unbending spirit. Many people couldn't take the strenuous workload, but Abiasaph was strong and set an example for others. Caath was proud of his father, but he was also concerned. He'd never been harsh or short-tempered like he'd been in recent weeks. Caath craved the gentleness that his friends, Tola and Salma, received from their fathers. He'd never seen that gentleness in his father, and he knew he never would.

He could live with that. He, like his father, would be strong and unbendable.

Abiasaph walked to his rolled-up mat and sat on it, refusing to join the excitement pervading the community. He, too, desperately wanted to be free of their horrible circumstances, to move to a new land where they could start over, where Hebrews could be a nation unto themselves. He wanted freedom very much, but he didn't think it was possible or probable. Being vigilant, he noticed how quickly his countrymen deteriorated after putting too much faith in false hopes of deliverance, only to see them fail. He wouldn't yield. This, too, would pass.

As he sat against the hut wall, his son longingly stared at him. Caath saw his father's eyes were dark and not soft like those of a baby lamb. If they could speak, he felt his father's eyes would speak of sadness, misfortune, anger, and bitterness.

When Abiasaph spoke, his dark eyes glared, and his words showed he was a hard, strong-willed, determined, and deliberate man. Caath saw the two sides of his father and didn't know what they meant. He didn't see the controversy, how his father's quietness, deliberation, and determination seemed to war against his anger and sadness. There were others in the camp that did and were concerned for Abiasaph and his son.

Those in camp who had insight saw there was danger in Abiasaph's house—coming from his own mind.

* * *

Abiasaph had been a quiet boy in his youth. He saw what happened around him, and he stored the images in his mind without knowing why. He watched Jubal, his father, closely. As a youngster, he admired his father and wanted to emulate him. As he grew older, however, he realized his father wasn't what he'd thought. He wanted to understand him but never could. His father seldom gave him any time or conversation. He never passed along the traditions and stories of their fathers, and Abiasaph didn't know them. With his father's blessing, he stopped attending school at an early age and joined the slave labor work force.

Jubal, like many others, was bitter. He had nothing good to say about the circumstances of their lives, so he continually harassed and cursed the Kemet guards. That display of anger caused his death at an early age.

Abiasaph's grandfather, for whom he was named, was much the same way, filled with curses and anger. The young Levite wondered if he, too, would follow the mold cast for him by those who went before him. He hoped not.

He recalled how resentful he'd felt after his father's death. His father had been an angry man in his later years, especially after Abiasaph's mother died. When Jubal was killed, Abiasaph became extremely bitter and introverted. He blamed the Almighty One for taking his parents. He was also bitter, because his father could have saved himself if he'd controlled his temper. His abuse of the Kemet guards finally cost him his life. Jubal kept nothing to himself, always blurting out his feelings no matter where he was. He was constantly in trouble, and that eventually brought about his death.

Abiasaph wondered if his father were alive now would he have toned down his anger? The guards weren't as vicious in the early years. They often allowed Hebrews to vent their anger without repercussions. Jubal strained his relationship with the masters, and the result didn't surprise anyone. If he'd been alive now, he would be dead quickly.

In his mind, Abiasaph saw his father screaming and cursing violently after his mother died. He mourned much longer than the proscribed time, ignoring all who offered to help or give solace. Soon, no one wanted to help. Abiasaph remembered, with anguish, how embarrassed he'd been.

His father cried, wailed, and cursed constantly. He became a laughingstock in the community for his constant crying and wailing. He was doing it until the moment when the soldiers finally killed him. He'd been so full of hate, it was impossible for his mind and body to contain it. That uncontrollable anger needed release, and it came with a price. Abiasaph's shoulders slumped as he thought of those early years, then he dismissed them from his mind.

After Jubal's death, Abiasaph left the Levite community to live his own life. He wanted no contact with anyone who reminded him of his family. He and his brother, Adbeel, weren't close, and now he was gone, too. The elders of his clan, although gentle and understanding, couldn't convince him to stay under God's blessing, as they put it.

Abiasaph would make his own blessing. He built a mud hut in the Benjaminite community and began, at an early age, to harden his mind against the cruelty of the taskmasters and the elders' foolhardy promises. He vowed he'd never be broken enough to cry like his father did no matter how badly he was beaten. He would never become like his father.

When he was eighteen, he married Nehushta, the daughter of Arad, the Benjaminite. Her love was a weapon against the defenses he unconsciously built within himself. He was completely overcome by her gentleness and love, but he still maintained his philosophy against believing in the elders. He wouldn't indulge in false hope. He continued working in the slave force but Nehushta melted his hardness. For a little less than three years, he was the happiest man in the Goshen camp, but that, too, wasn't to last.

Nehushta died in childbirth. Once again, the muscular young Levite slipped back into his callous shell. From then on, he exerted his energies in one direction, striving to understand the system under which he lived. He taught himself to survive that way, and he passed it on to his son.

However, even Abiasaph, a hardened young man, was rocked by the strange happenings over the past year. There had been many plagues, and much ado over Mosheh, the son of Amram. Now, it appeared, there was another plague.

Abiasaph forced himself to think in terms of his and Caath's survival, wondering how hateful the masters would be after this delay.

*We'll have to be especially cautious at the brickyards,* he thought. *No talking, no rest breaks, and stay as far from the guards as possible.*

After such events, there was usually an increase in the beatings and number of deaths. Abiasaph would be careful, and he would prepare Caath, too.

He heard the Gnat outside talking to Shimri, the Behemoth. He hadn't meant to be so sharp with Isus earlier. He realized he had been more insensitive lately.

Caath brought him a large drink of fresh goat's milk. Abiasaph sipped the drink, enjoying it early in the morning. That was the best time to drink it. It was still cool and had a bitter, refreshing, crisp taste. Later in the day, it would curdle and would taste rich and thick. He leaned his head against the mud wall and closed his eyes.

"Abiasaph, son of Jubal, get out of your tomb. Ha! Sleep is for the old, you weasel. Come out and see my battle wound. It's a reason to drink the drink of the gods."

The voice was unmistakable. Abiasaph turned to see the Behemoth's large head stuck through the doorway. He stood and walked outside with him.

Shimri, the oldest son of the dying Zichri, had lived forty-six years in slavery. He was cynical about everything. He had convinced himself that for a Hebrew, living under these conditions, nothing should be considered serious or true.

Shimri was large for a Hebrew, with huge legs and a head twice the size of most. His full, black beard was always unkempt, and his large, bulbous nose was very noticeable within the coarse hair covering his face. He'd lost most of his upper hair, and baldness made him appear meaner. That appearance was aided by the many empty places in his mouth where he once had teeth. Those that remained were discolored, larger than normal, and one protruded over his lip. Knowing the effect, he smiled and laughed a lot.

"Abiasaph, put some life into that body, boy. We may have another free day today. No guards, whips, or curses but our own. Ha! Look, friend." Shimri turned so Abiasaph could see the long gash down his right leg from his knee to his ankle.

Abiasaph looked at him in confusion.

"Yes, they gave me one more last night after I left you," Shimri said. "There was no reason. They were just venting their anger. One day, my friend, I'll vent *my* anger and kill one of them for revenge. Maybe I'll kill all of them. Let's go and find the little frog from the south and drink the drink of the gods today."

"No, Shimri. You go ahead. I haven't decided yet how this day will proceed."

"You're always too serious, Abiasaph." Shimri bellowed with laughter. "Your son will die from being serious. Learn to live again. Only then will you have something to teach him. Come, while we're still able. Who knows what tomorrow may bring?"

"Thank you, Shimri, but I'll stay for now."

The Behemoth knew when his small friend had made up his mind, but he, too, could be stubborn. "Let it be, you maker of pharaoh's temples. I'll get drink for both of us."

He turned, still laughing, and hobbled off to find the tiny African exile the Hebrews called the Little Beer Man to purchase, as Shimri called it, the drink of the gods.

Abiasaph went back into his hut and sat by his son, who brushed freshly baked bread with honey and oil, a delicacy they didn't eat very often. Caath placed the sweetened, still warm loaf on a platter with some leeks and cucumbers and handed it to his father. Abiasaph smiled at his nine-year-old son.

"What's the occasion, Caath?"

Caath shrugged. "Even if the soldiers come, Papa, we have a few hours of freedom. That's reason enough to have a special meal."

The Levite and his son ate quietly. Abiasaph, his eyes closed, visualized the day's work. Caath, glancing at his father, wanted to talk, but he knew that wouldn't happen. Caath enjoyed the special attention he gave his father that morning. He just wished things were different, so they could laugh and have time to play.

He didn't want life to be the way his father explained it, but he knew his father was right. That was their lot. The only way to have victory was to recognize it as such. Too many of the people hoped and wished. As a result, their work was good sometimes and bad other times, and that was why they were beaten.

He'd heard his father say that often, adding, "I'm not beaten, my son, because I have accepted my lot in life. I don't like it. I hate it. I hate those who lord over us, but I know this is what I must do. I have no other choice. I know what I must do to stay alive and well, so I do it."

Caath smiled, thinking how wise his father was. He taught his son many things, including not to cry. He overheard many Hebrews remarking about that when he was beaten a few weeks earlier, he didn't cry, even though it was hard. He obeyed his father, and he knew he was better off for it. He had much to be thankful for.

He filled the washbasin with water and carefully placed it beside his father, then he checked the fire, made sure everything was in its place, and took the last drink of milk from his cup.

"Papa, can I go find Tola until the guards come? We'll keep watch for them."

Much to his surprise, his father looked up and nodded.

"Thank you, Papa." Caath hurried outside. "I hope they don't come at all today," he yelled as he ran off to meet his young friend.

Abiasaph lay back against his mat, watching his son bound happily through the doorway. His head drooped, and he soon fell asleep.

\* \* \*

They walked slowly around a vast field. Abiasaph had to admit it was a magnificent yield again that year. He worked hard on his fields and fruit yards. It was satisfying to see such beautiful results.

He stopped and leaned against the slight trunk of an almond tree. He smiled, pulling Nehushta closer and kissing her soft neck. She said something wonderful, as she always did, but he didn't hear her. He was pleased to be where he was, with her beside him.

She broke away, laughing, and ran to the tall palm tree at the edge of the yard. He slowly walked toward her. Wrapping her arms around his neck, she kissed his lips. They sat under the shade of the palm tree. A gentle breeze blew through it, caressing them as they caressed each other.

Enraptured by her genuinely shy smile, he ran his fingers through her long, smooth hair ...

\* \* \*

"Abiasaph! Abiasaph! Wake up, you snoring jackal!"

Abiasaph jumped, then got up and rubbed his eyes. He wondered why he couldn't be left alone, but he walked outside to join the Behemoth.

It was obvious that something drastic had happened in the city. No guards had come. Most of the people utilized the free day for themselves. Some repaired huts and tents. Some grazed their herds, while others mended broken folds. Many were excited, and celebrations were in progress everywhere.

The two men sat by the well. The Behemoth had two large skins filled with bitter Kemet beer. He handed one to his friend.

"Abiasaph, the world has gone mad. Our tormentors are being tormented, and the more troubles they receive, the more hateful they become. I've said it before. If old Aaron and Mosheh are behind this, we should sack them like quail and turn them in to Mi-Sakhme. He would cure them of these games, wouldn't he?"

He paused and pointed at the city. "I wonder what they're doing now. Are they responsible for that black cloud? Do you think we might really be rescued? I stopped believing a long time ago. What's the answer, son of Jubal?"

"Shimri, I don't wish to accuse anyone. I can't say who's to blame. It's true that I don't understand this. I know what I see, though, and that is that our lot's becoming worse, not better. That's my answer to the well-wishers. What we must consider, friend, is what will we do when this strange thing passes? We don't know what that black thing is doing to our enemies. Is it just a cloud? If so, they'd be taking us to the labor yards. Is it blinding them? They'll be angrier than ever. Is it hurting them?

"Suppose, Shimri, they make our tasks even more impossible and punish us like Shelomi. Do we stand by and let them? We can't fight. That's certain. I don't know why the city is black, so I think about what will happen when it's black no more. That's more important."

"You speak like a seer, Abiasaph. Let's make you the head of your clan. Then you can argue against those who think foolishly. Ha!" He stopped talking long enough to take a large drink from his goatskin bag, spilling some down his rough black beard and onto his broad, curly-haired chest.

"Now, Friend, let's speak of more important matters. We must consider the possibility that no chariots will arrive at our camp today. What will we do with ourselves?"

"The sheep fold needs repair. We didn't mend it the last free day we had. If your brothers work with us, we can do it in one day."

"No, no. Bah, I say! Today, we'll drink the drink of the gods. There'll be another day for repairing sheepfolds. Think about this, you labor-loving slave of Pharaoh. If we work all day at the fold, tomorrow we might be beaten to death by Mi-Sakhme and his she-goats. Our work will have been for nothing. While we lay dying, we would have to ask ourselves, 'Fools, why didn't you take advantage of the free day yesterday and enjoy yourselves?' No, my friend. There will be no mending today, just celebrating."

The two men laughed. Abiasaph drank more of the strong liquid and stared at the thick, black veil hanging over Avaris.

"You have a strange way of looking at things," Abiasaph said. "We're trapped in a country that isn't ours, and everyone wants to run away. We don't run by leaving the country, we run by going into ourselves. My father did that in his own way. You also do it. I guess even I do it. We're a strange people, aren't we?"

"We are, and we're being oppressed by an even stranger people. Cheer up, Abiasaph. I have a new song. I made it while walking this morning to find the Little Beer Man. Let me take a moment to remember the words, and I'll sing it for you."

The Behemoth only sang while drinking. That wasn't the first time Abiasaph heard him sing a song. To the surprise of many, Shimri didn't sing in the same voice he used for speaking. He had a gentle, pleasant singing voice, one that was easy to listen to. It was higher than his speaking voice, too. That seemed odd at first, but it was enjoyable.

After a few moments, he was ready and began his musical interlude.

"Pharaoh thinks that he's a god;
He dances with his naked queen.
But poof! The light has gone away.
There's no one now who can be seen.

Darkness, darkness, black and cold
Makes the Kemet men grow old.
They beg us, 'Please, please take our gold.'

The Hebrew troubles burn our hearts.
Our joy is lost in this strange land.
So celebrate a new free day
With the drink of the gods in our hands.

54

Darkness, darkness, cold and black.
They're trapped like quail in the sack.
So let's just leave and not come back.

When the blackness lifts, what will we see?
Will the Two Lands still be black and red?
Will Ramesses want to murder us?
Or will his people all be dead?

Darkness, darkness, full of fear.
Give me a goatskin full of beer.
The drink of the gods will still be here.

The drink of the gods, the drink of the gods,
The drink of the gods, I say.
The drink of the gods, the drink of the gods,
We'll drink to the fill today.

He paused, humming the melody, and then he repeated the final verses. When he opened his eyes, he looked at his friend for approval. "Did you like it? Join in, my friend. Sing with me. It's a song for today."

Even Abiasaph had to smile at the uncharacteristic change in the Behemoth when he sang. "Not I, Shimri. You sing. I'll listen."

He repeated the entire song, enjoying himself immensely.

* * *

Hor-em-heb, the likable former Egyptian priest, walked casually through the encampment. He exchanged words with many of the Hebrews, enjoying the liberty of the free day and participating in the excitement of the moment. He came upon the unlikely twosome near the well of Benjamin: Shimri, massive-shouldered, broad-chested, full-bearded, with his deep, coarse voice echoing through the community, talking animatedly with Abiasaph, the small, slight, strongly built Levite who spoke seldomly and quietly.

Hor-em-heb stood twenty-five feet away, watching the two men, amazed when Shimri suddenly began singing. He couldn't make out all the words, because the large man sang so quietly.

When he finished, Shimri looked up and saw Hor-em-heb standing to one side. Knowing the man had been a priest under the pharaoh, Shimri mocked him good-naturedly by called him God-man.

"God-man!" He laughed. "Come join us."

Abiasaph watched Hor-em-heb walk over and squat carefully on the ground beside them. The man used a walking stick, his leg having been severely chewed in a bear attack years earlier. The wound forced him to sit in an odd way.

As usual, Shimri was inconsiderate. "God-man, if you danced like that for old King Seti, he would have put you in his harem, and you wouldn't have to drag around here using a stick. Here, brother. Drink to the gods with us."

Hor-em-heb smiled and shook his head, turning down the request. "It seems that you're less intrigued by the newest occurrence than your neighbors. Could it be you haven't understood what this means?"

"Tell us, God-man. What has happened?" Shimri asked.

"Shimri, I'm not a Hebrew, but I know your God's promises concerning these things. Surely, you've heard of them, too."

"God-man, don't argue with me about gods. You're much too wise, and I'm a mere slave. Tell me what happened. That's all. What is your opinion?"

Hor-em-heb smiled. "My opinion matters little, my friends. Those who know your God don't offer opinions. They seem to know what's happening, and they understand the pattern of these strange events. Their answer is that the God of Abraham is coming to take you from the land that has borne you sorrow for your children and bitterness for your harvest."

"Is that what you say, too, God-man? Can't the Almighty One deliver us without all this foolishness? If He's such a great God, why have we been waiting angrily without any sign of Him?"

"Shimri, isn't the blackness a sign? I would answer you, friend, with the answer given me by Alumai when I asked a similar question years ago. The God of the Hebrews doesn't do things the way His people do. If He did, He'd be no different than they are. Not only is He different, He's Almighty. That's why He's called the Almighty One. Therefore, He does things in an almighty way. The reason we don't always understand Him is because we, unlike your God, aren't almighty.

"That is also why the men of Kemet can't understand these things. Their gods aren't mighty, either, and they aren't accustomed to things being done in such an unusual and majestic fashion.

"I believe what your elders say. I eagerly await the expected deliverance."

Abiasaph looked at him and smiled. He sincerely liked the white-haired priest. He remembered when Hor-em-heb first came to their encampment and moved into Alumai's house, where he still lived with Libni, Alumai's grandson. From the beginning, Hor-em-heb let everyone know how much he appreciated their generous hospitality. His gentle manner and likable personality won him instant friendship.

It seemed he didn't mind slavery at all. Abiasaph never heard him complain, but he never quite understood why the man chose to live in Goshen with the Hebrews. Once, he held a high office in the Black Land. He had wealth and leisure, two things Abiasaph had never experienced. The Levite also hadn't known how much Hor-em-heb believed in the Almighty One. Though he married a Hebrew woman, he wasn't Hebrew, and it was strange to hear him expound so strongly about the Almighty One and the people's supposed deliverance.

Hor-em-heb's physical problems had taken their toll, however. He was sixty years of age, and his once-black hair had turned white during the last few years, making his red face seem even redder. Although that face showed wisdom, it also showed his years.

Abiasaph shook off his reverie, eager to resume the conversation with his companions.

Hor-em-heb was talking. "...and is it not the same, my young friends, with every other plague we have witnessed? Our captors have an explanation for everything, yet our Hebrew elders tell us it's the hand of their God. Do you remember the plague of flies? Isn't that a good example of what I'm saying?"

Hor-em-heb paused, seeing he had their rapt attention. "Some acquaintances of mine who live in the city told me that the flies appeared suddenly in great swarms, causing much discomfort. You know, of course, there were no flies in Goshen. Did you know what went on in the houses of the people in the city, even in the court of the pharaoh?

"The large flies entered every house in the Black Land. It was as if that were their purpose. There were more flies inside the houses than out, though the land was filled with them everywhere. It was almost impossible to eat, because the flies filled the food vessels even as they were being prepared.

"It was a difficult experience, my friends. The weakest among the people of Kemet became severely ill. As with the other plagues, the people soon congregated into large groups, calling to their gods for deliverance. The gods of the Two Lands demand absolute cleanliness in worship, however, so they couldn't hear the petitions of the people. How could the people be clean in a plague of filthy dog flies? When it ended, we were told that the gods finally answered the people of Kemet and delivered them. I for one know that wasn't the case.

"Of course, if the plague was sent by your Almighty One, as your elders say, then I wonder if the gods of the land were able to do anything at all.

"Not everyone here believes that, do they? I find it strange that your people aren't of one mind on this. You quarrel among yourselves at a time when you should be unified because of your bondage.

"As you two look at the curtain of darkness covering the land, is it an omen of good or bad? Consider this—when it ends, the pharaoh will explain it away. Your own leaders will say it was your Almighty One preparing you for your great deliverance. If this plague is like all the others, you'll still be here as slaves. You won't be able to understand once again. Will you choose to believe anyway? What have you decided?"

Shimri, who wouldn't give in to Hor-em-heb, simply grunted.

Abiasaph shook his head. *The only sure thing,* he thought, *is that no one really knows the truth about what's happening. There are too many possible different answers.*

Embarrassed, he said, "Hor-em-heb, you've asked the wrong man. I don't know, but I have a question for you."

Hor-em-heb nodded.

"This Little Beer Man who sells beer to our friend, Shimri. Do you know of whom I speak? He looks and talks funny. Where's he from? How did he get such a strange name?"

The Behemoth was instantly alert, interested in anything that had to do with his favorite subject—the drink of the gods.

"I can only tell you what I've heard regarding that. Supposedly, the Little Beer Man came to the Two Lands in a merchant ship from Libya. My understanding is he came from somewhere in central Africa, but, when he was sold to one of the grand houses of Kemet, no one knew his name. He offered none, either.

"Of course, they gave him a name. I don't know if I ever heard what it was. Eventually, after serving in his new house for a few months and gaining favor with his master steward, he suddenly emerged with a new name for himself. He called himself Mugolla Who Is of Mugolla and proclaimed himself one with the people of Kemet and a worshipper of the gods of the land.

"I can't tell you how he went about choosing such a name. It's not Egyptian. He's a strange one. He needs no entertainment, because he can entertain himself. From what I understand, greed and dishonesty were his downfall. Otherwise, he seemed to have attained a high place among the stewards in the grand house that purchased him. Wouldn't life be boring, my friends, if there weren't such strange characters as Mugolla around?"

Shimri grunted, stood, and belched loudly, much to his delight. He looked down at Hor-em-heb. "If there were no taskmasters, killings, beatings, whips, tax of half our harvest, and giant monuments to build to the great god king of the Two Lands, then maybe life would be boring. As it is, life isn't boring. It's sad. The little duck from the south, the Beer Man, whose head is as big as his body and whose mouth is never closed, maybe he tells stories while he sleeps."

Shimri laughed. "He entertains us, my God-man friend, and he brings happiness to overcome the life we're forced to live. He can call himself anything he wants. If he changes his name and calls himself something else tomorrow, that matters little, as long as he brings us plenty of his excellent beer."

Abiasaph had to smile at his exuberant friend's laughter. Hor-em-heb wished them well. With Abiasaph's help, he rose to leave, but Shimri waved him back for a moment.

"Wait. I have more to say. After hearing your words of beauty about many things, I have come to a conclusion. We Hebrews have been given wisdom concerning these times. You men of Kemet have been given the gods and drink of the gods. With my Hebrew wisdom, I decree we should drink the drink of the gods."

He laughed and walked off with the two empty skins to find the Little Deer Man again. Hor-em-heb smiled, nodded to Abiasaph, and limped toward the house of Libni.

Abiasaph sat quietly, wondering why he allowed himself to waste so much of his free day.

# CHAPTER THREE

# THE INVESTIGATORS

Eldad stood outside Mosheh's small tent. He came to speak to the Hebrew leader but found his tent empty. The old Judaite chieftain wondered where the man was.

He walked toward Aaron's house, though he felt strongly he wouldn't find him there, either. Eldad wondered if the two Levite brothers were aware of what was happening. *They must be,* he thought. *This plague of darkness can be seen no matter where one is. It's likely they even brought it about.*

As he approached Aaron's house, he saw Phinehas, Eleazar's son, standing outside, staring at the wall of darkness.

"I seek Aaron and Mosheh," Eldad said. "Are they here?"

"Grandfather left with Mosheh early this morning. He didn't say where they were going."

"Then they saw the darkness?"

"Yes. It was here when we awoke. I heard them discussing it as they left."

Eldad thanked the young man and walked toward his own community at the center of the encampment. The other Hebrew leaders were already on their way to meet Eldad and discuss the latest development. Though he would have liked Mosheh's insights concerning the darkness enveloping the land of his enemies, he would be satisfied to meet with the other Hebrew leaders without him. The Almighty One would give them wisdom. Of that, he was confident.

His own thoughts weren't as settled as he would have liked. Of course, they would have to investigate the newest development to determine what it was and what damage it might have done. They had a good group of chieftains. He knew there would be no difficulty with the meeting.

They met and filled the large tent called the Tent of Meeting, pitched near the edge of the community of Judah. Eldad looked around the room intently. He raised his arm to gain the men's attention, and walked to the center to address them.

That wasn't the first meeting of its kind the men attended. The darkness was the ninth plague that struck in the past year. Each plague seemed worse than its predecessor. In some instances, Mosheh informed the elders of what the Almighty One would do in advance. Other times, like the present, the plagues struck without warning and with startling effect. On those occasions, the elders met hastily and called a conference to determine what they should do.

Eldad told them that Mosheh and Aaron weren't available, but they knew of the latest phenomenon. He shared his own thoughts concerning the darkness, and then opened the meeting so others could share theirs.

After much discussion, the Hebrew leaders decided to send a contingent of men to learn what the darkness was. Eldad called on Caleb, the son of Jephunnah, of the tribe of Judah, to lead the expedition.

"Caleb, choose six trustworthy men and learn what you can about this darkness. Has it caused any damage? Are there any injured among us? Where does it begin and end? What effect does it have on the people of Kemet? Why haven't they come for us today? Until we hear from Mosheh, we want to know whether this, too, came from the Almighty One.

"There's much to learn, so be vigilant. When you're satisfied, report back without speaking to anyone. Swear your men to secrecy until we speak with Mosheh. Go in peace, Caleb, and may the Almighty One guard you."

The other leaders nodded. After some conversation, they left the Tent of Meeting and went their separate ways.

Caleb was a young man to be given such responsibility. Although he was an overseer in the slave force, he didn't consider himself a leader. He was a humble man who spent much of his free time instructing and playing with his son. Eldad knew, as did the others, that when Caleb was given a duty, he would definitely carry it out.

Caleb began selecting the men he would take with him. Soon, they gathered at the edge of the Judaite community and started toward Avaris. It seemed to Caleb that the darkness began near the city's outer wall and ran along the desert, deep into the Black Land. He decided to begin his investigation at the approach to the city near the number-four brickyard. Much of the wall area was desolate, but that section was closer to where some of the people of Kemet lived. He assumed they could learn more from them.

He was filled with apprehension and excitement as he walked. He didn't know what he'd find at Avaris and almost feared finding out. Simultaneously, he believed strongly that the plagues came from the Almighty One through Mosheh's hands. He believed, as did most of the elders, that the deliverance of the Hebrew people was at hand. Reminding himself of that, Caleb overcame the fear of the unknown that began gnawing at him.

The men spoke little as they walked. Caleb's mind was filled with questions. They faced the ninth plague brought by the Almighty One, if it truly came from Him.

*How long will He continue to harass the pharaoh and his people?* Caleb wondered. *If this is the deliverance that our father Abraham spoke of, when will the actual deliverance take place? How much longer will the pharaoh's people allow him to deny Mosheh's requests? Won't they rebel?*

The young Judaite brought his mind back to the task at hand. After a long walk, they reached their destination. As they neared the brickyard, Caleb turned to one of the men closest to him.

"It looks quite different at this distance, doesn't it, Bezaleel?"

Bezaleel nodded quietly and stood in awe of the sight before him. Caleb and his men were less than one hundred yards from the darkness, and the enormity of the plague was overwhelming. When they stood at the edge of their encampment and looked at the black wall, it resembled a giant veil hanging loosely over the city, reaching toward heaven. They assumed that as they neared, its real shape and color would become visible, but that hadn't happened.

At close range, the wall of blackness was as black as it appeared from the camp. It was pure black, and it made the young Hebrew men uneasy.

"Listen!" Caleb whispered. "What's that noise?"

They stopped talking and tried to discern the sound.

"Bezaleel, how would you describe it?"

"It's difficult. If it's coming from the people of Kemet, I might say it was groaning or crying out. If the sound comes from the darkness itself, what is it?" His face showed fear.

"Caleb," another man said, sensing danger, "is he correct? Is that sound coming from the darkness itself? It's a very strange noise."

"I don't know. Let's continue and find out."

"Caleb," another man called, "have you noticed that as we come closer, the darkness hasn't lightened in color? It's still blacker than anything I've seen. It also becomes more fearful with every step we take. There seems to be a power to it."

"Yes," their leader answered, solemnly. Caleb moved forward cautiously. Looking around, he saw the fear on the men's faces as they huddled behind him. He rallied them closer, encouraging them.

They didn't fear the darkness, because they felt it was another plague from their Almighty One. Their fear came from the fact that they were coming closer to the city, and they didn't know what was happening. If they met guards and soldiers, what would they do? Would they be more angry than usual?

Caleb forced a smile and motioned them forward. They stepped ahead cautiously, and the closer they came, the louder the noise was.

Again, he stopped, looking at his men in amazement. "It's the people. Listen! I hear crying, yelling, and moaning. That's people calling out. Maybe they're crying to their gods for deliverance from the plague of darkness. I wonder what it's doing to them."

They sat and listened to the strange noises coming from the black plague.

"I hear screaming, too," another said, "and much crying. Caleb, what is it doing to them? What's going on? Can the darkness be causing pain? Dare we go closer?"

"This is a strange thing, indeed. Whatever is happening, it's causing great trouble for the people of Kemet. I don't know why. The voices sound far away, but it's hard to tell. Could the darkness absorb some of the sound? That's possible.

"Remember, Men, this plague was probably sent by the Almighty One and isn't designed to harm us, only our oppressors. Let's continue. There's much to learn, but not so much to fear."

In a few minutes of careful walking, they covered the remaining distance and reached the wall of darkness. Caleb stood five feet from it with his men a few yards behind him. From where he stood, he felt a strong force coming from the darkness. The power was strong enough that he didn't want to venture closer. The men backed away, leaving their leader alone. Since their concern was well-founded, Caleb allowed them to retreat.

He heard loud moaning that usually accompanied the red men's petitioning their gods. *As I thought,* he mused, *they're in terrible agony, but from what? Is this the Almighty One's power I feel? Is the darkness attacking the people of Kemet somehow? Can it be giving off some kind of pestilence such as befell the people earlier?*

He sighed, uttered a quiet prayer to the Almighty One, and stood perfectly still, watching the darkness. Even at such close range, the wall retained its pure black color. He could see why no one had entered or exited it. It looked impenetrable. That helped him make his next decision.

"Men," he called, "I'm going to enter the darkness. I must see what's going on inside. I'll go alone. No one else must enter no matter what. I'll call out to you when I'm inside, so stay close. If anything happens to me, I'll try to let you know. If I can't return, wait no longer than half an hour, then tell Eldad what little we have learned."

The brave man from the tribe of Judah turned and looked at the great trial that faced him. He took one hesitant step forward, and each successive step was more difficult. The power emanating from the darkness held him back.

65

*Is this the power of the Almighty One?* Caleb wondered. *If it is, should I attempt to move against it?*

That thought vanished quickly. He was under orders from his chieftains and the Almighty One Himself. He would proceed.

After two more short, cautious steps, he was within an arm's reach of the black veil. He turned to look back at his men and forced a smile. They were perfectly still, their eyes on him.

Slowly, moving his arm against the invisible power, Caleb reached out to touch the black wall. He immediately jumped back, startled. He hadn't expected to feel anything, but the darkness had a definite texture. It felt as if he were touching something solid, not just air.

He took a deep breath, released it, and turned toward the wall again, moving cautiously closer. Standing directly in front of it, he touched it again and felt calmer. With difficulty, he moved his fingers inside, feeling around, opening and closing his fist as if trying to hold onto it.

"Caleb, what is it?" his men asked. "What have you found?"

"Are you all right?"

The tall, partly bald young man slowly pulled his hand from the plague and looked at it. Confident he hadn't been hurt, he turned and walked back to his men, then sat among them to talk.

"You saw for yourselves," he said. "The power that comes from the blackness nearly kept me from approaching. It's hard to move against but not impossible. When I first touched it, it frightened me. It feels like something other than just air or darkness. It's hard to explain, but it's not just empty air. It's made of something, but I don't know what that is.

"When I put my hand in it, I felt its thickness. It almost seemed as if the darkness was moving. I can only imagine what it must be like on the other side. I don't know if it's a thick wall or if the black continues into the city. If it's a wall, we still don't know why the people are in such agony."

"Shall we report back to Eldad now?" one asked eagerly.

"Ha! If we did, Joseph, we wouldn't have much to report. I don't understand anything about this plague yet. We've learned little. I believe we must go into or through it."

"But you don't know what will happen to you if you do that. No one has yet gone into it or come out. I don't think Eldad requires that of you. Please reconsider."

"Joseph," Caleb said, laughing, "where's the courage of your grandfather? Maybe, like your father, you'll be wise and talented instead of brave. Now we know why Eldad chose me to lead this group instead of you. If he had chosen you, we'd be on our way back to the community now, alive and well, with nothing to report. Be brave, my friend. The Almighty One goes before me. I'll return."

Caleb inched his way back to the plague. He forced himself against the black power until he penetrated its wall and stepped into it. It amazed him as his right leg, then his left, disappeared. Once inside, he stood perfectly still. His first impulse was to move out immediately. He felt as if he was suffocating, but he chose to stay put. The shrieking was much louder, though still muffled. The people of Kemet were obviously experiencing a great horror, but he didn't know why.

His men, seeing him disappear, began calling to him. To his amazement, their voices sounded very distant.

"Caleb? Can you hear me?"

"Speak to us, Caleb!"

"Are you all right? Has anything happened to you?"

"Yes, I hear you," came Caleb's welcome but muffled reply. His voice sounded very distant. "It's difficult to speak. My throat burns from it, but I'm all right."

The men listened, but those were the last words they heard from him for a while.

Caleb was having an incredible experience in the darkness. What he saw, or couldn't see, was almost unbelievable. He rubbed his eyes and tried to make himself see more clearly, without success. Everything around him was as black as it had been outside. He turned his hand over in front of his face but couldn't even see the outline. He felt stunned.

As he stood there contemplating his plight and his next move, he became more aware of the incredible power of the darkness. On that side of it, the power was stronger than outside. It was as if heaven had fallen on him. He felt immobilized, held by that strange grip.

He didn't panic and forced himself to relax. Considering the possible danger, he reminded himself he was secure with the Almighty One on his side.

He attempted to sway to one side but couldn't move. *Whatever this power is, it's greater than anything I've encountered,* he thought.

When he spoke to his men, black air filled his lungs making it difficult to speak and causing much distress.

*At least the air isn't harming me,* he thought thankfully.

Still, it controlled him. He couldn't move.

*No wonder the people of Kemet haven't left,* he realized. *They're trapped like I am.* He considered that. *Or am I?*

He forced his arm outward to see if he could touch anything. After a few attempts, he was able to slowly extend his arm. He touched nothing, but knowing approximately where he was, he realized there wasn't anything for him to touch.

He tried to step forward. The blackness kept him from moving normally, but he was able to proceed slowly and with difficulty. He closed his eyes and quietly thanked the Almighty One. With the God of Abraham, Isaac, and Jacob, there was nothing to fear.

He wasn't far into the darkness, so he would be able to leave fairly easily, but he expended a lot of energy just taking a few steps. He listened to the noises from the city. They seemed distant, but he couldn't tell how far away anyone was.

The people were obviously experiencing what he encountered when he tried to speak with his men. It amused him that so many of the people of Kemet weren't smart enough to stop yelling. He wondered if any knew they could still move. None had yet left the darkness. He didn't know exactly what was going on in the city, so it was possible their situation was worse than his.

He decided to move toward the city. It took many minutes as he forced himself to take a few steps. After going only a short distance, he tired. Movement was harder than he thought.

He rested for a few minutes, and tried again. For the next hour, he moved slowly toward the city. Due to how long it took, he lost sight of how far he'd gone. It seemed he was too far from the people to reach them in a reasonable amount of time, so he decided to sit and listen awhile.

Even sitting down was a strange experience. At that closer distance, and being in the darkness, he could more easily discern what was being said. He listened for many minutes and heard many people cursing. He heard Mosheh's name mentioned with animosity several times. It was obvious the people of Kemet weren't having a good time. They petitioned their gods, and some of their words were tinged with anger and fear.

Caleb was a brave young man, but he determined he'd gone far enough. If he went too far, his life might be in danger. He stood, turned around, and started back the way he came.

It took a few hours, and when he finally reached the end of the black plague, there was no warning whatsoever. Suddenly, his foot left the darkness, and he was outside.

His men watched incredulously as a foot, then a leg suddenly appeared from the black wall. When Caleb was completely out, he walked slowly back to his men and sat down feeling very tired.

"Are you all right? Were you hurt?"

"No, I'm fine. Let me rest a moment. Then I'll tell you what happened."

"You almost fell over when you came out. What happened? You looked like someone was pushing you."

"No. I met no one. The darkness is difficult." He took a brief rest, and then said, "Moving against it requires much effort. That's why I almost fell when I came out. I feel as if I had just completed a full day's work at the quarries. The darkness is almost impossible to penetrate. It's a fearsome power."

He rested for a few more minutes, and then related his experiences and what he decided while in the blackness.

"What will Ramesses do when this plague lifts? Will it be worse for us again?"

"Yes, brothers," Caleb answered. "I fear that when this is over, it will be worse than ever. It probably doesn't matter what this plague is or how it affects the Egyptians. The pharaoh will be so angry and frustrated, that no matter what happened to him, he will want to retaliate. That will be very difficult for us."

"Well?" Belazeel asked. "Shall we report?"

"I've learned enough to give a report. This is definitely the Almighty One's work. There are people trapped in there, and they are very bitter. It's extremely difficult to move or speak, but it can be done with patience. That's all I know, but it's more than our chieftains know.

"Let me rest a little longer, then we'll walk along the edge of the darkness before returning. I've seen enough of this plague for a while."

Caleb's men did as he suggested. They regrouped, investigated a little more, and walked back toward Judah, where Eldad and a small group of elders waited patiently. The return trek was less fearful for the men, but it also had less laughter. Many were filled with wonder and doubt. They knew enough not to want to investigate further. Each had plans for what he wanted to do with his free day.

# CHAPTER FOUR

# THE GNAT

After leaving Abiasaph, Isus walked back to his house, though he didn't go inside. He wasn't ready for Tirzah, his wife. He wanted to think. He walked to the sheepfold and sat beside the gate. Most of the people in the community were still excited over the new plague. They didn't notice the Gnat sitting alone.

It had always been that way. No one liked him. In a much later time, he would have been called mildly retarded. He desperately tried to absorb the words of wisdom he heard from the men he worked with or lived near. He excitedly tried to display that wisdom for others, but it never came out right. His thoughts, more often than not, were desultory. Sometimes, others teased him. Most often, they just ignored him. No one liked him very much.

Isus, a Benjaminite, was short and slight. He wasn't strong, but he didn't shirk his responsibilities on the work force. That, at least, earned him some respect from the other Hebrew slaves. After marrying Tirzah, he, with the help of the men of Benjamin, built the small hut in which he still lived. Forty-four years old, he wondered if any of the decisions he'd made in life were the correct ones. Nothing had turned out right. He wasn't popular as a young man, and he reluctantly learned to keep to himself.

He married in his thirty-fourth year, hoping marriage would bring him out of his shell and gain him some consideration from the community. That didn't happen. Ten years wasn't that long, but he sometimes felt he'd been married forever.

Abiasaph, the Levite, was already living in the hut beside him when Isus moved in. They'd been neighbors for ten years, but they weren't close.

He wondered about his neighbor. It wasn't normal for him to speak sharply like he had earlier. *Is it possible he sees some truth in the things I said?* the Gnat wondered. *Could his pride have kept him from admitting it? I'm right about the plagues. I'm sure of it. Too many others in camp believe the same thing. This plague is from the Almighty One. Abiasaph has strong ideas about our bondage, too. He forces them on young Caath.*

That disturbed Isus. He felt deep love for the boy. He couldn't give his love to his own son, because Tirzah was barren. He loved his neighbor's son and believed Abiasaph was destroying him. He was teaching the boy to be hopeless, but there was nothing Isus could do about that. Caath would never believe anything that disagreed with his father, so it was useless to talk to him. If Isus reached out to him with truth and guidance, it had to come through Abiasaph, and that wouldn't be easy. Gnat's neighbor was a stubborn donkey.

Tebaliah's old, scraggly sheepdog ambled slowly up to the Gnat and brushed against him. The Gnat turned his head and looked at the sad animal.

"Have you seen the latest plague, old friend? It's the Almighty One come to rescue us, and you, too, from the Egyptians. I've contemplated this all night, and that's my decision on it.

"So what should we do, you ask?

"You've come to the right person. It's good I can give you some of my valuable time. Pay heed. Stop trying to better your situation with our enemies. It won't look good for you if the others see you making a place for yourself in the houses of Kemet.

"What? What did you say?

"Yes, that's certainly a change from what we once thought, isn't it, old friend?"

The old dog raised its head, cocked it, blinked, and turned to walk out of hearing range. He lay down and closed his eyes. Even the animals didn't want to listen to the Gnat.

Isus crossed his legs and sat staring at the lifeless city. He listened to many people and heard many different thoughts about their situation. He wondered if he figured it out right.

*How fortunate for Tirzah that I'm wise enough to consider the various theories and can pick the truth from among them.* Although he allowed himself such generous thoughts, he knew Tirzah disagreed. She didn't respect him for his wisdom or for anything else. She didn't even like him. *Well, I don't really like you, either.* Still, he put up with her and knew he would continue to.

He wished he could walk into his hut, clap his hands for her attention, and say, "Tirzah, I have the final, absolute truth. Listen to me."

*That would do it,* he thought. *If I have the truth, I can gain her respect and that of the rest of the community.*

As much as that would answer his problems, it presented another problem of its own—what was the truth? As soon as he thought he had it, someone else came up with another theory, and he would become lost in considering it.

He sighed. Heavy thinking tired him. He wasn't accomplishing anything. *Oh, well, the chieftains will determine what we do, regardless of what I think. What does it matter?* He remembered hearing Shimri say the same thing. Was it true? He didn't know.

"Why should so few make such important decisions for so many?" Shimri had asked.

The Gnat agreed.

Those thoughts and others whirled in his mind. He wanted everything to fall into place to give him understanding. The more he thought about things and tried to find clarity, the more confused he became.

He moved away from the sheep gate as Tebaliah moved his herd out of the fold.

The young shepherd smiled at him. "Good day, Isus." Tebaliah was always polite and courteous.

The Gnat grunted a reply. He watched the Simeonite intently, noticing his care for his sheep. As Tebaliah moved down the path, the Gnat resumed his sitting position, leaning against a corner post, looking feeble, his hands clasped loosely in his lap, his shoulders

sagging under his burden. He placed his head in a comfortable position, closed his eyes, and allowed himself a few minutes of fantasy.

* * *

"Good day, Tirzah. May we come in, please?"

"Oh, it's Eldad and Aphiah. What brings you learned, esteemed
elders to my humble home?"

"Tirzah, we've come to seek the wisdom of your blessed husband,
but we see he isn't here."

"No, my lords. Isus was called to the house of the pharaoh, the
great Ramesses himself, just today. Didn't you see the parade? He
rode into the city on a golden chariot sent by the pharaoh to retrieve
him. They, too, hope he can solve a problem they're having. I don't
know the nature of it, honored chieftains, but I'm sure he'll return
this evening. I'll tell him of your request."

"Has Mosheh been to visit him lately?"

"Why, yes. He and Aaron spent considerable time with him
yesterday. Of course, they wanted his opinion about the terrible
plagues that have fallen upon the land. It was clear they were very
satisfied when they left. My wonderful Isus was able to calm them,
and he freely granted his wisdom."

"Thank you, Tirzah, most fortunate of wives. If you would please
mention to Isus that we've been here, then when he has rested after
his return, he can send for us, so we, too, can partake of his excellent
wisdom. May your house be blessed this day."

* * *

The Gnat smiled broadly. He opened his eyes to see if anyone
was watching, but he was alone. Then he saw Shimri coming up the
path. The Gnat stood and walked hurriedly over to intercept Zichri's
eldest son.

"Shimri! How's your father this day?"

"If I said he was dead or wrestling with Hupham, the lion, what
difference would it make? Little Gnat, you buzz just to hear yourself make noise. You aren't concerned about my father. What if I

asked you how your wonderful Tirzah was today? What would you think? You'd think I'm interested in your large-bellied woman! No. Enough meaningless talk."

He laughed and slapped the Gnat's back hard, knocking him down.

"Why aren't you celebrating, Gnat? Don't you know this is a free day?"

Isus forced a laugh, knowing Shimri joked with everyone. "Shimri, my friend, I have almost forgotten about that. Has anyone decided what's happening? What's causing the frightful thing over the city?"

"Frightful? There's nothing frightful about it. It's surely just a large sandstorm blowing in from the desert, or maybe one of those thousands of gods decided he wasn't being worshipped properly. Possibly his tomb isn't big enough, and he became angry enough to kick up a dust storm such as the red men have never seen before."

Although Shimri knew that was possible, he didn't really believe it. He knew that the Gnat would cling to everything he said, though, so he tried to speak seriously, which wasn't easy. It was difficult not to laugh as he created his story. He'd heard enough about the gods of Kemet from the Beer Man and also from his former wife, a foreigner from Kemet, to create a story that would put Isus' mind in complete turmoil. He relished the idea and quickly gathered his thoughts. After a brief pause for effect, he began.

"Isus, I've spoken with Little Beer Man, Mugolla-sekh-mugolla, the dwarf, and the old red extortionist who lives in the community of criminals. They're sure that the gods killed King Seti, because he began building that great city for himself. The sun god, Re, and his love goddess, Hathor, commanded him to rebuild the city and fill it with large temples and tombs so they could spend eternity there. Seti, as we know, didn't obey this command. He served the god Osiris and provoked the others to jealousy. They vowed vengeance.

"We saw what happened to King Seti. He lives forever in an unfinished tomb. We contend with his son, Ramesses, and he's been more forbidding than Seti. The gods Re and Hathor have watched and waited patiently as Ramesses and his beautiful queen Nefertari have taken the land for themselves.

"You know that everything we build gives honor to Ramesses. He's become a giant in the world. We've heard of the battles between him and the Hittites. That fool of a king has moved into the land beyond the desert. It's said he has decided to conquer the world and has proclaimed himself a god greater than the gods of the land.

"He forgot about the jealous gods of his father and their promise of vengeance. Re, the bright god of the sun, and his beautiful Hathor, queen of all that brings joy to men's hearts, have filled themselves with hatred. They covered the land with plagues—rain falling in blocks, filth and famine, weeping, and death. But through all this, the blind, heartless Ramesses sees only his naked Nefertari dancing before him.

"In the heat of their anger, Re and Hathor have lifted every grain of sand from the desert floor and have tossed them into the wind to be blown through the land for a season. They tossed them into the sun to block its light. That's the cause of the darkness. So you see, there's no mystery. You just need to understand the gods."

The Gnat was stunned. That was an entirely different view than anything he'd heard Shimri express before. He spoke carefully. "Where'd you learn this? What effect does it have on the elders' words, that the people of Kemet and all their many gods are false and shouldn't be considered by us?"

"True, Isus, but look how many Hebrews have adopted the people's style of worship and joined it with our own, which was handed down to us by our fathers. One's right, and the others wrong, so our elders say, yet we've joined them.

"What has the God of Abraham said about that? Nothing, Gnat. The red people don't believe in our God of Abraham, Isaac, and Jacob. Our elders don't believe in the gods of the land, but if there are gods at all, then the gods of Kemet are the more powerful ones. There are more of them. If gods are responsible for these plagues, then it must be the jealous gods who are causing them. Let them fight. We need the relief from our burdens."

The Behemoth paused, proudly laying his ill-conceived story to rest. He walked away, leaving the Gnat with his mouth open.

Isus was deep in thought. He would have to put aside his previous conclusions and consider the new information. Why did things have to be so difficult?

He stood in the path for a long time, trying to make sense of his swirling thoughts, but he failed. He needed more time. Finally, he walked into his small hut and sat by the fire pit. Tirzah had started the day's baking earlier, but then gave it up and slept noisily a few feet away. He refueled the fire and absentmindedly continued making bread.

He knew there was a possibility that Shimri wasn't telling the truth. *Shimri lies so often,* he thought. *But he did repeat the words that Little Beer Man said earlier. Now I must consider the possibility that the gods of Kemet are pouring out their anger upon their own land. That would certainly explain why we're being spared.*

What a magnificent theory that was! The Gnat wanted to explain it to someone right away, but he had to think it through more clearly. He had to reconcile this new knowledge with the fact that the Hebrew God was responsible for all the things that had happened.

"How can I do that?" he muttered, the enormity of the task almost more than he could bear. He felt the pressure in his mind rise to a breaking point. He hated it when he couldn't control his thoughts. It was frustrating when they got out of hand. His head hurt. His thoughts became chimerical.

He walked to the door, and Tirzah stirred behind him. He knew by her groaning that she was awake.

"Isus," she moaned, "how miserable I am. If only I could have some peace in my suffering. Bring me bread to eat, Isus. I must have strength. Bring me your skin of milk."

He quietly gathered a platter of unleavened bread and his skin of milk and gave them to his wife.

"Pour the milk into the cup for me, Isus. Can't you see I'm ill?"

He obediently poured the cup and handed it to his overweight wife.

"Every day while you work in the sunshine and enjoy the companionship of men, I rot away in this ugly house of mud. I'm too weak to work or get help when I need it. Today, you're finally here to care for me, and I have to yell at you to get anything. Is that how much you care, Isus?"

He didn't bother reminding her that despite her constant complaints of illness, she always took part in every Kemet celebration. Though they were in bondage to the pharaoh, the Hebrews were still invited to the feasts and celebrations in the city. Tirzah hadn't missed one yet. She filled herself on the wonderful food that was given away.

He was content to let her rant. He'd stopped listening years earlier, though he still waited on her, which was easier than arguing.

Isus thought about the early years of his marriage. Their union began gloriously, but that hadn't lasted. It was obvious early on that Tirzah wouldn't produce a child. Her barrenness became an embarrassment to both of them. She began making up illnesses, none of which could be verified by the physicians, and she wanted everyone to feel sorry for her. She spent most of her day eating and was soon very overweight, and soon her imagined illnesses became real.

As years passed, she became increasingly involved in her own suffering and became a bother to everyone. Isus believed it was people's distaste for her that caused his lack of self-respect within the community.

He looked at his wife and realized she was yelling his name.

"Isus, be attentive when I speak to you! What's going on out there? What have the people decided about the new thing?"

The frail man sighed. He dreaded the questions, because once he began talking, he wouldn't be able to stop from saying everything he knew, and he didn't have it all sorted out yet. It was too late. Tirzah wanted an answer.

"It seems there are two beliefs about it. Many, as I told you before, believe the Almighty One of our fathers is bringing judgment on the red people in answer to our prayers."

"I don't want to hear such foolishness! What are the sensible men saying? What about the red men, the criminals and exiles who understand this land?"

"I believe I may have the answer. I've been thinking seriously about these things and have spoken to others who agree. We've decided that the gods of Kemet are responsible. They're pouring out their anger upon their own people."

"I don't care what you think. I've been hearing that for too long. What do the people say?"

He took a deep breath. "Tirzah, allow me to finish. I was about to say that the people agree with me. They, too, feel certain it's the gods who have brought about these terrible things. I can't explain the reasoning, nor can they. It has to do with Ramesses not following the commands of the gods and not including the gods in the bounty he has received from his military victories. I truly don't understand why the gods would punish them now, when the pharaoh is so near to conquering the world. Nevertheless, that's my present thinking."

"Good. That's certainly better reasoning than what we've been hearing from our own so-called wise men and their tales. What then? Will life be better for us when the gods of Kemet are finished with their punishment? Think about that, Isus. When the calm comes, it might be a good time to consider joining the red people if we can. A peasant in Kemet is better off than a chieftain in the house of Jacob."

She was feeling better. It seemed the conversation lifted her spirits. "Bring us meat to eat today, Isus. If it's necessary for you to go into Avaris to build later, then you'll have time to hunt now. It's good for me to have meat more often than you supply it. I wonder if you're truly concerned about my well-being." She paused, clutching her bosom, and made an expression of pain. "It would be good to have a little wine now. Get it for me."

He pulled down the goatskin curtain that hung over two acacia poles separating the sleeping area from the rest of the hut, then went to where he kept the tightly sealed skin filled with fermented grape juice. It was secured among the twisted reeds that were the house's frame.

He took his father's favorite cup, which he potted, and filled it half full of the strong, reddish drink. He looked into the cup and took advantage of the brief respite Tirzah allowed him.

"What are you doing? I'm waiting!"

He thought of a well-known proverb. *As the going up a sandy way is to the feet of the aged, so is a wife full of words to a quiet man*. He smiled, drank some of the warm wine, refilled the cup, and carried it to his wife full of words.

Isus, hearing Shimri bellowing outside, walked to the hut door. The big man laughed as he dragged Abiasaph from his house. It looked like he carried two large skins filled with something, probably beer. Shimri liked beer. The Gnat watched the two men walk to the well and sit down.

He badly wanted to walk out and hear them offer him a place beside them. He closed his eyes and thought how nice that would be.

"Isus, Isus, dear friend! We've been looking everywhere for you. Please, join us for drink and talk. We can't discuss things properly without you."

That conversation would never happen. He opened his eyes and looked longingly at the two men. He never sat with them or drank Kemet beer with them. He longed to be like the other men in camp. *Maybe someday,* he promised himself.

As he looked beyond the men, the strange blackness surrounding the land sent a chill through him. He shook his head, depressed by the confusion in his mind.

"Isus!" Tirzah called.

*Will there ever be a day when she doesn't call me?* he wondered.

"Bring water so I can wash my hands. If you don't get meat soon, the day will be over, and I'll be without. Where have you stored your quail sack? Maybe that boy, Caath, would like to go with you. You like him. However you choose to do it, don't waste time sitting and thinking like you always do. It's early. The hunt should start now. Maybe you could ask around and find other men who are going out to hunt. You could join them. That makes success certain. What would you do if I fainted for lack of meat?"

He tried to envision that. *At least it would be quiet.*

"Are you listening to me?" she shouted. "My wine cup is empty! Isus!"

He walked back inside, put out the fire, stood silently for a moment, and walked back outside again. He sat by the door of his hut. Isus, the son of Jogli, of the tribe of Benjamin, shut his eyes and wondered why he'd been born.

# CHAPTER FIVE

# OSHEA AND THE TEARLESS BOY

Caath was a quiet boy. Raised without a mother, he didn't have the same balance during his early life as his friends. He knew only what his father said, and his father had grown bitter after Caath's mother died. His father took the loss hard, though he didn't allow himself the luxury of a long mourning period. He adjusted quickly to raising his son alone but decided how he'd do it. He accepted advice from no one. He and his son would learn to survive in a cruel world, and they'd do it their way. He would teach Caath how to live without the sorrow, weeping, and complaining he heard from everyone else. Abiasaph would survive quietly, the best way, and would teach his son likewise.

Caath was only nine, but he was forced like all the others to work in the brickyards with the men. He learned to work hard enough to escape the whip and to please his taskmasters. He accepted punishment and cruelty without tears. He never cried under any circumstances, following his father's hard-and-fast rule.

Caath always obeyed his father, but Abiasaph wasn't completely satisfied. Caath didn't have the hardness that his father wanted to see. Toughness would be for his son's protection, especially as he grew older. He tried desperately to instill this trait in his only son.

What Abiasaph didn't realize was that, even though Caath never knew his mother, she had a great impact on his character. Being carried by her allowed him to acquire some of her more admirable traits, most notably her shyness and gentleness. Even with Abiasaph's instruction and strict hold on Caath's life, the young boy never lost those characteristics. He remained quiet, gentle, and very shy.

Generally, Caath wasn't a happy nine-year-old. His father was a serious man, so Caath became a serious boy. They never played together or had fun, and they seldom laughed. Abiasaph was a staunch, hard father, and Caath was an obedient, quiet son.

On the day of darkness, though, Caath felt different. It was another free day. At least, it was starting out that way. There were no guards, brutal work, or punishments. He looked at the day with great anticipation, longing to enjoy himself and be a nine-year-old, nothing else. He felt happy.

He found his friend, Tola, at the outer edge of camp, tending his father's sheep. "Tola," Caath yelled as he waved to his friend.

He ran to meet his best friend. They were glad to be together again. They knew it would probably be for just a short time, but they'd make the best of it. Tola invited Caath to graze sheep with him.

Caath was a good worker. Tola knew he could rely on him and didn't have to worry that something might happen to displease his father. He liked being with his younger friend. They felt a lot older than they were and usually had good conversations about many things, especially during the past year, with all the troubles in the Two Lands. They lived in a very grown-up world that lacked a proper child's environment. They were forced to adjust.

"Caath, have you taken a good look at the blackness yet?" Tola asked. "The more I look at it, the stranger it seems. At first I thought it was a sandstorm. Actually, I heard someone say that, and it seemed like it might be, but my father said it was something special, like another plague. I don't know. All I've done this morning is stare at it. I'm not sure I believe it's really there."

They laughed. Caath admired his friend. Tola appeared a lot older than his eleven years as he leaned on his shepherd's staff.

They'd always been friends, but, until recently, they hadn't had much time together except when working under the pharaoh. Since the plagues started, however, there had been a few free days. No guards came to march them to work, so the boys spent a lot of time together working and playing.

Play was something they'd had little time for in their short lives, so when an opportunity presented itself, they enjoyed it immensely. In their circumstances, play often consisted of nothing more than walking through the fields, kicking stones. They were content just to be together.

Caath noticed Tola's donkey grazing with the sheep. He enjoyed riding it, and Tola occasionally took him with him when he rode.

"I see you have old Amasai with you today," Caath said.

"Yes. We can ride later if you want."

"I'd like that." Caath grinned.

Tola pointed at the black city. "Have you talked with your father about any of this? What does he say?"

"Papa hasn't said anything yet. You know how he is. He waits and looks at things a long time before deciding. When the other plagues came, everyone thought they had them figured out, but Papa said nothing. Most of the men said the Almighty One had come to take us from this land for a sacrifice or something, but it wasn't long until each plague passed, and we were still here. Then everyone looked foolish for what they said.

"It's been that way every time. Remember our last free day, when hail tore up the land of Kemet so badly? Papa said it wasn't a good omen. He said it wouldn't last, and we'd be marched away the next day, then it would be worse than before. He was right, too.

"This morning, I heard him speaking to Isus. He told him that blackness would make things worse, not better. Papa said the guards will still come today or tomorrow, and we'd better be prepared. They'll be angrier and meaner, and our lives will be much worse. Are you afraid?"

"A little. It's hard to be brave. Did you hear about Shelomi, the Asherite? My father says he's badly hurt. The physicians might not be able to help him. He also said he heard some men in our community saying that last night, two men of Manasseh were killed near the

Great Sea in a fight with soldiers of Kemet. They may decide to kill us all one day. You've heard about them putting some of our babies in jars and hiding them in temple walls?"

"Papa said that isn't true."

"My father says it might be. Even if they haven't done it, they've done *something* to the Hebrew babies. They were taken away and never returned to their mothers." Tola sat on a large, flat rock protruding from the hillside where he watched the sheep.

"Have you ever thought about what boys like us did before there was slavery?" Caath asked. "My father says Hebrew boys were supposed to become men at an early age. Too much play interferes with teaching and wisdom. He says it was many generations ago that Hebrew boys played games and enjoyed themselves. What do you think? What did boys do before there was slavery?"

Silence surrounded them as they tried to envision the impossible.

"I don't know," Tola said finally, "but I think I would have enjoyed it. Being free, I mean. Do you think the Almighty One will rescue us?"

Caath shrugged. "That would be nice, but Papa doesn't like me to think about such things. Isus told me once that when our families first came to Egypt from the desert where we used to live, we were good friends with the Egyptians. Boys like us went to school instead of working as slaves. He seemed to think that boys played a lot, but he didn't know what they did."

"Salma used to go with his mother to the festivals in Kemet," Tola said. "He saw a group of boys playing in a field by themselves, using a ball of some kind. Once, while his mother was shopping and visiting the booths, he stayed to watch a group of boys for a long time. He said they seemed to be having fun."

"What was the game? How'd they play it?"

"He wasn't sure. He said they sometimes threw the ball and tried to catch it, and sometimes they kicked it. They ran around a lot and seemed to have fun. He wanted to join them, but he couldn't. They didn't wear sandals while they played, either. Sometimes, they laughed hard, like they were having fun. Salma said it hurt inside when he saw that.

"He cried when he told me about it. He said he wanted so badly to join the boys and their game. Some saw him, and they yelled at him and called him names, so he left to find his mother."

Caath couldn't understand why anyone would cry about a game, but he'd been raised differently than the other boys in Goshen. Tola's story made him wonder what it would be like to play like that. He looked at his friend and shook his head. "If we weren't slaves, would we have games like that?"

"Oh, yes, Caath. More than that." Tola became excited. "If we weren't slaves, we could have races, games with balls, and games with animals. We'd have so many things to do, we'd never get any work done."

They laughed at that. One who didn't know their circumstances would never have realized that the short reverie of two friends was a rare, precious moment. Nor would someone notice the healing the boys received from their time together.

They sighed deeply. "Your father's right about one thing, Caath. Things are getting worse. What will they do to us next? My father says it would be better to die quickly than to be beaten like Shelomi. When I think about that…yes, I'm afraid. I'm only eleven years old. I don't want to be hurt like that."

Caath, seeing how worried his friend was, wanted to help Tola not be afraid. His father taught him the importance of being strong and not letting things make him weak. Mostly, his father taught him not to cry. That helped a lot, especially earlier when he had been beaten by the Kemet guard.

"Do you remember when I was beaten?" Caath asked. "We talked about it afterward, remember?"

"Yes. I'll always remember that."

"I really meant what I said then. I never knew what I'd do if I were beaten like that, but because Papa taught me not to cry, that kept the beating from being even worse. When you cry, it's like you're saying, 'This hurts so much, I can't accept it.' Then it becomes like you think. When you decide not to cry, it's like saying, 'I don't care what you do to me, it won't hurt enough to make me cry.' Then it doesn't hurt so much. It's hard to understand, but when I did it, I saw it was true.

"When the guard started whipping me, I wanted to scream and call Papa, but I knew he was in the quarries and couldn't hear me. When the whip first struck, it felt like someone cut me with a knife. Then I remember what Papa said. I didn't think about it, I just remembered everything he taught me.

"He always said the beatings wouldn't kill me, and I'd have to go back to work again, and he was right. Papa always said to let them do whatever they wanted, and it wouldn't be so bad. I told you before how I looked right into that black guard's eye. I just looked. He became angrier and hit me three more times, but I still didn't cry. I know now I'll never cry no matter what they do to me."

"Caath," his friend asked in amazement, "what happened when you stared at the guard? Why did he get angrier?"

"Papa said later the guard was probably a little afraid, too, when I stared back at him. They aren't used to that. I'll tell you one thing. If I ever saw that guard in the dark of the night, I could pick him out just by looking at his eyes."

"Wow. You could go into the blackness right now and find him just by looking at his eyes?"

Caath laughed. "I don't ever want to see him again, Tola."

"Are your wounds healing?"

"They are a little, but Papa said they'd never go away. I'll have the marks forever, and I won't forget."

Tola smiled proudly at his friend. "You know, you've picked up a new name since that happened. I've heard people call you the Tearless Boy."

Caath had heard it, too, and felt embarrassed by it. He laughed to hide his shyness and looked for another topic to discuss. "Who's that?" He pointed toward the marshlands below.

"I think its Oshea. He built a small altar there a long time ago. He said the Almighty One spoke to him about something important, so he built the altar to remind him of what they talked about. He prays there a lot."

"How do you know all that? Have you spoken with him?"

"Not really. My father told me the story."

"Who's with him?"

88

"It might be Tebaliah, the lame one. He and Oshea are good friends. You know Tebaliah, don't you? He lives near you. He and Oshea are together a lot."

"Can we go there?"

"Sure." Tola smiled. That sounded like a good idea. "We can ride Amasai, and we'll graze the flock that way."

Caath hoisted himself on the donkey, and Tola climbed on behind. The young shepherd called out to three of his sheep, and moved the donkey slowly toward their destination. The sheep he called bleated loudly, then followed. The rest of the flock followed behind.

They soon reached the area where the two men were praying. The boys jumped down from the donkey. Tola counted his sheep; then he and Caath sat on the ground and watched quietly as the men prayed. Oshea and Tebaliah were both sprawled on the ground in front of the altar.

Caath wondered how the Almighty One had met Oshea there and spoken to him. He also wondered if the Almighty One looked like a Hebrew. Was he red with funny hair like the people of Kemet? Caath guessed He would look like a Hebrew, because he was the Hebrew God. If He were the Almighty One, where'd He come from? How'd He get there?

Caath didn't know much about the Almighty One, because his father didn't mention him. He knew that most of the boys were taught stories of old about Abraham, Jacob, and Joseph. Caath wondered about such things, but he never pressed his father to teach him, because he knew best. If it were important, his father would tell him at the right time. It seemed like he should know something about the Almighty One, though. Everyone else did, or so it seemed. He had a lot of questions he wanted to ask Oshea—if he and Tebaliah would ever stop praying.

The boys sat patiently, being respectfully silent. Finally, the men stood, brushed themselves off, and saw the boys.

"Good morning," Oshea said, walking toward them and smiling. "What brings you young men to our place of worship?"

Caath and Tola exchanged a look, and Tola cleared his throat. "We wanted to see the altar, Oshea, and to say hello to you and Tebaliah. We're getting a lot of free days lately, aren't we?"

Caath never had the chance to speak with Oshea before. He'd heard his name mentioned often, because his family was highly respected in the encampment. Elishama, the Ephramite chieftain, whom Oshea called his grandfather even though he wasn't, was considered the wisest man in camp. Caath's father hadn't said much about that family, and Caath knew his father wasn't very fond of them. His father believed they were wishing for the impossible and didn't see things clearly. Papa was usually right. Caath would soon know for himself.

He already knew Tebaliah. Their families shared the sheepfold and raised their herds together. Tebaliah thought like Oshea and wasn't regarded too well even by his own family, but he'd always been nice to Caath, and the boy liked him.

Oshea and Tebaliah sat down beside the two young shepherds.

"You young men have come to visit with us," Oshea said. "Good. We like that. Tebaliah and I are good listeners." He smiled and waited.

Caath knew that if he said nothing, Tola would speak. He wanted it that way. Like Oshea, he was a good listener, too. He had a few questions for Oshea, but he was too shy to voice them.

"My father says this darkness over Avaris is another plague," Tola began. "He says many people believe different things about it, but we're supposed to believe the Almighty One is doing this to punish the pharaoh and his people. Caath's father says that will just make them angrier, and they'll punish us more. Now it's worse than ever. I'm not brave like Caath. I'm afraid of what will happen. How long will these plagues last?"

Oshea looked at the boys, studying their faces. "I see both of you have wise fathers. Both of them are correct in what they say. Caath, your father has noticed that with each passing plague, the pharaoh becomes crueler and makes our work more difficult. That's because he refuses the Almighty One's direct orders to him, so he must endure the Almighty One's anger. The pharaoh directs his anger at us, because he knows the Almighty One is our God. He isn't used to having someone control him the way our God has. Each time the Almighty One punishes him, pharaoh becomes angrier. He can't fight the Almighty One, so he takes it out on us. That won't last much longer, Caath. The end of this will be soon.

"Tola, your father has noticed that not everyone believes the same way concerning what's happening. Let me explain why.

"We've been in slavery for many years. Because of the harsh treatment by the Egyptians, many of our people no longer believe the elders and chieftains of the tribes. They have lost hope and their respect for their leaders. We've been told that the Almighty One will take us from this land, and the plagues are His way of bringing that about. Many of our people have heard that said too often, so they've lost patience. They'd don't see it happening, so they no longer believe it, even if they once did.

"It's happening, though. I can see it, because I understand. The Almighty One said many years ago that this time would occur, and I know He won't deceive me. As every new thing happens, I accept it as His work, making His promise true.

"That might be difficult to understand, so let me tell you the entire story in case you haven't heard it. Many months ago, before the plagues began, Aaron and Mosheh came to the camp to speak to the elders and chieftains. Aaron told us about a meeting between Mosheh and the Almighty One.

"The Almighty One told Mosheh that He knew what was happening to us here, about our slavery and sadness. He promised that He'd soon come to take us away from this situation. He said He'd take us to a new land that would be better than this one. Mosheh said it would be filled with milk and honey. Doesn't that sound good?"

The boys envisioned sweetened bread with lots of honey and cool, refreshing milk, and nodded.

"Many of the elders didn't believe what Aaron and Mosheh told us, so Mosheh took his staff and threw it on the ground. When it touched the ground, it turned into a snake and crawled around the tent. The men almost hurt themselves getting out of its way."

Tola and Caath were wide-eyed and astonished. Tola had heard part of the story before, but not in such detail. Caath hadn't heard any of it before.

"When Mosheh reached out and grasped the snake's tail, it became a staff again. Aaron explained that was a sign to prove they were emissaries of the Almighty One, and that He would keep His promise. Let me ask you something, boys. Do you think you would have believed them if you saw that stick become a snake?"

"Yes!" they said in excitement.

"That was how I felt, too, but not everyone did. The message went throughout the encampment to the head of every house. If you'll remember, most of the encampment came to the Judaite community where we mourned in sackcloth and with ashes because of the way we'd forgotten the Almighty One and His promises. Even then, many of our people were only doing it because it was expected. They worshipped outwardly with words, but not inwardly with their hearts.

"A short time later, the overseers were beaten badly. If you remember, some of our men had the bottoms of their feet stripped off by the guards' whips. It was a terrible sight. Adriel and Kemuel still can't walk. Many others are still seriously injured. Because of that, some of the overseers stirred up the men in camp, blaming Mosheh and Aaron for the beatings.

"When Mosheh and Aaron returned to camp after visiting with the pharaoh, they were almost stoned. Do you know why? Those troublemakers never really believed the Almighty One's promise to begin with. All they believed was what they saw with their own eyes.

"Let me explain something important about the Almighty One. He doesn't show Himself to us the same way we see each other. We won't see Him walking down the path. We can't look into the sky and expect to see Him waving to us, so we can't believe according to what we see, or there'll be nothing to believe. The Almighty One is hidden from our eyes but not our hearts. Maybe he's hidden from our sight because we turned away from loving, worshipping, and understanding Him. Our father, Abraham, knew the Almighty One well. He walked and talked with Him. Our fathers, Isaac and Jacob, also knew Him, but we've turned away. Look at us!

"We worship the gods of Kemet with the people of Kemet. We've changed the way we were taught to live by those who came before and passed it on to us. By the look of things, it appears we've become one with the people of this land, even though they lord over us because of our heritage and position as slaves. We aren't the same people we once were. But we're a very special people, something our forefathers told us. Because our lives have become so full of sadness and anger, we no longer choose to believe the stories that made us who we are.

"Hear this, young men. When the Almighty One visited Mosheh, He told him that for all future generations, He would be known as the God of Abraham, Isaac, and Jacob, the God of Israel. He would be called the Lord. Not the God of Oshea, Tebaliah, Jeser, or Abiasaph, but the God of Abraham, Isaac, and Jacob. That is because they believed Him when He told them things. We haven't done that.

"The Almighty one told Mosheh that when Ramesses asked him who it was who commanded him to let us go into the wilderness and sacrifice, who it was who sent the plagues, Mosheh should tell him it was *I Am*. That was the name the Lord told Mosheh to use. That might sound funny to you, but it's important to realize that our Almighty God wasn't just the God of our fathers, he's our God, too. That's why His name is I Am, not I Was.

"The bitterness in the Hebrew men has made them turn their backs on the Almighty One at a time when He's actually rescuing them from the Egyptians. Caath and Tola, the Almighty One is keeping His promise. He sent Mosheh to confirm it to us, but He never sent a messenger to cancel it. The more times Mosheh and Aaron come to bring us news from God, the more hateful we become toward them, blaming them for all that's happening to us.

"We can see the Almighty One's love for us in the plagues if we look hard enough. The plagues have only hurt the people of the Two Lands. We felt no damaging hail. There were no festering lumps in our land, but they were on the bodies of the soldiers of Kemet. We have no sickness that's beyond our physicians' knowledge. Our herds haven't been touched by pestilence. The only trees that still stand and bear fruit in all the land are here in our encampment. Some of our people don't see that, even as clear as it is.

"Let me explain it another way, because I want you to under-stand this clearly. I'll give you an example. When the early green fruit appears on the trees, the leaves soon follow, correct?"

"Yes," they replied.

"When the early green fruit falls to the ground, what happens next?"

"I know!" Caath said. "The second fruit follows with nice juicy figs to eat. Yum!"

They laughed.

"Think for a moment that Tebaliah was on the other side of the city where the plagues destroyed the land so badly. Somehow, you were able to talk to him, and you told him what you just said about the fig trees here. He looked around him, saw only dead and dried trees ruined by hail and eaten by locusts, so he says, 'No, boys, you must be joking. I'm sorry, but that's just not true. There is no second fruit. I can see for myself. There's no fruit at all. The trees are dead.'

"It's easy to understand why he doesn't believe you, because he doesn't see what you see. Does the fact that he doesn't believe you change anything? Does the second harvest of nice, juicy figs disap-pear just because he doesn't believe you?"

"No," Tola said. "Tebaliah doesn't understand that our land wasn't destroyed by hail."

"That's true." Oshea paused to make sure he had the boys' full attention. "In the same way, many of our men don't believe the promise of the Almighty One, which was given to us by Aaron and Mosheh. Just as Tebaliah didn't believe you about the fruit, because he didn't see what you saw, so do many of the men in our camp not believe that the Almighty One will deliver us from this land. Like Tebaliah, they don't see what we see.

"Just because they don't see it doesn't mean it's not true. The promise hasn't disappeared, just like the figs didn't. It's still here, and it will happen. Instead of looking at the plagues, hard work, and beatings, it would be better for us to look at the promise.

"If we continue looking at the promise of the God of Abraham, Isaac, and Jacob, our eyes will be opened by Him, and we'll see things differently. We'll see the promise taking place. It's definitely happening.

"You see, it's easy if we have this understanding. It's more difficult for those who don't. They are angry, bitter, and sad, because they have no hope. It's important for us to have hope. Because of that, Tebaliah and I are happy. The day of our God is coming soon."

Caath was shocked. He'd never heard anyone explain the plagues that way before. He looked at his friend, who seemed to have the same feelings. Caath wanted desperately to say something. He didn't want the conversation to end, but he didn't know what to say. He wondered if his father knew this. He guessed not. If his father knew, he probably would have told him about it. If his father believed that way, he wouldn't instruct Caath as he'd done in the past.

Caath looked at Oshea and remembered something he wanted to ask. "Oshea, what happened here when you met the Almighty One and built this altar? Was that the same Almighty One that Mosheh spoke to? Where does He live? Is He a Hebrew like us?"

Oshea grinned at the boy's innocence, then he placed his hand on his shoulder. "Yes, Caath. There's only one Almighty One. He lives in the heavens." He pointed toward the clouds, and the boys looked as if expecting to see a house floating there.

"It was here at this place," Oshea said, "that the Almighty One spoke to me two years ago. He reminded me of the promise he made to Abraham, and He told me what He wanted me to do about it. The rest I can't tell you, because those were things the Almighty One wanted to say just to me.

"I come here so I'll always remember what the Almighty One said. I want to worship and thank Him. He's truly the greatest God in all the lands on the earth. We need only remember the stories of old to know that.

"The Almighty One's promise is happening right now. You can be sure of it, and we're part of it. If the guards come tomorrow and beat me so badly I can't walk, it won't change the Almighty One's promise. It will only change the shape of my feet. I'll still see His promise."

Oshea stood, took Tebaliah's hand to help him, and said, "Thank you for visiting with us. We must be on our way now. Say hello to your fathers for us."

Tola and Caath sat under the tree silently for a few minutes, amazed by what they'd heard. The story was completely different from what most of the men in camp said. Tola planned to discuss it with his father, Jeser, hoping he could explain it as well as Oshea.

Caath, however, hid the whole thing away in his mind. He wasn't sure what to do about it and doubted his father would let him explain. It dawned on him that if Oshea was right, then his father was one of those who didn't believe in the promise. That was difficult for Caath. He would never turn against his father, but he wanted to believe what Oshea said. The more he thought about it, the surer he was that his father was definitely one of those who didn't believe in the promise of the Almighty One to rescue them from that land. He wondered what he should do about that.

As the two boys put their thoughts in order, Libni and his wife, Vophsi, approached just as Oshea and Tebaliah started walking away.

"Tebaliah!" he called to the crippled Simeonite. "Are these your sheep, my friend?"

"No, they belong to young Tola here."

"Young man," Libni said with a smile, "whatever you've been doing, it hasn't been in the best interest of your father's flock. Have you noticed where your sheep are?"

Tola turned and saw some of the sheep had left the flock. He'd been so engrossed in the conversation with Oshea, he'd forgotten to watch them. "Oh, my! Caath and I can round them up quickly. They haven't gone far."

"Wait, boys," Oshea said. "Looks like we have a visitor. Look there."

The boys saw a small, muscular leopard stalking two lambs that had left the safety of the flock. The two shepherds reacted immediately. Tola grabbed his wooden club, and Caath reached for some large stones. They moved quietly but quickly toward the helpless lambs. Oshea and Libni followed in case the boys needed help. Tebaliah found a smooth stone the size of his hand and placed it in his sling.

Fortunately, the land was open. Wild animals rarely stayed long in such areas, especially with people nearby.

The leopard sensed the danger. Its ears pricked, and it looked toward the young warriors coming its way. Caath began throwing stones toward it, but he was too far away to do any good. Then he heard the sound of Tebaliah's sling, and he turned toward it.

The young Simeonite swung the sling around his head, and released the stone. It glided through the air and landed only two feet from the leopard, bouncing once before striking its face. The leopard jumped, turned, and saw Tola. It darted across the field in a flash and was soon out of sight.

With Oshea and Libni's help, the boys quickly brought the flock back together.

"You boys are brave," Libni said, standing beside them with an arm around their shoulders.

"A shepherd must protect his flock," Tola said modestly, "but it was easier being brave with you men here. I hoped the leopard would run like that. I'm glad you were here, too, Caath." He nodded toward his friend.

"Boys," Libni said, smiling, "the way a good shepherd protects his flock is how the Lord God protects us. A shepherd can't always save all his sheep from danger, but he will always save the flock. When it's time, he finds them new, better pasture. Likewise, the Lord God has protected us, His people. Even though many of us have lost our lives, we're still a great congregation. He's ready to take us to new pasture. Be encouraged by the lessons you've learned as a shepherd. You'll be better men for it."

Caath and Tola remounted Amasai and herded the sheep toward the community. Libni and Vophsi joined Oshea and Tebaliah. The four adults walked casually along the marshlands.

"That's the tearless boy they speak of, isn't it?" Vophsi asked.

"Yes," Oshea replied. "He's a brave one but shy, too. Abiasaph, his father, is a hard man. He may make a man of his son too soon." He shrugged. "But then, who am I to decide such a thing? We should pray for Abiasaph. God will give him wisdom concerning his son."

They chatted amiably as they walked. The two young friends, however, planned games to play when they had the sheep back to the grazing area.

# CHAPTER SIX

# ABIASAPH, THE TORN ONE

Abiasaph walked into his hut, glad to get away from Shimri and his drinking. He unrolled his mat and laid it on the hard ground. Hopefully, he could get some extra sleep. Sleep was difficult for many in Goshen. The slave work was strenuous, and the days were long—as were the memories.

He still found it hard to believe the guards weren't coming, but the day was half-over, and they hadn't arrived. He knew, though he didn't agree with it, that there was a chance that what was being said about God delivering the tribes could be true. Every new event pointed toward that possibility.

He decided to think about more pleasant things - his wife, Nehushta. His heart grew heavy as he thought of her. Life had been wonderful while she was alive. When he thought about her, which was often, he didn't see her in the deteriorating state in which she spent her last months. Instead, he saw her as a healthy young woman, often more healthy than himself.

Because thinking of her often brought sorrow, he enhanced his memories to bring joy. Even if his memories weren't always factual, they comforted him.

It didn't always work that way, though. Sometimes, he remembered things exactly as they were. When that happened, he suffered, but he couldn't stop remembering. He accepted the fact that suffering came with his memories. This day would be another of those times.

As his mind drifted back in time, he saw again her magnificent smile when he discovered she was pregnant. That was one of the best days of his life, along with the day they were married. He remembered walking through the doorway of the hut that evening. As tired as he might have been, he always perked up when he neared his house, because Nehushta was waiting.

She had her back to the door as he entered, and, when she turned, her face glowed as if a bright light shone on her.

⊪  ⊪  ⊪

"Abiasaph, oh, Abiasaph! I have wonderful news. Come to me, my husband." She opened her arms to him.

Although he had had a difficult day, he no longer felt tired. He knew she loved him. She was always happy when he came home, but that night was special. He didn't know why, but something showed in her smile and love.

He walked slowly toward her, took her in his arms, and kissed her gently. Abiasaph wanted just to look at her. She was so beautiful when she smiled. He held her at arm's length and admired her for several minutes, seeing how radiant she was.

"Nehushta," he said softly, "I'm so in love with you. You're the only reason I have happiness in life. You know that, don't you?"

"Oh, Abiasaph, how could anything compare with what you've done for me? What would I be without you? I could never have had this opportunity."

"What opportunity? What are you saying?"

The young daughter of Arad, the Benjaminite, smiled at him, her face shining with happiness. She cupped his face in her hands and told him the wonderful news. "Abiasaph, I'm with child. Isn't it wonderful, glorious news? It'll be your son, my husband. I know it. Oh, Abiasaph, I'm so happy for you. Father will be happy, too. We must go tell him soon. We've honored our agreement—you will have your son."

He was stunned. He couldn't speak or move, but tears welled inside him. It took all his strength to hold them back. He wouldn't yield to them even in such a glorious moment. He was proud of his restraint, and he vowed he would teach it to his son.

"Nehushta, how thankful I am. How incredibly thankful I am. We were so sure it wouldn't be. I'm so happy to think we'll have a son."

He pulled her close and held her for a long time without speaking.

\* \* \*

He turned on his straw mat. Sleep wasn't coming easily. He needed to use the free time to rest, but he couldn't rest with thoughts of Nehushta so vivid in his mind. He remembered how they'd spent that evening reminiscing about their marriage and the few years they'd had together. They were happy years, but they hadn't begun that way.

\* \* \*

He was fifteen years old when he first saw Nehushta, though he'd known her all his life. Many of the other young men joked about her lameness, but he simply felt sorry for her. It wasn't her fault. She'd been born with one leg too short, and her foot never formed properly, making her limp when she walked. He knew she was aware of the jokes, and that was why she stayed by herself so much.

As he watched her tending her father's vegetable garden, he suddenly saw, for the first time, how attractive she was. He was impressed by her attitude. She was kindly toward everyone, even those who teased her. He saw her differently from that moment on, but he didn't do anything about it. He felt embarrassed and shy around her.

Six months later, he finally gathered the courage to speak to her. It was early morning, and she carried a small water jug to her father's tent. Abiasaph felt his heart pounding as she drew near.

101

"Nehushta, daughter of Arad, be careful as you carry that. This way is becoming more difficult to walk every day." *Oh, you fool!* he thought to himself. *Of all the things to say, why'd you pick that? She'll think you're teasing her about her lameness like the others. What a fool you are!*

She smiled and thanked him, and he wondered for a long time how that short conversation had affected her.

That one exchange of words, however, did something to him. From then on, all he thought about was Nehushta, and the feeling grew stronger over time. Eventually, he knew he loved her, but did that matter? He had no father to arrange a marriage for him, and he was divorced from his clan. Since he chose to build his own hut and not be governed by others of his tribe, there was no one who would speak for him. He'd never have the courage to approach Arad alone. Even if he did, he knew he'd be speechless.

It would never work. He would never have her, yet she was all that mattered to him. Without her, he wondered if there was any reason to live.

Just being alive didn't mean much to him. Being under the pharaoh's rule was a miserable existence. He saw life with Nehushta as a way to escape the hatred and bitterness that filled him, but he feared he'd never have it. He didn't even know if she loved him, but he knew he loved her. For the following year, he thought about her every day and dreamed of her every night.

He didn't speak to her again for a long time, but, whenever he saw her, he stopped and looked at her until their eyes met. He said, "I love you," with his eyes as hard as he could.

He didn't know if she understood, but they always smiled at each other. His heart ached, wanting to be with her. Eventually, he convinced himself that she cared for him, too. Maybe she even loved him like he loved her. That meant he had to see her father. There was no other way.

Two years had passed since he first saw her in the garden. Finally, he felt he was bold enough to speak to Arad. For months, he planned what to say. Those were exciting months, as he plotted out his eventual life with Nehushta.

It was a depressing time, too. He continually found himself believing it would never work. He and Nehushta were destined to smile at each other from a distance for the rest of their lives. When he had those thoughts, his heart wanted to break.

Finally, it was time to approach her father. It was the time of planting, and, at late evening, when Abiasaph walked toward Arad's tent. The old man sat outside alone and saw Abiasaph coming, so he motioned him to sit. It felt wonderful being greeted as an adult.

"Abiasaph," the old man growled, "good evening to you. Sit with me, and we'll talk of many things."

He called Nehushta to bring them food. To Abiasaph's delight, she soon appeared at the tent door with a platter of bread and two cups. Abiasaph was especially pleased when Arad offered him wine. That was a sign of acceptance.

"Hushta, bring us wine tonight," Arad had said. "Abiasaph and I might visit for a while."

Arad did that on purpose for Abiasaph's sake. He wanted the young man to know he considered it an honor to talk with him. Abiasaph could use the encouragement—he was a sorrowful young man.

Arad offered the food to Abiasaph, and paused before speaking. "Abiasaph, your heart is laden with thought this evening. You came here to discuss those thoughts. Go ahead, my young friend, and hold nothing back. I will listen carefully."

Abiasaph looked up just as Nehushta appeared with a wineskin. She glanced at him and smiled, then saw her father watching her, and shyly handed the skin to Arad, disappearing back into the tent.

Arad saw the young Levite observing his daughter. Many men in camp considered it a curse to have a female child permanently injured at birth. Arad seldom discussed his feelings about her to anyone, but he saw something in the young man's look that intrigued him.

"She's a good daughter, Abiasaph," he said. "She never complains of her affliction, and she works hard. It's sad that she's twisted like that, for surely otherwise she'd make someone a good wife. Even if she were to marry, I fear she'll be barren. But enough of that, my friend. Let's talk about your concerns. What brings you to my humble dwelling?"

"Arad," he said boldly, "I've come to you to talk about Nehushta." He cleared his throat, feeling his heart pounding inside his tunic and wondering if Arad could see it. He glanced down and was glad there was no obvious movement. When he saw Arad's inquisitive look, he decided not to explain. He just took a deep breath and went on.

"Arad, I have come to ask you to make a pact of marriage between your daughter, Nehushta, and myself."

Arad didn't seem upset. Abiasaph didn't know how the old man felt about his statement, but at least he'd said it. He felt good and very relieved to have it out in the open.

Arad was very surprised by Abiasaph's words. He wondered why anyone would want to marry a lame woman. The old Benjaminite sat motionlessly and stared at Abiasaph. He tugged his beard for a few moments, and answered slowly.

"Abiasaph, why do you want Nehushta for a wife? She's injured, and we don't know if she can bear children. She's a mockery among the young men in camp, yet you ask for her to be your wife. Why?"

Abiasaph felt very bold. He knew he could say what he had to, so he spoke clearly and slowly to make sure Arad understood. "Arad, I'm not one who has ever mocked her. When I hear the other men make fun of her, I become so angry I want to fight them. I've never had unkind thoughts toward her. I want her for my wife, because I love her. I don't see her affliction as the others do. I see her gentleness and kindness, and I see her love."

Arad understood that. He knew Abiasaph well enough to know that the young man needed someone to love and understand him. It was clear Abiasaph had seen some of Nehushta's hidden goodness. Arad knew, of course, but he didn't think anyone else had seen it. He also knew he wouldn't be able to make a marriage contract for her if he refused Abiasaph's offer.

He looked sternly at the young man. "What can you give to secure this pact? Have you considered that? You have no family or herd. Should I hire you to pay for her, like Laban hired Jacob, our father? No. We're all the pharaoh's slaves. We share the same difficulty, and we spend our days working for others, not ourselves. So, then, what will you offer? Have you considered payment?"

Abiasaph knew he had nothing, so he hung his head, rubbing his forehead with his long fingers as he wondered what to say.

"What is your offer?" the old man asked again.

"I'm sorry, Arad. You're right. I have nothing of my own to offer, but I'll let you set the price. Whatever you ask, I'll meet it. If I must do what Jacob did, so be it."

"How can you do what Jacob did? Will you stop working for the pharaoh? Will he excuse you, so you can purchase a wife? Think what you're saying."

"I'm sorry. I'm not exactly sure what you mean. What did Jacob do to secure his wife?"

"Abiasaph, don't you know the story?"

"Tell me again, please. I remember it, but I have it confused with some of the others," he lied. "My father died a long time ago, and I haven't thought of such things in a while."

Arad eyed him warily, wondering if he didn't know any of the old stories. He knew that Abiasaph's father died when the boy was young. Maybe he hadn't shared their traditions with the boy, or maybe Abiasaph was telling the truth and didn't remember. He watched Abiasaph carefully as he spoke.

"Jacob, our father, the son of Isaac, was sent by his mother, Rebekah, to the house of her brother, Laban, that he might secure for himself a wife from her own stock. Remember how he reached the well at Laban's property, saw Rachel for the first time, and immediately loved her? After meeting with her father, Jacob agreed to work for Laban seven years in return for his beloved, and he did.

"It was a large price to pay, but that was how much he wanted her. When the seven years were over, Laban deceived Jacob and gave him his eldest daughter, Leah, instead. Jacob reluctantly took her and agreed to work additional years for Laban to have Rachel, too. He loved her that much."

"I'm like our father, Jacob," Abiasaph answered. "I love Nehushta so much that I'll accept any price you set."

"Think what you're saying. Sometimes, matters of the heart affect our thoughts. We say things that we later regret. Do you still want me to set a price?"

Abiasaph didn't hesitate. "Yes. You make the contract, and I'll abide by it. I, too, like our father, Jacob, loved Nehushta when I saw her for the first time."

Arad didn't answer. It was clear how much Abiasaph cared for his daughter, but he didn't know why he wanted to marry her. She was a curse from God, an outcast. Arad had already accepted the fact that she'd stay with him for her entire life, and now this young man wanted to marry her. Arad suspected there was a lot about Abiasaph he didn't understand. He studied the young Levite quietly.

Abiasaph knew exactly why he loved Nehushta. He was filled with compassion for her. In her, he saw a mirror of his own suffering. He thought of himself as a man without happiness. He never enjoyed himself and seldom laughed.

He hated the pharaoh for controlling his life. He hated his own people for letting it happen. He hated the Almighty One, because the people spoke of Him as being so great, yet He didn't do anything to change their sad situation. He had no father or mother to love or love him in return. His youth was fleeing, and there was no enjoyment in it.

He saw Nehushta's situation as even worse. She was afflicted. People avoided her, but that didn't seem to bother her. At least, she didn't show it. She loved. Somehow, Abiasaph knew that the gentleness and love came from her affliction. He was almost certain that, if she were whole, she'd be the same as the other Hebrew girls, but she was different. Abiasaph loved her because of her affliction, not despite it. He knew Nehushta could give him love and something to live for.

Arad smiled. Abiasaph was clearly serious. He didn't want to miss such an opportunity, because he doubted he'd find another. "Abiasaph, we can't enter into a contract as others would, but I offer you a pact. I believe you'll be pleased by it. Take Nehushta for your wife, and, in return, give me a grandson. That is all I ask."

Arad smiled at Abiasaph and held out his hand.

\* \* \*

Abiasaph awoke abruptly. He opened his eyes, and his pleasant reverie vanished. He looked around the hut and leaned over to look through the doorway. It was still day. He had much work to do, but he wanted to remember Nehushta more. Those were the only enjoyable moments he had. Nothing else was important.

He closed his eyes and blocked out the guilt that ate at him, thinking again of his wife.

It was wonderful. He remembered clearly every moment they were together. In his thoughts, he saw her contagious smile. Because of her great love, his days at work didn't consume him as they had since her death. Long marches back to camp were a joy, because she would be waiting with outstretched arms and a radiant smile.

Nehushta lived for Abiasaph. He was her entire life. He lifted her from the pit of Sheol and gave her a new life, filled with hope. She wanted to meet all his needs and told him that many times. She enjoyed being needed and wanted, and Abiasaph both needed and wanted her. She was aware of his insecurities and overcame them with her endless love, vowing never to give him a reason to stop loving her. As long as she loved him, nothing could hurt him—not the Egyptians, the guards, the soldiers, or physical pain.

Why did it have to end?

Abiasaph didn't usually think of unpleasant things concerning his life with Nehushta, but the images pushed at his mind, trying to come through. He didn't want to see her like that again, but he couldn't help himself. The pictures unfolded before his eyes.

He gave in. After wiping sweat from his forehead, he settled back against the mat and closed his eyes.

\* \* \*

She sat at the spinning tool, large with child, strain evident on her face. He wanted to believe the pain came from the child, but he knew that wasn't true.

Arad died several months earlier, not knowing if his contract would be fulfilled. It was a great loss for Nehushta. She had wanted so badly for her father to know she could bear his grandson.

Now the issue was in doubt again. The extra weight created severe suffering for her. She hadn't been able to walk for over a month. The knots in her thighs and down her side kept growing. Her face was aged and worn, but for Abiasaph, she always smiled. She loved him and forced her magnificent love to show through her pain and suffering.

Abiasaph didn't want to believe that such a thing could happen to her. Out of frustration, he became angry with the physician and midwives. The physician was helpless. Finally, as he'd known it would, the time came when the elders put Nehushta away from the community because of her disfiguration and continuous fever. Abiasaph left his hut and stayed with her in the lonely tent pitched far outside camp.

⊪ ⊪ ⊪

He tossed and turned on the mat, perspiring heavily. He began to recall their conversation in the tent. Desperately, he tried to rid it from his mind, but he couldn't. His heart sank, and heaviness overcame him, as his thoughts moved forward. He loved her so much. What happened to her wasn't fair, though he knew that life for any Hebrew wasn't fair. But why Nehushta? Why did it have to happen?

\* \* \*

She motioned him to sit beside her. It was hard for him. He didn't want to leave her, but he couldn't stand to see her in such pain. Deep in his mind, he knew she would die, but he refused to believe it. More than once he awoke in the night screaming, "No!!"

He looked at the pitiful sight of his sweet Nehushta, then walked to where she half-sat, half-lay on the mat, and knelt beside her.

"Abiasaph." Her fingers moved down his cheek, and she smiled as she whispered his name.

*How can she smile?* he wondered. *It's impossible, but she smiles for me.*

"Abiasaph," she whispered, "I'm certain we'll have a son. I've been told that it will be so. That'll make up for anything that might happen to me. You'll have your son. That's the most important thing."

She coughed in great pain. Abiasaph placed his hand on her cheek and comforted her as best he could. Her face burned with fever. He watched tears run down her face, some for joy at having a son, and some because of her intense suffering.

He looked at his wife, and, for a brief moment, she was as radiant and warm as he remembered, her smile lighting the tent. He called her name and reached for her, but her features changed, and he realized he'd been dreaming while awake.

He looked at her again and saw her lovely smile was forced. Her face was no longer attractive. Swelling disfigured her lovely features, but her smile was still there. Every hour, the pain grew in intensity. He couldn't wish her back to health. She was as she was.

Abiasaph was heartbroken. He loved her so much. Softly, he caressed her swollen face. "My little flower," he said, his voice cracking. "My Nehushta. If you carry a son, I'm happy, too. That's wonderful news, but that's not the most important thing. There's something more important that comes first—you. I need you. You must stay with me. You're more important to me than a son. I need you to love me, to be with me every day."

He stopped abruptly and looked at her inquisitively. "Who told you that you're carrying a son? How can you be so sure?"

"The Almighty One, Abiasaph," she whispered. "We have forgotten Him, but He hasn't forgotten us."

That wasn't surprising. Abiasaph hadn't thought about Him in years. As a boy, he was told that the Almighty One was the special God of the Hebrews. He demanded sacrifices and worship, and, in return, He protected the people. Abiasaph never paid much attention to that kind of talk, because he knew the Almighty One wasn't protecting the people very well. He didn't need to learn more about Him. Abiasaph blamed Him for the deaths of his parents and the slavery of the camp.

Now his wonderful Nehushta, whom he loved, said the Almighty One told her she'd bear a son. Abiasaph wanted to be angry, but he wouldn't do that to her. Instead of speaking, he laid his head against her large stomach, filled with child and disease.

"I love you, Nehushta," he said. "Please, don't leave me. I love you so much."

He wanted to cry but refused. He wrapped his arms around his sick wife and held her tightly, wondering why the physician couldn't cut the sickness from her and let her live as before. He buried his head in her lap and repeated his lament.

"Please don't leave me, Nehushta. Please stay with me, my wonderful, wonderful Nehushta."

They stayed that way for a long time, Abiasaph resting his head against her stomach, pleading with her, while she ran her fingers through his dark hair, smiling and comforting him.

\* \* \*

Abiasaph opened his eyes again and rolled his head on the mat. Perspiration covered his forehead and face. He closed his eyes and felt his heart sink to new depths that brought searing pain to every part of his body. He moaned as he saw himself coming home from the workyards and walking to his tent on that final day.

\* \* \*

The physician stood away from the tent, waiting patiently. Abiasaph knew something had happened, and he stopped, fearing to come closer. He didn't want to hear the man's words.

The physician slowly walked toward him and placed his hand on the young man's shoulder. "Abiasaph, you have a son, my friend, a healthy son. He's with the women of your tribe. You may go there whenever you wish. The boy has no afflictions." He forced himself to smile.

"Nehushta?" was all Abiasaph could ask.

The physician held the man's shoulders with strong hands, and the look on his face told Abiasaph what he dreaded to hear. "She's dead, Abiasaph. It's just as well. Her affliction grew worse as the child broke free. I'm sorry, my friend."

He paused and stepped back. "Abiasaph, because of the disease, we must burn the tent. Come with me, and I will take you to your son."

"Where is my Nehushta?" he asked softly.

The physician lowered his eyes, unable to look at the grief-stricken Levite. "In the tent," he said slowly, shaking his head to the question Abiasaph didn't ask.

The two men walked slowly toward camp.

* * *

Abiasaph jumped up from his mat, wet with perspiration. He walked out the doorway and entered bright sunlight. After a long drink from his water skin, he tried to clear his mind and bring it back to the present.

*I'll check the sheepfold,* he decided. *There's much work to be done there. That's what I should do.*

The sad young man walked slowly down the path, clutching his side, trying to relieve the ache in his heart. As he walked, he tried to convince himself to forget the only thing in his life worth remembering.

# CHAPTER SEVEN

# LITTLE BEER MAN

S himri was drunk again. He sat in a small circle with Shobab, his brother, and some others. Mugolla–sekh-mugolla, the Little Beer Man, was the center of attention and had complete mastery of his audience.

A strange sight, he came from one of the southern lands years earlier, but he never said where. He was only a little over three feet tall. When he moved, he waddled more like a duck than walked like a man. His dark-green eyes were long and slanted, and he had no eyebrows. His hair was black, like the Egyptians, but it grew in all directions. When he cut it, he always did it poorly. His strange appearance captivated his audience as much as his story-telling ability. Knowing that, he continued his tale with great animation.

"And so, the mistress of the house was in great difficulty over the thievery. She couldn't, by the gods, go to Mi-Sakhme with a complaint. Her lord, in his mercy, had granted her a request of great proportions shortly before when he placed a handsome young peasant into the office of the estate scribe, a high position for a peasant. The mistress feared that the scribe, who was her newest plaything, would be suspected of the thievery.

"However, Petephis, the chief overseer, was in command of the estate. The mistress told him of the theft and assured him the scribe was beyond suspicion. Before then, I had gained the position of chief purchaser for the estate, a fine position. I, therefore, took orders from no one but the captain."

He grinned through his oversized, nearly toothless face, relishing his control over his audience. As usual, the number of listeners increased as the tale progressed.

"Young Hebrew men, Mi-Sakhme was thinking death when he finally learned what happened. Petephis, through my words to him, and despite his mistress' wishes, had accused the young scribe before Mi-Sakhme. The captain would have fed him to the crocodiles were it not for her intervention.

"She, lying again because of her love for the young man, spoke to her lord and said he was beyond reproach. Mi-Sakhme, unable to resist her provocative smile, and knowing that the scribe was a beautiful young man who would give the captain more prestige, relented from his murderous intentions, and the scribe was released back to his mistress' bedroom.

"With all the lying being done, no one knew who the thief was. The only person who was deceived was the captain. Isn't it ironic that in pursuit of justice, a myriad of injustices flowed freely and without restraint?"

"How'd you eventually get caught and sent here?" Shobab asked, glad for the welcome interlude that helped keep his thoughts from Shelomi's terrible beating the night before.

"Caught?" The Little Beer Man laughed. "I was never caught, Hebrew lad. They would never have caught me. The wise one from the south is too intelligent for that. Petephis, who was my dear friend and superior at the estate, allowed his loyalty to me to run dry and ruin our friendship. He became suspicious of me and watched me closer than ever. Much to my disapproval, he began questioning me.

"Soon, I'm sad to say, we were no longer friends. He realized that only the two of us were in the house when the thief was active. He didn't know how smart I was when he decided to match wits with me. When he accused me, I replied, 'Petephis, my trusting friend and general, if it has to be that one of us is guilty of those crimes as you say, and since I'm innocent, then it allows that you are the guilty one.

By the gods, would that it isn't so. I don't want to believe that of my friend.

"'You're a respected man, a noble among stewards. Why would you do such a thing to your lord, the captain, who has treated you so well? Wait, Petephis. My heart tells me a different tale. I'm thinking of feeding you to the crocodiles too soon. Just because we were the only ones present at the time doesn't mean either of us is a thief. Think for a moment. If I'm innocent, and so are you, what is the answer? Could it be there has been more than one thief over the years? We must believe that for your sake. I won't be so harsh as to allow you to accuse yourself in such a way. If you say so, my master, I will believe that you and I are both innocent of any wrongdoing. We'll have to wait for the gods to bring forth the guilty ones.

'If I agreed with you, my friend, and assumed that you had, in fact, masterminded this thievery that has endured for so long, then I would have to admit I've been deceived by you for years. Yet, no one deceives me. I'm the small wise one from the south, and what the gods didn't give me in height and weight, they made up for in intelligence, wisdom, and guile, to say but a whisper.

'I haven't been deceived, and, therefore, you aren't guilty. We must look elsewhere for the thieves. It's not one of us. No, don't thank me,' he said, spreading his arms out in a gesture. 'It's my pleasure to serve you in this way.'

"He was speechless, young listeners, and wasn't willing to match wits with me. My mastery of the mind kept me from certain death in that confrontation. I found that the mistress, in her lust for her scribe and to excuse him from guilt, accused *me* to Mi-Sakhme. Me, the wise, small one from the South. Would he accept such an accusation against a popular servant like Mugolla-sekh-mugolla?

"My friends, the mistress painted her eyes with enticing antimony, she poured sweet-smelling ointment on her head, and she adorned her hair with beautiful ostrich feathers brought from Africa, then she went to see her master wearing nothing but a leering smile," he explained, lifting his eyebrowless eyes. "Under those circumstances, he would believe whatever she said, and he did.

"Soon thereafter, Petephis had me exiled to keep me alive. Mi-Sakhme would have had me killed, but he always took Petephis' advice. Though he couldn't prove it, Petephis was certain I was in charge of the thievery that went on for so many years. Because of our long companionship, he disposed of me through exile instead of death. He had Mi-Sakhme sign the letter of exile against me, but, as usual, he didn't know what he was signing. I kept my life, as much from my own wit and wisdom as from the luck of the gods, to say but a whisper.

"Hear this, Hebrew friends. Petephis could have been a little jealous of me. Though I operated under his leadership, everyone who came into contact with me was impressed and wondered why I was kept in such a low position, even though, as chief purchaser of the estate, I was very high among the other servants.

"Petephis may have wondered whether I was in line to replace him if Mi-Sakhme chose. There aren't many in the Two Lands with the wisdom, wit, and willingness that I, the small one from the south, possess. Its possible Petephis chose to exile me to protect his position. Well, his and the captain's loss is your gain, my friends. Don't cheer. I'm far too humble.

"So here I am as your reward." He laughed. "Now I can teach you how a young man should live in this great land."

"Ha!" one of the Hebrews said. "Would you, a foreigner, teach us how to live? We don't even serve the same gods."

"Foreigner? Gods? I'm no foreigner, you young fool. I'm definitely of Kemet, a son of the Two Lands. And what do you know about gods? The Two Lands invented gods! I was born in the deepest south, in what is known down there as the highlands. I traveled years to reach the lower land and was left here in a trade caravan. I knew nothing about the land of Kemet at that time, but I became one of the people, and it was clear to me that the gods of the land were certainly more powerful than the gods of the rest of the earth. They've turned the pharaohs into gods themselves. Who could be more powerful than Amun? Who has more wisdom than Re, the god of the sun? Where are your gods? You're in slavery to the great Pharaoh Ramesses, and no one has rescued you. Don't speak to me of gods."

The men were silent. Shimri, who was drunk, only vaguely remembered his conversation with the Gnat the previous day, and how he chided him while speaking of Re and Hathor.

"Yes, little man with the big mouth," the Behemoth roared, "we know all about gods. Re started a sandstorm, and it has blackened the sky. Take him some beer, Little Beer Man, and soothe his headache. Then we'll have light again." He laughed.

"Sir, what are the palaces like in which you served?" young Tola asked. "Are some of them really as big as our entire camp?"

"Yes, little babies, you wish to know all about the small wise man and the grand estate over which he once presided. In truth, I'll tell you of the grandest estate in all the Lower Land, with the exception of Ramesses' own palace, the palace of the great god king himself. The estate I speak of is the estate of the captain of the soldiers, Mi-Sakhme, the friend of the Hebrews." He laughed.

The Hebrews knew who Mi-Sakhme was. As the captain of soldiers, he was responsible for the entire army of guards and taskmasters who presided over the Hebrew slave force. He was the one who issued the cruelest orders, often resulting in death or severe injury to the slaves. Not only did the Hebrews know Mi-Sakhme, they hated him passionately. Mugolla-sekh-mugolla, completely devoid of compassion, and staring at Tola, Caath, and their friend, Salma, didn't care how his manner of speaking might affect the boys' minds.

"Yes, babies, it's a grand palace, a house that includes everything a man could want for his happiness, to say but a whisper. Let me begin. Sit back. What a shame you aren't little red boys. I could give you some beer to enhance your listening ability, as they do in the Kemet schools. Take heed.

"Mi-Sakhme, the royal captain of the soldiers, built one of the most glorious palaces in all the Lower Land. It was majestic for its size, but it was also beautiful because of the magnificent touch of his honored purchasing officer. You know who that is, don't you?" He opened his slanting, browless eyes wide, his mouth gaping as if ready to swallow anyone who came too close.

"Stop your stupid boasting, you half-grown duck," Shimri snorted. "Get on with it. We want to be entertained, not bored."

"My honored little ones," Little Beer Man said, ignoring the drunken man's comments, "it was he at whom you gaze with such startled eyes today. I alone, the wise and shrewd one from the deepest south, was the purchasing officer for the estate, to say but a whisper. I, who occasionally received small help from others, made the palace such a beautiful place to visit and live."

"What did it look like?" Salma asked.

"Lie back your heads and prepare your hearts for a treat unlike anything you've ever tasted, one that will bring a smile to your stomach. I'll teach you of the great ways of the people of Kemet. I'll enhance your imagination and let you see in your mind what you would otherwise never know. I'll tell you of the honored estate of the captain, Mi-Sakhme, friend of the Hebrews. Ha! Do you know where this palace is, little babies?"

"No," they said in unison.

"Of course not. Your teachers have sheltered you from all that really matters, but I won't allow you to go to your graves without proper knowledge. Hmmm. Well, then. Do any of you little ones work with rebuilding the great city?"

"Yes," Caath said. "We all do. I work at the brickyards, and Tola and Salma work in the fields and carry mortar."

"Ah. Well, then, if you were to walk along the river in the same course the ships take toward the quarries, southeast from Avaris, if you continued for several hours at a reasonable pace, you'd soon come upon a pathway marked with stones that takes you from the river to Mi-Sakhme's estate. After some time, you'd see a beautiful brick wall standing more than three cubits in height, with gates on each side. That magnificent wall surrounds the palace grounds of Captain Mi-Sakhme.

"You'd naturally stop and stare for many minutes before proceeding into the grounds, because of the magnificence and beauty of the estate. It's a sight to behold, one that would make your eyes widen. As you walk through the front entrance, you immediately see a small temple to the god Anpu, the Opener of the Way. There, you must do homage and beg for the safety of Mi-Sakhme, your honored host.

"What is that look upon your faces? It's obvious you don't understand the gods. Please don't compare the true way of worshipping the gods of the Two Lands with your primitive Hebrew God and your own worship. Listen to the small wise one from the south, and you'll understand. You shall learn of the gods as you learn of the beauty of Mi-Sakhme's estate. You'll even learn the proper worship of the gods.

"Again, babies, remember that it's important to do homage at the temple of Anpu. Don't overlook that important act. When you leave the temple, if you look toward the south, you'll be mystified by the beautiful formal gardens that control your gaze. I myself, the wise purchaser, had a great investment in their reaching such uncompromised beauty.

"Magnificent palm trees line the entrance to the gardens. There, you walk upon smooth jade stones that shine like gold but with the color of green. They're called green gold. I bargained them from a trader who came from far beyond the Sea of Red Earth. It took him three years to bring the amount I needed to finish the gardens. Of course, the means for purchasing such expensive stones was not difficult. Whatever I desired to make the estate more beautiful, I had the authority to obtain regardless of price."

Mugolla-sekh-mugolla paused for a moment, his head raised as he looked into the heavens, allowing everyone within sight the chance to see how important he was. His goal accomplished, he smiled and continued.

"The gardens are filled throughout with sycamore fig trees that yield fruit tenfold above others in the land. Everywhere you look, your eyes are treated to jasmine and chrysanthemums among the many beautiful flowers and plants adorning the gardens. The wonderfully scented myrrh trees, brought from the land of Punt, were my favorites. Yes, the gardens at the house of Mi-Sakhme are glorious, to say but a whisper.

"In the center of the gardens is a grand lotus pool with the most refreshing water in the Lower Land. The pool is for wading and enjoyment and is filled with exotic fish brought from far-away lands. Of course, that's to be enjoyed only by the master and his mistress and their special guests. How often I would see her lounging at the pool, her favorite place to relax and entertain.

"Then, as you pass through the gardens moving south, you come to the games area. We might stop our tour for a game of backgammon. Do you play?"

The wide-eyed boys shook their heads. Salma wondered if that was the game he saw the Kemet boys playing at the festival months earlier. Shobab smiled, enjoying the effect Mugolla-sekh-mugolla had on the children.

"The game area has a high fence around it with a low gate to take you to the next section. That's the play area for pets. Yes, the captain's house has many pets. The captain and his mistress are fond of animals, and they wanted their pets to have a place where they could run and play without feeling captive. What things you can have if you are wealthy! When I was at the estate, we had monkeys, cats, and geese. Some of the servants were allowed dogs. There were antelope, too, but they became lost before I left. Petephis had a pet monkey that amused everyone. I wonder if that little entertainer is still there? He was called Watch Me, and that's what we did when he began to play. Those among the servants enjoyed Watch Me often, and so did I."

"I've heard King Ramesses has a pet lion," one of the boys said. "Is that true?"

"Ha! Anyone who has a pet lion had better have an iron tunic, too," Mugolla answered. "I haven't had the pleasure of spending much time at the estate of the great pharaoh. In his presence, one must always be prostrate with lowered eyes, so it's difficult to know much of what happens at the grand palaces of the god king, but you're right. From what I understand, our great pharaoh has a pet lion, but I don't think that's a pet I'd play with. Pharaoh Ramesses has many acquisitions he keeps just to say he has them. The golden-maned lion is one such.

"Back to our tour. Then, my children, as you continue your walk around the main quarters, you come to the storehouses. You'll see the huge slaughterhouse, where animals are killed and hung, waiting to become tasty meals for the captain and his guests. Next is the bakery. Ah, little Hebrews, your mothers know nothing about baking bread compared to the bakers on the estate. The breads and cakes will cause you to eat until you are gorged. They have the finest herbs and spices, some brought from Asian lands, to create delicacies of which you've never dreamed.

"Then we find the brewery and workhouses. That is where much of the estate's work is done. I could talk to you for hours about the brewery and how I mastered that art and eventually taught the brewers my own magnificent secrets. I'm still renowned for the graceful art of beer making, in which I do excel, to which Shimri can attest.

"Being a drinker of great discrimination, I thoroughly enjoyed drinking the beers brewed on the estate. In my leisure time, I inquired how it was done, only to find, much to my dismay, there wasn't a brewmaster among them. They simply followed the instructions like one building a stone gate. As I had time, I spent more time there, learning the trade. Once I mastered the technique, I began experimenting with other herbs and plants to create the perfect brew. Of course, I succeeded. There's no one in the Two Lands who can brew like the small wise one from the south, to say but a whisper."

Little Beer Man paused to reflect on his achievements, sighed and continued.

"In the various work houses, slaves slaughter and prepare cattle for the main table, make bread and cakes, store and dry vegetables, make dyes for clothing, and store grain in the silos. Many men and women work there.

"A little farther from the work quarters are the stables, where they keep work animals and the captain's chariots and horses. Those chariots are always polished until they shine like the sun. The chariot horses, unlike workhorses, are pampered as if they were the captain's children. Those horses receive the best feed, are washed daily, and even have their own physician. A chariot horse in the house of the captain is better off than a chieftain in the tents of Goshen. Ha!

"As we proceed around the estate, we soon come to the kitchens, where all the magnificent food is prepared. There you will also find the stairways leading to the servant's quarters. I and a few other important members of the captain's staff had our quarters in the rear of the main house, not in the servant's quarters.

"What grand meals were served from those kitchens! Cattle and duck, the largest and best fish, and hippo. The finest meats were served every day, with platters of vegetables from Kemet and from around the world."

"Sir," Tola asked, "how'd you become an officer in such a grand house?"

"Ah. An old proverb of my land teaches that *the learned man rules himself.* Having learned how to turn my extraordinary wisdom into shrewdness, I was able, to the delight and advantage of my overseers, to establish myself in positions of regard and self-rule. Heed me, young babies, and you can do the same.

"Being not as tall as other men, I was first noticed by Petephis, the grandest of lords and chief overseer. Our friend Shimri, who loves to share his wit with all who will listen, has more than once referred to me as the pygmy.

"My friends, the truth is, years ago, when Mi-Sakhme sent Petephis to the great trading center in the Upper Land, he was accompanied by the equally faithful steward from the pharaoh's estate, the venerable Menna. Menna had a list of purchases he was to make for Ramesses, the famed sire of one hundred children. Among his goals was to purchase some palace soldiers, or bodyguards, from Sardinia and some gray pygmies from Central Africa.

"I believe Menna accomplished all those things, but I had a terrible time convincing him I was a magician and an entertainer from the Asian highlands. I wasn't a pygmy. I was less tall than others but not less wise. What I lacked in size, I made up for with the sharpness of my mind. Menna eventually understood and released me, and kept only the African pygmies for the pharaoh's pleasure.

"At my first encounter with Petephis, I entertained him with my wit and wisdom. I juggled six balls simultaneously, never letting one fall. I learned wonderful feats of magic that I displayed, much to his satisfaction, not to mention the others who were interested in purchasing me. Petephis was very impressed and made a wise decision, purchasing me then without knowing exactly what he'd do with me but knowing that it was a wise decision nonetheless.

"From that day forward, I made sure that Petephis knew of everything I did that would bring glory to him and the estate. I counseled him on whom to purchase for the staff, and he soon saw my counsel was wise. It was only a matter of time before I was named to a high position, becoming the chief purchaser in the palace.

"Now, let us continue our grand tour of the estate. As we stroll along the rear of the estate, we see a large pool that first appears like another wading area, but beware! This is a terrible place, filled with crocodiles for the captain's pleasure. Because of the high overhanging lip around the pool, an island appears in the center of the pool for the crocodiles to lounge upon, creating a striking scene for those who visit the estate.

"Beyond the crocodile pool is a large porch extending from the house that fills the entire west wing. That porch is an extension of the main bedroom and living quarters for the captain's lovely mistress. I don't mention her name, because of a belief of hers that her name should never be spoken aloud by anyone beneath her. As the daughter of a priest of the land, she knew things about the gods of which we have no knowledge.

"The mistress often had luxurious dinner parties that began in the central rooms of the palace but always ended in the large porch area. It would be filled with people to the last corner. They were such magnificent parties, with dancers, blind flute and lute players, harpists...."

"Blind?" Tola asked. "Why would she want blind flute players?"

"I saw that at some of the festivals," Shobab said. "They had blind musicians, but I never knew why. I just assumed they learned their craft and then lost their eyesight."

"No, no, my friend, it's not that simple," Mugolla-sekh-mugolla said. "The blind flutists and harpists are considered by the elegant as the most desirable. What great attraction could a sighted flute player be? A blind one who plays well attracts much attention from those who see and hear.

"That practice began many years earlier when the queen filled her house with blind musicians. She was taken with their abilities, and that tradition is still practiced. The cost meant nothing. The means were granted us to obtain whatever was needful for the estate or our mistress' yearning. When entertainments were the course of the day, she preferred blind musicians. We often sent servants to other lands at her command to bring back musicians. Some played instruments that no one in Kemet had ever seen. That raised our mistress high in the eyes of others, knowing to what expense she went to provide them with such grand entertainment. Do you understand?"

Caath looked at Tola, leaned over, and whispered, "Do you believe all this? It sounds strange."

Tola smiled and shrugged, then they looked back at the Little Beer Man, eager to hear the rest.

"Yes, the parties were bountiful, and, of course, I arranged them all. Oh, the dancing! The mistress went to any end to have the finest dancers. She brought in beautiful, acrobatic, high-kicking dancers who wore very little clothing. When they entertained, all other festivities stopped. The men loved watching them, and the women watched for other reasons." He laughed.

"You babies would become lost in such a house. There are rooms for everything—separate harem rooms for the concubines of the master and Petephis, different dining rooms for different kinds of dinners, and three central rooms, each of which would hold ten of your Goshen houses.

"There are bedrooms for everyone and every possible guest, even a furniture room to show off recent acquisitions. As you may have assumed, I, as the wise purchaser, was partially responsible for the grand furnishings that caused the room to be so renowned. There are temple rooms filled with shrines and temples for various gods, including the favorite gods of the master and mistress. There are bathing rooms for them and for their guests, sitting rooms, four dressing rooms, and hallways that are large enough to hold a complete Hebrew family, to say but a whisper.

"Yes, Mi-Sakhme's estate is among the grandest in the land. I miss it, and it certainly misses me. They'll never have another purchaser like myself. That's sad. In all likelihood, they have regretted it many times. They have other servants and officers. I hope they honor the palace the same way I once did."

Salma spoke hesitantly. "We've heard that many of our people who left us work in the houses of Kemet. Were there any Hebrew servants in your house?"

"Yes. There was Ebebi. I purchased him soon before I departed. He was a shrewd one, becoming one of the people to gain favor with Petephis."

"Ebebi?" Tola asked. "That's no Hebrew name. I never heard that one before."

"Ah, yes. The man was a Hebrew, but not a good one by your standards. I don't remember his Hebrew name, but it seems that he deceived his way into the position of overseer while he was a Hebrew by continually speaking against his Hebrew brothers to the soldiers. Many of your men were beaten seriously because of him. He boasted about it to the rest of us. He must have assumed that would gain him favor. When the Hebrews became suspicious of his behavior, he arranged to be considered for placement in the captain's house as a servant.

"To prove his sincerity, he was to bring to the captain the hand of a Hebrew whom he had slain. Ebebi did that, and Mi-Sakhme rewarded him by granting him an interview with Petephis for a position in the house, which, of course, I had already arranged, anticipating the captain's approval."

Mugolla-sekh-mugolla glanced quickly at the adults in the audience to see their expressions. He knew they wouldn't be pleased with such information.

"It should be stated, my friends, that at the time, Petephis and I had no knowledge that Ebebi had killed one of his own and sliced off the man's hand just to please the captain. I've always been a man of peace. As you have seen since I joined you here in Goshen, I have no interest in fighting or killing, but we did, in fact, grant Ebebi a place in the servant's house. After he accomplished the murder, the captain awarded him the name Ebebi, a name of the people, at Ebebi's request. By now, he might have a good place in the house."

Caath was startled by the story and became angry with Ebebi for treating his fellow Hebrews in such a way.

The Little Beer Man continued, speaking of various parties and entertainments he remembered, or presided over, but Caath's thoughts were elsewhere. He thought over what Oshea said earlier. He wanted desperately for his father to understand the Almighty One as Oshea did. He felt tremendous respect for his father and trusted and believed him. For the first time, he began to doubt his father's wisdom concerning the long months of plagues.

Caath couldn't remember having such a longing as he felt then. He wanted to know everything there was about the Almighty One, Abraham, Joseph, and his own fathers. He wanted very much to believe, like Oshea, that very soon the camp would be free of such horrible slavery, and he wanted his father to believe it, too.

Caath thought his father would probably like to hear the story of the Hebrew man who became a person of Kemet. He would tell him later.

Shobab, the youngest of Zichri's three sons, tired of the conversation. Seeing his brother's condition, he tried to persuade Shimri to come home with him. Shobab knew there was work to be done at their house, and Tebaliah might tell their father of Shimri's drunkenness.

Shobab had no desire to be involved in another family argument with all its' shouting and cursing. He was still partially numb from the previous evening's events. He thought of Shelomi and his terrible beating, though he desperately tried not to.

Shobab had also heard earlier that more men were killed in a fight with Kemet soldiers near the Great Sea. *What's happening?* he wondered. *Every day, it's getting worse. More and more of us are being murdered by angry soldiers, all because of the plagues. Who's right? Is Libni correct? Is the Almighty One coming to get us out? If so, why are there so many killings?*

It was too much for him to figure out, especially then. He had to help his brother, and he kept thinking of Shelomi. He couldn't get the image of his face out of his mind. It had been stripped away like a fish being skinned, and the look of horror on his face was one Shobab would always remember.

After much encouragement, Shimri bid good-bye to the men and boys and left with Shobab toward their hut. They met Tebaliah, who inquired of their doings.

"Father desires us to repair our house this day," Tebaliah said, "while there's still light. He asked me to come to you."

Shimri felt a deep dislike for Tebaliah. It stemmed partly from the injury Tebaliah had, which prevented him from working with the rest of the men. That occurred years before when he was injured working in the sheep fold. Tebaliah never fully recovered. His left foot was badly twisted, and he couldn't walk without a stick. Shimri resented him for not participating in their forced labor and had already told Shobab about it.

He also disliked Tebaliah's strong belief in the Almighty One and his spending so much time with Oshea, the son of Nun. Shimri's lifestyle was in direct contrast with that of his brother, and they argued often.

The drunken Behemoth brushed past Tebaliah, knocking him off balance. "You have the right to talk to us, do you? Shobab and I have toiled with our hands and backs for many endless days, and today, you toad, we have some rest, and you order us back to work? Are you now a soldier of Kemet, footless one? Are we, who are important, to be controlled and ordered about by you, who are nothing?"

Tebaliah, seeing his brother was drunk, didn't reply. He was concerned about Shimri's drinking. Their father might die soon, yet he and his brothers still fought.

Shimri stood over Tebaliah, spraying him with his wet, slurred speech. "Well, what is it? Do you have something to say to me? Say it, so I can strike you down for good."

"No, Shimri, my brother. It's not my nature to say anything to you that would upset you. It's my duty to inform you what our father asked me to say. If you're tired from your drinking, then Shobab and I can do the mending while you rest. It's of no concern to me. I won't say anything to our father about it."

"You crippled fool! In your weakness, you're like a woman and can't do a man's work. You waste your time and have become a teacher of magic and the gods. You've decided, you weakling, that the rest of us, who have important things to do, should heed you. You're mad. We have no desire to hear these same precepts and laws you've decided to follow. When did you become someone who anyone should follow? You're no son of our father."

Shimri's drunken condition played havoc with his ability to make his point, although it allowed him to say what was in his heart.

"You're darkened in your thinking to allow yourself to be influenced by Oshea, someone no one wants to see or talk to. Why learn from one such as he? The blind ones like yourself who speak of things that can't be seen or felt should open their eyes and see. You're still blinded by the words of that old man, Mosheh. Where was he while the rest of us suffered, when your foot was mangled? Now he comes in here with his stories and magic, but they aren't true." He laughed before continuing.

"Go and listen to Little Beer Man. He, too, has stories that mean very little but are nice to hear. You can sleep while listening to that little pygmy. His speech is attractive. Listen to him, oh brother of waste, and add his tales to your great thoughts of the Almighty One." He spat out the name.

"Shimri, wait," Shobab said. "Be not so unfriendly, Brother."

Shobab usually agreed with Shimri, but he knew that Shimri was speaking through his drunkenness. His speech didn't even make sense. Shobab also wanted peace in their family.

"Shimri, Tebaliah's right. Let's go mend the house. If you wish, elder brother, you may rest. Tebaliah and I can make the repair. It's getting dark and will soon be time for the evening meal. We'll awaken you then."

"Curse you and your righteousness!" the Behemoth shouted. "Both of you!"

He threw a punch so hard he almost fell, and he grabbed Tebaliah's neck with one hand and Shobab's shoulder with another, throwing them down with one thrust of his powerful arms. He cursed them, and all the bitterness, unforgiveness, and guilt that burdened him came lashing out at the brothers who lay helplessly on the ground.

He looked scornfully at his brothers lying at his feet, unable or unwilling to move. He was filled with hatred, but he didn't really want to hurt them.

"Get off your tails, you frightened geese. I won't hit you. In my drunken condition, I can still mend a hut while you two decide where to start, so stop soft-talking about my sweet drink of the gods. By the gods themselves, I'll have more to drink, and we'll still mend our father's house.

"Tebaliah," he said, pointing at him and shaking the finger slowly, "we'll hear no more talk about Mosheh or the Almighty One or the plagues, or I'll cripple your other leg."

He reached down and pulled them both to their feet. Shobab retrieved Tebaliah's walking stick. With Shimri leading, the three brothers walked back to their hut where their father, Zichri, lay slowly dying.

# CHAPTER EIGHT

# OLD ABRAHAM

The three men walked slowly through the large camp, which still bustled with activity, though evening had arrived. They drew smiles and waves from many they passed. They were three of the camp's chieftains, men who might ultimately decide the fate of the entire people.

Eldad, the chieftain of the tribe of Judah, painfully watched his people suffer for eighty-nine years. As he walked, he looked around curiously at the children of Israel. He stroked his long beard continuously, a habit from his younger days, and wondered why his people, who'd been oppressed for so long, couldn't unite at such a time as this.

He realized many men of Goshen didn't honor the Lord or look to Him for guidance. The stories of Abraham and Joseph that gave strength to Eldad and others had little impact on so many of the others. The years of slavery had altered their thinking and their ability to exercise their faith.

Though they certainly had the desire, Eldad knew they'd lost the will to be free, having been slaves all their lives. He longed to see oneness in their thinking and was saddened by their lack of confidence in Mosheh. Still, he felt great understanding and compassion for his people.

*I love them, Lord, even in my anger. Could You do less?* he wondered.

He walked on, stroking his beard and smiling at everyone. As he did, he offered words of encouragement in his coarse voice.

"Young man! Yes, how is it with you today? Be preparing yourself, my youthful friend. Let not the day of our Almighty One come upon you and find you not ready. Shalom."

Aphiah, the Ruebenite, stood taller than the other two. The added height was an advantage, because he enjoyed being noticed. He wasn't very well liked, though he held the honored position of chieftain and teacher in his own community. The children secretly said that if everything Aphiah said about himself while teaching was removed, there wouldn't be enough words left to make a dung cake.

Eldad, Aphiah, and Mishael, the chieftain of Issachar, arrived at the large tent that housed Elishama's family. They called the old man's name, and his granddaughter came out with a basin of water to wash their dusty feet. They entered the central room of the tent and bowed to their respected friend.

Elishama motioned them to sit. His granddaughter brought out a large platter of leeks, cucumbers, dried dates, and loaves of bread. She handed each a cup of spiced milk and left the four men to their business.

Elishama was a descendant of Ephraim, the son of Joseph. Like Abraham before him, he never wavered in his beliefs regardless of the circumstances that surrounded him. Because he was humble, there were many within the Goshen community who didn't know of the old man's many accomplishments.

In his younger years, he was a stalwart in camp, a man who stood up to the guards and soldiers in the work force. He fought vigorously to get the Hebrew slaves a measure of respectability with their Egyptian slave masters. He also fought against the terribly stiff tax charged against the fruits of the fields the Hebrews owned or managed. He was a man who encouraged his brothers every day and helped keep their hopes up, awaiting the coming of the Almighty One.

In his older years, Elishama was honored not only because of all he'd done earlier but because he was considered the wisest man in camp, one who seemed to know the Almighty One well. He was highly respected for his unwavering belief regardless of circumstances. Though he was respected by most of the men in camp, to some, he was just as highly misunderstood. Some of them mocked him and called him Old Abraham, because of his age and great faith. Others used the name out of respect. No one, however, used the name to his face.

As was his custom, he sat quietly and waited for the others to speak. Eldad sucked cucumber juice from his fingers and looked into the old man's eyes.

"Elishama, my friend and counselor, you must be aware of what happened to Avaris and the rest of the land around us. It's been covered with a darkness unlike anything we've ever seen. You must know we investigated this thing."

Elishama nodded. By then, everyone knew what had happened.

"When it became obvious there would be no soldiers or work today," Eldad continued, "we decided to send Caleb, the son of Jephunnah, to take a closer look at this plague. His report sounds strange to our ears, but not so strange considering what's been taking place over the last few months. To you, perhaps it won't sound strange at all."

Elishama hadn't been at the tent meeting earlier that day, but he'd heard from others in his clan about Caleb's journey and return. He'd been waiting for Eldad's visit to hear the full report. "Please go on," he said.

Eldad related what Caleb found and told them. " ... so, when he finished his investigation, he was able to move out of the darkness back to where his men were, but it was very difficult. He concluded that it is yet another plague sent by the Almighty One. One reason he thinks so is that although he experienced difficulty in the darkness, it wasn't enough to fill him with anguish like he heard in the voices of those of Kemet.

"I agree. We haven't spoken with Aaron or Mosheh for days and had no warning this was coming. However, it seems to be the hand of the Lord. Once again, Elishama, the plague affects our enemies and gives us freedom.

"However, it is with much sadness that I must inform you that we elders, once again, were divided in our opinions. We're a strange people. I know that the Lord is preparing us further for our deliverance from this land. Many of the elders agree, but not all. We aren't united."

Eldad stopped speaking and looked intently at Elishama, wondering if he would reply. The elderly Eldad looked forward to his friend's words. He, too, considered the Ephramite elder the wisest man in the camp. His words always carried much encouragement. Aphiah, however, seized the moment and spoke first.

"Elishama, take counsel with my words, I pray. The things that our honored chieftain, Eldad, has told you are the well-thought-out opinions of most of us who have the responsibility to think for the rest of the camp. Possibly, it's time to call the people together and let them know we have everything in hand. That would dispel their concerns."

Old Abraham paid little attention to the self-righteous Ruebenite.

"Our people," Eldad said, "are caught in a swirling wind. They don't know what to believe. I think they want to believe as we do, that the time of deliverance is near, but they're frightened. They're torn between their fear of Ramesses, his soldiers, and their hatred for Mosheh, which is actually a misunderstanding. Our people need counsel, but they're afraid of hearing it.

"When we speak to them about what the Lord's doing and how Mosheh has been sent to lead us out of here, we simply anger them further. How do we bring them together? How can we help our brothers? At a time like this, they need our leadership, but there's much rebellion. Will the people be ready when the Lord is ready to take us from here? I honestly don't know."

Old Abraham spoke almost in a whisper, but he spoke clearly enough for them to hear him. "The promise has been given to us, my friends, that we, the Hebrew people, will be rescued from our bondage by the Almighty One. He will deliver us into a land overflowing with all good things. I have never doubted that, nor do I doubt it now. It will happen as the Almighty One said. Our people will be delivered from the hand of Ramesses. If they believe, they will be rescued. If they don't, they'll still be rescued. It would be well if all were prepared, but they won't be. However, that doesn't change the Unchangeable One."

Eldad was greatly encouraged by those words.

Mishael rubbed his coarse hands on his face. "Elishama, how does this new plague affect our belief that the Almighty One is coming for us? Is it further assurance? Is it drawing us closer to that time? Many people say that Ramesses will lay an even harsher punishment against us. Our people can't take much more persecution."

"Mishael, we need not make any judgments until we've heard from Aaron and Mosheh. If they're communing with the Almighty One, then we need only to see what it is that He, through Mosheh, has to tell us. I will tell you this—in my opinion, the Almighty One isn't yet finished showing His power to Ramesses.

"Surely, this is His hand bringing forth darkness over the land. All the signs point to that. He isn't slack. You can be certain of that. Remember how many times our God has shown His power to Ramesses, and the stiff-necked pharaoh has stood his ground, thinking he's keeping the Almighty One from doing what He chooses? Ramesses, too, will become a believer, but it will be too late. We can be patient. The Almighty One is in control.

"Remember, Mishael, we were told by Aaron that the Almighty One would have us take spoil of our captors, the people of Kemet, before we depart. We haven't done that yet. Let us be filled with belief and still be patient. We must not get ahead of the plan that has been laid out for us.

"Also remember that the Almighty One has held the promise of deliverance since the time of our father, Abraham. That should make it certain that He's not going to be hurried in bringing it about. We can be at peace and watch with expectancy."

"That is wise counsel, Elishama," Eldad said, running his fingers through his beard. "It is, however, a difficult thing for men to have patience in such times. They don't have our understanding. We wish to counsel our people in this manner, however. We want them to believe and be at peace and watch, as you say, with joy and expectancy.

"Will the people receive counsel from us? Will they respond favorably to anything we say in this matter? Many men in camp are angry and impatient. They don't understand what the Lord's doing and want revenge. We aren't looked upon favorably by everyone in the camp. Dare we attempt to continue in this manner?"

Elishama nodded as if agreeing in his mind. "Counsel, my friends, when it isn't dispensed with care and consideration, is like water poured into a broken cup. In the same manner, the ears of the wise counselor are larger than his tongue. He keeps his wisdom safe and gives it only to those who have the key, which is an honest, searching heart.

"While we wait patiently for Mosheh to bring further instructions from the Almighty One, you'll find those who seek the wisdom you have. When you do, open your place of safekeeping and give them wisdom from your storehouse. Where you see wisdom and counsel bearing fruit, there will be behind it one that has guarded the Lord's secrets well and hasn't wasted them.

"Many men think they have much wisdom to impart. Those who truly have it are slow to give it away, for they know it's not theirs to give. True wisdom comes from above and isn't spoken in a haughty voice. Those who proudly display their wisdom are, in fact, displaying their own foolishness. At best, they will make others as foolish as themselves."

He paused, looking at the three men sitting with him, and then he closed his eyes to gather his thoughts. The men waited reverently for him to continue. The elderly Ephramite looked at Eldad, forced a half-smile, then looked at Aphiah who moved uncomfortably in his seat when Elishama's staring cut into his heart.

"I don't hesitate to say to you, my brothers, that we live in a time unlike any time that has passed in our history. We're witnessing things that can't be easily understood. Our people, whom we love, have allowed confusion and anger to separate them from us. I believe that as we draw closer to the time, men throughout the encampment will look more seriously for the truth. We have that truth, not because we're wiser, but rather because the truth was given to us by our fathers and confirmed by the Almighty One through Mosheh and Aaron.

"It's time to put aside our own concerns. There's no room in Goshen for greed or pride among our leadership. The Almighty One of Israel would have us sacrifice those things on the altar, even more than an unblemished lamb. If we don't have the people's respect, they won't listen to us."

Aphiah squirmed, his restlessness becoming more obvious.

"You're correct, Eldad," Elishama continued. "Our people are filled with questions now. What the Almighty One is doing has been seen. I believe that many who were angry earlier are now frightened. Those who would have stoned Mosheh to death eagerly await his next instructions, though they don't say so outwardly. Our men are like a large flock grazing in the wilderness with no shepherd to call them in at night or keep them from danger. The God of Abraham has brought Mosheh to us to unite us and be a shepherd for our people.

"Remember, my friends, that once even some of you were very much against Mosheh. Some even turned the people against him. Have you considered why you did that?" He was speaking of Aphiah.

"It was because of envy," Elishama said. "In our pitiful state, we, as leaders, should be prepared to sacrifice everything for the cause of our people. Mosheh is a good example of that. He gave up the throne of the Two Lands and hid in the desert until the Almighty One called him—all for the love of our people."

"But honored chieftain," Aphiah said, speaking loudly and with a red face, "please remember that none of us had seen or heard from Mosheh for many years. We knew only of his early life as a man that was raised in the pharaoh's court, our captor and enemy. He was a military warrior who led the red men in battle, the same men who are our hated enemies. Mosheh left Kemet and hid for forty years, living peacefully, while we who remained were overworked, beaten, and murdered. I ask you, were we to believe this man just because he said he was sent by God? Did you believe him at first? I think not.

Uncharacteristically, Elishama raised his voice as he answered Aphiah's challenge. "I, too, know of the early years of my friend,

Mosheh. I didn't pass judgment on him based on that knowledge, however. Instead, I considered the testimony of his father, Amram. He told us how Mosheh came to be raised in the king's palace. It was the Almighty One Himself who commanded Amram to hide the child from the guards' swords. It was the Almighty One who preserved Mosheh's life. Have you considered that, Aphiah?

"He became a great commander of the army, as you said, saving the land from invasion by many enemies, but I also considered if it was possible that Mosheh was chosen to be a warrior against the invading nations so he wouldn't have to command the guards who beat and killed his own people.

"Then, too, Aphiah, how do we respond to Mosheh's testimony of his encounter with the Almighty One in the desert? We can't dispute his story because of the signs he performed before us.

"You see then that I *did* believe Mosheh and Aaron when they came to us. I haven't doubted what they said. You did, my friend, even when you first heard it, and that was because your heart was of stone. You weren't interested in the future of our people. You were only interested in yourself. The seriousness of our troubles hasn't touched you the same way it has touched others. If you don't change your thinking and attitude, you can be of no service to your people during this period of strife."

He sighed and softened his voice. "Aphiah, I don't often speak harshly, but it's necessary for you to understand the truth about yourself. We're a people devoid of ambition because of what we've experienced. Your great achievements to our people are but a sieve filled with chaff tossed into the wind. To gain the people's respect, you must have compassion, understanding, and genuine love like Mishael. You must show kindness and gentleness, and you must be bold in your conclusions concerning the Almighty One, like Eldad, but those things aren't part of your nature.

"They can be, however. You know the truth. The great virtue of humility, which was so prevalent in our father Abraham, has escaped you. Please remember, our gracious God is a merciful God. He would like nothing better than to help remold you so you can be a strong tree to help shelter our people. It won't be easy for you.

You're a proud man. We're your friends. At this time, brothers, we need each other, and we need all of us to help lead our people."

Elishama fell silent. Aphiah, however, was outraged. He couldn't believe what he'd just heard. The man had embarrassed him in front of his peers. His mind raced. Who did Old Abraham think he was, talking to him like that? He was a teacher, a man highly respected for it. He was also the finest herdsman in Goshen, and the people knew it.

The tall Ruebenite chieftain rose from his mat. Without speaking, he turned and stormed out of the tent. The three remaining Hebrew leaders watched him silently.

Elishama felt no remorse. He was saddened but not surprised at Aphiah's reaction. Elishama knew he hadn't spoken in anger but in truth.

Once Aphiah was out of sight of Elishama's house, he stopped, sat on a stone bench beside a large field of maize that was just sprouting, and forced his mind to relax and let his anger subside.

What had gotten into Elishama that would make him speak to him like that? Old Abraham had never done that as long as Aphiah had known him. He'd never spoken like that to anyone.

Aphiah was wise enough that he wanted to consider what Elishama had said, because he knew the old man was wise, but his pride had been attacked, and he hadn't yet accepted that. Wounded, he wanted to lash out.

Elishama was wrong. Aphiah was well respected in the community, and the things he had accomplished were important. The people listened to him because of who he was. He would have a positive effect on them. He would be among those leaders who helped prepare the people for the Lord's rescue.

He relaxed. His confidence in himself brought his pride back to the danger level, where it usually operated.

Elishama must come to him and apologize. He had no other choice. Once he realized what he'd done, he would repent and seek Aphiah's forgiveness. He considered how to handle that. Certainly, he would forgive the old man. Otherwise, he'd fall into disrepute with the other elders, but he would demand a full apology. That would work to his advantage, but he must think it out.

The proud Ruebenite didn't have enough humility to accept Elishama's criticism honorably. He sighed, laid his head back against the wooden bench, and reviewed the words that had cut him so sharply.

"You doubted what was said, even when you first heard it, and it was because your heart was made of stone. You weren't interested in the future of our people. You were only interested in yourself. The seriousness of our troubles hasn't touched you the same way it has touched others. If you don't change your thinking and attitude, you can be of no service to the people.

"It's necessary for you to understand the truth about yourself. Your great achievements are to the people but a sieve filled with chaff tossed into the wind. To gain the respect of our people, you must have compassion, understanding, and genuine love. You must show kindness and gentleness, and you must be bold in your conclusions concerning the Almighty One. Those things aren't part of your nature."

*What? I don't have compassion and genuine love?* he wondered. *Is that possible? I'm a proud man, but I have good reason. I've accomplished much under the worst circumstances, and I should be proud. Compassion? Well, maybe I don't have as much as Eldad, but he can spend all day thinking about his people. I must spend time taking care of my business. That doesn't mean I'm not compassionate. I'm just not as compassionate as Eldad. Understanding? Genuine love?*

Deep inside, he knew he had to consider what Elishama said. His earlier thoughts of the man's apology were wrong. He knew it. Maybe he would consider becoming more understanding and compassionate. It wasn't as if he didn't want to be more compassionate. After all, he was a leader of the Hebrews. It was his duty to help prepare them for what the Almighty One did. He felt genuine love for them and cared about them. He understood they needed help.

He would think it over. He would be a good leader, and he would prove to Elishama and the others that he was as good a leader as any in the camp. Maybe Elishama would still apologize.

\* \* \*

"Hopefully," Elishama muttered, "he'll think seriously about what's been said to him."

"I'm sure, Elishama, that you don't need my encouragement," Eldad said, "but I believe you were right. Aphiah could have responded differently than he did. It was his decision to be offended, rather than corrected. Possibly, we'll be rid of him and his self-righteousness."

"Do you think so?" Elishama smiled.

Eldad sighed. "No. He may bring more trouble now than before. How do we deal with him?"

Old Abraham ran his hands over his pure-white beard. "We don't need to deal with him any longer. We'll let the Almighty One do that. I believe he has a decent heart. Give him time. What he needs is time to think.

"There are more important things for us to do. We don't know exactly where we are in the Almighty One's plan and promise. There may be more beatings and killings, or we might be at the threshold of leaving our sorrows behind. Either way, we need to be prepared so we might help prepare others.

"Regardless of the thoughts of those who've chosen to rebel, we need to be of one mind concerning the things Mosheh has brought us from the Almighty One. We need to be sure in our thoughts that He's coming soon to fulfill His promise to our father, Abraham. We need to know that our enemies, Ramesses and his people, are feeling the wrath of our just and holy God. We need to be bold yet gentle as we present these things to the people.

"This encampment won't be united, my friends, until we, the chieftains of the tribes of Israel, are united. Eldad and Mishael, walk among the people. Talk with them. Encourage them, but hear me. As you converse with them, don't listen just to their anger, bitterness, and disappointments. Listen also to what speaks beneath those feelings.

"Is there fear behind their angry words? Is their discouragement a blanket that covers their lack of knowledge of the Almighty One and the truth? It's possible that we should attempt to give back to our people that which they lost through years of slavery. Remember, a Hebrew who has lost his awareness of the Almighty One is only half a Hebrew. We have the other half. Be wise and dispense your wisdom and knowledge gently and cautiously.

"Listen with large ears, my brothers, and you'll know to whom you should give understanding."

The elders nodded.

"Come, Mishael," Eldad said. "There's much to be done while we still have freedom in the camp."

The men rose and bowed to their honored host, nodded to his granddaughter and left the tent. They walked enthusiastically through the camp. Eldad encouraged those with whom he came into contact, and Mishael spoke comforting words to them. As he walked and spoke, Mishael also wondered what was going through the Almighty One's mind.

Was he really just biding His time, waiting for the right moment to deliver them, or was He trying desperately to rescue them and have difficulty doing it? He hoped no one would ask him that.

# CHAPTER NINE

# IDBASH, I LOVE YOU

Caath, not intending to be away so long, was surprised to see how quickly evening arrived. He walked slowly to his father's hut and stopped outside, listening. When he heard nothing, he peered in through the doorway and found the hut empty. He walked inside and started tidying up. Cooking grates and other utensils lay where he and his father had left them earlier. Gathering them in his arms, he took them to the well to wash them, bringing the water jug along to be refilled.

The young son of Abiasaph felt good, though a bit uncertain. Spending the day with his friends, Tola and Salma, put him in a good mood. He didn't know what love was, though he'd heard the term often enough. He was beginning to believe that, if there was such a thing, he felt it in his relationship with Tola. No matter what they did together, it was enjoyable.

He stopped for a moment to look at the black curtain surrounding the land. He wondered what the truth was concerning the plagues. He and Tola talked about it earlier that day, but what left the biggest impression on him was what Oshea told them as they sat by the altar near the marshes. But then, as he listened to the Little Beer Man, his thoughts became confused again.

He had many questions. He wanted to understand everything and felt his father could help, but he was no longer certain his father knew all the answers.

He finished his chores at the well and balanced the full water jug on his head as he carried the cooking utensils back to the hut. When he approached, he saw his father moving about inside.

Abiasaph turned and looked sternly at the boy, though he said nothing. Caath meekly brought the things into the house and placed them in their proper places. Abiasaph turned and walked to the far corner of the hut where a tiny lamb lay on his mat.

Caath saw the lamb immediately. "Papa, what happened? Is it hurt?"

"No, no." Abiasaph smiled. "It's just another lamb that has refused its mother's milk. This is the one born yesterday. It's the days in which we live, Caath. The old men of the community say that seldom, in times past, were the animals so full of rebellion. Now it seems common." He nodded to his son, including him in the caretaking of the frail animal. "We'll keep the lamb here tonight. When the guards come in the morning, be sure to place her with her mother."

"Yes, Papa. If the guards don't come again tomorrow, shall we keep the lamb here in the hut to feed it?"

Abiasaph paused, not having considered that possibility. "Yes, if you keep her with you, you may graze her close by. Don't take her far, or she'll learn wanderlust, and you'll lose her. Treat her kindly. She'll follow you, and, in time, become a good lead ewe."

"Papa, can I name her? Please?"

Abiasaph laughed. "You've become the namer of the entire flock, haven't you? Go ahead. What shall it be?"

Abiasaph enjoyed having a light moment with his son but knew it wouldn't last. He'd spent his day feeling restless. He spoke briefly with Hor-em-heb, the white-haired former priest of Kemet, and left that conversation more confused than relieved. The man's speech was gentle but was very convincing in his argument favoring Mosheh and Aaron.

Coming from someone who'd been trained in the temples of Kemet, that was startling to hear. Abiasaph cleared his mind of such thoughts and watched his son as he searched for a name for the newest member of their flock.

After a few moments, Caath's eyes lit up, and he turned to his father joyfully. "I know, Papa. I have a name. Actually, I have two. I'd like to call her Ulam when she grows, because she'll be the lead ewe, but even more, I'll call her Idbash, because she's colored like honey and is sweet to hold and care for. Ulam, come here! Idbash, come! Yes, I've decided. It'll be Idbash."

He cuddled the lamb and pressed its soft face against his. "Idbash, we'll make you our lead ewe. Come, let's have some milk."

He poured milk from the goatskin into a cup and carefully fed it to the lamb. He enjoyed himself. It was good medicine for him, and Abiasaph knew it. He watched approvingly as his son pampered the young animal. He let him play with it for a long time before stopping him.

"Caath, it's time to put Idbash to sleep for the night. Make a bed for her and come. We must talk. I'm hungry. While you played today, your papa worked in the sheep fold."

Caath built a small bed for Idbash, gently laid her down, patted her soft head, and bid her good night. He began to prepare a meal for himself and his father. Abiasaph pulled two large fish from a jar at the door and handed them to his son.

"Papa, where'd you get these? Did you go on the hunt?"

"Ha! No, I wasn't hunting today. Michael, the son of Joel, came by and left those for us. He said that had you gone with him, those were the two you would have caught. You were busy playing with friends, so he caught enough fish for his family and more. You should have stayed here this morning. You could have gone with him and enjoyed yourself."

Caath knew he wouldn't have enjoyed himself as much as he did being with Tola. He hadn't had such a good day in a very long time. Although he always enjoyed being with Michael, who was seventeen and someone Caath felt close to, being with Tola was better.

Caath finished cooking and brought a platter to his father, then set one on the ground for himself. He brought two cups of milk spiced with honey to sweeten the sour taste.

145

Abiasaph looked at his son for a long time. He had a lot to tell him but didn't know how to begin. That was unusual. Abiasaph was rarely unprepared.

He cared for his son but had never been able to tell him. When his beloved Nehushta died in childbirth nine years earlier, Abiasaph had, without realizing it, harbored bitterness toward Caath. When he realized that several years later, he repented within himself and tried to treat the boy with more love and respect, which was difficult. Abiasaph never developed a love for his son. He always felt a responsibility to train and prepare him for life, but until that moment, it never occurred to him to tell him he loved him.

Abiasaph loved only one person in his life—Nehushta. When she died, love died. In the years since he recognized his wrong attitude toward Caath, he treated him more kindly and tried to enjoy him more. He was convinced he loved him as best he could. Though he often sensed an emptiness in their relationship, he attributed it to Nehushta's death, not to a lack within himself.

But now, he felt empty. He wanted to put his arms around his son and hold him, but he couldn't. Caath was becoming a man. More than ever, Abiasaph had to instruct him in the hardness of life.

He sighed, staring at the boy, who enjoyed the evening meal. They didn't have meat very often.

"Caath, we must talk of things that won't be easy for you," Abiasaph said. "They are things you're hearing much about. It might be difficult for you to understand me after hearing so many things from others, so I'll give you a direction to follow. Take heed."

Caath saw that his father was serious. Though he often instructed Caath, they seldom had long conversations. He looked forward to it.

Abiasaph tugged at his waistband, contemplating his words. "Caath, I'm not changing my own ideas concerning the things that have been happening. Those things I have already taught you, I still want you to follow. Concerning the work we're forced to do, we must consider that tomorrow, the guards will probably be here early and angry. We must be prepared to work harder than usual and say nothing. They'll be looking for someone to beat. Those things haven't changed.

"However, we must also consider a new thing. These strange happenings haven't been without a force or reason. I'm sure of that. Some say, as you know, that the Hebrew God is doing these things to punish the people. Others say that Mosheh will lead us out of Kemet to a new land where every day will be a free day. Yes, I've heard those things, but I don't believe them. They're too easy. Things have never been easy for the Hebrew people. That isn't our way. What is happening now, it won't be easy, either.

"The Hebrew God, the Almighty One, is distant from me. I'm not like Old Abraham and the chieftains. Strange things are happening, and soon, an answer will appear. I see it like the flood season. You watch the waters rise and rise, and you know they'll stop, even at the edge of the bank, no matter what others say. Finally, they reach the point of flooding and roll across the land with mighty force.

"That's what I see now, Caath. I have watched these things occur and have thought about them, although I haven't said anything. I know what the others say, but I don't believe as they do. However, the waters are still rising. What will happen? Will we learn that our chieftains are right? I don't think so, but something will happen soon, and it might be worse for us than now.

"It's hard to believe that the Almighty One will save us from our torment. If that's His desire, why hasn't He done it already? I've heard so many things about Him, but I haven't seen anything of Him, so I can't believe that. Do you understand? It's hard for me to say these things. I've been unable to make my own thoughts clear, so I'm having difficulty telling you. It's necessary for you to be prepared for more sadness, because we can't rely on stories for our deliverance.

"Let's consider the possibilities. If the plagues stop, and peace reigns in the land, will pharaoh relent in his hardness toward us? Will his anger be greater? Will he attack like a hungry bear in the sheepfold? How can we prepare for that? Have you considered that? If we knew that our task of building the city tomorrow would be even more difficult, how would we manage?

"Remember how the people responded when we were ordered to make the same amount of bricks while supplying our own straw? Many lost their lives out of stupidity and stubbornness. Now we make bricks with less straw and they're still strong. If we work, we make the quota. We could have done that at the beginning and been spared so many deaths.

"We must be wise, my son, not foolish. The Hebrew people have proven that wisdom and hope don't mix well. As we look at all that has happened in recent months, we can assume the next move is the pharaoh's. We must be prepared for what he'll do. We don't know what it'll be, but we can be ready to accept it, knowing that no matter how impossible it seems, we can solve it and still survive."

"Papa, I can do that. You've taught me how to make myself work no matter how hard it is. I won't cry or feel sorry for myself, but Papa, shouldn't we also prepare for the things the elders say? Oshea says it's no longer a question that the Almighty One will free us from the land. It's certain. He says it's important to rehearse the old stories, sacrifice, and pray. He built an altar near the marshlands, and Tola and I saw him and Tebaliah lying before it, praying for a long time. He said that especially now, praying, sacrificing, and believing the promise are more important than anything else."

Abiasaph slammed his fist against the ground. "No! Oshea doesn't think deeply enough. Yes, he's a respected man, and things may turn out as he says, but it has to become clearer first. It's not important to prepare for something we aren't certain of, when there are things we can be sure of."

"But Papa, Oshea is sure of the taking out of the people from the land. He says the Almighty One promised our father, Abraham, many years ago that He would take us out of the land." He desperately wanted to get that point across. He wasn't disagreeing with his father, he just wanted to make sure his Papa understood everything everyone else did. He wished he could explain it better, but the more he talked, the angrier his father became.

"Think, Caath! How could Abraham hundreds of years ago have known we'd be here? Remember, it was Jacob, after Abraham died, who brought us here when there was famine throughout the rest of the world. Even he didn't know we'd stay here and be put into slavery."

"Yes, Papa." Caath strained, trying to think what to do. There was much he wanted to tell his father, but he couldn't hurt him, or he'd become angry, and the talk would end. In an attempt to soothe his father, he spoke softly.

"Papa, you've never told me the stories of old about Abraham, Isaac, or our father, Jacob. I know about Joseph only those few things I've heard from Tola and Salma. I've never heard about the promise the others mention. You told me once, Papa, that you never bothered with learning those things because they aren't important. I believe you, Papa. I know what you've taught me is true and important, but it also seems important to know those other things so we can decide what we should do."

Abiasaph, angered, jumped up from the mat and spilled his cup of milk. He walked toward the door, cursing quietly to himself. He knew Caath was speaking the truth, but it hurt to hear it from his son. That kind of thing wasn't in Abiasaph's idea of a father-son relationship.

He turned and shouted, "Boy, get up!"

Startled, Caath jumped to his feet. Abiasaph strode toward him, grabbed his shoulders with two strong hands, and shook him as he shouted, "You're the boy, understand? I'm the father. I don't want to hear you say anything else about Oshea or Mosheh or their God. Do you hear me? I don't want to hear anymore!"

"Y...yes, Papa."

Abiasaph's hands fell limply to his side. He walked toward the opening and looked out into the evening, which was growing darker by the minute. It was still light, though, compared to the blackness hanging over the city of Avaris.

Caath regained his composure and walked to where Idbash lay. He stroked her soft back, staring at his father, no longer concerned for his own safety but fearful for his father. He didn't know what was happening to him. Why couldn't he see Caath wasn't against him?

He agreed with what his father taught, but he wanted to understand more. What could he do? He sighed. He had to let his father calm down before talking with him again.

Abiasaph went to the wineskin and filled his cup, and walked to Caath and the lamb feeling calmer.

"Caath, I don't wish to hurt you, but you must consider that I'm your father, and I know what's best for you to understand and think. You're still a boy. If you allow too many thoughts to fill your mind, you'll become confused. Look at Isus. He wants to believe everything he hears. As a result, he doesn't know what to think.

"As for Oshea, you know I've never been a friend of his. He and others like him are a different kind of Hebrew than we are, even though we come from the same loins. We're made from a different nature than they.

"Heed me, Son. We're like outcasts. You need to understand that. It's not for us to visit others in camp. It's hard for me when you go with your young friend, Tola. His people are different, too. I didn't have a friend at your age. I spent no time playing. The life we face isn't for boys, it's for men. Those who allow their sons to be children will lose them. You don't understand that yet, but I've lived for thirty years and know it's true.

"We have no heritage, no family to belong to. We're alone, and we must think by ourselves. We have only each other. We no longer have my brother, Adbeel. He's become a thorn to us and has made our lot even worse. We no longer have a clan, either. It's the best way. It's just you and I, Caath, and we must do our thinking with that in mind."

"Papa, we herd with Shimri and his house. Don't we have a pact with him, Tebaliah, and Shobab?"

"No," Abiasaph said sharply. "I would have no part with them if I could. Shimri has become a thorn in the camp. He's my friend, but every day he loses more of himself to the gods of drink. Tebaliah is worthless after his injury and because he believes in hopeless things. Shobab can't think for himself, because he's too young. What good are they to us? We stand alone, Caath. That's best.

"Take heed now, and I'll explain to you what pharaoh and the brick making and the land of Goshen have taught me. Standing alone has taught me to depend on no one else but myself. It'll be the same for you. You'll be better able to live and work and will survive when others fall. You'll learn to see life as it is and not waste your time dreaming of things that can't be.

"Oshea speaks of the future, but the future we face is just tomorrow. We must be prepared to meet the guards and their whips. We face a long day toiling under the sun. Do you understand?"

"Yes, Papa."

"Do you want to question me now?"

"Yes," he said warily, "but if I do, it's only because I want us to work things out together. I believe that it's just us standing alone. I don't want that, but I accept it. You've taught me to be strong, and I will stand with you. I question because I want us to have the answers.

"Can it hurt to learn the stories of old? Even if we stand alone, apart from the others, can't we know those things? When I hear Oshea speak of them, I don't think about listening to him and not you. I know that the things you teach are good, but inside, when I hear about the Almighty One and Abraham and Joseph, I feel it's something I should know. I feel an emptiness inside, because I don't understand those things. Papa, I know I'm not making much sense. I don't know how to say what I'm thinking."

He shrugged and decided to stop. He couldn't find the right words, and his Papa would never understand.

"I, too, don't understand those things, Caath, but I don't believe we need to. As I said, it's enough just to be prepared for each day." He cleared his throat, finding it difficult to continue. "I'll think more about this. We'll talk again some other time."

The troubled Levite left his hut feeling embarrassed and confused. He walked toward the sheepfold so he could be alone to think.

Caath watched his father go. He glanced out at him occasionally as he finished cleaning the hut, wondering what was happening to him. He sipped his father's wine and found it smooth but sour. He shuddered and poured it back into the wineskin.

He walked through the doorway and sat in front of the hut, leaning against the mud wall. Then he looked back around the doorway and clapped his hands softly. "Idbash! Come, Idbash!"

The frail lamb scurried out the door and into his lap. He hugged the lamb tightly and sat quietly looking into her eyes. He stroked her soft body with his small, rough hands. He felt something special coming from Idbash and decided it was love.

Tears formed in his eyes, but he fought them off and overcame the emotion. He was glad he could keep his tears inside like his father taught him.

He thought about his father's outbreak of anger, then about Oshea and Tebaliah and the conversation earlier that day. Then he put it out of his mind. It was too confusing. He held Idbash's face in his hands and looked into her soft eyes. He sat that way, gently petting her, for a long time. She cocked her head and laid it against his shoulder.

Then Caath said something that he'd never said to anyone before in his life. He spoke quietly, wanting no one to hear, but he meant it.

"Idbash, I love you."

Caath was amazed at hearing those words. He had never said them before. They sounded funny, but they felt good. He was glad he'd done it.

He looked up into the clear, dark sky and wondered about Oshea's God. He closed his eyes and held Idbash close as he said, quietly, "Almighty One of Oshea and Tebaliah, can you hear me? If you can, please help me to be strong like Papa taught. Help me to stand alone with him, the way he wants, and please help him decide to let me learn the old stories.

"Almighty One of Oshea and Tebaliah, if You're really coming to take us from this land, would You please take Papa, Idbash, and me with You? Please, Almighty One, take us with You."

# PART TWO
# THE SECOND DAY

# CHAPTER TEN

# EBEBI

M i-Sakhme, the captain of the guard, was certain it wasn't a great dust storm as his counselors had first suggested. It was different, strange, and frightening. His mind whirled with unanswered questions. *What's causing this horrible plague of darkness? What can I do about it?*

He'd done nothing since the previous day when the darkness began. He wondered what the situation was with his estate and people. How were the soldiers doing without his leadership? Were they at the work sites? How was the pharaoh handling it? Had he met with Mosheh, that meddler, yet? Was that even necessary? Was the darkness another magic act from that old, smelly, sand crosser? How far did it extend? Was it just at Mi-Sakhme's estate? Were the Hebrew slaves at work?

His thoughts were desultory. He felt the effect of the darkness physically and mentally. He hadn't slept. He tried to calm himself and organize his thoughts. The previous year had been emotionally draining. His estate was in a shambles. The moment he began repairs from one of the plagues, another arrived that was even worse.

The current one affected him personally. When he tried to call for Petephis, his chief steward, the thick air almost choked him. Since then, Petephis had come to him, but then he left. With talking being so painful, Mi-Sakhme had remained quiet since.

*At least most of the screaming is over,* he thought, thanking the gods.

He didn't know where his mistress was, though he knew she was safe somewhere on the estate, probably in her rooms. He didn't know if he'd lost any of his people to the darkness. He hadn't heard any official reports from soldiers or stewards. Seeing the situation, that was understandable. He didn't want to lose more people, though. He'd already lost thirteen important soldiers and servants and countless others to the string of disasters.

The plague must have been brought on by the old prince, Mosheh. It had the characteristics of the other calamities. He wondered if the Hebrews were experiencing the darkness, too.

What was wrong with his pharaoh? Why wouldn't he give in? The Egyptians wouldn't be able to continue much longer this way.

As a result of the plagues over the past year, Mi-Sakhme had lost almost all his cattle, his gardens and fields were destroyed, and thirteen of his soldiers and servants died. It would take years to rebuild his estate.

To make matters worse, the people were rebelling. The soldiers weren't responding to discipline as readily, and two had the gall to assault him near the city gate. They were no longer willing to work for the same wage as before, claiming the circumstances had changed. They acted as if the plagues were his fault. Fortunately, his personal guards overcame the troublemakers.

How much longer could the situation go on? Everyone had been touched by the plagues. No one lived a normal life anymore. People were unhappy and short-tempered, and there was talk of eliminating Ramesses for someone who would give in to the Hebrews.

Mi-Sakhme shook his head. That would never happen. Ramesses would remain pharaoh until his natural death. No one would find enough support to kill him. Ramesses was the strongest and most popular pharaoh the land had ever seen, and he would remain in control.

The real question was whether the pharaoh would be forced to give in to Mosheh. Ramesses didn't give in easily, but if he didn't, the people would continue to be harassed by the plagues. What could be done?

Mi-Sakhme pitied himself. He felt as if he were losing his mind. Trying to remain calm was becoming a monumental task. Thousands of people looked to him for help, wisdom, and advice.

What could he give? He didn't know what to say. Although he didn't know any more than anyone else, he had to give an answer. He prayed the gods hadn't forgotten him and his people and would deliver them.

He wondered if he believed in the gods anymore. He wasn't certain, but at least no one was running to him for an answer to the current plague. He found that sarcastically amusing.

He wanted to call Petephis, who was probably nearby, but would he hear him? Mi-Sakhme couldn't yell anymore due to the pain that came from talking in the blackness. It was like being strangled, yet he wanted to speak to someone. He was becoming more frightened by the minute.

"Petephis?" he asked softly.

"Yes, my lord. I'm nearby. Keep calling my name, and I'll come to you."

The man's voice sounded as if it came through a sieve. A few minutes later, Mi-Sakhme felt a hand touch his shoulder. He turned toward it, but he saw nothing. Even at close range, the blackness was complete. Nothing had changed since the plague began. That, in itself, was amazing. And frightening.

Suddenly, a disturbing thought came to his mind. He wondered if he were blind. He prayed not. He had too much to live for. His weakened mind needed assurance and encouragement.

"Petephis," he whispered, "can you see me?"

"No, my lord. Everything is thick and black, but I'm here beside you." He gripped his lord's shoulder again.

Mi-Sakhme sighed in relief. It was a comfort to know that Petephis was blind, too. Mi-Sakhme had to remain sane and wait for the blackness to lift, but it was difficult. The ordeal had a profound effect on him. He was completely helpless, and, for a brief moment, he wished he had a lower servant there to scream at and relieve some of the pressure.

He told himself to stop thinking like that. "Is it another day, Petephis, since this began?"

"Yes, my lord. This is the second day since the darkness came upon us."

"Can we move at all? Is it wise for me to move? Will I be harmed?" Oh, the pain that came from speaking, but he had to have answers.

"It would be better if you didn't move unnecessarily, my lord. It's almost impossible to move about. When I decided to come to this side of the house to be near you, I found it extremely difficult. It's better to sit still. As was the case with the other misfortunes, this will pass soon, I'm sure."

"Thank you, Petephis." In an unusual gesture, he reached out and patted Petephis' shoulder. At least his chief steward understood him and was reliable.

He wondered how long the situation could last. He would go mad if it didn't end soon. No one could sit in the dark like that forever. There had to be something he could do.

Petephis knew his master was capricious. And he was concerned that he might over-react. He decided to stay close to him, if possible.

Mi-Sakhme needed to arrange his thoughts clearly. Everyone depended on him. He had to do something, so he thought of the previous plagues. All came about because of that dreaded Hebrew, Mosheh.

Was it possible that the darkness had been caused by something other than Mosheh's magic? No, that was unlikely. Mosheh was to blame. Curse those Hebrews! Their god had certainly been working for them lately. Why hadn't the Egyptian gods done something?

He considered that seriously, but he only found more questions. Could the Egyptian gods be angry with them? Could they be angry with Ramesses? Had he angered them somehow, or had Mi-Sakhme brought down their wrath? What was the answer?

He thought for a while and decided the gods were angry with something or someone. If he knew what it was, then he would have the solution.

He pondered that revelation, listing the chief officials in his staff, then his officers, then his servants. Wait! Why hadn't he seen it before?

"Petephis!" He nearly choked on the thick air.

"Yes, my lord?" He hadn't moved. The two men were close enough that their shoulders touched.

"Petephis, don't we have a Hebrew among the household servants?"

"Yes, Master, the one now called Ebebi. He was a Hebrew at the beginning."

"Have him brought to me at once. Make sure a few of my soldiers come with you."

Petephis nodded and moved away.

Mi-Sakhme relaxed. Why hadn't he thought of that earlier? He'd been suffering in a nightmare for over a day, and all along, the answer was in his house.

He knew that when he rid his house of the Hebrew servant, the gods would withdraw their anger and would smile upon him again. Light would return, and his discomfort would vanish. The gods didn't want any Hebrews on the estate while they were fighting the Hebrew god. He must send a runner to the pharaoh and tell him the answer he'd found. Surely he would be rewarded for finding divine intervention. He felt better already.

He hoped Petephis could locate Ebebi. He could be anywhere on the estate, and Petephis might not find him in the darkness. Then what?

Mi-Sakhme knew he couldn't last much longer. His mind was doing strange things. The pressure felt strong enough to make his head explode.

"Petephis, you must find that Hebrew slave—quickly."

Wait! He knew Petephis was an organized servant. He would know exactly where the Hebrew was. Everything would be all right soon. He just had to relax and leave it to Petephis. He was capable.

It would be good to get some sleep. When the light returned, there would be much to do. He had to tell Ramesses that he was the one who saved them from the darkness. His shoulders relaxed, though his eyes remained open.

In the prime of his life, the overweight, fearful man sat at his writing table convinced that the mighty gods, in their gratitude and mercy, were ready to end the plague and restore light to his estate once he found the cause of the terror and eliminated it.

It amused him to think how simple it was, and he was amazed that he realized the truth while all the sages missed it. Petephis had to find that slave! Everything depended on it.

Mi-Sakhme's thoughts slowly slipped into oblivion, and he slept.

\* \* \*

It was a huge task, one that would take Egypt's best if they wished to win. It was decided to call in Mi Sakhme, the captain of the pharaoh's guard.

He quickly gathered his elite troops and found the camp pitched far from the outskirts of the Two Lands. He was greeted warmly upon arrival. The remainder of the pharaoh's special regiment didn't look very good.

"Mi-Sakhme, my friend, how good that you and your men are here," the pharaoh said. "This has been the most treacherous of the battles in which I've been involved. As you can see, I've lost many of my best soldiers. Our situation is severe."

After Mi-Sakhme and his men were fed and rested, he met with Ramesses and his field officers to discuss strategy.

"We're certain, Captain Mi-Sakhme, that this brutal enemy will attack by nightfall. They know we've been badly hurt, and they'd be fools not to try to finish us off. What's your suggestion? What plan can you create to save our lives?"

"My dearest king, I'm somewhat surprised that you're still considering the possibility of defeat now that we are here. We've never failed before. Every battle we've fought has been won by a wide margin, and these infidels will fare no better. The gods haven't let us down, my king. They've simply been waiting for those to whom they have given great abilities. We'll overcome the enemy. Never fear."

"I'm sure you are correct. You always bring victory, and this situation will be no different. I have something else to speak with you about. I've met with my counselors, and I'm concerned about my ability to continue operating as the king of our great land. The injuries I've suffered worry me. I can no longer lead our great nation, and we'll need a strong military man like me—or you. Would you be willing to become the next pharaoh and rule our nation?"

Mi-Sakhme was pleased. He knew for some time he would eventually become pharaoh. The gods confirmed that with him earlier. They hadn't discontinued his position as the greatest warrior in the history of the land, so he hadn't thought about being pharaoh very often, but here he was and it appeared that it was time.

Ramesses was prepared to step aside. He knew that one couldn't stop fate. He saw that Mi-Sakhme must take over. It was natural.

"Yes, my lord, I'm prepared to accept your throne whenever you choose to step aside. Let's not worry about that right now. We have a battle to win. I must go prepare my troops."

As the humble captain left the tent, the pharaoh shook his head in disbelief. He turned to his counselors and generals and asked, "Is there a greater man in all the Two Lands? I think not. We made a wise decision."

\* \* \*

Adbeel was a Levite by birth, but his parents died young, and he and his brother, Abiasaph, were the only two who remained from the immediate family. Abiasaph chose to move away from the Levite camp, but Adbeel accepted the invitation of old Samuel and lived in his house.

Adbeel feared the Egyptians. He saw many of his brethren seriously injured and beaten by the Kemet guards. As an overseer among the Hebrew slaves, he was in constant communication with the head guards. On one such occasion, he gave the guards the names of his Hebrew companions who were causing dissension among the slaves. Those men were immediately beaten, resulting in more than one death.

Though Adbeel hadn't intended for that to happen, he was too far into the traitorous game to turn away, so he continued informing the guards about certain Hebrews.

He eventually requested asylum and asked to become one of the people of Kemet. His request was passed to Mi-Sakhme, the captain of the guards, who brought him to his estate to be interviewed by Petephis and his chief purchaser, Mugolla-sekh-mugolla, the foreign dwarf. After much discussion, they decided that if the man proved himself, he could become a slave at the estate.

They decided to ask Adbeel to kill one of his fellow Hebrews and cut off the hand, bringing it to Mi-Sakhme to prove he was sincere in his desire to leave the Hebrew slave force and deny his heritage.

It wasn't easy for Adbeel to accept those terms, but he realized it was his only chance for survival. If he stayed, someone would find out he'd been responsible for many of the recent beatings and deaths. Besides, he couldn't take slave work anymore.

After meeting Mi-Sakhme's demand, Adbeel was brought to the estate and changed his name to Ebebi. That was nearly one year earlier. He worked in several capacities in the servant force and considered himself one of the people of Kemet. He missed his own people, but, because of what he'd done, he couldn't go back, and he accepted that. He was a good servant to his master, Petephis.

\* \* \*

Mi-Sakhme awoke, startling himself, and remembered his situation. How different reality was from his pleasant dreams. He remembered Petephis had left to find the Hebrew, but Mi-Sakhme didn't know how long he'd been gone. If Petephis didn't find the man, the plague would never end. Everything hinged on finding Ebebi. That was the single most important thing happening in the entire land.

"Master? Where are you?"

"Petephis?" Mi-Sakhme soon felt the reassuring touch of Petephis' hand.

"Master, I have Ebebi with me."

"Thank you, Petephis. I have the answer to the blackness. We'll soon be out of this plague." He coughed, feeling severe pain in his throat. "Come here, Hebrew, and bow before me. I won't speak loudly to you."

Ebebi obeyed.

"Ebebi," Mi-Sakhme whispered, "your presence on the estate has angered the gods. Don't you know that our gods and your Hebrew gods are at war? That's where this horrible darkness has come from. It's a weapon of war. You've hidden from me, so I couldn't remove you from the grounds, but it's no use. The gods of Kemet have given me wisdom concerning your trickery. We found you. In our house, I can appease the gods only by removing you. It's necessary to save our land. Petephis, do away with him immediately."

He paused, feeling great discomfort from speaking, then added, "Bring me wine, Petephis. I shall retire soon. Tomorrow, there will be much to do."

Ebebi was horrified. "Master, please hear me! I'm no longer a Hebrew. I'm Ebebi of the Lower Land. Please repent of this order." But even as he spoke, he knew his plea was futile.

Mi-Sakhme felt himself shaking. He was on the verge of solving the crisis, and he felt all the evil in the world warring with him. All he wanted was to remove the Hebrew so his gods could save him.

He had to remain calm and allow everything to work itself out. Then he heard Petephis speaking, although he didn't catch the words.

"Speak again, Petephis," he ordered.

"Would it be better, my lord, to exile Ebebi to the Hebrew camp instead of killing him? If we kill him, his body will remain here and might continue to anger the gods. After what Ebebi has done to them, the Hebrews will certainly carry out your orders. Let Ebebi's curse be on them."

"Yes. Exile is better. Do it quickly. I'll hear no more of this. Send for my wine, Petephis. I must rest." His body slumped in the deep wooden bench. He felt relieved and knew he'd done the right thing.

In a short time, the Hebrew would be gone. He wondered how long it would take Petephis to get the Hebrew off the estate. What did it matter? It was done. He praised the gods, knowing his servants would honor and love him for saving them from the blackness.

"Mi-Sakhme, the savior," he muttered. "That sounds good."

Now he could sleep. He'd had little rest lately, but his work was finished. He closed his eyes and immediately felt relief from the tremendous burden he'd been under.

* * *

With much difficulty, Petephis and the soldiers walked Ebebi to the entrance. Petephis was pretty sure that was the entrance into the pet's garden, but he wasn't certain. They'd become lost leaving the master's quarters, and he fell and cut his leg. When they resumed their journey, Petephis wasn't sure which way he was going.

Presently, though, they came to the exit. The mild-mannered Petephis wished Ebebi well and warned him to leave the estate completely, or Mi-Sakhme would demand his life.

Ebebi moved through the blackness, stunned by the sudden change in his life. There had been no warning. As he walked, he kept his hands out in front of him to protect his face as he pushed forward.

He was frightened. Although he'd been on the estate for almost a year, he still didn't know it well enough to navigate in the dark. The darkness was dreadful and very thick, making it almost impossible to move. He forced himself to take one step after another.

It might take hours to leave the estate. Movement was slow and difficult at best. He pushed along, occasionally touching what he guessed was the wall of the main building then what seemed to be part of a gate, but that didn't help. There were gates all throughout the estate. He had no idea where he was or where he was headed.

Suddenly, he realized he was no longer Ebebi. Once he left the estate, his only chance of survival would be if his Hebrew relatives took him back. He had to think of himself as Adbeel, not Ebebi.

His mind raced. He wondered what could have caused the captain to make such a decision against him. He'd never done such a thing before, even when the horrible plagues came. Ebebi wasn't the cause of the darkness. Once Mi-Sakhme had time to think it through, he'd realize that, but it would be too late. His decision was final.

There would be no reprieve. Ebebi had to think in terms of being a Hebrew again. Would the Levites take him back? They had to. There was nowhere else he could go. The red people hated Hebrews, and he couldn't go to them. He'd never find another position in a house of Kemet once word of his exile spread. Even if he found a position, Mi-Sakhme would eventually hear of it and order him killed. He had to go back to Goshen.

Adbeel anticipated being a Hebrew again. He would have to work under the same overseers he'd caused so much trouble. Would they remember him? Maybe not. His traitorous deeds had been done in secret.

He wondered if anyone knew he killed Nohah, the Danite, and cut off his hand? He shuddered at the thought of the consequences of that, but no one knew. The murder had been attributed to the soldiers of Kemet. Cutting off a man's hand after killing him was a Kemet tradition. At the time, it seemed a small price to pay for his freedom.

"Freedom? Humph! This is freedom?" He thought further about the consequences of being recognized. Suppose they learned who he was, and that he had killed Nohah? Then what?

The answer was simple. He would lose his own hand and suffer accordingly. When his suffering was completed, he would be killed.

Adbeel fully understood the danger of going back to the Hebrew camp, but he had no alternative. Besides, there was hope. The Hebrews were understanding and compassionate.

"Maybe I can convince them I was forced to enter Mi-Sakhme's estate under duress and have worked there in imprisonment for the past year. That would be good." He could claim he used the darkness to escape.

He nodded, but the plan was forming well. He just had to think it out carefully.

Who should he approach when he finally reached camp? He couldn't see his brother, Abiasaph, nor could he visit Assir, the elder. He would want a life for a life.

Then he remembered Samuel and nodded. However, Samuel had been very ill. He hoped the man was still alive. Adbeel couldn't remember if he'd heard any news of his death. Samuel was the perfect choice. Adbeel lived with him before leaving for Mi-Sakhme's estate.

Slowly, he recalled what happened. Samuel had been ill, but he was probably still alive. He had the reputation of being the clan's peacemaker.

He felt a sense of release, almost as if he'd broken free of something. He wondered if, deep down, he hadn't always wanted to return to his family. During his stay at the estate, he never felt the freedom he initially sought. Working there was just another form of slavery, much like being a Hebrew, but he enjoyed being one of the people of Kemet. At least there were no beatings.

He had to become accustomed to being a Hebrew again. It was clear he had a lot to think about during his long walk.

He wondered how far he'd gone. Not far, he guessed, judging by his slow pace. He'd been walking through an open area for a while, his outstretched hands encountering nothing. Adbeel became fearful. He wanted to touch something to know where he was. It was tiring moving so slowly in the dreaded darkness.

If he could hear something, he'd know where he was. He stood and listened for a while, but he didn't hear anything—not voices or animals, just an occasional wail from someone in the house. The darkness stifled all sound, making it hard to judge distance. There wasn't even any wind.

He had to be near the outside wall. If he could just touch it, he'd be able to follow it to the main entrance. Adbeel moved forward through the blackness, gaining a little with each step, but he must have crossed the courtyard already. Or had he? If so, that meant the outer wall was near. He considered slowing down, but he wasn't moving fast enough to hurt himself even if he ran into the wall.

What would Mi-Sakhme think if the darkness remained even after he left the estate? Adbeel knew it would. The gods wouldn't intervene just because he left. If Mosheh's God, the Almighty One, caused the darkness, he doubted that the gods of the land could do anything about it.

It would be interesting to hear the Hebrew side of the story for all the plagues. He'd heard that many of the plagues left the Hebrews untouched, but Petephis added that had been a rumor, nothing more. Of course, Adbeel never knew if anything was true. By the time stories filtered through all the people on the estate, most of the content had lost credence. He wondered how the Hebrews were faring in the darkness.

That was another thing he'd have to contend with. How would he even find Samuel or Goshen in the dark? He'd need the luck of the gods.

"Where's that brick wall?" he muttered. "I have to be near it by now. Can it be that I haven't walked as far as I thought? No, that's not right. Maybe I'm walking along the wall, not toward it. That must be it."

He stopped, turned to the right, and felt certain he'd locate the brick wall in moments. As he moved forward in the new direction, though, he felt uneasy and sensed the need to be cautious. He ached from forcing his way through the blackness. He was tired, and he hadn't even left the estate grounds yet.

He made each step lightly, feeling danger nearby. He began to fear the darkness more than before. He began pleading with the gods of Kemet, then the Almighty One.

He moved his arms, desperately trying to touch something, stepping forward cautiously. Without warning, his foot suddenly touched empty air. Frantically, he tried to discover where he was, and then he hit the water.

He started to go under and beat at the water with his hands. "By the gods, I can't swim!" he shouted.

He thought fast. The edge of the pool had to be near, but which way? Then he realized he wasn't in the wading pool, because this pool was much deeper. He should have touched bottom by now. He must be in the pool of crocodiles.

"Oh, by the gods, I'm with the crocodiles!!"

Adbeel reached in all directions, trying to grasp something. He kept going under and was barely able to get his head out by kicking and splashing as hard as he could. He didn't realize his frantic actions were an invitation to the crocodiles. In unison, they slid into the black pool from their island and moved toward the ripples.

"Oh, gods! Where's the edge!" he screamed.

He flailed wildly.

"There!" He felt it. It was right in front of him. Grasping the protruding lip over the edge of the pool, he pulled himself toward it. He tried to push out of the water too soon and slid back in.

"Oh, gods!" He had to calm himself. He needed a good, solid grip, and then he could get out. He finally held on and knew he had it.

He bobbed once or twice to get some momentum, then, with all his remaining strength, he forced himself up. Then it happened.

"My foot! It has my foot! Aaaaah!!!"

Somehow, he pulled himself over the edge and out onto the bank, dragging himself from the water's edge. He moaned horribly, clutching the remains of his foot. A crocodile had torn most of it off.

"Oh, gods! I'm going to die!"

He didn't know if his foot was bleeding, but it must be. The pain was terrible. All his toes and half his foot were gone. He held the mangled remnants, rocking back and forth, moaning softly. He stayed in that position for some time, crying.

Finally, he regained his control and forced himself to think. He had to wrap his foot, but with what? All he wore was a loincloth.

He stripped off his loincloth, leaving himself naked. His sandals had slipped off while he was in the water. He carefully wrapped the garment around his damaged foot, having heard that it was important to wrap a wound tightly.

The pain and throbbing were extreme. He needed relief. What was the sense of bandaging it? He would probably die from the pain. He never knew anything could hurt so badly. He sobbed uncontrollably. What could he do? He couldn't walk. How could he find Samuel or leave the estate?

The thought came that he might lose his mind, but he wouldn't let that happen. He had to stop and think clearly. What could he do? He had no gods to pray to, and there was no one to help him.

Adbeel cried out, but the thickness of the air prevented it. He would show the gods. He'd go back to Goshen and find Samuel without them. Slowly, he calmed himself. He had to fight off the pain and think sensibly. He refused to die.

The bandage seemed tightly wrapped and was still dry in places. Maybe he could still make it. He had to find the outside wall, but that meant crawling. At least now, he knew where he was.

He thought for a moment and visualized the courtyard. The wall was only a short distance away. He took a deep breath and pulled himself toward it. The pain was almost too much to endure, but he wouldn't give in no matter how far away Samuel was.

He cursed the darkness, the gods of Kemet, the Almighty One of the Hebrews, Mi-Sakhme, and Ramesses. He even cursed himself.

All the while, he dragged himself toward the wall, knowing he would reach it soon.

Pain filled him.

# CHAPTER ELEVEN

# THE BEHEMOTH

S himri stretched his massive arms and yawned noisily. He rolled off his sleeping mat and looked through the open window. It was late morning, but he heard no other sounds in the house. He walked to the loosely hung curtain that provided privacy for the sleeping room, pushed it aside, and lumbered into the large central room of his father's house.

His brothers, Tebaliah and Shobab, were gone. *Have they prepared food for me?* Shimri wondered. *No. There's no meal left for me, you jackals!*

Disgusted, he stomped to the far corner of the room, pushed aside the lid of the rough wooden shelf that stored their food, and found a large piece of melon and some bread. He poured a cup of milk and walked to the doorway, then sat and ate.

"Another free day," he said, wondering if he should be angry, happy, or not care.

*What shall I do today?* he wondered. *Another free day, another day to drink and forget. Another day to run from the pharaoh and his ugly red people, and to run from Mosheh and his stupid ideas. What's better than drinking? Tomorrow, I might be dead.*

He nodded. When he stood again, he turned toward the inside of the house having heard his father moan. The large Simeonite walked back into the house and through the curtain to Zichri's sleeping chamber. He looked down at his dying father for a moment. The room smelled like death.

*What a waste,* he thought. *There's nothing left of the old man, no strength, yelling, or fighting, just a poor, dying fool.*

He walked to his father's bedside and touched his shoulder. "Father, I'm here. What can I bring you?"

Zichri waved his hand in the air, reaching for his eldest son, then let his hand fall. His speech broke occasionally as he tried to talk. His voice was barely a whisper.

"Shimri, you drink too much, more than I ever did. You're even angrier than I was. Why have you kept your children from me at my dying? Where are they? I have no laughter in my house, just fighting and arguing."

"Father, your ears no longer hear as they once did. Don't trouble yourself with what you can't see or hear."

Zichri coughed violently.

"Shall I send for the physician, Father?"

The old man slowly regained control of himself. "No, no. I'm already dead. The physician can do nothing. My time is near. Look in on me often Shimri, so I don't pass without you."

Zichri waved his hand, dismissing his son. Shimri patted his father's shoulder and left, taking his drinking goatskin as he walked out of the house and down the path to the community well to wash his face. His neighbors were busy working, cleaning, and talking. It seemed everyone was doing something.

The Behemoth realized he'd slept long past the morning hour. It amused him that Tebaliah and Shobab hadn't dared wake him earlier. They were probably at the sheepfold, but he decided not to go there yet. Abiasaph would want him to work, and he wasn't ready for that.

*I'll purchase one skin of beer,* he decided. *That'll be a good start for a free day. Then I'll go to the sheepfold.*

He found the Little Beer Man easily. After a casual greeting, the small man agreed to fill his guest's goatskin.

"I'll sit and talk with you while I drink this one," Shimri said. "Then I must refill my skin and be off to see my people."

"What's your pleasure, Shimri? What shall we speak of? Shall we rehearse the mighty deeds of our great Pharaoh Ramesses, or shall we debate the intentions of the gods? Do you desire to hear of my exploits in the house of Mi-Sakhme, friend of the Hebrews, or shall we speak of the vast woodland of the deep south? Do you wish to argue about Mosheh and his tricks?"

"Ha! You'll get no argument from me concerning Mosheh, dwarf. He's no friend of mine, nor is he my leader or instructor. He's brought only torture and anger. He's no deliverer."

"Then what is this hope your people speak of? Surely, there are those among you who believe Mosheh is your rescuer."

"They love being disappointed. They hold on for something they can't see, hoping desperately for something that won't happen, even though they've been proven wrong many times. Still, they cling to their false hope and talk of deliverance only to be disappointed every day.

"Abiasaph, the Levite, is a wise man among my people. He, too, knows there's no deliverer. His talk is of survival, Beer Man, and it's not just talk. He knows how to stay alive. No one beats him. He dares not complain about the work, but he hates as much as the rest of us. When pharaoh comes for us again, Abiasaph will be ready, just as always. The others will receive what they ask for and will lose their hope once again."

Shimri spoke in a falsetto voice as if imitating a woman. "'Oh,' they will say, 'We were so certain the Almighty One was coming this time. Now we must go back into slavery again.'" His voice returned to normal. "They bounce from sadness to sadness, gaining nothing.

"Bah, I say! There's no rescuer, and there won't be any. We're still in slavery. A free day isn't given to us to build false hope. It's not given us so we may rebuild our folds and houses, nor was it given us for rest so we may be better workers when we return. Abiasaph's right, Beer Man."

"What of you, Shimri? Are you prepared like your friend? Are you ready to go back to work under the guards?"

"I'm never ready to build the pharaoh's dreams. I'll take whatever they give me, be it a heavy workload or a thousand lashes.

"I'm alone, Beer Man. No one else shares my thoughts. I don't believe in miracles like Oshea and Tebaliah. I'm not interested in surviving unwounded, as is Abiasaph. It takes far too much effort to be that prepared. This is our lot, and I accept it.

"No, I'm tired, wounded, and sick. I fought with vengeance against your pharaoh and his goats. I haven't won even a small battle."

He handed his empty goatskin to Mugolla-sekh-mugolla, who obligingly refilled it with dark, thick liquid. The Beer Man wondered what would happen if that large man ever lashed out with full vengeance. He was very big and strong and could probably kill with his hands. Mugolla decided not to upset him.

Shimri took a long drink and continued his solemn discourse. "I'm old before my years, Beer Man, without any future. My children have been stolen by my wives, and I seldom see them. The warmth I once had in my heart for them, my friends, and my people is gone. My father, who's dying, does so without my love. My brothers are equally useless.

"What kind of life is ours? We sleep at night to gain enough strength for a new day of work. We look forward each night to another day of sweat under the whips of Ramesses and Mi-Sakhme. How I hate them!

"We eat not to enjoy food but to stay alive, so we might present the pharaoh with his treasured trophy. We're afraid to die. We want to live, but living has become worse than dying.

"I'm a hater, Beer Man. I hate the pharaoh, the people of Kemet, Mosheh, and his friends. I even hate life and myself, but my hate isn't as angry as it once was. Even that has softened. Do you know why? It's because I no longer care like I used to. I no longer even feel the need to stay alive. There's no hope but Mosheh's false hope, and that's not for me.

"These are free days, and I want to forget who I am, where I am, and what I am. When I drink, I have happiness, forgetfulness, and less hate and troubled thoughts. My sadness is gone."

He paused and looked at the little man, who listened intently, frightened by the big man's words.

"Shimri, my friend, I understand you even though others don't. I am very like you. I have no rescuer and have lost all hope. I live only because I'm alive. Though my happiness is false, it's better than nothing.

"You may be the wisest of your people, Shimri. When whatever is to happen finally comes, you won't be disappointed. Your friend, Abiasaph, may have a better way, but it's not the best one. He chooses to survive, but life isn't eternal. Only the gods and pharaohs have immortality, not us. Abiasaph will be dismayed, because his survival tactics will someday fail.

"By the gods, I tell you that forgetting isn't easy. Living isn't easy for either of us, but beer is the god of forgetfulness. We must give her a name, for she surely answers when we call. With her at our side, life becomes bearable, does it not?"

The Behemoth, deep in thought, handed his goatskin to the Beer Man, who smiled and, as he had been doing, partially refilled it.

"I have a song," Shimri said softly. "Yesterday, as I sat drinking, I began singing. I made up the song and sang it many times. Why should I live working under your pharaoh? Why should I put up with my false-hope brothers and angry, dying father? Why should I listen to the ridiculous dreams of the dreamers? There's nothing there for me. I'd rather drink the drink of the gods. That gives me a way of life without bitterness. Drink is better than false hope, because with drink, I can forget that I'm a slave and a Hebrew."

He stopped talking and closed his eyes, then he sang in his quiet, gentle, sad voice.

> I am no longer Pharaoh's slave,
> Buried in sadness and shame.
> I've broken through the grave of death
> And have taken a new name.
>
> I found a cave in the enemy's field
> Filled with skins of beer.
> While others cry and die away
> I drink, and there is no fear.

"The drink of the gods," she says she is
And she'll take me to freedom faster,
But she lies, for she has kept me a slave,
And now she's become my master.

But if sadness is to be my living god,
And death to be my fate,
Then I'll die while drinking the drink of the gods,
For with her, I have no hate.

Shimri finished his song and sat quietly. Mugolla, astonished by the solemn song, waited before speaking, too.

"Shimri, you're a master, too. Your song is a wonderful lament. I'm surprised and pleased. Will you allow me to perform my mastery for you? I'm making beer today. I can start now. Will you join me and learn my art?"

"No, dwarf. I'm on my way to see Abiasaph. Your speech hasn't put me in a good mood. I enjoy your storytelling but not your companionship. Be off with you."

The Behemoth stood and walked back toward the community. Little Beer Man stared after him as he disappeared behind the houses. Shimri was mean, and his mouth held hard words, but they were alike.

Regardless of what Shimri said, he liked and needed the Beer Man's companionship. They needed each other. Shimri would be back soon enough.

The Behemoth was surprised with himself. He usually didn't let anyone know his inner feelings. He swung his arm in disgust. Why did he say such things to that loud-mouthed dwarf? He shouldn't lose control like that. If his weakness became known, people would mock him.

He sat beside the path and leaned against a large sycamore. Why did he feel so sad? Did he have to hate to have revenge against his father, Zichri? Where was his happiness? Beer didn't make him happy. He lied to himself, and the gods of drink lied, too. His song was true.

A small dog ambled by, eyeing him carefully.

"Come here, dog. I won't hurt you. Come on."

The animal trotted up and placed its paws on his large legs. He petted it gently. Anyone who came across that scene would have been amazed to see the loud, angry Simeonite gently petting a mangy dog.

"There, you see? I'm not a mean Hebrew. I'm gentle like a goat or lamb. Sit with me, little dog, and I'll tell you the sad story of Shimri, who doesn't want to live."

He caressed the soft fur on the dog's neck and recalled his early life and the things that shaped his personality.

\* \* \*

In his earlier years, Shimri'd been a likable man in the Goshen camp. Though he wasn't serious in his devotions to the Almighty One, he accepted and followed his people's traditions. His great wit made him popular with most of the men. He constantly had cruelly humorous things to say about their tormentors, the soldiers of Kemet. His witty blows at the pharaoh kept the men amused and was a source of encouragement to the otherwise downtrodden work force.

His father, Zichri, however, was a cruel man. Bitter because of the conditions of their lives, he harassed young Shimri often for being so good-natured. Even the Behemoth's marriage didn't escape his father's wrath.

After months of preparation and anticipation, Shimri's wedding day arrived, and a celebration began. It was late in the day, and the girl was brought out to meet her betrothed. Zichri's drunkenness and abusive manner had been an embarrassment throughout the day. He reached out and tore the veil from the girl's face, breaking a long and sacred tradition. He maligned her with vehement curses and fought the men of Benjamin, her tribe. The Benjaminites angrily took her away and refused to allow the marriage.

Zichri, before then, had already been unbearable to most of the camp, except for his own family. His actions at the wedding were something Shimri would never forgive. Soon afterward, to hurt his father, he wed a daughter of a Kemet exile, the people Zichri hated most. The fact that the marriage didn't last didn't change Zichri's feelings.

As the Behemoth grew older, he slowly acquired his father's traits. He, too, became cruel. Though he displayed his humor as often as before, it exuded anger, bitterness, and hatred. He no longer entertained the rest of the community. He drank excessively when he could and no longer cared for others. He broke most of the Hebrew traditions, transgressed the laws, and made fun of everything the Hebrews held sacred. He denied the existence of the Almighty One, and, though he believed little about gods in general, expressed more belief in the Kemet deities than any other. He knew that would bother many, and he enjoyed doing so.

To him, life was misery, and he wanted to see the traditions of his people completely forgotten. He was a slave. To survive, he needed to spend every moment not in bondage doing things that brought pleasure and enjoyment—or, at least, distraction. That became his goal and justification for indulging in drink as often as he did. To keep himself from falling into any traps of belief, he constantly ridiculed everything that others held dear.

\* \* \*

"Curse you, Zichri, my father," he said. "You're the cause of all my troubles, but you've given me no joy to soften my hate."

He closed his eyes and petted the dog absent-mindedly.

"Where's the fondness I once had for my children? Where's the gentleness that once filled my heart? Where's the mother of my youth I once loved?"

Tears formed in his eyes and spilled onto his cheeks, running down into his coarse, matted beard. Slowly, he stood and shook his head. He brutally kicked the dog, making it yelp and run. He grabbed his skin of beer and continued toward Abiasaph's hut.

He sneaked up behind Abiasaph, who was working in the sheepfold, and whacked his back with a huge hand. Startled, Abiasaph turned to defend himself and saw the large Simeonite roaring with laughter.

"Abiasaph, if I were a Kemet guard come to take you back to work, I would have crushed you by the time you turned. You're getting slow. It's time for you to rest. Come, I've brought beer."

"Rest. Shimri? You haven't even started working, and you want rest. What are you resting from?"

"I've worked as hard as you, finding Little Beer Man and having to put up with his story telling just to get some beer."

"I'd say you've had more than a skin already. You're right, though. I'm ready for a rest."

The two men walked to a large sycamore tree near the sheep fold and sat under it. Abiasaph took a small sip of Shimri's beer.

"Abiasaph, Little Beer Man told me you're like the well-wishers. Even though you don't dream false dreams like they do, you prepare yourself to be a model slave and protect your life. He says your careful preparations will gain you nothing. Your day will come, and all your wisdom will be for naught. Answer him. Are you like my Tebaliah? Do you prepare in vain?"

Abiasaph smiled. "Need I have an answer for Little Beer Man? Who is he that I should answer him? Are you so confused in your thoughts that you'd go to an exile for counsel? You're beginning to sound like the Gnat."

"Wait now, you, sharp-tongued dung thrower! I haven't gone to the dwarf for counsel. Don't you know me better than that? Do I need to ask anyone for counsel? No. I never will, either.

"I was sitting with that little duck, receiving my portion of beer, and he ranted on as he does. He spoke of Mosheh, his lies to the people, and how they'll be disappointed in their impossible dream. Then I spoke of you, telling him how you answer such people and how you haven't been taken in by their loose talk of deliverance.

"He told me that even you would suffer disappointment, because as our lot becomes worse, so will your preparations become more difficult. When the pharaoh drops his iron hand upon us and ends our misery for good, your preparations will have been for naught."

Abiasaph thought for a moment. "What has he suggested I do? Drink beer all day?"

Shimri laughed. "You must have been listening. That's exactly what he said. We must forget our miseries while we can and get what pleasure we can from life. Who knows what tomorrow will bring?"

"That's true," Abiasaph answered. "Tomorrow, no doubt, we'll again be at the work site. Let's repair the sheep fold today while we can."

"No, no! It's a free day, not a work day. I won't be taken in by Mosheh or by you. Come walk with me. We'll walk through the camp and speak with the others. Let's see what they're doing and thinking. We'll go by the community of robbers, find the Beer Man, and refill our skins. A walk will be good for your back and your mind. You work too much. This is a free day. Don't act like a slave today, my friend. Act like a free man."

"But Shimri, we aren't free. We're slaves to the pharaoh no matter what happens today. Tomorrow won't be another free day."

"Be that as it may, we'll fix the sheep fold later. I'll help. I give my word."

Abiasaph picked up his skin and joined his herd partner. Shimri was right. A walk through the community sounded like a good idea.

# CHAPTER TWELVE

# ABISAPH'S REVENGE

Mishael met Oshea at the Judaite pathway, and the two men walked along the path leading to the outer edge of camp.

"What is it Susi wants with us, Oshea?" Mishael asked. "Is there some trouble at the camp border?"

"I've been told someone has come through the darkness from the city of guards outside Avaris and has asked for me."

"Through the darkness? Didn't Caleb say that was impossible?"

Oshea shrugged. "Caleb said he experienced much difficulty moving in it, so I don't know. We're almost there. We'll find out soon."

As they approached the gathering, Susi came to meet them.

"Oshea, Mishael, thank you for coming. There's a soldier of Kemet, a Nubian, who tells us he came through the darkness to reach our camp. He says he no longer wants to be an enemy of the Hebrews but wants to become one with us."

"Why did he ask for us?" Mishael asked.

"He's very frightened. He says he knows both of you, because you're overseers in the work force, and you've spoken to him before. He says you're the only two Hebrews he doesn't fear."

"Well, let's see how we can help the man," Oshea said.

The three Hebrews walked to the small circle of men gathered around the tall, black Nubian soldier. Pharez, the physician, was bandaging his arm.

"Oshea, Mishael," Pharez said, "good day. This man says he was attacked by an animal while traveling here through the darkness. It's not a serious wound, but I'm glad you're here. I wish to hear his story."

The tall, strongly built soldier relaxed noticeably when he saw the two Hebrew leaders. "Hebrew friends, I need your protection, please. I'm weak, tired, and hungry. Coming through the black air was the most difficult thing I've ever done, and I almost didn't make it. Please help me."

Mishael asked someone to bring food for their guest, then led the Nubian to a bench in front of a large tree. "Sit and rest, my friend. You're safe here. Food and drink are coming. Please tell us why you're here and what you'd have us do."

The Nubian sat and leaned against the tree. Despite Mishael's words, he didn't feel safe, but at least he'd reached Goshen.

"My name is Orusi," he began. "I was brought from Nubia many years ago to work as a soldier in the captain's guard. As you both know, I've been working with the slave force at Avaris. Both of you have spoken to me about your Abraham God. Do you remember?"

"Yes, we remember," Oshea said. "You haven't always been so responsive as this, but I'm happy to see the change in you. Please continue your story. We're anxious to hear it."

Orusi's eyes darted nervously from side to side as if expecting trouble. "Mishael, I haven't been able to forget what you said about your Abraham God. As a child, I remember my mother saying there is a God who is greater than all others. She said someday, that mighty God would show himself, and, when He did, He was the one I should follow and obey.

"I've always feared the gods of Kemet, but I never saw magic and power like your Abraham God has shown. I've watched carefully as the plagues came, wondering if He were the true God my mother meant. I've listened carefully to what you've told me about your Abraham God, and I've become very concerned, because you're so certain he's coming to take you away.

"When the black air came, I was sure it was your Abraham God blinding us so He could help you escape. I knew He's been protecting you while we've been tortured with His magical powers, and I knew you wouldn't be blinded like we were. At least, I hoped so. I knew He would be protecting you again. I sat in my house and came to a very difficult decision.

"I left my wife and son, who's away at school, and fought my way through the black air until I found your camp. I was afraid you'd be leaving with your Abraham God, and I might miss you. I was surprised and happy when I found you still here. I would like to join your people and become a Hebrew. I believe that your Abraham God is the one I must follow."

"Orusi," Mishael asked, "how'd you move through the darkness? You're obviously exhausted. Tell us about it."

"The black air is the reason I can barely talk. I never worked so hard before. When I awoke yesterday, the black air was all around me. It frightened me, and I thought it was attacking me. It's black like that everywhere in the city. I don't know how far it goes, or if Mi-Sakhme or Ramesses have it at their estates, but the city of guards was filled with it.

"Everywhere I looked, it was there. I was sure that your Abraham God had once again terrified us with a form of magic or power. I wanted to tell Him I was no longer an enemy, that He was the one I've been looking for, but I didn't know how. I sat still for many hours, afraid to move, then, when I tried to move, I couldn't.

"It's hard to understand if you haven't been in the black air, but it seemed to control me as if it were a god. I was never so fearful in my life. I thought I would die, but, after I saw the black air did nothing to me, I chose to attempt this journey and hoped the Abraham God would understand."

"What happened after you decided to come here?" Oshea asked.

Orusi looked around and began to relax, although he was still fearful. As he spoke, two Hebrew women came with food and drink. He ate quickly as he answered Oshea's question.

"I left quietly, without telling anyone. It's extremely difficult to move in the black air. Every step took effort. In time, I learned the necessary pace. It was easy to leave quietly, because there was much commotion—screaming, yelling, and cursing everywhere.

"After some hours, I knew I'd left the city of soldiers. I lit a torch to guide me the rest of the way, but the torch wouldn't burn in the black air. It's very strange, this black air of your Abraham God. However, if He wishes to frighten the people of Kemet, He has succeeded. They're ready to turn against the pharaoh. I heard many remarks as I left, although people sounded as if they were speaking with closed mouths. When I was alone on my way, I tried to talk, but speaking in the black air hurt my throat, so I quit.

"Once I was away from the city, I moved closer to the marshlands to determine how far to come, praying I wouldn't meet any poisonous snakes or crocodiles. Fortunately, I didn't."

"How'd you hurt your arm?" Mishael asked.

"That happened while I walked. I brought no food with me, because I didn't know whether the black air would affect food. After some hours, I became hungry, and I knew I was near your area, so I reached out to find some trees or bushes. I didn't know your land wasn't covered in blackness. I thought it might not be, but I wasn't sure.

"I touched something, and I reached to touch it again, but it wasn't there. I didn't know what it was. That frightened me so badly, I couldn't move. Then, in my fear, I sensed it was a wild animal, so I shouted, hoping to scare it off. Instead, it lunged and took my arm in its jaw. I hit it and knocked it loose. Then it was gone.

"By the sound of its growl, it must have been a jackal or wild dog. My arm hurt badly, and I knew I'd lost some flesh, but I couldn't see and didn't know how badly I was injured until I came to Goshen."

"An animal would probably have the same trouble seeing that you had," Oshea said.

Orusi smiled. "I'm sure you're right. I know how fortunate I was. I didn't think about it while I was in the black air, but I realize I could have become lost or fallen in the river. The most amazing thing is that the black air ended without warning. The brightness of day in Goshen hurt my eyes when I stepped out. I turned and saw I was facing a black wall. When I tried to walk, I fell over, because I used too much force, as if I were still in the black air.

"I was very relieved to see you were still here. I can't tell you how I feel, because it's too much to talk about. I must ask if you will allow me to be part of your people and to follow you and your Abraham God to a new land."

Orusi turned his head to look as three men approached— Abiasaph, Shimri, and Shobab walked boldly forward.

The Behemoth pointed his finger at Orusi and demanded, "What are you doing here on a free day, enemy, drinking our milk as if you were a guest?"

Orusi jumped up as Shimri stepped toward him. Both were large men, but Orusi was clearly terrified. He glanced to see if the others surrounded him, but they hadn't.

Oshea stood and walked toward Shimri. "This man has just traveled through the blackness to escape from our enemies. We've accepted his story and him. He's no longer an enemy. He's a friend."

"Friend?" Shimri bellowed. "The soldiers of Kemet are murderers! What will he do when the rest of them come to make us work? Will he become a slave, toiling and sweating beside us, or will he pick up his whip and be a soldier of Kemet again? No! This man ran from the terror in his own land, hoping to find comfort here. When the plague is over, he'll leave. Your kindness, Oshea, is sickening."

"Shimri, we've heard him talk. We believe him. He won't turn against us."

"Bah! I won't trust him, even if you do." He started toward Orusi, swinging his large fist at him, but the Nubian, a trained soldier, sidestepped and countered, swinging his fist and striking Shimri's chest.

The Behemoth tumbled backward. Before he could retaliate, four Hebrew men pulled him away.

Abiasaph watched the encounter with interest. He had no love for any Kemet guard, and it wouldn't have bothered him if Shimri broke the Nubian in half. Then, as the men pulled Shimri away, Abiasaph suddenly realized who Orusi was, and he moved forward slowly. Although Abiasaph was smaller, he was filled with anger that made him seem large.

"I know you, guard of Kemet!" he said. "You're the one who beat my son with your whip. He pointed you out to me. You beat a nine-year-old boy until his blood ran, and you smiled!"

Orusi backed away. He feared for his life, but he must make the man understand. "I'm sorry, Hebrew. I'm no longer that kind of man. I was under orders and did what I was told. I'm sorry...."

Abiasaph leaped at him, slashing his face with his fist. He punched Orusi twice more before the man fell. Abiasaph fell on him, digging his knees into the man's shoulders and pounding his already bloody face.

"I withheld my anger in your land, but now you're in mine!" Abiasaph shouted. "My son still bears your scars!"

Oshea and Susi were barely able to pull Abiasaph off the man. They acted quickly, but Orusi had already sustained great damage to his face. Someone sent for the physician as Oshea and Susi pulled Abiasaph farther from Orusi. The Behemoth, held firmly by four men, shouted encouragement to his friend.

"Abiasaph, you little Levite warrior, you beat him good! Someone get beer! We'll celebrate. Abiasaph, the lion killer, has made his mark."

Abiasaph didn't feel like celebrating. Oshea and Susi sat him under a tree to calm him down. They talked, but Abiasaph didn't hear them. He wondered what happened. He'd never lost control like that before. What was wrong with him?

He took a deep breath and raised his head, seeing Mishael standing before him.

"Are you all right?" the chieftain asked. "I think you lost your mind for a moment."

Abiasaph nodded.

"I understand why. If my son had been beaten like that, I might have done the same thing. I don't know. My friend, I must ask you to forget this matter. Revenge in its fullest isn't a law. This man has asked to live in our camp, and you must continue to live your own life and forget what happened. It will take hard work, but you must do it. No one can do it for you.

"You don't have to associate with him if you wish, but don't carry your anger with you. Don't let Shimri's loud barking revive it, either. We can't change the past, but this man wants no more trouble, I assure you."

Mishael patted Abiasaph's shoulder, and he nodded.

Hor-em-heb, standing to one side, walked over to Abiasaph and placed his hand on the Levite's shoulder. Seeing Abiasaph was calmer, Mishael walked back to Oshea, who watched Pharez bandage the Nubian again.

The two Hebrew leaders walked out of earshot of the Nubian guard.

"Are we mistaken?" Mishael asked softly. "With so much turmoil in our camp, can we allow him to stay with us? Won't his life be in danger? Our men are wound as tightly as chariot springs. This could be a mistake."

"You may be right, but Orusi is very fearful. He's not an enemy like Ramesses. He was likely sold into the guard by merchants. Keep him close to your own house and protect him. We'll speak to grandfather about this."

That sounded wise. Mishael waited for the physician to finish with Orusi, then he took him to his home.

* * *

Hor-em-heb squeezed Abiasaph's shoulder. "Hello again, my friend. I'd say only one small thing, if you'll allow me."

Abiasaph nodded.

"You're probably thinking you'd like to go off somewhere and drink. In truth, you shouldn't be alone right now. I'm sure you'll agree. As long as you're with someone who won't try to counsel or judge you, it will be best. With that in mind, I invite you to come with me. I'm kind enough to be a friend but not wise enough to judge.

"I'm on my way to the house of Libni to engage in a much-desired meal of fresh fish and cucumbers. Vophsi excels in such meals. Please join me. You're probably hungry. Vophsi has been working with the physician, and she can soothe your battered hands."

Abiasaph looked down at his bloody hands and realized they hurt. The old, white-haired priest had a friendly smile. Even Abiasaph, whose mood was anything but gentle, couldn't resist such a warm invitation. He nodded and stood to leave.

He looked at Orusi, who lay on the ground with a wet, bloody cloth over his face, and felt only slight satisfaction. He and Hor-em-heb walked away toward the house of Libni. Abiasaph's body shook from excitement.

"Where's your son, Abiasaph? Would he not like to join us?"

"He's at the sheep fold, I think. We need not look for him now." He lifted his hands and examined them, indicating he didn't want Caath to see him like that. Hor-em-heb nodded and led the way.

Abiasaph was surprised, walking with the white-haired priest. It wasn't like him to mingle with others. He wanted to go home, dress his wounds, sit quietly, and think, but he knew he couldn't. Deep inside, he desired Hor-em-heb's friendship, and he trusted him.

It was years since he'd eaten at any house other than his own. The thought of fish and cucumbers sounded good.

## CHAPTER THIRTEEN

# GODS, GODS, EVERYWHERE GODS

Libni and Vophsi were outside the house when Hor-em-heb and Abiasaph arrived. Seeing Abiasaph's condition, Vophsi immediately took him inside to clean his hands.

"Oh, my, Abiasaph. What have you done? Here, let me make up some wet cheese to soak your hands in."

While she tended Abiasaph's wounds, Hor-em-heb explained to Libni what happened.

"I'm glad you brought him with you," Libni whispered. "He might need some friends right now. We'll do what we can."

With his hand wrapped in smelly, wet cloth, the Levite rejoined them.

"Aha," Libni said with a laugh. "I see you've been introduced to the sour-milk method of healing. Vophsi knows her medicine. If you can stand the smell, it'll heal your hands."

Abiasaph felt at ease around the two men. They were well liked in camp, and both were soft-spoken. He wouldn't have any trouble while visiting them. When he smelled the fish cooking, he realized how hungry he was.

"How old is young Caath now?" Libni asked. "These young ones grow so fast."

"He's nine years old," Abiasaph replied, "and you're right. He must grow up early to survive. He's a slave like we are, no longer a child."

"It surprises me to hear you say that. I saw your son yesterday, when he visited with Oshea, and he appeared to be a normal child."

"I teach my son what I believe he should know. I don't like Oshea instructing him in other things. Now Caath is confused, but that will be hard for you to understand, because you two both agree with Oshea."

"That's true," Libni said. "We don't want to interfere with your right to raise your son your own way. Please forgive us if we gave that impression. You once asked why our friend, Hor-em-heb, left Kemet to live with us as a Hebrew. It might be a good time for you to know the answer to that." He smiled at his white-haired friend.

"Go ahead, Hor-em-heb," Abiasaph said. "I've often wondered about that. Why did you choose the life of a slave over your high position in Kemet? If I had such a choice, I might choose otherwise."

Abiasaph wondered what caused the man to change his life so dramatically. Hor-em-heb had been a priest under the pharaoh and was held in high esteem, part of the royalty and nobility of the Two Lands. There were women of his own people he could have married instead of Alumai's daughter.

The priest settled into a comfortable position on the cushioned mat. "It wasn't a quick decision. It took months of studying and pondering before I left Menpi and moved to Goshen. Most of my time was spent comparing the gods I served there with the God you serve here. My study surprised me. It's difficult to become knowledgeable about the gods of Kemet without becoming more confused. The more I learned of your one God, the more I became convinced of His reality."

"How'd you find out about our God?" Abiasaph asked.

"It was Alumai's daughter who first introduced me to your Hebrew Almighty One. I was in the city for a feast day and celebration, and I happened to see two beautiful Hebrew girls. One was Libni's mother, the other, her sister, Timna. Timna smiled at me, and my heart was no longer my own."

Abiasaph smiled, but he understood. He experienced the same feeling when he first saw Nehushta.

"I was unable to spend time with them that day, but I made certain to come again the next. When I saw them again the second day, I convinced them to guide me here. I wanted to look into your Hebrew traditions as part of my studies. On the pretext that I, an Egyptian priest, was interested in learning of the Hebrew God, I soon found myself sitting at table with the venerable Alumai. As you may have guessed, if you knew him, he spoke to me of the God of Abraham, Isaac, and Jacob with such force, I was stunned by what I heard.

"Though my head swam with thoughts of Timna, I was filled of thoughts about the Hebrew Almighty One, too. I returned to the temple and studied all I could about the gods of the Two Lands."

Abiasaph was surprised. "Certainly a priest would know about the gods? How could you be a priest and not know?"

"A good point. I had much knowledge regarding the gods of the Two Lands, but Egyptian gods aren't stable like your Almighty One. I wanted to be very sure, so I studied all I could about the gods, from their beginnings to the present. I searched the wisdom of those before me, all that the scribes had recorded of them. The more I studied, the more I wanted to hear about the God of Goshen, and I wanted to see Timna, as well. Back to Goshen I came. That time, Alumai sat with me for two days, speaking of the Almighty One. When I left, I was almost convinced.

"I think, Abiasaph, that if I were to tell you about the gods of the Two Lands, you'd understand how I reached my decision."

"Yes," Abiasaph said quickly, wanting to know more about the Almighty One and enjoying the setting. There was no pressure on him to respond. It was just story telling, like with the Little Beer Man. Maybe it would be an opportunity for him to learn some of the things he didn't know.

"Certainly, having lived here all your life," Hor-em-heb continued, "you've acquired some knowledge of the gods of Kemet. Like most Hebrews, I imagine it left you confused. Is that correct?"

"Actually, I have paid very little attention to talk about gods. I know that many people fear those many gods, and they believe their gods to be responsible for just about everything that happens, good or bad. Though I've heard some of their names, I know very little about them."

"Our land is filled with many gods, as you know," Hor-em-heb went on. "What you may not know is that there are nearly as many stories of the beginning as there are gods who were said to have begun it. As I was taught, Atum was the first god. When the world as we know it began, Atum already existed. He had no beginning. The world formed around him. Atum had a world in which to live and preside over, and he created two pairs of gods. The first pair was Shu, the god of air, and his mate, Tefnut, the goddess of moisture. The second pair was Geb, the god of earth, and Hut, goddess of the sky.

"Geb and Hut, through god birth, bore Osiris, the god of vegetation. He taught our people the arts of agriculture and building. He eventually married Isis, the goddess of fertility, and she bore Horus, known today as the falcon god.

"Osiris, however, was later killed by his younger brother, Set. Isis recovered his body and restored it as best she could. Set tore it to pieces, and one piece was never found. Osiris descended into the nether world and became the ruler over death and men's souls. He was avenged by his son, Horus, who eventually killed Set. Horus, then, became the ruling lord of the Two Lands.

"If that seems a bit confusing, you should know that priests today are taught differently from that. The new teaching is that Ptah was the first god. He, in turn, created all the other gods. Ptah ruled from the city of Menpi.

"Does that mean that we who are older were taught incorrectly?"

Abiasaph shrugged. He didn't know the answer, but he didn't want to speak. The story mesmerized him, and he wanted to hear more. He carefully lifted fish to his mouth. It was difficult eating with his hands bandaged, but the meal was very tasty. He enjoyed it, and he motioned Hor-em-heb to continue.

"I think not," Hor-em-heb said. "We weren't taught incorrectly, and neither were those who came after us. You see, the nature of the gods of Kemet is that they are at the mercy of the ruling kings. If a new pharaoh chooses to change the status or order of the gods, the gods must respond.

"In the years since the beginning of our land, many pharaohs have had their own favorite god to guide them and rule over their leadership. When that happened, the positions of the gods changed. The gods have little control over this. Only the pharaoh can change the status of the gods. That's one reason why the pharaohs are considered gods by many people.

"So a new generation of priests will learn about the gods based on the pharaoh who reigned at that time. Who's right or wrong? The answer is no one.

"Let me add to your confusion. Of course you know about Re, the sun god. Not long ago, he was the ruler of the land, not Atum or Ptah. It was Re, and stories of the ruling gods warring with each other are plentiful."

"How many different gods are there in Kemet?" Abiasaph asked.

"You've probably heard of Anpu, the opener of the way, and Heqet, the great midwife goddess. The exiles in this land speak frequently of Sobk, the god of water, and Hapi, the rain god, don't they? You may have heard of Thoth, the god of learning. Certainly you know about Hathor, goddess of love. She's known throughout the land. There are many gods. There's also Anubis, the divine embalmer, and Amon, the present god of fertility. In the land of sand, my friend, there are gods everywhere.

"To the people of Kemet, the gods have control over their entire lives. The gods decide whether a thing may be done on a particular day or in a particular way. Isn't it interesting that the gods of Kemet must have an image made of them to receive proper worship? It's the same with the gods of other lands I studied. Only here in Goshen have I found a God without images.

"As I studied deeper about each of the gods, I found that even here in the red land, we once, many years ago, had only one god, just like you. I don't know if that was the same Almighty One that Abraham knew, but I'm sure it was only one god.

"Somehow, in the hundreds of years since, with all the kings becoming gods, and the priests having to invent gods to fit each new king, we've turned our one god into many. These gods, in their mysteriousness, have created terror in the hearts of the people. Early in the history of the Two Lands, I believe we worshipped only one god for many years. I wish I knew why and how that changed."

"But if so many of those gods were invented by the priests and never existed, where do they get their power and magic?" Abiasaph asked.

"That's a difficult question, my friend. Most of the power and magic visible in our land is done by magicians and sorcerers, the wise men in the pharaoh's court. Their power has always been attributed to the gods, but not every god imparts that power to a magician.

"Listen to a surprising comparison. The power that comes from the gods of Kemet always carries fear with it. The gods strike fear into all people. The people then worship for fear of death. The power I've seen associated with your Almighty One causes your people to be strong and have hope. That is, of course, limited to those who have understanding of your God. They worship Him out of respect. The fear that comes from your Almighty One is for those who don't know Him. The worship of the gods in my land has always been based on fear, not respect or admiration.

"Our people, Abiasaph, are very fearful. Our magicians strike more fear in them with their acts. Since I've seen the acts of your Almighty One, I no longer marvel at the magicians of the pharaoh.

"When I considered all these things, I was amazed at the difference I found in my thinking. The Hebrew God seemed very much like what I expected the original god of the Two Lands to have been, the difference being that your Hebrew God seems never to have changed. The stories passed down through your generations about Him aren't as confusing as the stories of our gods. Though your people are fearful, too, I believe, after talking with Alumai, that it's because of the hundreds of years you've lived in this land, subjected to cruelty and slavery. Many of your people have become accustomed to seeing the rites and worship of the people. They're used to witchcraft, sorcery, and magic. They've lost the uniqueness they once had in the worship of their God. I'm sure, after hearing from Alumai, that the Hebrew nation that came to this land under your father, Jacob, was much different than the present one.

194

"I found that in earlier years, the Hebrew life, lived under the guidance of your Almighty One, was simple and uncomplicated, and your people weren't fearful. Your father, Abraham, was a fierce warrior who stood his ground against any adversary. It isn't that way now, as you know.

"So, my friend, I have never regretted my decision to marry Timna and become one with your people, the Hebrew nation, especially now, when we could be so close to leaving for a new land of our own."

Abiasaph wanted to hear the entire conversation that passed between Hor-em-heb and Alumai, but he was ashamed to ask a foreigner about his own people's God. He wondered how he could learn more. He needed to know if he planned to keep his promise to Caath.

"Hor-em-heb," Abiasaph said, "it's difficult to believe that you'd leave what you had in order to become as we are. Is serving the right God that important?"

"Yes. It definitely is. A true people must be centered around its God, for a true God is a controlling factor for any nation.

"Your God of Abraham, for example, though He has allowed you to suffer these many years, has chosen this time to rescue you from your troubles. He must certainly have the capability to do that, or He wouldn't be so certain. Mosheh and Aaron, your leaders, have made it clear that the God of Abraham is in complete control.

"You see, now that I'm convinced that your Almighty One is the most powerful God of all, I have little difficulty understanding or believing His instructions, for I'm versed in the knowledge of gods. That's what impresses me most about the God of Abraham. To those that He has given understanding, there's no confusion, doubt, or haughtiness. Because of your God, your leaders have hope and believe He will keep His promise. The people of the land wish that their gods would do the same, but there's no hope. Everything is left to the god's mood at the time."

Hor-em-heb sat quietly for a moment, then looked at Abiasaph. "In the temples, you see, even the most learned priests are just as confused as the peasants, although they act differently. They have knowledge, but it's only of things of which they aren't certain. I

195

know, because I was knowledgeable, too. When I passed that knowledge on to others, it was to bring to light my own greatness as much as to help those in need. It's a difficult task to keep the gods separated or satisfied and the stories arranged properly. I often imparted knowledge to others while not being certain myself.

"Many times we'd be called in to be with the pharaoh during a time of important decision-making. He would want information about his predecessors and their actions during similar situations. That part was easy. All we had to do was read the parchments.

"Before he made a decision, he wanted our opinions on whether the appropriate gods would be favorable to his actions. We gave that information based on guesswork, coupled with the guesswork of priests who performed before us. We always counseled the pharaoh with trembling knees, knowing that our lives were in his hands.

"Here, in Goshen, I find that those of your people who are most learned about your God have an assurance and boldness about them that contrasts with our priests. There isn't boasting among men like Eldad and Elishama as there is among the high priests of the temple. Your great men are humble. The great men of Kemet are proud and haughty. You can see that my decision wasn't that difficult to make."

Abiasaph sat quietly and pondered the man's words. He thought of those in camp who fit the description—Old Abraham, Eldad, Oshea, Mishael, Libni, and now Hor-em-heb.

There were quite a few such men. All had the assurance Hor-em-heb mentioned, along with peacefulness. Even Hor-em-heb had it. They were at peace. Having peace of mind under their current circumstances wasn't usual, and it was something Abiasaph certainly didn't have. He was disturbed about many things. He needed answers and couldn't find them. He, too, needed peace in his life.

"How's your hand feeling now, my friend?" Libni asked.

Abiasaph lifted the bandage and looked at his hand. "It looks as though your wet cheese has done the job again. The swelling's reduced already. My hand still hurts, but it's not as bad as before. The other hand is fine, just a few cuts."

"I'm glad to hear it. Keep your hand wrapped in sour milk, or cheese, as you call it, and it will heal even more quickly." Libni was glad to see Abiasaph relax during the conversation. He was one of many in the camp who were more concerned than necessary. He thought of Shelomi and shuddered, his concern showing.

"Have either of you heard more about Shelomi?" Libni asked. "I went there this morning, but there was no improvement."

"Yes," Hor-em-heb said, wiping his mouth. "I'm sorry. I should have told you sooner. I talked to Pharez, the physician, before we came here. He said Shelomi's condition isn't good, and there's little he can do. There was considerable loss of blood. Shelomi can't speak. He lies in his bed, his eyes open, filled with fear. It sounds as though he may not be with us much longer as we prepare for our departure from this land. That's very sad, my friends, isn't it?"

It was a report all had expected but none wanted to hear. Such a report created confusion in Abiasaph.

"Excuse me for asking," he said, "but I'm troubled by something. If the Almighty One is so powerful, and He can do all those things to the people of Kemet, and He cares so much for us that He's prepared to take us to another land, why can't He intervene and stop all the beatings and deaths? How does Shelomi believe in the Almighty One, when, it appears, that he won't be here when the deliverance takes place?"

The others sat and pondered the difficult question. Finally, Libni spoke deliberately and quietly. "Abiasaph, your question is one of the most difficult of all questions at this time. It would be wonderful if we had a God who chose to give us a perfect world, where everything happened the way we wanted, where no one became sick and died, all had the best food to eat, and we were allowed to live where we wished. However, if no one was injured, no child died at birth, no one became angry or cursed, there were no wars, and crops always were bountiful, that would be wonderful! What an existence! What a land! We would be popular, because we'd live in paradise.

"Our God hasn't promised us an easy life, or that we'd live forever. Because there are sicknesses, He gave us physicians. Because crops aren't always plentiful, we learned to barter. Think about it, my friend. If the Almighty one is able to do these things to the pharaoh and the people of the Two Lands, while also protecting us as a nation, He truly is powerful. I can't answer why Shelomi lies in terror in his own bed, or why your Nehushta died while bringing your son into the world.

"We look around, and we see that without the intervention of the Almighty One, we would be subject to the pharaoh for how many more generations? Perhaps forever. We'd have no future as a nation. Our God stands between the pharaoh and ourselves. He's protecting us. He'll take us out as promised. We must believe and hope. That is our greatest weapon."

Abiasaph was deep in thought. He was glad he asked, and he was just as glad Libni answered. He had a lot to think about. He wanted to change the topic, having had enough information for one day. Thinking about Sheloml and those who'd been beaten bothered him.

"Libni, I noticed in walking this morning that you need some mending and rebuilding of your well and fences. Would you like help with that work while we have free time? Caath and I can work with you, if you'd like."

"Thank you for the offer. I've thought that out carefully. In one respect, I believe we'll be rescued soon, so it's useless to fix such things, but you're right. Since we have the time, we should do mending wherever necessary. I accept. If we're fortunate tomorrow again with another free day, you and Caath can come when you choose, and we'll finish the mending. Vophsi will create a mouth-watering meal for you both.

"When Alumai, my grandfather, was alive, he often talked about the time in which we live. Whenever we talked about the Almighty One's deliverance, grandfather told us a dream he had as a young man.

"In the dream, grandfather saw a great hand come out of the heavens and move downward toward the land. It came slowly, its palm open. As it neared, he saw it was large enough to hold the entire Hebrew people, and he knew it was the hand of the Almighty One come to take them out of the land.

"As the hand drew closer to the land, it caused the wind to blow, and the land reacted strangely. People were tossed about, some of them injured. He watched in amazement as many of his brothers and neighbors shook their fists at the heavens and cursed the wind and the destruction. He called out, explaining it was the hand of God come to deliver them, but no one heard him. They grew more bitter, cursed, and shouted blasphemies at God. They also began to curse grandfather.

"Finally, amid a mighty tumult, the hand reached the earth and swept the Hebrew people up and out of the land. As he watched the deliverance take place, he said he almost couldn't believe what he saw. There, held in the hand of the Almighty One Himself, the Hebrew men and women fought to get away. They cursed the hand, not realizing it was a noble act of God.

"It's happening now just as it did in grandfather's dream. Very few among us are aware of just how great a thing the Almighty One is doing. True, it's hard to understand if you look at our position, for we're no more than slaves, and poor and cruelly treated ones at that. I choose to see it differently. I see the promise of the Almighty One unfolding clearly and more quickly than you can imagine. It's exciting, Abiasaph, a good time to be alive.

"You can see why I'm more concerned with properly preparing our people for the deliverance and may have allowed my fences and houses to become shabby."

Abiasaph smiled, stood, and thanked his friends for their hospitality and conversation. "I must leave you now. It's getting late, and I don't know where my son is. Libni, if we're still in camp tomorrow, we'll help you with your mending."

Vophsi looked at his hands and assured him the swelling was gone. He would have the full use of it soon. It still hurt, but he hadn't noticed the pain in a while.

The young man nodded to his hosts and left the tent. As he walked out, he overheard Hor-em-heb and Libni speaking of Shelomi's sad condition.

"Poor Shelomi," Abiasaph said softly. "He probably won't live to be rescued by the Almighty One. Poor Abiasaph! I will probably live to see it, and I don't even understand it."

He thought over what Libni said but didn't agree with the man's philosophy about work. Regardless of one's beliefs, there were jobs that needed doing. One didn't stop eating, so why stop mending? He and Caath would help. The job would be easy, especially since Hor-em-heb and Libni would help him. He sighed as he walked.

The difference between them was that Libni understood and believed in the deliverance, and Abiasaph didn't.

He thought of Alumai's dream and wondered if he was one of those who fought to be free of the hand of deliverance. As he slowly walked back toward his community, he realized he probably was.

# CHAPTER FOURTEEN

# SAD NEWS, ABIASAPH

Adbeel felt no pain. His movements were mechanical, and his mind felt shattered. His half-foot and leg were swollen to twice their normal size, but he'd already forgotten about them.

*I've been crawling for days, or maybe it's just been hours,* he thought, cursing the darkness.

Then he realized he didn't know how long he'd been in his present circumstances.

*What happened to the time?* he wondered. He didn't know where he was, how long he'd been there, and what he was doing.

*Calm yourself! I must force myself to think. Think, Ebebi!*

He remembered seeing Horus, the falcon god. He attacked Ebebi, who barely escaped with his life. Was that possible?

*No, that must have been a dream. My foot! Yes, I remember. My foot was damaged.*

He reached down to touch it and screamed. He'd forgotten how badly it hurt.

*What are they doing to me?* he wondered. *Why am I allowing them to hurt me this way? My head hurts so badly. Horus must have injured that, too. He left me with a constant ringing sound as a reminder.*

"It won't work, Horus!" he shouted. "I won't fall into more of your snares! You may have the upper hand now, but I'll best you in the end."

Touching his head, he knew he was perspiring heavily, and he needed rest, but there was no time. His head hurt badly, and his foot and leg were worse.

"Keep walking, Ebebi," he told himself. "We won't give in. There's plenty of fight left in us. I'm thirsty, Petephis. Is there anyone who can bring me a drink?

"I remember now. There was a blackness. I remember seeing it. It was a cruel but effective means of warfare, Horus, but it hasn't worked. As you see, I've overcome it. The odds are in my favor. What? Yes, you injured my leg, but that, my honored adversary, is why warriors have two legs.

"Petephis, please bring me drink. I'm very thirsty. I'd like wine, Petephis. I must plan our next campaign. Bring Mi-Sakhme. I have orders for him. Where's my wine?"

Adbeel lurched forward, cocking his head upward. "What? Who's this? Who are these men, Petephis? Are they friend or foe? Your Ebebi needs wine. Your Ebebi..., Uh ... your Ebebi ... uh, I can't remember."

The two Hebrews stopped, hesitant to go farther. Adbeel scowled at them and beckoned with his hand.

"Aha! Is the enemy in such difficulties that he must send spies disguised as slaves? That makes me laugh. Enough of this. Petephis, rid me of these men. Bring me wine. I must prepare my plan of attack. Horus will give no quarter. I must make immediate plans."

The old Hebrew looked at the strange sight before him. "Petephis, did you say? Is that not a name of Kemet? Who are you asking for? Aren't you Adbeel, the Levite, brother of Abiasaph?"

The words startled Adbeel. He cocked his head to one side, then the other, staring at the two men. *Adbeel?* he wondered. *Did he say Adbeel? Am I not Adbeel? Then who's Ebebi? Who are these men? Why do they look at me like that? Where's Samuel? Isn't he supposed to meet me here? Who's Adbeel? Who am I?*

"Adbeel," the old man said, "what happened to you? What's wrong with your leg and foot? Where are your clothes?"

202

It was clear that Adbeel had lost his mind. The old man put his hand on his grandson's shoulder. "He doesn't look well, does he, Gemalli?"

"Petephis," Adbeel said, "rid me of these interrogators immediately. Ebebi must rest. Send for entertainers and more wine. Send for Adbeel, too. I must see who he is. He's likely a spy for old Horus, that crafty god. Bring more wine. I must rest."

Adbeel laid down his head and closed his eyes.

* * *

Pharez and Oshea spoke quietly about Shelomi's worsening condition. The physician lowered his gaze. Shelomi's situation bothered him. He was filled with fear. He'd seen such looks before. Those who had it never recovered. Pharez knew Shelomi would die, but he didn't want him to die in fear like that.

"I don't think he'll last much longer," Pharez said. "I can't be certain. There are things he's suffering from that I have no control over or answers for.

"We remedied his outward appearance. That would eventually heal, though he would have permanent scars. But he's been injured inside, too, where we can't see. Something in his mind is damaged. He has lost the ability to speak, and he lies there on the mat with his face horribly twisted and eyes open constantly. Fear fills his gaze. I think he still sees the soldiers coming at him with their whips and clubs. It's very sad.

"I've gone to him often to let him know I'm here, but I can't be sure he knows it. We tried to make him as comfortable as possible. We feed him, but all he can eat is a small amount of broth or milk mixed with herbs. I'm sorry, but I can't offer any hope to his family and friends."

Pharez stared into the late evening sky. "Oshea, he's only one of many. How long can this go on? Have Mosheh and Aaron come with any more information about our deliverance from this torment?"

Eldad and Gemalli arrived, interrupting them. The chieftain summoned Oshea as he approached the large tent.

"I have disturbing news," Eldad said. "I should speak with you and Elishama."

Pharez left them, and they went immediately into Elishama's tent. After a short greeting, Elishama summoned his granddaughter to bring a skin filled with water.

"I've chosen to report this to you, Oshea, because it is very strange," Eldad said. "You're friends with Abiasaph, the Levite, aren't you?"

Oshea winced. "Eldad, I'm sorry to say Abiasaph has few close friends. Shimri, the Simeonite, the son of Zichri, would probably be his closest friend. Abiasaph's a quiet man who keeps to himself."

"Then let me tell you what we saw, and possibly we can find the wisdom to determine what to do about it.

"Gemalli, here, the son of my Joel, was walking with me outside the encampment, and we found a naked man crawling toward us on the ground. As we approached, we saw he was hurt, and we eventually saw his foot had a loose wrapping around it filled with dirt and sand. The poor man had lost his foot. His legs were badly torn and swollen, and he was bruised all over.

"Where his foot had been, his leg was now three times its normal size. His elbows and legs were bleeding badly, and there was much dried blood, as if he had been bleeding for some time. He looked horrible. When we came close enough to see him, he looked up at us with eyes filled, not with horror, but with insanity.

"It was Adbeel, the son of Jubal, the brother of Abiasaph, the Levite. This man called himself Ebebi, and he called out to someone named Petephis. These are Kemet names, so I don't know what it means.

"As he spoke, it was clear his mind was gone. He ranted about a war he fought with someone. I didn't catch the name of his enemy, but he kept asking Petephis to bring him wine. He was clearly out of his mind.

"Finally, he lay back his head, stopped crawling, and closed his eyes. We found he was dead. We stopped on our way to ask the physician from Issachar to bring his body into camp."

"You haven't found Abiasaph yet?" Oshea asked.

"No. I thought you were a friend of his, and you might be the one to tell him."

Oshea looked at Elishama, wondering if the old man would agree. Though he wasn't Oshea's grandfather, he always called him that. "Grandfather, Shimri wouldn't be the right one to tell Abiasaph about this. I'd like to go with Eldad. I've been thinking about Abiasaph since I spoke with his son, and I'd like to be of assistance to him."

Elishama nodded.

\* \* \*

The two men reached Abiasaph and Caath's hut, where they sat finishing a late meal.

"Abiasaph?" Oshea called. "May we visit with you for a short time? We have news."

The young Levite rose from his mat and walked to the open doorway. He motioned the men inside.

"Caath, bring milk for the men," he said softly.

Caath obediently left. He was excited to have Oshea in his house, but he saw by his solemn mood it wouldn't be a joyful visit.

The men sat in a circle around Abiasaph's small fire. He thought they were there to discuss his fight with the Nubian. "What has brought you to visit us?"

Eldad reached over and laid a coarse hand on Abiasaph's knee. "It's sad news, Abiasaph, that we have to offer this day." The elderly man paused, looked at Oshea, who nodded, and began to speak.

"Abiasaph, earlier this evening," Oshea began, "Eldad and his grandson were walking near the edge of the camp and saw a young man crawling along the ground. As they approached him, they recognized him as Adbeel, your brother. He was obviously mad and had been injured. He died before Eldad and Gemalli could help him."

Oshea paused. The hut was silent. Caath brought cups of milk and a large platter of cut melon and set them down before the men. He sat behind his father and listened.

"Eldad, did he have anything to say before he died?" Abiasaph asked. "Why was he coming here? What happened to him?"

Abiasaph found he couldn't say his brother's name. Even at the news of his death, he still had bitter feelings toward the man.

"Yes, he spoke, but I'm afraid his words were no help. They held no meaning. He had already lost control of his mind. He spoke of someone named Petephis and kept calling himself Ebebi, a Kemet name. However, we were sure he was Adbeel.

"His foot had been torn off, and the physician said the pain probably caused him to lose his sanity. He must have crawled through the darkness for hours, assuming that is from where he came."

Abiasaph sat quietly. Behind him, Caath became excited. Knowing his place, he was silent, but the others noted the effect on him.

"Abiasaph," Oshea said, "I believe Caath may have something to say. He has held his silence out of respect for us, but it might do to hear him."

Abiasaph looked at his son and motioned him to speak.

"Papa," Caath said excitedly, "the little man, Mugolla, was speaking about a Hebrew slave in the house of Mi-Sakhme. He mentioned the name Petephis as an overseer of the estate, but the Hebrew slave was called Ebebi. He said he came to the house of Mi-Sakhme one year ago."

Abiasaph turned and caught Oshea's eye. They knew it was about that time that Adbeel had disappeared. Some thought he'd been killed. Abiasaph was red with anger and embarrassment, but he listened to his son.

"This Mugolla didn't remember the man's Hebrew name, Papa, but his Kemet name was Ebebi. According to Mugolla, Ebebi was a horrible man. He had to kill a Hebrew man and bring the hand to Mi-Sakhme as proof he did it. Ebebi did it, Papa. He killed one of our people and cut off his hand."

Abiasaph held up his hand to silence his son and hung his head in shame. He knew it was at that time that Nohah, the Simeonite, had been found murdered with no hand. Everyone thought the Kemet soldiers did it, because it was a cruel tradition of theirs to kill and maim like that. Abiasaph couldn't look at the two elders, because he knew they remembered, too.

Eldad rose from his sitting position and went to Caath and Abiasaph. He put a strong arm around Caath's neck and hugged the boy while patting his shoulder. "I'm sorry, Abiasaph. Don't blame yourself. You aren't responsible for your brother's actions. Let's just assume that he, in remorse, was coming back to repent. The Almighty One has made restitution—your brother's life for Nohah's. We can put it to rest and forget it. Let's not speak of it further."

"Your words are of no use," Abiasaph said. "If Little Beer Man knows those things, as soon as he hears of Adbeel's return, he'll tell everyone."

Eldad looked around, catching everyone's gaze. "Then let us speak no more of it. The name of Ebebi will not be mentioned. Adbeel lost control of his mind by the time we reached him, so we can't be sure what he said. He also ordered his steward to bring him entertainment and wine. There he lay, naked and injured, far from any house. There was no steward with him.

"My friends, it would be wisest to leave this conversation to the sand dust of the desert and proclaim only what we know for certain, that Adbeel has returned but, sadly, died."

He looked to Abiasaph for approval. Abisasaph stared back in amazement. He couldn't understand why they wanted to protect his and Caath's name. They weren't important people in the camp, and they didn't even share the same beliefs. He'd never been Oshea's friend, so why would he attempt to comfort Abiasaph?

Everything that happened that day left him feeling unbalanced. He didn't know what to do or say, but he was glad Eldad decided to keep the information quiet. Abiasaph nodded and remained silent.

The two visitors stood. Each gripped Abiasaph's shoulder, patted his back, and prepared to depart. Eldad told him where Adbeel's body was being kept. Abiasaph assured him he'd go there immediately.

Oshea squeezed Caath's shoulder and smiled warmly at him. He then turned to Abiasaph and made an astounding offer. "Abiasaph, my grandfather's house is always open to you. You're welcome if you'd like to come and speak to us, or if you'd just like to listen to my grandfather speak, as many other men do. You're also welcome just to come and sit at any time."

The men left the hut and returned to their own community.

Abiasaph and Caath stood quietly for a few moments, taking in what happened. Caath began to clean the floor, taking the cups and platter to the well to wash. When he returned, he refilled his father's cup with milk and poured some for himself.

"Papa, do you like Oshea now?"

Abiasaph turned and looked at his son, then they smiled at each other. He gripped Caath's shoulder. "Yes, son, I think I do. It was good of him and Eldad to visit us under such strange circumstances. It wasn't necessary, but it was very kind of them to grant us that comfort."

He helped his son tidy up the hut. "Now, Caath, go get Idbash. He can come with us. We'll see how well you taught him to listen to you."

Caath called his lamb, and it immediately sprinted from the far end of the hut and leaped into his arms. They left the hut and walked slowly to the house of Issachar, the physician, to preside over the burial of a family member.

# CHAPTER FIFTEEN

# MOSHEH

The two elderly men sat quietly in the tent. Night was upon them, and they would sleep soon. Mosheh had just returned from speaking with the Lord. His brother waited quietly, wondering what their instructions would be.

Aaron sometimes found it difficult to believe all the things that happened during the past year. He remembered the day it began.

\* \* \*

He'd been to the festival in the city. Festival days were proclaimed as free days for the slaves, and Aaron attended them when he could. He enjoyed the various forms of entertainment. Like the rest of his Hebrew brethren, he also enjoyed the food. Aaron was enthralled by the stories of the many gods of the Two Lands. The festival days always included much worship of the Kemet deities. It was an interesting spectacle, and that day, he enjoyed himself.

Upon returning to camp, he went into the desert to commune with the Almighty One, as was his custom. As he sat in the sand, contemplating the stories of his God handed down by Amram, his father, he suddenly felt overcome with remorse. He was keenly aware that his interest in the gods of Kemet was unsatisfactory to the Almighty One. He tore his clothes and lay prone on the sand, repenting of his wrongdoing.

After more than an hour, feeling clean and close to God again, he stood and started back to his tent. As he walked, he felt a powerful presence around him and stopped perfectly still until the feeling passed. Nothing had been said or done, but he knew he was to pack a goatskin and journey into the desert early the next morning.

He told no one. Quietly, he awoke and followed the instructions that came to him and began his trek into the open desert. After many hours, he saw a man in the distance. Drawn toward him, Aaron walked to where the man sat. As he approached, he cautiously looked him over. He was old, like Aaron, a shepherd. The shepherd smiled as they met. Aaron didn't speak, but the man offered him food and drink, and he accepted.

Aaron immediately liked the old man, who was very gentle. He spoke quietly and slowly.

The two old men ate and rested. They made small talk, and Aaron enjoyed the rest after his long walk. While they sat on the ground, looking up into the beautiful calm sky, the man turned and called Aaron by name. Startled, Aaron looked hard at the other man.

"Mosheh! My brother! It's been so many years!" he said.

"Yes, Aaron. It's been nearly forty years. I have a family in this land. It's good to see you."

They embraced and spent a long time sharing memories. After finishing their meal, Mosheh motioned Aaron to rest, because he had much to tell him.

"Much has happened since we last spoke. I would have been killed by the Egyptians had I stayed in Avaris forty years ago. Our Almighty One had other plans. It took me forty years to learn why the Lord sent me here. We'll be coming back to Goshen with you. I've spoken with the Lord, and He's ready to deliver our people from bondage."

"That's wonderful news, dear brother! We've been waiting for so long. Things have become much worse. The masters show little mercy. Why has the Almighty One sent me here? He told me to come to the desert."

"You're to be my voice, Aaron. I can't speak well in my late years. It's not like the old days, when I was trained to lead and manage and speak in the land of the pharaoh. Those responsibilities were easier then. I've become softer, and I haven't spoken much for many years. I have little to say to my sheep." He smiled. "The people of Goshen may not hear me, but they'll hear you. The Lord gave me His instructions, and you are to be our voice to the people and to the pharaoh.

"The Lord has told me that He has seen the troubles you mentioned. He, too, is no longer willing to have us battered by the pharaoh and his soldiers. He's ready to take us from that land to a land of our own, the one that was promised to our father, Abraham.

"Come. You must meet my family. We're going back to Egypt. We'll sleep tonight, then tomorrow, we'll finish our journey to the land of Goshen."

\* \* \*

Aaron shook off his reverie and wondered, as he had so often before, why God chose him to be Mosheh's voice. He hadn't been very dedicated in his worship of the God of his fathers. Elishama and Eldad were more devoted, so why had the Almighty One called on Aaron for such a task?

He didn't know, but he was certainly enjoying his part. The role he played brought him a greater respect for the Almighty One. The whole experience was thrilling—and a bit frightening.

Mosheh was different. He had a deep relationship with the Almighty One, and he loved and respected Him. Aaron hadn't come to know God in that way, but he hoped he would. Sometimes, he thought it would never happen. He was too changeable. Sometimes, he even agreed with the troublemakers in camp, thinking he and Mosheh had acted wrongly. Then Mosheh would be upset with him.

He no longer had that problem. With each new plague, Aaron became more aware of how close they were to their promised deliverance. He prayed it would come soon, before he and Mosheh died at the hands of their own people.

He no sooner finished that thought than he saw his weakness. At the age of eighty-five, he should be stronger than that. With the Lord's help, he would be. He prayed God would forgive him.

Mosheh hadn't spoken since his return. He sat at the back of the tent, leaning against a support pole sipping warm goat's milk. He looked at Aaron, waiting until their eyes met.

"The Lord has spoken to me again," Mosheh said. "We're near the time of His final act of judgment against this land and its people. Tomorrow, we'll speak with the elders. The Lord is preparing for the deliverance. It will happen soon. As He promised earlier, He'll slay the firstborn of everyone in the land, rulers, peasants, even animals. All will die at the Lord's hand."

"Did He promise we would be spared?"

"Yes. The Lord will pass over the houses and cattle of His people. However, there are more instructions to come. All is not yet final. I'll tell you all that the Lord told me, but we'll do that in the morning.

"Go be with your family now. I will sleep soon. We'll rise early and talk again. Sleep well, Aaron."

Aaron rose and bid his brother good night, then went to his house where his family waited.

Mosheh sipped his milk. He heard someone playing a lyre nearby, and the music was soothing. He thought of his early years, raised in the Egyptian way. He learned to play many musical instruments and became an accomplished musician. He rose slowly, pushed his way through the tent opening, and walked outside.

He laid out his sheepskin mat on the ground, resting it against a large sycamore tree, then stretched out on it with his hands folded behind his head as he leaned against the base of the tree. He looked up and shook his head in amazement. The starry sky was beautiful but ominous in comparison to the black plague that covered the rest of the land. He pondered the might and power of his God.

He reached around to swat away a bug from his face. As his fingers ran slowly across his rough, wrinkled cheek, he thought back to his boyhood. His fair complexion had been an embarrassment. He wanted so badly to grow older quickly, so he could finally attain a look of manhood. Once he had grown, though, there were no longer any questions of his manhood.

He smiled as he recalled his years in the palace. Mosheh reached around and smoothed out the mat. He drank the last of his milk, tossed the goatskin into the tent, and relaxed.

\* \* \*

Mosheh was called the First Prince of the Two Lands, next in line to succeed the king. He couldn't remember his earliest years, but he marveled at the story his brother Aaron told him about being hidden in the basket as a baby.

Mosheh was born at a time when a cruel edict from the pharaoh was being carried out in Goshen. All male children under the age of two years were to be killed. The pharaoh's wise men predicted that a Hebrew child born at that time would grow and rise up against him, causing great damage to the Two Lands.

Mosheh's mother, Jochebed, placed her son in a basket of reeds in the shallows of the Nile near where the pharaoh's daughter bathed. She found the basket and decided to keep the baby and named him Mosheh.

Mosheh's sister, Mariam, hid in the reeds and came out, offering to find the princess a Hebrew mother to nurse the baby. As a result, Mosheh was reunited with his mother for a few more years.

The pharaoh's daughter took Mosheh into the palace where he was raised as an Egyptian and became the heir to the throne. He remembered, with bitterness, his days of schooling at the temples of On. Scorn for his people and for Israel was drummed into the minds of all the young boys. The recognition of the inferiority of the Hebrew race was essential knowledge in the training of the young royals. Although Mosheh wasn't bitter then, later, when he learned the truth, he recalled his youth with bad memories.

A proverb stated, *The ear of the student is on his back, so when he is beaten, he listens.* Mosheh, like the other boys, learned to listen. Being from a royal house, he also studied at the school of scribes, which was considered one of the more honored professions in the land. He learned to play various musical instruments and attended a military school, where he became an accomplished archer and expert chariot driver.

Mosheh knew he was different and often spoke to his psuedo-mother, the princess, about it. She wasn't completely truthful with him, but there were enough hints from servants for him to understand he wasn't really an Egyptian prince. He also had vague memories of another woman. He'd spent his earliest years with her. The more he thought of his origins, the more thoughts of Jochebed came to mind. Mosheh was an excellent student, who learned all he was taught, but he never learned to hate his fellow Hebrews.

He was glad when his schooling was over. He attained great honor during his time as a prince for leading the pharaoh's army to many military victories. He didn't remember that with relish, though.

Seti, his stepfather, groomed Mosheh for the throne, but Mosheh wasn't comfortable around the foreign princes and the inflated egos of the court. As he aged, he knew he wanted no part of the royalty and riches prepared for him. He felt a stronger kinship with the people of Goshen.

His brothers often teased him that he wasn't a true Egyptian. His features were more Hebrew than Egyptian. That was obvious to him, too.

Finally, he consulted his mother again, who reluctantly told him the truth. From that time on, he went to Goshen as often as he could, secretly meeting with Aaron and having the truth verified. One day while driving along the river, he saw a Kemet guard whipping a Hebrew slave. He stopped his chariot and demanded an explanation for such brutal punishment.

The answer changed his life forever, because the guard said, "I don't need any reason to beat a slave. These Hebrews are lazy and belligerent." He picked up his whip and returned to the beating.

Mosheh was furious. He jumped off his chariot and beat the guard's face with his fists. He grabbed his throat and threw him to the ground. The soldier's head struck a large rock, which killed him instantly.

Mosheh saw that the only witness was the Hebrew slave and his working partners, two other Hebrews. He dug a large grave in the sand and buried the Egyptian, and turned to the slaves.

"I am Mosheh. Like you, I'm Hebrew. Though I was raised in the king's palace, I haven't forgotten my heritage, and I'll help you whenever I can."

The two Hebrews who helped their fallen comrade paid him scant attention.

"You're one of them!" one said. "You can't fool us with an act of kindness, if that's what it is. We're Hebrews, and you're Egyptian."

They turned and walked toward the encampment, helping their injured friend.

Mosheh was crushed. He jumped into his chariot and drove back to his house, wondering how long it would take before word got out that he'd killed a guard. That would mean death. Since he became an adult, there were many in the court, including his half-brothers, who looked for opportunities to destroy him. Finally, he decided to leave the Two Lands and run as far away as he could.

* * *

Mosheh moved on the mat, opening his eyes and looking up at the sky. The musician still played in the distance. He thought about the years he spent shepherding Jethro's flocks in the wilderness and smiled at the comparison. After being held in high esteem in the Two Lands, he was considered nothing in the wilderness, because of his decision to shepherd with the women and children instead of becoming a warrior with the other men of the tribe.

*What would they have done if they knew of my background as a military captain?* he wondered.

Those had been good years, though. After all the excitement of Kemet, the years of learning, parties, entertainment, and commanding the pharaoh's armies, he welcomed the slow, easy life of a shepherd. It gave him the chance to balance his thinking. Under the pharaoh, he'd been bold, confident, and daring. As a shepherd, he became gentle, quiet, and less proud of his achievements. He enjoyed that much more.

That was why it came as a surprise when the Almighty One appeared to him from a fire in the middle of a dry bush that didn't burn up.

*Why did God choose me?* he wondered. *I was no longer a leader of men. I became short in my speech and had the calm life of a shepherd. Why would He call me to be His spokesman to the pharaoh and the children of Israel?*

He was doing exactly that, regardless of his qualifications. He made mistakes, and he wondered why the Lord endured his complaining and impatience.

*If You, Lord, were as impatient with the children of Jacob as I've been with You, they'd be dead by now. Not only have I been impatient, I've been obstinate, too, especially at the beginning.*

He complained to the Lord many times that he was the wrong man to send as His messenger. When he thought about it, he became embarrassed and shook his head in disgust.

*At least my stupidity and slowness caused me to learn to develop a much better understanding of these people. I become angry at their rebelliousness and obstinance, but I also am filled with compassion for them. I see in each one a little of myself. They'll develop, Lord, each in their own time.*

He noticed over the past year how many of the Hebrew families had returned to the Almighty One. There were those who still worshipped with the people of Kemet, but he began to see why the Lord took so long to bring about his promise.

*The people wouldn't have been ready to leave the land one year ago,* he realized. *They'd have turned back and rebelled at the first setback. I question if they're ready now, but at least they're more ready than before.*

The elderly Levite moved around, finding a more comfortable position. He recalled the Lord telling him he would be a shepherd again, moving the Lord's sheep from one pasture to another, and he smiled.

*The children of Israel* are *like sheep. Some move immediately when they hear their names called, while others drag along slowly. Some have to be carried, while others lag behind and invite danger. They're doing the same thing in their response to the Almighty One and His promise. Now, Lord, You tell me to be a shepherd again, this time, to lead Your people into the land promised to our father, Abraham.*

Mosheh shook his head in wonder. *Well, the Lord sent Aaron to speak for me. That's good. Aaron's more eloquent than I, and he has the people's respect.*

He noticed that even Aaron had developed many of the ways of the red people. Often, the two men disagreed. Mosheh wondered if Aaron was sent as punishment to him for the way he angered the Lord. That thought made him smile. That wasn't true, or course.

He thought of the events that led to the present. *How can this pharaoh be so stone-hearted? Doesn't he realize he's fighting against the I Am, the Lord, the God of all Israel?*

He remembered seeing the pharaoh the first time nearly one year earlier. Ramesses had exploded with anger when Mosheh and Aaron refused to bow down and do homage to him before speaking. When they dared to look into his face, Ramesses flew into a rage. He'd hated Mosheh for a long time.

*How that ignited his anger,* Mosheh thought. *Could the pharaoh's unwillingness to obey the Lord be partly because of our first act of defiance?*

He thought of his people's long history. Whenever the Almighty One decided to fight for them, they didn't just win, they won mightily.

*Pharaoh will be surprised by the time this is over,* Mosheh thought, thinking of their ultimate victory. *Will he be killed? Will the Almighty One spare him?*

He thought of the plagues the Lord had brought. It was almost like a dream with so many miraculous things happening, yet he knew it was real, and it was still happening. The darkness over the land was another of the cups of God's wrath poured upon that oppressive people. Still, the pharaoh stubbornly refused to acknowledge the Lord's power. That would end soon.

The Lord had spoken to Mosheh about it earlier that evening. *Pharaoh will reject the Lord's demand again, and the Lord will bring one last plague upon the land, slaying the firstborn of people and animals. Then and only then will the pharaoh send the children of Israel from the land. He'll do it with a strong hand. So the time has come. It's only a matter of days.*

*Are the people ready to receive this word? Will they believe this time? Will there be any who won't come? What of the foreigners who sojourn among us? I need to ask the Lord about that.*

He still had questions, but he'd be content to let them remain idle until the Lord, in His own time, provided the answers. His concern for his people wouldn't be idle, though. He loved the Hebrew nation. He spent many years away from them because of other circumstances, but he missed their fellowship.

Mosheh rose and walked to the pathway near his tent and looked into the dark sky. It was dark but lighter compared to the heavy blackness that hung over the rest of the land. He raised his arms, palms open, and, with his low, coarse voice, spoke slowly and confidently to his God.

"God of my fathers, Abraham, Isaac, and Jacob; God who has claimed His people, the children of Jacob, as Your own; God eternal, to be known forever as the God of Abraham, Isaac, and Jacob, the Deliverer of Israel; Lord God of Israel, who has shown Your power to the gods of this land and caused them to tremble and flee before Your face, harken to me, Mosheh, Your lowly servant.

"Remember Your promise to our father, Abraham, Lord. Remember the words You gave to me, Your humble servant. Remember the words that we spoke at Your bidding to the elders of Your people and to the pharaoh. Remember, God of Abraham, Your mercy and leniency toward Your people, the children of Israel.

"I ask You to remember Your words, Lord, because that's our only hope. You've sent me to Your people, but Lord, who am I that they should put their hope in me? No, Lord. Our hope is in You and Your promise.

"I stand before You, Lord, a coward, a man who ran from his enemies, unwilling to stay and die as so many of Your people have done, yet You showed me Your mercy, Lord. You've retrieved me from the treacherous jaws of an easy, uncaring life.

"I'm grateful, Lord. I'm willing to suffer and die for my people, but had not Your mercy been greater than my apathy and transgression, I would have no part in this great thing You're about to do.

"Now, Lord, I see this people, too, uncaring, afraid, unbelieving, not prepared for Your great deliverance. They're at odds with each other, without respect for those that You have placed in their command. They defy us, Lord. They're deceived, filled with bitterness, and still honor gods of clay.

"Let not Your wrath against the stubborn and unbelieving of Your people keep them from partaking of the richness of this victory. I entreat You, Lord, to honor Your word in its completeness and have compassion on this people. Show us again Your mercy."

Mosheh lowered his outstretched arms and wiped tears from his eyes. He stood quietly for a few minutes, and slowly raised his head toward the black night. He dropped to his knees, keeping his head and eyes in position, and spoke to his friend, God. His voice was filled with anguish, and his speech was broken.

"Lord, God of Abraham, hear me! This, Your people, is a stubborn one. We've told them all that You've commanded us. You, Lord, with Your strong hand, have performed signs for them that would have astonished our father, Abraham. You've protected them through the plagues, a sure sign of Your love for them. Still, Your people are as unmovable as a donkey.

"They've tried to kill your servants, Mosheh and Aaron. They've spat at us and mocked us. They haven't and won't hear our words. Lord, are we angry? No. I, too, love this, Your people, with a father's love.

"Lord, they also spit at and mock You. Are You angry, Lord? Will You take all of this people out of the land, even those who defy You? Lord God of Abraham, I see this people as sheep without a shepherd. They've been captured by a cruel enemy. He leads them in hatred, not love, and they follow him, unknowingly. Don't hate them, Lord. They've lost their will to be free. The enemy has tried to force them into his mold. You, my God, have cast their mold years earlier, when You promised our father, Abraham, that his seed would become Your people.

"This, Your people, Lord, have forgotten Your promise. They see Your mighty acts and hear Your words, Lord, which we've spoken unto them, and they still say, 'We're caught in a snare, and there's no way out.'

"Almighty One, God of our fathers, God of the promise, the people may not listen to us tomorrow. The words You've given us for them are excellent to us, but they also will be hard for the people. My heart, Lord, tells me that many among them won't partake of Your great provision. Have mercy on them, Lord. Don't take us from this land unless You take all of us. If one must stay behind to avenge Your anger and justice … then let it be me."

The rugged old shepherd stopped pleading, buried his head in his hands, and wept. Slowly, he walked back to the sycamore tree and leaned against its trunk.

Mosheh had spent most of his life away from his people, longing to be with them. Now he was there, but in a capacity he never would've chosen. He looked out into the night sky and saw the Lord's majesty in the vastness above, even though part of his view was blocked by the recent plague. It was magnificent.

He closed his eyes and cupped his hands in his lap, sitting quietly and thinking about the enormous love the Lord had for His people. A picture came to mind.

He saw the Lord, mighty, surrounded by fire. He reached out, filled with love, to the entire Hebrew encampment. He saw the children of Israel. Some ran, fearing the fire and cursing the intense heat. Others carried on with their lives as if the fire didn't exist. Some knelt, hid their faces, and removed their sandals, showing respect for the Lord. Mosheh knew the situation in Goshen was exactly like the one in his mind.

*These people don't love You or fear You,* he realized, *yet You've promised to deliver them, anyway.*

He opened his eyes and looked around at the quiet, restful community. "This is, indeed, a holy place and time. And look, Lord. All Israel sleeps."

He thought about his people for a long time and began to weep. A great hand reached down from the heavens and touched his head.

Instantly, Mosheh slept, and the hand disappeared. As he slept restfully, a single tear fell onto his long, wet beard.

# PART THREE

# THE THIRD DAY

# CHAPTER SIXTEEN

# THE PLAGUES

Caath awoke and looked through the open doorway at a new day. He jumped up and ran to the door. It was already light in Goshen, but a thick, black cloud still hung over the rest of the land.

*Three days in a row!* he thought happily. *The soldiers have stayed away again. Praise be to the gods! No, praise be to the Almighty One.* He wondered if the Almighty One could hear his thoughts.

He called Idbash, and they went to the well to draw water. Caath wondered how his father would be that morning. The previous day had been strange. He knew a lot was happening in his father. He was changing, but Caath couldn't see in what way. At least his father liked Oshea now.

They left the well and started toward the sheepfold. "Come, Idbash. We must get milk for Papa. He'll be awake soon."

As they walked, something emerged from the shadows, startling Caath enough to make him drop his jug. Then he realized it was his father.

"Papa! You frightened me! I thought you were asleep."

"No. Sleep didn't come for me last night. I've been walking through the community and thinking, but I'm hungry now. I'll get the milk. You prepare a meal."

Caath, with Idbash at his side, picked up the water jug, filled it at the well, and returned to the hut to start a meal. His father was very troubled, perhaps over his brother.

*No,* Caath decided. *Papa was troubled yesterday even before he learned of Adbeel. I don't know. I don't like seeing him like this.*

Abiasaph finished the milking and closed the goatskin. He sat by the gate, knowing Caath wouldn't have the meal ready yet.

He was perplexed. He stayed awake all night, thinking and wondering, figuring and deciding, but he still had no answers. His heart was heavy. He wanted to know, if only for Caath's sake, what to do about the plagues and the Almighty One. His normal way of thinking didn't satisfy him anymore. Abiasaph realized it was probably true that the Almighty One was behind the plagues. And if there was to be deliverance, Abiasaph wasn't sure if he and his son would be part of it.

After all, he removed the Almighty One from his life and thinking years earlier. Would He allow Abiasaph to reconcile that mistake? If He did, how would Abiasaph go about it? Who would he ask?

He wouldn't go to the elders. He was no longer close to any of them. He thought of Old Abraham, who seemed a kindly old man, and was considered by many as the wisest man in camp. He wanted to talk with him, but why would he speak with someone like Abiasaph? He doubted the old man even knew his name.

Still, Oshea said to visit him, but he didn't want to walk up to his tent and announce himself. He didn't know what to do.

He was also upset over Adbeel's return. He had developed a deep hatred for his brother over the last few years, but that softened when he saw his brother's body. What horrible pain and torment had he gone through? Still, he couldn't forgive Adbeel's killing of Nohah and moving to a house of Kemet, especially the house of Mi-Sakhme, the murderer. Even if Eldad kept that news from the rest of the camp, it was too late for Abiasaph. He knew the truth.

He was concerned over his inability to control himself. He shouldn't have fought the Nubian soldier, but he hadn't liked how the man had beaten his son. As he pondered all those things, he knew the real problem was he couldn't find the answers he wanted about the Almighty One. For the first time in his life, he wanted to sit with his son and tell him the old stories about Abraham, Joseph, and Levi.

Where could he learn those tales? How could he teach his son what he didn't know? If all those stories were true, how would he instruct Caath? He didn't even know them himself.

"Papa!"

Looking up and seeing Caath motioning him inside, he walked into his hut and sat down with his son.

"Caath, we should be wealthy and living in a palace. Then you could prepare a meal like this every day."

"Papa," Caath replied with a grin, "if we ate like this every day, we'd soon be tired of it, and it wouldn't be so enjoyable. Besides, we couldn't be in a palace. You said we were different. Our life is to be lived away from the rest of the people, just you and me. Do you remember?"

Abiasaph glanced at him. Yes, he remembered. He continued eating. "Finish your meal, Son, and go work at the sheep folds. I need to be alone to think."

Abiasaph finished eating quietly and alone. He put away his utensils and sat on his mat with a sigh. He was tired but knew he wouldn't sleep. He had too much on his mind. He thought about the plagues. Had they all come from the Almighty One? The Kemet task-masters showed a cause for each plague after it was over. Abiasaph believed them, so who was right?

He remembered Hor-em-heb asking him that same question. The man had his own answer, but Abiasaph didn't. Maybe, if he could decide what the source of the plagues was, that would be a good place to begin thinking. There would be no more reason to learn about the Almighty One, if, in fact, He hadn't brought the plagues, but if He had....

That was what he needed to know. He reconstructed the plagues in his mind, hoping for a clue to help clear his mind.

The first plague turned the water red and undrinkable. Mosheh and the elders said it turned to blood, but it came just before the annual flood, nearly a year earlier. Abiasaph smiled as he recalled the events.

When the river was at its lowest, right before the floods each year, it often became reddish in color because of the red earth at the bottom. Many fish died in the shallow water, and the water wasn't fit for drinking. Many men, including Abiasaph, assumed that was the normal course of events when the plague came, only it was stronger than usual.

It happened early in the day, or so others said. He was at the quarries, working, and heard nothing about it until he reached the brickyards at the end of the day. Some of the guards complained, because they had no water to drink.

It was only after they returned to camp that he heard the story of Mosheh striking the water with his rod in front of Ramesses as he came for his morning worship.

At that time, Abiasaph, like many others, was more amused than excited by the story. The next few days, however, bore out the truth of the plague. There was no water to drink anywhere. He heard that even the vessels that had already been drawn with water had changed to a dark-red color, supposedly by the magic of sorcerers who matched Mosheh's power. The water became bitter and undrinkable, with a strong, unpleasant odor.

Eventually, the guards made the Hebrew slaves dig new streams near the river from which to draw fresh water. That water was clear and drinkable. Because of that, the story about Mosheh lost credence. Many Hebrews disliked the old man and blamed him for the increased workload laid on them over his arguments with the pharaoh.

Regardless of what the elders wanted everyone to believe, it was normal for the river to be in that condition at that time of year. Perhaps it was worse than usual, because of the competition between Mosheh and the pharaoh's magicians. There was no proof it was a plague from the Almighty One. When it was over, the Kemet guards emphatically stated it wasn't a plague.

Abiasaph smiled as he realized how much he enjoyed seeing his tormentors experience such discomfort. If any good came from it, it was seeing the guards suffer and letting them have a taste of what the slaves felt every day.

He stretched out his legs and tried to remember the next event. Then he recalled the incredible image of frogs. How the Gnat had responded to that plague! He never heard such complaining and wailing.

A short time after the first plague, frogs overflowed the river and filled the land, but there were more frogs than anyone could recall seeing before. They were everywhere. It seemed there were more in Kemet than in the camp, though.

The Hebrews were told that the frogs filled the houses of the people in Kemet and even slept in their beds. They were found in baking chambers and cooking pots. Abiasaph wondered if that was true. He hadn't seen the houses, so he didn't know. Hor-em-heb indicated the story was true, but the situation in Goshen wasn't bad.

Later, when the frogs died, the Hebrews had to gather them and heap them in large piles at different locations throughout the land. Abiasaph was working at the gate to Avaris and remembered how filthy that job had been. The stench was terrible, and he shivered at the memory. Someone said Mosheh had brought the frogs from the river, and that Ramesses' magicians again matched his skill and copied him. That was why there were so many.

He considered that. Did that qualify as a plague from the Almighty One, or was it a plague from the pharaoh's magicians? If they hadn't tried to match Mosheh's magic, wouldn't it have been normal for that time of year? Frogs always spilled from the river during the floods. The timing wasn't exactly right, but it was close

Abiasaph wondered if there would have been much said about either situation had Mosheh not performed his magic and the Egyptian magicians copied him. Frustrated, he slammed his fist into the ground.

"I still know nothing!" he said angrily.

The Levite stood and poured a cup of wine as he paced the small room. He rolled his sleeping mat into the form of a chair and placed it against the hut wall. He sat on it, resting his head against the wall, staring into his cup as he swirled the wine, seeing how close it could come to the top. He took a deep breath, exhaled loudly, and continued thinking.

The slaves had just arrived at the work site early one morning, and he stood with Shimri and Samuel, waiting for their work orders, when they heard a scream.

He remembered looking around, straining to find the source. Samuel, open-mouthed, pointed to the ground around them and saw it was covered in lice. They seemed to have risen from the desert floor and filled the area.

The guards ran in all directions, trying to escape the lice, which seemed to prefer them more than the Hebrew slaves. The guards screamed and cursed, and Abiasaph watched, incredulously, as swarms of lice enveloped the guards and taskmasters. Some were completely covered in them. Although the situation was uncomfortable and sickening to the Hebrews, they didn't have the same trouble the guards did.

Abiasaph remembered swatting at lice until his arms ached, and they were still on his body when he returned to camp, but that was mild compared to what the guards encountered. The situation was so bad that before the end of the day, the taskmasters sent the slaves back to Goshen and told them they'd be sent for later, but it never happened.

That was their first free day, or part of one, from the plagues.

Because of that day, Abiasaph got a lot of work finished. Having no guards over him, he was able to rest or take a drink when he wished. He had enjoyed himself, despite the manual labor.

Who brought the lice? The magicians weren't involved like with the water and frogs.

The elders called it another plague from the Almighty One, while the guards said the plague was natural and their gods removed it. It was hard to make sense of the situation. The lice showed up, created an upheaval, and then disappeared.

He thought about the plague of lice, wondering how to explain it. It certainly wasn't a normal thing. Why would the Kemet gods do such a thing to their own people then take it away?

He put aside his questions, sipped his wine, and returned to his recollections.

The next day, after the free day because of the lice, they were put back to work. All the Kemet guards and officers wore nets over their faces, but, though it helped a little, that didn't keep the lice off. They swatted, slapped, and cursed all day. The horses were troubled, too. The Hebrew slaves weren't allowed to wear nets. That was an unpleasant memory. Eventually, the lice disappeared, and life returned to normal, but the guards were harder on the slaves after that. Again, many Hebrews, including Abiasaph, blamed Mosheh.

He shook his head at the feeling of strangeness that accompanied that memory. The feeling was partly from frustration, because his recollections weren't producing any answers.

The next plague was an infestation of dog flies. Hor-em-heb had been talking about that with Abiasaph and Shimri only a day or so ago. Abiasaph was in the quarries when that plague occurred. Swarms of flies came out of nowhere in numbers too great to count.

He and a large group of men were pushing a boulder toward the floating raft when they heard a roaring sound. They saw a mass of insects attacking the area as if poured from a giant container. The sky was dark with them. It was terrifying at first, because no one knew what it was.

It was impossible to work. The flies caused great difficulty to the red men, Nubians, and foreign guards. The Hebrews got very little done, but it was worse for the enemy than them. All over the city, guards screamed and cursed the flies. The flies bit and raised large welts, and the day ended earlier than usual.

They went back to Goshen, where there were no dog flies at all. The following morning, no soldiers came to camp, because too many guards had taken ill. It was another free day.

He rememberd bitterly that many of the Hebrew men rejoiced, proclaiming it the day of the Almighty One's deliverance. They said the days of slavery were over. Those were the ones who suffered the most the following day when the guards came. Not only did the Hebrews have to work again but the work was more strenuous, the beatings more severe. The guards were outraged, because the flies infested their houses and swarmed on their children for two nights, while the Hebrews were untouched. Abiasaph decided he wanted no more tales of the Almighty One and His deliverance.

The guards beat the Hebrews regularly after that. Every day, someone was badly hurt, and men died. Many of the Hebrews became terrified, while others were insanely angry. Abiasaph thought it out and chose to protect himself and his son.

The problem came from the Hebrews' attitudes. They couldn't adjust to slavery again after convincing themselves it was over. The same ones who'd been celebrating God's victory soon were ready to stone Mosheh to death. The old man had to go into hiding.

As Abiasaph sipped his wine, he realized there was no explanation for that plague, either. The Kemet officers said the flies came because of all the dead frogs. The Hebrew elders attributed it to the hand of the Almighty One. Nevertheless, the Hebrew slaves had to burn the heaps of dead frogs.

One thing was different with that plague. There were no flies in Goshen at all. If the gods of Kemet were responsible for the plague, they would have had no reason to spare the Hebrews. Could it have been from the Almighty One?

The troubled Levite rose from his mat and walked outside his tent. He folded his arms and stared out at the sheepfold, seeing Caath kneeling at the gate, playing with Idbash. The boy caught his father's stare and quickly grabbed his cleaning tool to run back inside the fold.

Abiasaph smiled, walked back into the tent, and poured another cup of wine. He sat down on his mat again to think.

After the insects, the plagues stopped for a while, and many thought they were over. The taskmasters continued to work the Hebrews bitterly, and beatings were many and severe. Most stopped paying attention to Mosheh. Those who'd been excited over their expected deliverance had nothing to say.

It seemed life was back to normal. The Hebrews were even invited to the next festival, as if none of the plagues had happened. There had been a good flooding, and a good sowing was in progress. People settled into their normal work habits, and talk of deliverance was almost silenced.

Then came the sickness of the animals. It was the kind of pestilence that usually occurred with major dust storms or when heavy dust stayed in the air a long time. That pestilence, however, was far more grievous than in previous years.

Many animals outside the encampment were afflicted and died. Camels, horses, cows, ass, and sheep lay dead all over the Two Lands. Even domesticated animals were found dead, including monkeys, geese, and pet lions. Wild animals and beasts in the wilderness didn't die, and neither did any animals belonging to the Hebrews. Once again, their part of Goshen was spared.

By then, the people of Kemet were arguing among themselves. There was much talk among them about Mosheh, whom many feared, especially the peasants. Guards and officers, however, spoke little of Mosheh. They'd felt the impact of the plagues and were more irritable than before. It became even more difficult for the Hebrews to go through a day without experiencing their masters' ire. Mi-Sakhme, the captain of the guard, seemed to have gone berserk. He lost much of his fortune to the plagues, and he took it out on the Hebrews through his guards.

Abiasaph began to question himself, trying to sort out his conclusions, if any. If the Almighty One sent the plagues, why had He done it? If it was to free the Hebrews, then why were they still slaves? Abiasaph didn't understand. How could the Almighty One lay harsh judgments on the people of the pharaoh and protect the Hebrews, then watch and do nothing while the soldiers and taskmasters beat and killed them, making their lives more difficult and bitter every day? Those two thoughts didn't go together.

He was almost willing to give credit to the Almighty One for causing the plagues, but he didn't understand why. Talk of deliverance didn't satisfy him.

He sipped more wine and thought back again. The next plague was easy to remember. He was making bricks at the brickyard beside the temple site one morning. The taskmasters were talking with him and Caleb, the Hebrew overseer, explaining the amount of work required that day.

Suddenly, the man who spoke gasped for air, and two huge boils grew on his throat as the others watched. When they reached the size of a man's fist, they stopped growing, and the taskmaster fell over, screaming.

Abiasaph shuddered. He'd never seen anything like it before. It was horrible, even if it was done to an enemy. From the cursing and horror they heard throughout the brickyard, Abiasaph and Caleb knew others were experiencing the same thing. Many died from the plague, while virtually all were taken ill. As the boils reached their full size, many burst, spewing out a thick, yellow liquid. It was sickening to watch. The men who were attacked screamed with pain.

Again, the Hebrews were sent back to camp, and free days followed. There were many deaths in the Lower Land from the boils, and the Hebrews were told that Mosheh had sprinkled ashes toward the heavens, because Ramesses still wouldn't let the Hebrews go into the desert to sacrifice and celebrate as Mosheh demanded. When the ashes came back down, boils broke out on the pharaoh, his wise men, and all his servants. Then they appeared on the guards, soldiers, and taskmasters.

He gulped more wine. Why had the Almighty One brought the boils? Was it to punish the pharaoh? The more he was punished, the more punishment he gave to the Hebrews.

He shook his head, disappointed at his lack of progress. None of it made sense. He remembered seeing the ugly boils and the uglier thick yellow liquid that squirted from them.

When the plague ended, there was no explanation from the Kemet guards. There was only more anger, hatred, threats, and worse beatings.

The guards vowed that if the plagues didn't stop, they'd kill Mosheh, then the tribal chieftains, and then all the women and children. They would move all slaves into the city, taking them away from their families, making them experience whatever plague Mosheh called upon the people of Kemet. They'd be forced to work night and day with very little food. All privileges would be stripped from them, leaving them no animals or food of their own. There would be no more Hebrew religious services or permission for them to attend Kemet festivals.

The plagues continued, but the threats were never carried out. Abiasaph wondered why. After the boils were gone, and the Hebrews were put back to work, another plague came quickly.

Hail came at night after the slaves returned to Goshen, and they were glad, because the hail was devastating. Abiasaph saw what was left of the land after it was over. It was the most severe destruction he'd ever seen or imagined. Any man of Kemet who hadn't been indoors was killed. All the cattle in the fields died, trees were uprooted, and vegetables and fruit were ruined. It was sad seeing such waste, even if it happened to his enemies.

From the camp, they heard pounding in the heavens and saw fire running along the ground, which was frightening. He could barely imagine what it must have been like in Kemet. It had been loud, too. He and Caath thought the world was ending.

He also sadly remembered that after the free day that time, the Egyptian taskmasters were merciless, blaming the Hebrews for all their misfortunes. Though many of the Hebrews joined the guards and blamed Mosheh for their troubles, that didn't lessen the guard's damage against them. They even beat the old and wounded who worked the grain fields. Samuel, the gentle, old Levite, was beaten to death. He hadn't done anything wrong or even spoken to the guard who murdered him. That was a sad time for the house of Levi.

There were often Kemet guards, however, who softened their attitude toward the Hebrews. Some became frightened of Mosheh. Old Soft Eye at the brickyards suddenly became easier on the slaves. Many of the Nubians, always a superstitious lot, were less cruel. It was clear they were very frightened. The Kemet guards, being Egyptians, made up for it, taking out their bitterness on the Hebrews.

When the plague of hail ended, and the Hebrews were back at work, Abiasaph was one of the few who was prepared. He was one of the rare ones who escaped the angry guards' wrath. Mi-Sakhme, the master of the guard force, was even more incensed than before. As far as Abiasaph remembered, that still didn't justify the worsening conditions for his people. If it was their God doing those things, why couldn't He do something about the cruelty from Mi-Sakhme and his band of murderers? Abiasaph didn't understand it.

*I'm wasting my time,* he thought. *Remembering all this doesn't help. I'm torn between two different ideas, and I badly want to know the truth.*

He stood, took a long drink from his goatskin of water, having earlier put his wineskin away, and shook his head in disgust. He couldn't stop the memories. He wanted an answer, and he was willing to look at each plague to find the truth.

He stared blankly at the brown mud wall of his hut, a simple cloth attached to the top of the wall to drape down and add a touch of beauty to an otherwise dreary house. That was the one thing he still had that Nehushta made, and it turned his small hut into a home. He wasn't really thinking about her, though.

He slid to a sitting position and remembered, with a touch of fear, the more recent plague of locusts. A strong east wind brought them into the land. Usually when locusts came, they swarmed with the south wind, but not that time. They just kept coming and coming. It was terrifying. Locusts were knee deep in the fields, and, when they finished their feast, there was nothing left of the land. They devoured everything the storms left.

Abiasaph actually saw a Kemet guard suffocated by the locusts. They covered every inch of his body, and, as he screamed for help, they filled his mouth. His eyes bulged as he fought for breath. It was an agonizing death.

Abiasaph shuddered. Many others died the same way.

After a few days, a strong wind carried the locusts completely out of the land. It was clear some powerful force was behind the attacks on the red people and their land. The intensity of the plague of locusts was beyond imagining. Even then, after a few calm days, the Hebrews forgot it all. The harshness of the taskmasters and the unrelenting beatings and killings took precedence, and Abiasaph was no different.

As with every other plague, the Hebrew leaders, through Mosheh and Aaron, acknowledged the Almighty One as the responsible party. Abiasaph wondered why the pharaoh hadn't ordered Mosheh killed. That didn't make sense, either.

Now they had a strange darkness covering the land. The slaves had at least three free days because of it, but what would happen next? How would the people of Kemet react? They wouldn't be happier. What would Ramesses do? Mi-Sakhme was probably out of his mind. How many would he kill in revenge?

Abiasaph knew that many friends and neighbors would probably die at Mi-Sakhme's hands once the plague lifted. There were many questions and no answers.

He thought of Oshea and Libni and some others who were so strong in their faith. They didn't have Abiasaph's problems. They had peace. He had no peace or answers.

*Oshea's different from me,* he thought. *He thinks differently. He sees things and knows things I don't.*

That was part of the problem. He needed to know what Oshea knew. Abiasaph walked to the door and decided to go see Old Abraham.

# CHAPTER SEVENTEEN

# KEMET, THE BLACK LAND

Throughout the Lower Land, Egyptians struggled horribly with their newest adversity. Though called the Black Land for a different reason, it truly became a black land with the advent of this most recent plague. Most of the people were still in their homes. There was no reason to leave, and, for most, it was impossible to move. A few brave souls struggled against the darkness, thinking that it was only in their area, and that they'd find light elsewhere, but they soon learned differently.

Many of the Kemet guards lived in a small community just north of Mempi, across the Nile from Goshen. Word had gotten out that the latest problem was more magic from the hand of Mosheh, the former Egyptian prince, and it was a cover for the Hebrews to cross the Nile and attack the guards.

Fearing for their lives, the guards armed themselves with whips, swords, and clubs. Their leaders met to determine how to handle the threat. They decided to post guards around the city to protect it from anyone attempting to attack. As best they could, they tried to accomplish that feat.

In various places throughout the city, guards held their posts, attempting to protect their families and friends. Amid the confusion and fear, their actions spelled disaster for many.

One guard, nearly insane from fear, bumped into someone as he moved slightly from his position on the city's perimeter. Fearing the worst, he shouted that the Hebrews were attacking and stabbed at the intruder, grabbed his neck, and beat him with his club. The man shouted, but, in the blackness, the guard couldn't hear his words.

Fear controlled him. He clubbed the intruder until he was dead and his face mutilated. It turned out the man was a friend and neighbor, but the guard wouldn't learn that until later.

However, the damage had been done. As soon as the other guards heard the first one scream about an attack, word spread, and people relayed the message that the Hebrews were in the city, attacking everyone. People swung large wooden clubs wildly, lashing out with knives and whips. The battle raged, and confusion reigned. There were some places where calm prevailed, but most of the city exploded in battle. Many members of the guards' families died in the melee. It took hours for cooler heads to prevail and restore order.

Eventually, the remaining guards realized there were no Hebrews in their city. They were stunned. They were alone with their sorrow. For many, because of the darkness and the difficulty in moving or speaking, they didn't know if their own families were safe, dead, or injured, and there was little they could do about it.

Many left their posts to seek loved ones, but few found them. They couldn't see or hardly move through the terrible black thing that covered their land.

* * *

Mi-Sakhme slumped into the large bench and called, "Petephis? Are you still here?"

"Yes, Master, I'm with you. Can I get you something to drink?"

"No, no. Have we determined that the Hebrew has left the property? I must know."

"Master, I have servants checking the entire grounds, and Ebebi hasn't been found. We can safely assume he's left the area."

Mi-Sakhme was mystified. He'd been certain that the darkness would lift the moment he removed the Hebrew. What had gone wrong? He'd been so sure. Now he was out of ideas and didn't know what to do.

Perhaps this was another plague from the Hebrew prince, Mosheh. Of course, there was always the possibility that what Mi-Sakhme had done was correct, but the gods weren't that easily satisfied. He hoped they would remove the darkness soon.

"Petephis, have we heard from the pharaoh? Have there been any messengers?"

"No. We've heard nothing from our great pharaoh. We can assume he's in the same difficulty we face. I've tried to send someone to him, but we've had no reply."

Mi-Sakhme leaned his head against the deep bench. "Bring me strong drink. I must rest. Keep my cup filled. Perhaps I can sleep. I need it."

He was deeply troubled. His entire household looked to him for leadership, but he had only questions, not answers.

Why didn't Ramesses get some answers from his wise men? Surely they, the magicians, and the gods couldn't all be quiet concerning the terrible darkness. Ramesses had to have the answer. Everything that Mi-Sakhme worked for hung in the balance—wealth, power, and respect. He was one of the great men in the Two Lands.

What would happen if the Hebrews and Mosheh continued harassing the pharaoh like this? If Ramesses gave in and let the Hebrews go into the wilderness, they weren't likely to return. Even though Ramesses would send soldiers to bring them back, the whole relationship between the Egyptians and the Hebrews would change.

If the Hebrews never returned, the pharaoh would force his own people to finish the building projects. That would create much consternation. The only salvation would be if Ramesses spent money to buy laborers from the south. What would happen to Mi-Sakhme then? Would he retain his high position? Ramesses had the capacity to eliminate him if the situation continued going wrong.

Mi-Sakhme feared for his life and loss of stature. He loved his estate. Often, in past months, before the terrible interruptions, he walked for hours around his estate, looking at the beauty his wealth had bought. He enjoyed the gardens, which were totally destroyed.

What would happen to it all if Ramesses lost to Mosheh? Mi-Sakhme didn't want to think about it.

Petephis brought a cup and handed it to his captain. Mi-Sakhme took a long drink and drained the cup, then handed it back. Petephis immediately refilled it and returned it, no easy task in the blackness.

Mi-Sakhme's life was in Mosheh's hands. There was nothing he could do. Taking another long drink, he felt the need to sleep and forget.

"Bring me a blanket, Petephis. I'll rest now. Make sure there are guards nearby. I must sleep."

The captain drank from the golden cup, then closed his eyes and prayed for sleep.

\* \* \*

Ramesses sent messengers to Mi-Sakhme, to the priests in Mempi, to the Hebrews in Goshen, and to the gate of Avaris. He had to know what was happening in his land. At the moment, he was huddled in his central meeting room with Menna, his faithful chief servant, and his wise men. Ramesses, too, was troubled but remained obstinate, refusing to give in to Mosheh and his God's magic. He was the great Ramesses, and he would overcome this interruption just like all the others.

Though they'd been meeting for over an hour, they had no new information, nor had his wise men been any help. They'd been quiet for several minutes. Although it wasn't the normal time for his banquet, Ramesses was suddenly hungry.

"Menna, send to the kitchens and have a meal prepared for us in this room. Tell them to prepare something good. Your king is hungry. We have major decisions to make, and we must eat to retain our strength. Have beer brought, too."

It was difficult having to manage a country in total darkness, not to mention meeting with his advisors without seeing them. Eating and drinking would be difficult, too.

His favorite sage was an old priest from On named Tupenthal. In the earlier meeting, which was held under the worst conditions with the difficulty in speaking, Tupenthal was the only one who had any meaningful ideas.

Tupenthal had known Mosheh well in the past. Like Ramesses, he was troubled by recent events.

"Tupenthal, come and speak to me regarding Mosheh and these devastations," Ramesses ordered.

The priest moved closer to his king until their arms touched. It was difficult to speak, but he'd been commanded, so he must. "Oh king who lives forever, my thoughts are similar to what I shared earlier. Mosheh was a great warrior. The only man in the Two Lands to outstrip him was you, my lord. If we could assume he'd attack us in the same manner in which he operated as your father's military leader, then it would be easy for us to plan against him, but he comes to us meek and humble. That's not the same Mosheh who led Seti's armies to great conquests.

"How, oh, king, do we prepare to fight someone who comes with no power but displays power like we've never seen before? The God he serves isn't like the gods of the Two Lands. We've called upon our gods to intervene against these terrible acts without success.

"It's difficult, ruler of the Two Lands, to believe that our gods are powerless against Mosheh's single God, but we haven't received any instructions from our gods. We have no history regarding such things as we're experiencing now. If our gods are waiting for a better opportunity to overcome Mosheh's God, then we gladly stand aside and allow them to do so. But it appears, my king, that our gods don't have the ability or will to fight Mosheh's God.

"How long, oh king, can we put up with these terrible onslaughts against the people and the land? At what point do we say we can take no more?"

"Tupenthal, we need wisdom. We'll find the answer to Mosheh and his power. We won't give in. At some point, he, too, will tire of losing and will give up. Then we'll win. For now, we need wisdom.

"Don't speak to me with fear. I refuse to have any seers or wise men that allow fear in their voices. I'll have your heads and will feed you to my lioness. You've been appointed as the medium between the gods of the lands and your god king. It's your responsibility to prostrate yourselves before the gods and learn what's happening in our land. Do you think our gods favor this? Never! Our gods aren't powerless. Don't you know our history? Tupenthal, you stay with me. The rest of you, go! Don't come back until you have the wisdom of the gods to break Mosheh's spell."

Ramesses stopped. It hurt to shout like that, but he had to get his point across. He was the leader of the Two Lands, and people needed to hear his voice. Now he was tired.

"Tupenthal, your king must rest. It's been difficult for us all. When Menna returns with the banquet, wake me so I might eat."

The great ruler of the Two Lands closed his eyes and rested. He had many decisions to make, and he needed his sleep.

* * *

The beautiful Nefertari sat quietly in her bedchamber. Menna visited her hours earlier and assured the queen that all was well under the circumstances. Her children were safe, and servants were with them. There was no need for her to become concerned. Ramesses was meeting with his advisors throughout the day and would solve the newest dilemma.

Menna sent a guard to stand outside her room in case the queen needed protection. Her handmaidens were nearby in case she needed anything. She needed only to call the guard, and he would call for her women.

The guard wasn't thinking about protecting the queen, however. He thought of the times he'd seen her, always scantily dressed, each time smiling sensually at all the men she passed, knowing that they would love to have her but never would.

He'd been standing there a long time. The queen said nothing. He didn't know she was inside, but Menna said so. Possibly, she was asleep. He wondered how far away she was and if she was wearing anything.

Nefertari was becoming very impatient. Menna said everything was all right, but that was then, and this was now. She wondered how long it was since she spoke to him. Menna said he'd post a guard. Had he done it?

"Hello?" she called. "Is anyone there?"

"Yes," came a muffled answer. "I'm here, Queen Nefertari. It will take me only a few moments to come to you."

"Have you heard anymore from your king or Menna?"

"No. They're busy planning a counterattack, I suppose. Are you all right, my queen?"

"Yes, although I'm a little frightened. Who are you? Do I know you?"

"I've seen you many times, my queen, but you wouldn't know my name. I'm one of the palace guards and am at your disposal."

"Where are you? I can't tell by the sound of your voice."

"I'm close to you, my queen." He was excited to be so close to her—and in her bedroom. He reached out his hand and stepped forward. Soon, he touched her bare shoulder.

"Oh! Is that you?" she asked.

"Yes, my queen." His voice came closer, and his hand rested on her shoulder. "If you're afraid, my queen, I can come closer."

"I don't think that would be wise. Your pharaoh would be very upset if he knew you'd touched his queen. Resume your position outside my door."

It was too late. The guard was too excited. Her bare shoulder sent a chill through him. Was she dressed? He allowed his hand to slide across her neck and across her loose-fitting silk garment.

"No!" she shouted, trying to pull away, but his strong hands held her onto the bed. This couldn't be happening to her. She was the queen of Egypt. "Please! I'm your queen. Let me go. Don't do this to your queen."

"My beautiful Nefertari," he cooed. "You parade around half-dressed, teasing us with seductive moves, and now it's come back to haunt you. No one can hear if you cry out. The great pharaoh is too busy to be concerned about you, but I'm not too busy, beautiful Nefertari."

\* \* \*

Old Soft Eye, as the Hebrews called him, stood near the wading pool that the guards had built during the previous year. It was one of their great achievements to have something in their community that usually could be found only among the wealthiest people of the two lands.

There had been much commotion during the last two days. There was no telling how many of their number died after the false report of an attack by the Hebrews earlier. Certainly, many were injured, too. There had been a lot of trouble that year, and he wondered if it would ever end.

Soft Eye was one of the older, wiser guards and soldiers who lived in the community, and he tried to calm the people in the city. Even though it was many hours since the self-inflicted battle, there was still turmoil in places, and he called out every few minutes to see if someone was within hearing distance. If he received an answer, he went to the person and spoke to him, calming him as best he could.

He thought his efforts were effective. He spoke to many guards, wives, and children who were frightened or angry. Some were injured, and some knew they'd lost loved ones. Though he had no experience in such areas, Soft Eye became a counselor and peace-maker in the city.

It would take hours even after the darkness lifted to determine exactly what happened in the community. How many were dead? How many of the injured would die without proper medical assistance? How many of the injured would be crippled forever? What effect would it have on the children, already terrified by everything else that happened during the past year? What effect would it have on the other guards and soldiers? Their anger and hatred, kindled against the Hebrews, had grown stronger with each new act of devastation.

Soft Eye had studied the history of his nation. He was an older man, who wanted to know his people and country. His wife's brother was a minor priest at On. With his help, Soft Eye spent time studying the Two Lands. It amazed him that at one time, a Hebrew named Joseph had saved his country. Because of his wisdom, he was raised to be the second in command of the entire land, directly below the king. Joseph's people and the Egyptians were friends. It was ironic that now those two peoples hated each other. Soft Eye understood why, but he didn't agree with it.

He made it a point to be kind to the Hebrew slaves. After all, they were men like he was. They had wives waiting for them at the end of the day and children they hoped to raise. Most were good workers. What amazed him was how the Hebrews responded to his kindness. None hated him—their actions made that clear. He learned it was possible to accomplish more with kindness than through force.

But that wasn't how it was done in Kemet, especially not by Mi-Sakhme or the pharaoh, may he live forever as the god king of the land.

Soft Eye was confused by recent events. He occasionally spoke to the Hebrew overseers, who adamantly believed that their God, the Almighty One, was responsible for the calamities that befell his beloved Two Lands.

The pharaoh had a different story. He said Prince Mosheh, who was also a magician, was creating all the havoc, and it was the pharaoh's magicians who did more magic to offset that, making things even worse. In each case, the gods of the Two Lands eventually won out and life returned to normal, but there was a lot of damage done and many deaths. He'd heard about wars between the gods from the priests, but that was the first time he'd seen it in action. He was glad his gods were winning.

"Hello? Is anyone within hearing distance of my voice?" he called as he did every few minutes.

"Yes! Who are you?" a female voice asked. "Are you one of our soldiers?"

"Yes, I am. Please let me come to you. I can help you get wherever you're going. It's difficult moving in this terrible black storm. Speak again so I can find you."

He went about being a comforter in a land of major discomfort, a land that universally hoped the terror would be over soon.

# CHAPTER EIGHTEEN

# THE STORIES OF OLD

Abiasaph approached Oshea, who was building a large wooden carrying basket a few yards from his tent. After the customary greetings, Oshea asked, "Have you come to visit?"

Abiasaph nodded, forcing an embarrassed smile. "Oshea, do you think your grandfather would speak with me?"

"Yes, I'm sure he would. Come. Grandfather's in the tent."

Elishama sat on the floor, eyes closed, obviously relaxed, but he looked up when Abiasaph entered through the curtain and motioned him to sit.

Abiasaph glanced around the unadorned tent. There was a blanket rolled up in one corner and a red-dyed skin and cup sitting beside it. The rest of the room was empty except for Old Abraham and the cup from which he occasionally sipped. Elishama wasn't sure who the young man was who sat so uncomfortably with him, and he looked to Oshea for an answer.

"Grandfather, you remember Abiasaph, the Levite?" Oshea asked.

Elishama smiled. "Abiasaph, welcome to my house. Oshea told me he had invited you, and I'm pleased you've accepted his invitation. I'm sorry to hear about your brother. There are sad things happening among us now." He paused. "Are you and your son in good health? Do you have enough of what you need?"

"Yes. We've never wanted, Elishama," Abiasaph replied.

"Then how can I be of service to you today?"

Abiasaph cleared his throat. He felt uncomfortable, but he wanted to go through with his mission. "Elishama, I'm troubled about the things I see happening. I don't know much about the Almighty One. My son, Caath, wants to know of our fathers and the stories of old, but they were never taught to me. My father...well, he never told me the old tales. How can I tell them to my son?"

Old Abraham waited, making sure his guest was finished. "You have come to a good place with such a request. It's always enjoyable for me to talk about my fathers and their deeds and to rehearse the wonderful things of the Almighty One, the God of our fathers. Allow me to send for some food, and I'll begin."

Oshea was stunned. Why hadn't Abiasaph's father passed on the stories and traditions of his people? All Hebrew families did that. Suddenly, he wondered how many others were in the camp that didn't know the old stories.

Elishama pulled a cord hanging above his head. Abiasaph looked up and saw the cord had been strung around the walls and to an adjoining room, where it rang a soft bell. He was very impressed by that and filed the information away in his mind.

Elishama's granddaughter appeared a few minutes later with a jug of dark milk and platter of bread. Abiasaph sipped his drink and found it had been mixed with herbs and honey, giving it a pleasant taste. That was probably because of Elishama's age. He couldn't drink milk once it became bitter.

Abiasaph relaxed, and Old Abraham began speaking.

"You say you haven't been told the traditions and stories of our fathers, so I shall attempt to tell you the tale of our nation, Israel, from Abraham to the present. There's nothing I enjoy more than speaking of such things. Of course, we don't have time to tell all the things our fathers did, but you'll know enough to instruct your son." He smiled.

"Abraham was descended from Noah, the blessed one, who was saved at the time of the great flood. Abraham dwelt near the place where the two great rivers come together, in the land of Ur of the Chaldees. He lived with his father, Terah, and his brothers.

"The Lord, our Almighty One, spoke to our father Abraham and told him to leave his father and his land and journey to a new country where he would sire a great nation. At that time, Abiasaph, Abraham knew no more of the Almighty One than you do, but he obeyed. He gathered all he had in people and animals and left on his journey.

"When he reached the land of the Canaanites, the Lord appeared to him and promised him that his offspring would be given the land on which he stood. He built an altar there as a memorial of the Lord's visit and His promise. That altar remained until the time our father Jacob left that land to come to Egypt. Probably, it's still there.

"Soon after that, a famine came like the one our father Jacob experienced. Like Jacob after him, Abraham also journeyed here to this very land to purchase provisions for his large group. I have often wondered what he thought when he came to the city of priests and saw the great pyramids built by our enemies. It's said some of them were here even then. What a surprise to suddenly see such large structures reaching into the sky. They would have been visible for miles away. What did Abraham think? He probably wondered who could have created such large buildings and how could a nation of people move such large blocks of stone.

"I have often wondered what was going through his mind as he and his company reached this land. I have also wondered if the Lord let him know this was to be the land where his people would eventually be held captive. Probably not, because that was never passed down to us, unless Abraham knew and kept it to himself."

He stopped to take a slow drink from his honeyed milk.

"Our father, Abraham, stayed here for some time and acquired an even greater company of animals and servants. He was highly esteemed by the inhabitants of this land. When he left Egypt, he returned to Canaan a wealthy man, and there he pitched his tent and raised his flocks.

"Again, the Lord spoke to him, telling him to look around. All he could see in every direction would be given to him and his children. He would sire a great nation that would be as the dust of the earth in number. All this was being told while Abraham was still without any children of his own, but he believed the Lord. He moved his company to Hebron and built another altar to the Lord.

"Abraham listened carefully to what the Lord said. He didn't scoff at His promise of children, just because it seemed unlikely. He didn't ask how it could happen. He just quietly lived his life believing that whatever the Lord told him would be accomplished.

"Sodom was a city where Abraham's nephew, Lot, had taken his family to dwell. A group of kings from various tribes joined together and attacked the city and its surrounding cities, taking Lot and his people captive. When Abraham heard of this, he took his three hundred trained men and went after the kings and their armies. He was victorious and recovered all the people and their possessions, returning them to their cities.

"Abraham refused the bounty the king of Sodom offered, telling him, 'All that I have has been given to me by the Lord. If I receive your portion of the spoils, you would be able to say that you helped make me rich. If I refuse to take anything from you, then you can't deny it when I say that only the Lord made me rich.

"Again, Abiasaph, you can see how much Abraham depended on the Almighty One. He needed no reward for his victory. The Lord wants all of us to be like our father Abraham in that respect.

"The Lord God visited Abraham later that evening and brought him outside his tent, saying, 'Abraham, look up into the heavens and count the stars. So shall your offspring be. Your heir will come from your own loins.' Abraham believed Him, though Sarah, his wife, was barren.

"Then the Lord told Abraham about us, Abiasaph. He told him that his descendants would be strangers in a land that wouldn't be their own, and they would be enslaved and mistreated. Has it not been as the Lord said? Then He made a vow to Abraham. He promised those who punished His people would, in turn, be punished by Him. He would rescue Abraham's descendants and bring them out of that bondage with a great hand and with great possessions. He even said when it would happen.

"'In the fourth generation,' the Lord promised, 'I will bring out this people from their captivity into the land of Canaan again, which I have given to you.'

"So, Abiasaph, the Lord promised the land to Abraham, but He'll give it to us, for we are the present Abraham, his descendants.

We'll have the promise given to us, because we are the generation that has come full – the four hundred years has passed - yet we've never seen the new land.

"Four hundred years ago, the Lord spoke those things to Abraham. Four generations ago, Abraham received the promise from the Lord. He knew he wouldn't live to see that day, but he believed his unborn children four generations away would. Now, here we are, patiently waiting for the God of Abraham to bring it to pass. The plagues, which we've seen, are the Lord fulfilling this promise in His own way.

"Sarah, Abraham's wife, didn't believe the Lord would produce a child through her, and she knew she wouldn't have a family unless someone took her place with Abraham. She convinced him to lie with Hagar, her maidservant, and Abraham did. As the maidservant began to grow with child, Sarah became envious and hated her, but the Lord saw to Hagar. She conceived and bore a son, Ishmael, who was born when Abraham was eighty-six years old. Abraham looked to Ishmael to be the beginning of the great nation the Lord mentioned.

"When Abraham was ninety-six, the Lord appeared to him again and reminded him he would be the father of many nations. It was at this time that the Lord changed his name from Abram, which Terah, his father, gave him, to Abraham, because of that promise.

"He reminded Abraham that He would give to his descendants the land of Canaan in which to dwell. That was also the time that the Lord established the covenant of circumcision with Abraham. That is the sign of our covenant with the Almighty One. It's our way of saying, 'Yes, Lord, we've rehearsed the things that You and our father Abraham discussed and covenanted. We're Your people, and we're waiting for Your promise.' Now, Abiasaph, we perform the rite of circumcisions and don't even think of the Lord's promise. Do you see how far we've come from the truth?"

Abiasaph was totally absorbed by what he heard. He nodded then leaned forward to hear more.

"It was then that the Lord told Abraham that the heir wasn't Ishmael but would come through Sarah. She would bear him a son who would become many nations, even producing kings. We haven't yet had a king, so that means it's yet to come. I doubt it'll happen in this land.

"When the Lord reminded Abraham that his son would come through Sarah, he laughed, wondering how such an old couple could produce children. The Lord named the son Isaac because of Abraham's laughter.

"There was much sin in the cities surrounding Abraham. Because of it, the Lord destroyed some of them, including Sodom, where Lot, Abraham's nephew, lived. Because of Abraham's righteousness, the Lord saved Lot and his daughters—the only ones who escaped. Lot's wife had the opportunity to be saved, but she refused to obey the Lord's command and was turned into a pillar of salt, because that was where her heart was. That teaches us that the Lord can do what He pleases, even with entire cities. And this land of Egypt is not too difficult for him to handle, either.

"Abraham then moved to the Negev region, closer to where we live now. There he met Abimelech, the king of Gerar, who gave him many gifts and increased his possessions. It was there that Isaac was born. At that time, Abraham was 100 years old, while Sarah was ninety. Abraham's great company stayed in the land of the way of the Philistines for many years.

"Abraham had an heir as the Lord promised. Isn't it amazing, Abiasaph, that for all those years, God promised him a son, and Abraham never had one? Even after he lost faith and produced a son through Hagar, the Almighty One eventually gave Abraham the son he wanted and kept his promise. You see, the Almighty One chooses that which He will perform, and then He performs it. He doesn't necessarily rely on our obedience and faith, or lack of it, to determine whether he'll follow through.

"But the Lord wasn't finished with Abraham. When Isaac was a young boy…. Hmmm. How old is your son, Abiasaph?"

"Caath is nine years old."

"When Isaac was a boy a few years older than your son, Abraham was given a strange command by the Lord. He told Abraham to take his son and go to a mountain in the land of Moriah. 'There,' He said, 'you are to sacrifice your son as a burnt offering to Me.'

"How would you have responded to that?"

The Levite shook his head. "I don't know. That's difficult to understand. I would take much time thinking it over before I obeyed, and even then, I'm not sure I would."

"Well said, Abiasaph. Most of us would have difficulty obeying such a command. We might think we heard Him wrong, that He said something else, but Abraham didn't plead or argue. He simply obeyed. The Lord had always been just with him, and he knew his son was a gift from the Lord, anyway, so he obeyed.

"Remember, Abiasaph, Abraham knew the Lord had promised him a seed that would develop into a huge nation. If Isaac died, that wouldn't happen. Maybe he didn't understand what the Almighty One was doing, but he knew His promise was certain. He gathered a few servants, packed an animal, and took Isaac to the mountain, which was three or four days away.

"Abraham had a lot of time to think over the Lord's command. He and Isaac had much time to talk about it, but nothing was said. When Abraham finally arrived, he was still willing to obey.

"Let me say this about our father, Abiasaph. He knew the Lord. They fellowshipped together, walking through the fields and talking. He knew that the Lord had a good reason for each command He made, and he believed and trusted in Him.

"When they arrived, Abraham tied Isaac to the altar and began to plunge the knife into him when an angel stopped him. He said Isaac's life was no longer required. Abraham saw a ram trapped in a thicket nearby and used that for the sacrifice instead. Then he and Isaac worshipped the Lord together."

"Elishama," Abiasaph said, "I heard that story when I was younger, though not quite the same way. I often wondered why Isaac didn't fight his father. If he was three or four years older than Caath, he would have struggled to get free."

"That's an interesting thought. Let me give you two other things to consider. First, Abraham was a giant of a man and was among the strongest men of his time. Even in his old age, it would have been useless for Isaac to fight him. Also, the son knew of his father's trust in the Lord. When he asked about the sacrifice, I can almost hear Abraham saying, 'Be at peace, my son. The Lord makes no mistakes. He has promised a great nation to be born through you, and you have yet to sire. The Lord hasn't yet had His last word concerning the sacrifice.'

"That was an important test for Abraham, and he passed."

"But Elishama," Abiasaph protested, "why would Abraham's God test him in that way? If He hadn't stopped him or the knife slipped, he could have killed his son."

"The Lord wouldn't have allowed that to happen. He knew when to stop Abraham, and that's why Isaac wasn't hurt. Let me answer this way.

"Suppose you were going to build a city. Your plan was to build it complete with temples, halls, and palaces. First, you'd need a good overseer, wouldn't you?"

Abiasaph nodded.

"As you searched for a man for that position, whom would you choose? Someone who looked like he could do it, or someone who said he could? Maybe someone you were told could do it?"

Abiasaph thought for a moment, his eyes on the old man. "For such a job, I'd take time choosing a master. I'd choose someone who'd already built a city before, whose work I had seen and liked."

"Someone who had proven himself?"

"Yes."

"Well said. The Lord, too, was searching for someone to be the father of an entire people. Four hundred years later, those people would inherit a great land and become a great nation. He had already chosen Abraham for the task, and He was proving him in the same way you would have proved your overseer.

"Abraham met the Lord's requirements to be the father of nations. He believed the Lord when He said he would sire a son in his hundredth year. He trusted the Lord in every battle he fought. He knew all his possessions came from the Lord and believed the Lord when He said his descendants would inherit the land of promise and would be numbered like grains of sand. The Lord knew how faithful Abraham was, but Abraham didn't know about himself. For Abraham to pass his trust and faithfulness on to the coming generations, he had to know, too.

"The Lord knew He wasn't requiring Isaac's life, but He chose not to tell Abraham until the last minute. When they came down the mountain, Abraham knew he was faithful. He knew he could believe the Lord in anything. The Almighty One had proven him and instilled in him a faithfulness that would stand apart like a torch in the darkness for the generations to come.

"Likewise, for us, we're in the midst of a great thing. The Lord is in the process of taking us out of this land and giving us our inheritance. Like Abraham, it's likely that the Almighty One won't tell us exactly when we're going until the last moment. We're being proven just as Abraham was.

"I question whether even Abraham knew he would obey the Lord to such an extent as sacrificing his son. But when they came down from the mountain, Abraham knew. The Lord knew he was the man to be the father of the nation of Israel, and Abraham knew it, too.

"When they came down the mountain in Moriah, the Lord repeated His promise, saying, 'Abraham, because of your faithfulness, your descendants will be like the stars in the sky and the sand at the bottom of the seas. They'll become a great people and will overthrow and take possession of the cities of their enemies. The world will know that I have blessed them.'

"That is what we have to look forward to. Have you noticed how often the Lord reminded Abraham of His promise? We're no different, my young friend. We, too, must remind each other often of His promise to us.

"After 175 years of sojourning, Abraham died a peaceful death and was buried with Sarah at the cave of Machpelah, which he purchased earlier, near Mamre. Before his death, he sent his servant back to the land of his family to secure a wife for Isaac. He told his servant that the Lord, Himself, would show him whom to choose.

"The result was that Rebekah, daughter of Bethuel, became Isaac's wife. She, like Sarah, was barren. Isaac prayed to the Lord for her, and she conceived. She bore him twin sons. Even before they were born, the Lord told Rebekah that the older son would serve the younger. The firstborn was Esau. His brother, Jacob, followed, holding Esau's foot.

"Isaac loved Esau because he was firstborn and strong—a skillful hunter. Jacob, though, was loved by Rebekah, because she knew he was favored by the Lord.

"After a long day hunting, Esau came upon his brother feeling tired and hungry. Jacob was preparing a meal, and the smell caused Esau great anguish. Jacob offered Esau a trade, a meal in return for his birthright, and they made a pact.

"Again, famine swept over the land. Isaac went to see Abimelech, the Philistine king. Abimelech gave Isaac land in which to dwell during the famine. The Lord reminded Isaac of his covenant with Abraham, which was now a covenant with him. He repeated His promise to Isaac, that his descendants would be numbered as the stars and would be given all the land he could see and beyond.

"Isaac and his family grew and became so wealthy, King Abimelech eventually asked him to move away, because the Philistines were envious. Isaac journeyed to Beersheba, where again the Lord reminded him of the promise. He told him again that his numbers would increase greatly. Like Abraham, Isaac built an altar to the Lord there.

"When I think of these things, Abiasaph, it occurs to me that the Almighty One found it necessary to remind Abraham, Isaac, and later, Jacob, many times about the promise He made. Why? I believe it's because the Almighty One knew that we'd be in our current situation. The reminders to our fathers were actually for us, Abiasaph, not them.

"Later, in his old age, as he was dying, Isaac sent for Esau to give his blessing as the eldest son and heir. Rebekah clothed Jacob to appear as Esau and deceive his father, because she remembered what the Lord said when her sons were born. Isaac lost the use of his eyes by then, and he didn't see the trickery. He blessed Jacob, not Esau, and Jacob, our father, became the heir to the promise.

"Esau became very angry and wanted to kill Jacob, so Jacob left his people to live with his mother's family in Haran. The Lord appeared to him as he was on his way there and reestablished the covenant of Abraham with Jacob. Jacob, too, was told that his descendants would be as the dust of the earth in number, and all the land around him would be theirs. The Lord told him that He wouldn't rest until He performed the fulfilling covenant with His people.

"Jacob lived in Haran for many years. He met Rachel, Laban's daughter, and loved her. He contracted to work for Laban for seven years for her, but, when the time was over, Laban tricked him, just as Jacob tricked his father, and gave him Leah for a wife instead. Jacob had to bargain to work longer to have Rachel as his wife. Rachel, like the women before her, was also barren. God eventually smiled on her, as he did on the other matriarchs."

Abiasaph thought back to the day he met Nehushta's father, Arad. That was when he'd first heard that story.

"The Lord gave Jacob twelve sons, the first of which was Rueben, through Leah, his wife. Then Simeon and Levi, your own father. After Levi, Judah was born to Leah. Rachel became jealous and gave her maidservant Bilhah to Jacob. Through her, Dan was born. Then Bilhah conceived again and bore Naphtali. Then Leah's maidservant was given to Jacob, and she bore him Gad and Asher. Leah then conceived again and gave Jacob Issachar and Zebulon.

"So Leah bore Jacob six sons, and he had four more by the two maidservants, but Jacob had no sons by Rachel, the wife he wanted.

"As before, the Lord remembered Rachel, and she bore Joseph. Jacob then left Laban and took his large family and great possessions to return to the land of his father.

"One evening, as they traveled, Jacob awoke from a deep sleep and found himself wrestling with a man. They fought throughout the night, and Jacob overcame him. The man changed Jacob's name to Israel because of their wrestling.

"Israel and his family camped in the Canaanite land at Sechem. There, his sons Simeon and Levi killed all the men of that city, because they defiled their sister, Dinah. Because of that, the Lord told Israel to move his people to Bethel. There, the Lord again reminded him of the promise. He said kings would come from his loins, and they would rule all the land around them.

"They journeyed from Bethel and went on to Mamre, where both Abraham and Isaac had stayed. While on that journey, Rachel finally gave Jacob the last of his twelve sons, Benjamin, but she died during the birth."

Abiasaph remembered his beloved Nehushta, who died bearing Caath, and thought over what Elishama said. Even though his forefathers hadn't endured slavery and torture, they certainly experienced difficulties. Abiasaph hadn't thought of that before.

Seeing Abiasaph deep in thought, Elishama paused. "Shall I continue?"

"Yes, please."

"Joseph, the eleventh son of Israel, was hated by his brothers, because he was clearly favored by his father. When Joseph was seventeen, he was sent by Jacob to see after his brothers, who were grazing their flocks at a place called Dothan. In their hatred for him, they cast him into an empty well. Then they sold him to a band of Midianite merchantmen on their way to Egypt. The merchants paid the price of a slave for him. When they arrived, they sold Joseph to a royal officer, a captain of the king's guards.

"Afraid of what they'd done, the brothers took Joseph's coat and dipped it in goat's blood, then told their father that Joseph had been killed by a wild animal. You can imagine how hard that was on Israel.

"All that happened during the time when the Lower Land was held captive by foreigners. Its rulers were desert warriors. They looked more like Hebrews than the red land people and were known by the people of the Two Lands as the shepherd kings, or Hyksos. The Egyptians hated them.

"Joseph was put into the court dungeon because of a falsehood made by the wife of the officer who bought him. From there, Joseph was called to interpret a dream for the shepherd king. Joseph found favor with the king, because he was more like them than the people of the land. He interpreted the dream and warned the king of a famine that would last seven years. He told the king how to overcome it by saving up grain and food during the coming seven good years and putting it in storage silos. When the famine came, there would be food enough for all the people of Egypt and more. For his wisdom, Joseph was given command over the land, and he saved the world from a great famine.

"The shepherd king changed Joseph's name to Zaphnath-Paaneah, or *food for the living*. He also gave him Asenath, the daughter of the priest of On, for a wife. She bore him two sons, Manasseh and Ephraim, my own forefather.

"When the famine came, Israel sent his sons to Egypt because he'd heard the only food in the world was there. Joseph wasn't angry with his brothers when he saw them. He forgave them their earlier trickery, realizing the Lord had sent him ahead to preserve his family and save them from destruction. Because of the great famine, of course, the Lord also preserved the inheritance, the promise. If Joseph hadn't been there, our nation would have died out. Were it not for him, the shepherd king wouldn't have been predisposed to allow us to stay, and our fathers would have died in Canaan.

"Of course, Joseph *was* here. The shepherd king showed him favor and gave him all the land of Goshen, where we now live. Israel was 130 years old when he came to this land, and the land swelled with our people. Our fathers lived in peace and prospered greatly, and their families multiplied. Joseph became great in the eyes of all people, Hebrew and red men. He knew of the Lord's promise and commanded that when we leave, we're to take his remains and bring them to the land of his fathers. His body remains here, as you know, in the sycamore coffin that looks like a man.

"The shepherd kings became content. They ruled only the Lower Land and paid no attention to the Upper Land, where the captive priests had been exiled and continued to rule the people. The priests quietly raised an army, having learned from their captors, and, after some years, came back into this land with chariots and horses. They overthrew the foreign rulers and drove them out. Because we were a peace-loving people, we were allowed to remain.

"Many changes were made then, Abiasaph. The red people raised up a new king named Ahmose. He put all foreigners, including us, to work. We had to rebuild all the cities of the land. Every pharaoh thereafter became less enamored with our race. Had Ahmose treated us the way Ramesses does, we might have risen up against him, but the change was gradual, and we were allowed to continue our own lives without outside rule. We were even paid wages for working under Ahmose, so no one was that concerned about the forced labor.

259

"When our fathers settled in this land, they established communities the way you see them now. Most of us took on this new way of a settled life. Now, of course, it's an old way for us. This kind of life, however, has made us soft.

"When our father Abraham was prince over his tribe, he was feared among nations everywhere. He was strong and protective of his tribe and was a fierce warrior. We never fought for this land as Abraham did for his. We were never attacked by outsiders. The land was given to us freely, and we prospered in it and became a nation of soft people.

"When the priests and the army from the Upper Land came to recapture this land for themselves, we sat by and watched. They forced us into a new way of life, and we accepted it. Our fathers didn't know it would become so bitter and oppressive. Our father Abraham would have risen up and fought them if they attempted this against his people. Nevertheless, we were swept into slavery and a great taxation was put on the fruits of our land and our labors. It's grown worse with each pharaoh.

"There have been many wars since then, as pharaohs have tried to capture the entire world. That hasn't changed. Ramesses, until the Lord reigned him in with these plagues, took his conquering armies everywhere. He was overcoming the world, so they say. I often wondered why all the peoples of the world didn't join together to fight against the proud son of the river. They would greatly outnumber Ramesses' people, who would faint with fright.

"Now I know, however, that the Lord was waiting and watching, allowing the time to pass, so that His promise to our father Abraham could begin to unfold. Here's where the stories of your family become important, Abiasaph.

"I know you've separated yourself from the tribe of your father, Levi. Your reasons are your own. I won't ask why, but I will say this—we live in a time of restoration. Your brother saw it and was coming back to restore himself, possibly, but the Lord had vengeance upon him because of the man he killed. You haven't been a rebellious man like that. You can return to your tribe if you wish. That, too, is your decision.

"When our father, Israel, spoke to his sons at his death, he said many harsh things concerning the tribes' future. He said the Lord would scatter Levi's descendants throughout the land, separating them from themselves. You're an example of that. Mosheh, the son of Amram, is another.

"Mosheh was taken from his mother and raised as a prince in the house of pharaoh. Years later, he left his land and became a shepherd in the wilderness for forty years. Finally, at an old age, he was reunited with his people. The Lord sent Mosheh to us as an instrument to draw us out of the land of our enemies. Mosheh, too, was obedient to the word of his father, Israel, although he didn't know it. He was separated from his tribe and was scattered for a time in another land.

"When Mosheh and his brother, Aaron, came to us, they not only had a message from the Lord, they accompanied it with magnificent signs so we would know they were telling the truth. The Lord's message to us is simple. The four hundred years have passed, and the fourth generation is full. He has come to take us to the land of the promise.

"Don't ask me to explain why the Lord did things this way. I can only guess. He remembers His promise of old, though, and His time wasn't slack. He has been very precise. Mosheh told us we'd take goods from the people of Kemet before the Lord delivers us from this land, so we shall not go empty but as in victory. I think there isn't much time left before we see the start of that victory. We've had three days off from work. No one knows what tomorrow might bring. There may be more cruelty from the taskmasters and soldiers.

"For us, my friend, there's only one way to look at it. We must look for the Lord. Be strong and of good courage. Look for the next words of our leader, Mosheh. Instruct your son in the stories of Abraham and your fathers. Prepare yourself in sackcloth and ashes. Build an altar to the Lord and worship Him. This is an exciting time, Abiasaph. Don't let those around you who love to hate, fight, and bring confusion alter your thinking.

"The Lord has for us a land where now the Canaanites, Hittites, and Amorites dwell, a land flowing freely with all good things to eat and with pasture and water. Be hopeful. Life is just beginning for us."

# CHAPTER NINETEEN

# MURDER AT GOSHEN

Orusi, the Nubian guard, stared into the ripening barley field. *These fields are so small*, he thought. *How do they feed themselves after giving pharaoh his portion?*

As he walked, he noticed that was the case with most of the grain fields. They weren't as large as he would have thought. The gardens were small, too. There was a time when that would have angered him, because small harvests meant a smaller, and lesser, income and food for him and the other Kemet guards. Now he was part of the Hebrew congregation, and he had to see things from their viewpoint.

He stared at a tiny mud hut fifty steps away that led into the Issachar community. He took in the entire scene and saw that Goshen, indeed, was a beautiful land. From where he stood, he could see the top of the large tent of Mishael's clan, which was his home.

*Mishael is a good man*, he thought. *I'm fortunate he took me in.*

Orusi wondered earlier if the Hebrews would allow him to stay. It amazed him how gracefully they accepted him. When he thought of all the things the Hebrews had been through because of him and the other guards, he wondered if he would have been so receptive in their position.

Some Hebrews were filled with hate. They weren't all like Mishael and Oshea. That had been shown the previous day. There were others, however, who were as kind as Mishael and Oshea, but why? What caused them to show kindness and generosity to their enemies? Was it because of their Abraham God?

It was that thought that brought him to the edge of the grain fields. He listened intently to Oshea the previous evening, then to Mishael, as they explained the story of their Abraham God. He, too, wanted to go somewhere alone and speak to the Almighty One. He was a frightened, troubled young man who had many questions for Him.

He knew, too, that he had to do something about Abiasaph, the man who fought him. Since he intended to live with the Hebrews, he didn't want any enemies. He didn't blame the man. He would have done the same thing. He just wanted Abiasaph and his son to know he was sorry and he wanted to make restitution.

He was a good builder and should be able to make something that would please them, but how would he find the opportunity? Abiasaph would hate him for a long time and wouldn't accept his repentance and sorrow.

Orusi glanced back into the Issachar sector and saw no one watching. Mishael warned him not to leave the community, but he decided to go anyway. He felt that, perhaps he should go somewhere alone and commune with the Abraham God.

He passed by the many Ruebenite houses, aligned neatly beside the main path. He noticed that the Ruebenites lived mostly in houses, not tents, not like the people of Issachar. As he walked, he stayed as close to the fields as he could so he could duck behind the grain stalks if someone saw him. Fortunately, there were few people around, so he went unnoticed.

He slowed his gait as he entered the community of Simeon. His unanswered questions again took precedence. Why did the Abraham God stay hidden from the Hebrews for so long? Didn't He know His people were being cruelly treated? Didn't He see what Seti and Ramesses had done with His Hebrews? Oshea said that the Abraham God knew, which was why Mosheh was creating such a disturbance in the Two Lands. Now the Hebrews were preparing to leave, and the pharaoh wouldn't be able to stop them. Orusi didn't understand it, but he'd seen God's power, and it was fearful.

Why did his bad luck suddenly change to good? As he walked through the black air, he'd been certain the Hebrews had already left.

Not only was he surprised to find them there, he wondered if the good fortune came from the Abraham God and not the gods of the land. What would become of him? If the Abraham God was ready to rescue the Hebrews and take them to safety, what would become of Orusi? Could he believe what he'd been told? What if their God didn't take him?

Oshea and Mishael assured him He would, but Orusi was worried. He wasn't sure what the answers to his questions were. What of his son and wife? How safe would they be once it was learned Orusi left for Goshen? Depending on when the departure happened, perhaps no one would ever know. Many guards were killed or injured earlier. Who would know where he'd gone?

Though he left his family when he set out, he still cared about them. His wife could be in danger because of the problems in the city. He told her to stay in the house and not to leave under any circumstances. She would be safe. He no longer loved her, but he didn't wish her harm.

*I won't miss her,* he thought. *We aren't happy together anymore.*

He couldn't speak to her about meaningful things. He couldn't mention his thoughts of the Hebrew God, because she would have reported him to Mi-Sakhme, and he would have been killed. Her bitterness and hate for the Hebrews had already turned him against her. For some time, he was concerned that the Abraham God might be the God his mother told him to look for. But his wife refused to consider that her beloved pharaoh might be wrong about the plagues, regardless of what happened.

*No, I won't miss her, but I'll miss my son.*

He stopped and leaned against a young tree along the path. He sighed, slid down the trunk, and sat on the moist ground. He pulled his legs up to his chest and locked his hands around them as tears rolled down his cheeks.

*How I'll miss my son, but what could I do? I had no choice.*

Orusi couldn't have brought him. His son was in school and wasn't expected home for days even without the black air that came.

When Orusi decided to leave, he knew he'd never have another chance.

He was frightened, confused, and troubled, hoping he'd done the right thing. Mishael told him he could speak with the Abraham God. He said he often went off alone to communicate with Him. That's what Orusi wanted, too.

He stood and resumed walking. Soon he reached the area where the communities of Simeon and Benjamin met. He looked out across an attractive field. The grain was thick, and the field was larger than the others he passed.

He glanced both ways, hoping no one noticed him. He then disappeared into the field. However, Aphlah, the Ruebenite chieftain, and Joseph, his brother's son, sat beneath a tree a short distance away and noticed the tall, black foreigner's strange behavior. They'd been watching him since they saw him come down Simeon's path.

"Shall we follow?" Joseph asked.

"No. We don't know how dangerous he is. Oshea has fooled our leaders again. He shouldn't have allowed this man to enter our congregation. He's probably a spy for the pharaoh.

"We've got him, though. He didn't see us, and we'll stay right here. When he comes out, if his strange behavior continues, you may run to Mishael of Issachar and inform him of this."

\* \* \*

Abiasaph was tense as he walked toward the edge of the Benjaminite community. His chest became tight.

Strange things were happening to him. He wondered what it meant. He no longer felt like his usual self. The things he'd hated for so long now called out to him to believe in them. His life felt different now that he knew the same things Oshea, Elishama, and Hor-em-heb knew.

Why did he want to change? Many others knew the same things, yet they didn't speak of the Almighty One or the deliverance. What made him feel this way?

He nodded as he answered his own questions. Perhaps because he could now sit with Caath and explain the old stories to him. He felt relieved that he'd solved that problem. He would do it that evening. Caath would be shocked when Abiasaph began to tell him the stories. He would wonder where his father learned them so quickly.

Abiasaph smiled, looking ahead to that time with his son. Only a day earlier, he would have thought that impossible. As badly as he wanted to learn those things, he saw no way to accomplish it. He knew the stories now, and he could share them with Caath. That pleased him.

Was that the only reason he felt differently? No. Just that one thing hadn't changed him. He still wasn't a happy Hebrew and felt troubled about his brother, Adbeel. He hated him. The man deserved what happened to him, but he was his brother, too. He was probably in Sheol. Caath and Abiasaph were the only ones of their line left. That wasn't a problem for them, but was it a problem for others in the community? He remembered when he once enjoyed his brother's company. Would he suffer forever?

Then there was Orusi, the Nubian. Was Abiasaph satisfied after hurting the man? He might steal back to his own people. If he did, what would he do to Abiasaph when they met again? Suppose he stayed with the Hebrews? Abiasaph didn't think the man would fight him, but how did he feel about him? He didn't know.

The Levite's steps slowed as he realized the answer to one of his questions.

He knew what it felt like to feel a more complete Hebrew. Knowing the old stories filled a part of him that had been empty, but he never would have thought of it that way.

Suddenly, he stopped. There, ahead of him, by the Simeonite field, was Orusi. Abiasaph edged toward the cover of a small cluster of almond trees. He watched as the man looked around nervously, then darted into the field. Abiasaph watched him slip out of sight.

What should he do? Dare he follow the man? They'd be alone, and if he wanted revenge, he could have it without anyone knowing, though Abiasaph doubted the man would fight.

What would Orusi do if Abiasaph approached him? He might try to defend himself, and they'd end up fighting, anyway. It was difficult to know what to do. Orusi was part of their group now, but he was supposed to stay in Mishael's community. What was he after?

Was he planning something? Someone needed to learn what he was doing.

The scene troubled him greatly. If the Nubian was sincere in what he'd told Oshea and Mishael, there was no reason for him to be in that part of Goshen. He supposedly was staying with Mishael, and Abiasaph doubted Mishael would approve of the way the Nubian was wandering about the community. What was his purpose? Abiasaph didn't know, but every possibility he could think of was bad. Someone needed to know what the Nubian was doing.

Abiasaph knew he was too distracted to make a clear decision at the moment. It wasn't like him to be so confused, and he didn't like it. He needed to choose a course of action and follow it.

His uncertainty and fear finally caused him to make an unwise decision. He walked back onto the path, past the Benjaminite marker, and moved cautiously into the field.

* * *

"Joseph!" Aphiah said softly. "Look there."

"I see. Who is it, Uncle?"

"It's the Levite, Abiasaph. He's the one who tried to kill that soldier yesterday, but Oshea stopped him. Looks like he might finish it now."

"Do you think he'll kill the Kemet guard, Uncle?"

"I'm sorry. I shouldn't have said that. We don't know whether Abiasaph's planning such a thing. It doesn't look good, though, him sneaking into the field after that black man. It could be dangerous."

"What should we do?"

"Nothing. You're a boy, and I'm an old man. We couldn't stop anything from happening. It's important that we remain safe. Your father would never forgive me if anything happened to you. I must keep myself from harm, too. I'm an important man in the community. Many would be crushed if something serious happened to me. As I said before, we'll sit and watch. When they come out, we'll decide what to do."

* * *

Orusi walked leisurely through the golden field, feeling more secure away from prying Hebrew eyes. He picked off ears of grain and dropped them into his mouth, enjoying the crisp, fresh taste. He looked around and saw he was in the center of the field. He looked up into the clear Goshen sky, amazed at the contrast with the black air that covered his old land.

*What magic the Abraham God does,* he thought. *I'm surprised that I took so long to make such a decision.*

Still, he had questions.

He wondered how the Hebrews communicated with their God. Oshea said he spoke with Him often. Mishael said he went off alone to do it. If Orusi spoke aloud, would their God hear him? He wanted to speak about the wrong he'd done to the Hebrews. He didn't know he'd been fighting the Abraham God.

He didn't know what to do about it, or if the Abraham God would listen to him. Was he an enemy? Should he believe Oshea, who said he wasn't? Since he'd brought harm to the Hebrews, would their God be as understanding as Mishael and Oshea? If He allowed Orusi to leave with the Hebrews, what would happen if he tired of them and wanted to return home? What if the Hebrews tired of him? Would their Abraham God protect him? Suppose the troublemakers among them decided to take revenge against him? It was difficult to know if he was doing the right thing.

Orusi felt a desperate need to tell the Abraham God that he was no longer an enemy, but he didn't know how. He thought about the God's obvious power and magic. To fight all the gods of Kemet and show such control as He'd shown in the past year was more power than Orusi had ever seen a god display.

*How merciful is He?* he wondered. *How understanding will He be of my situation? Will He forgive what I have done? I'm frightened of you, Abraham God. More, I'm terrified.*

The tall Nubian lowered his head and went to his knees in the moist earth.

* * *

A few yards away, Orusi was being watched, every move that he made. The man nodded as he saw Orusi go to his knees. He wondered if the black man was praying as he remained slumped on the ground, his head against his chest.

Was he biding his time, waiting for someone, perhaps another soldier? Could they be planning something against the Hebrews? Was he waiting for a woman—a Hebrew woman?

The more he thought of the possibilities, the angrier he became. Neither man moved for several minutes.

Finally, the Hebrew made up his mind and slowly crept closer until he was only three feet behind Orusi.

Orusi sensed the presence behind him. Controlling his panic, he slowly looked to the right and left as far as he could. He saw nothing, took a deep breath, and looked directly behind him. When he saw the man's legs, he froze in fear.

Neither man moved. Orusi slowly looked up into the man's face.

At that moment, the Hebrew pounced, a sharp skinning knife in his hand. As he fell upon the Nubian, he drove the knife deeply into his chest, twisting and turning the blade until the man was dead. He glanced around quickly, then dropped the knife beside the body and ran from the field.

\* \* \*

Aphiah and Joseph waited long enough.

"It's not good, Joseph," the old man said. "We've seen and heard nothing. That's a bad sign. We'll enter the field cautiously."

As they walked forward, however, they saw Abiasaph run from the field. He darted behind some trees and disappeared from view.

The old man and the boy ran into the grain field, suspecting the worst. It took only a few minutes to locate Orusi's body, curled on the ground with a bloody knife beside it.

# CHAPTER TWENTY

# AN EYE FOR AN EYE

"O shea! Oshea!" The heavyset man walked quickly toward Old Abraham's tent. Oshea stepped out to greet him.

"Oshea, there's been trouble again with Abiasaph and that Nubian soldier." He slowed his pace and walked with Oshea to a bench near the tent, where he sat down, breathing heavily.

"Oshea, Abiasaph, the Levite, has killed the Kemet soldier. He stabbed him with a knife."

"What? Are you certain, Mishael?"

"Yes. Aphiah, the Ruebenite chieftain, and his nephew were there, but Abiasaph didn't see them. They didn't actually witness the killing, but they saw Abiasaph sneak into a grain field after Orusi. After a long time, he ran back out and hid himself. The two ran in and found Orusi dead. No one else had entered the field. It's sad, Oshea."

Oshea dropped his head. "Is there any other possibility? Abiasaph was just here this morning, visiting grandfather, and he was very excited when he left. He looked better than I've ever seen before. This is very hard to believe."

"I don't think so. Aphiah and his nephew are certain, and they're the only witnesses." He put an arm around Oshea's shoulder. "I'll call for a court. Will your grandfather preside?"

"I'm sure he will. I'll bring him. Thank you." Oshea rose and walked into the tent.

He saw his grandfather looking up intently.

"Did you hear what Mishael said?" Oshea asked.

The elderly chieftain sipped his milk. "I didn't hear enough to understand. Please inform me."

Oshea repeated the story.

"I find this difficult to believe," Old Abraham said. "The man who listened to me this morning is not a murderer. I'm certain of that. When I saw him, he desired to learn of the Lord. He was an empty well, crying out to be filled. As I spoke to him of our traditions, explaining the story of the Hebrew nation, he was like a calf suckling on its mother.

"The more I spoke, the more he wanted to know. I poured wisdom and information into him, and he never filled up. He is no murderer, Oshea. It would be very strange for such a man to leave here and then decide to kill someone. If what I saw in Abiasaph wasn't honesty and sincerity, he did an excellent job of fooling me, because I still don't believe he could have killed someone.

"This morning, I watched the Lord give understanding to a young man. He was glad to hear about the Lord and His deeds. The heart is only so large, my son. Usually, there isn't room for both goodness and hate. If his hate, because of his son's injuries, was enough to make him willing to commit murder, I didn't detect it. I have to wonder what happened to all the good things that filled his heart this morning. I'd like to see him and see if those things are still there. If not, then...."

"I agree, grandfather. I hope Aphiah's wrong, but it doesn't seem like it. Please allow me to take some men to arrest Abiasaph. I'd like to speak with him."

"Go, but first send Caleb to me. I'd like him to interview Aphiah and his nephew, and I want him to inspect the area. Maybe he'll find something that will help us understand this. If there's more information available, and if anyone can find it, Caleb is that man."

Oshea, doing as his grandfather asked, gathered four men and walked, praying silently, to Abiasaph's hut. When they arrived, Abiasaph was inside his hut alone.

"Abiasaph, please come out," Oshea said.

The Levite walked carefully through the doorway, eyeing the men. Oshea spoke gently but firmly, carrying out his orders.

"Abiasaph, we've been sent to apprehend you and take you to the gateway to stand trial. Do you know why we're here?"

Abiasaph nodded. The glimmer of hope Oshea held onto vanished.

"Why, Abiasaph?" he asked.

The Levite stood quietly staring at him, hearing Oshea's voice echo in his mind.

He said nothing. From the moment he arrived in his tent after leaving Simeon's field, he considered what might happen to him. He knew they'd come, and hearing Oshea's voice outside had been expected. Though he knew how desperate his situation was, it was difficult to know how it would unfold. He knew he'd be arrested and judged. He would probably give his life for that of the Nubian guard, but he didn't know exactly how it would happen.

He hadn't yet thought what the situation would do to Caath or how much he'd miss his son. He wondered how difficult it would be for young Caath to know his father was condemned to death and to watch someone kill him. Suddenly, he saw the magnitude of what was happening.

In moments, he saw his life — sadness as a child, bitterness when his father became a laughingstock, sadness again when his parents died, happiness when he wed Nehushta, extreme happiness to know he'd have a son, sadness again when Nehushta began to carry such pain, and the worst sadness when she died. After that, nothing.

He shook his head, feeling disgusted with himself. He wasn't feeling sorry for himself, just angry at what he'd done. He was sad to know Caath would have to go through what he'd experienced with his own father. At least he wouldn't make a fool of himself as his father had.

He would go on trial for killing the Nubian guard. Then he would be killed, and he'd lose his son. The circle would be complete.

He shook his head again and stared at the ground, thinking of the Almighty One, in whom he had just begun to believe.

*I don't understand this,* he thought. *Is this my punishment, Almighty One, for not believing in You all these years?*

Then the enormity of the circumstances began to affect him. Tears formed in his eyes, but he wouldn't release them, even in his dreadful state.

*You can kill me, Death, but you won't kill my spirit. I refuse to cry. You're no different from the Kemet guards. Do what you must.*

He stepped toward Oshea. "Let's go. I'm ready."

Abiasaph walked with Oshea and the men to the Judaite gate at the center of the encampment, where justice would prevail. Oshea tried to get Abiasaph to talk as they walked, but he had little to say. Abiasaph would remain there under guard of four men of Ephraim for a few hours, until the chieftains gathered to determine his fate.

Abiasaph sat on the ground, surrounded by his guards, and thought of Caath. He would no longer watch his son grow to manhood. He wouldn't be able to instruct him or see him fall in love. Like his father-in-law, Arad, he, too, would never see or know his grandson. Fate arranged a life filled with disappointments for him. The final act of a sorrowful, disappointing, unproductive life was about to be played out. He would die at the hands of those who, only hours earlier, had given him hope and a reason and desire to live.

He'd never sit with Caath and tell him the old stories. Earlier that day, that had been the most important thing in his life. Finally, he could satisfy his son's thirst for knowledge. Caath would be excited to hear those things coming from his father's mouth. The more he considered that, the more he hated himself.

He'd been stupid. There was no reason to enter that field. He should have known it would bring trouble. His instinct told him to go back to his hut, but he allowed his curiosity to win out. Because of his stupidity, he was a dead man, and his death would drain life from his son, too.

He wanted desperately to believe it wasn't happening, but it was no dream. *Is this justice?* he wondered. *How important is the death of one guard, who only hours ago was our enemy, tormenting and beating us? Who knows what was in his heart? He might have been part of a plan to create more trouble for us. He might have been a spy, attempting to learn what was happening in Goshen while Kemet is in darkness. He might have been waiting for a Hebrew woman. Why is his death so important?*

It didn't matter. The court would issue a decision, and it would be final. Mishael would make sure it was carried out. Abiasaph would be killed—an eye for an eye, or a life for a life.

As the elders arrived, Abiasaph realized how quickly the hours had passed. Except for the short time when Caleb came to speak to him, he'd been sitting where he was for almost two hours. Knowing his future, he wished time had passed more slowly, but it was too late. He looked to see who would determine his fate and sentence him to death.

The first man he saw was Mishael, the Issachar elder. He would be the blood avenger against Abiasaph. He'd always been gentle and nice before. The irony wasn't lost on Abiasaph, even in such dire circumstances. He smiled inwardly.

Then he saw Aphiah, the chief of the tribe of Rueben. *Why is he here?* Abiasaph wondered. *Will they allow that selfish madman to sit in this court? I'm doomed. If there was any possibility of hope before, it's gone.*

Uzza, the Levite elder who would speak for Abiasaph, was there, as was Jephunnah, the Judaite. Soon, Old Abraham arrived and called the men together. They took their proper places.

"Men of Israel," Old Abraham began, "this is not a happy time for us. Today, we must make judgment for or against Abiasaph, the Levite. He's accused of killing Orusi, the Nubian soldier, who just recently joined us and lived with the clan of Mishael. He was killed with this knife, found beside his body, in the field of Simeon. Aphiah, here, and Joseph, his brother's son, are witnesses, but not of the actual killing.

"Abiasaph, let me advise you of our law. If you're guilty, you'll be punished. If we find this has been an act caused by enmity, and if it's established that you lay in wait, as you've been accused, then your punishment will be death at the hands of Mishael, the avenger, or of this court, if he chooses not to seek revenge.

"If you're found innocent, you'll go free. There will be no charge against you, and no word will be sent to the community. Our judgment is final and won't be changed. Do you understand?"

Abiasaph nodded.

"Men of Israel, let us begin." Elishama raised his arms to the sky and closed his eyes as he began the proceedings with the proper prayer.

"Almighty One of the heavens, who is our judge, who has given us wisdom and reason that we might judge in Your place, hear us. We stand before you by our law to pass judgment on one of our own, which is also one of Your own, Lord. We seek justice that we wouldn't, without cause, deliver vengeance against our own. Likewise, Lord, we seek justice that we wouldn't allow a transgression like this to go unpunished. We honor You with our decision, Lord, our rescuer from the depths of Sheol. Come quickly for us. So be it."

The men nodded, and the trial began. Aphiah rose and gave his testimony. As was the custom, Uzza, the youngest member of the court, started the interrogation.

"Abiasaph, was not this Orusi, the Nubian guard from Kemet, among the men who beat your son Caath, earlier, at the city work site?"

"Yes."

"Was your anger kindled against him because of that beating?"

Abiasaph hesitated, wondering how to answer. Certainly, he hated the man who'd beaten his son for no reason, but he hadn't thought of going out of his way to find him and satisfy his revenge.

"Let me ask it differently. When you saw Orusi yesterday in Goshen, was your anger kindled against him then?"

"Yes."

"Did you not fight with him to satisfy that revenge?"

"Yes."

His answers were barely audible. He would have preferred not to speak and let them do whatever they planned, but he had to answer.

"So, Abiasaph, Orusi beat your son, Caath. In return, yesterday, you beat the guard. Is that correct?"

"Yes."

"An eye for an eye, Abiasaph?"

"Yes, an eye for an eye."

"So, if you were justified in exacting an eye for an eye, your revenge was full. Is that correct?"

"Yes."

"So, then, you had no reason to kill Orusi, since he hadn't taken Caath's life. Is that correct?"

"Yes."

Uzza wasn't convinced Abiasaph was innocent, but he had the duty of defending him as an elder of his tribe. He wouldn't ask directly if Abiasaph killed the Nubian, because he didn't know what Abiasaph might say. He thought he knew Abiasaph well enough to know he might tell the truth and accept the consequences.

Uzza turned to the other men of the court. "Men of Israel, I don't think Abiasaph is the kind of man who would take a life without reason. He's no lawbreaker. There was no vengeance here, because his vengeance was already full. We must recognize there is another explanation for this death other than what has been claimed. As part of this court's proceedings, I'd like to investigate this incident further to determine if there might be another answer."

Uzza sat, wanting to believe he had impressed the others. Mishael rose, looking at Elishama, not Abiasaph. "Elishama, this Orusi was a fearful man. I warned him not to leave our community, because of what happened between him and Abiasaph. I didn't feel that Abiasaph would attack him again, but there are others in the camp that might cause trouble. Orusi was unable to express himself very well. He doesn't know our language, so he could have gotten into trouble easily. Orusi chose not to follow my advice and left the Ephramite community.

"However fearful Orusi was, his disobedience to my counsel doesn't excuse the one who killed him. I don't think he was looking for a fight. The physician said Orusi didn't struggle with his killer. Whoever killed him must have been lying in wait."

Mishael turned his attention to the solemn Levite. "Abiasaph was it because of your son that you did this thing?"

Abiasaph didn't answer but stared blankly. When it was obvious he wouldn't speak, Elishama intervened.

"Abiasaph, you must answer Mishael."

"I have no answer for that question."

Mishael paused, looked at Old Abraham, shrugged, and sat down. "There's no reason to continue asking questions."

Elishama looked at Jephunnah, but he declined the invitation to question Abiasaph. Elishama began his own questioning.

"Abiasaph, you told me this morning that you were planning to relate the stories of old to your son this evening, correct?"

"Yes."

"Had you changed your mind on that, or were you still planning to do it when Oshea came to bring you here?"

"I had still planned to speak with my son."

The chieftain raised his eyebrows slightly. After a brief pause, he asked, "Abiasaph, is Aphiah's story correct? Did he see you running from the field of Simeon, hiding as you went?"

"Yes."

"Why? Please answer me. Why did you run like that?"

"I was frightened."

"Why were you frightened?"

Abiasaph sighed and turned to look at the men in the circle. It seemed to him their minds were already made up. It showed on their faces, but he answered, because he had to.

"The Nubian was dead. I knew I would be suspected of killing him if I were seen there, so I ran, hoping to reach my hut before anyone saw me. I didn't know Aphiah was nearby."

""Abiasaph, did you kill Orusi, the Nubian?"

"No, Elishama. He was dead when I found him."

Aphiah jumped up and waved his arms. "No! Are you going to allow this man to lie like this? We saw him, Elishama. He's adding transgression to transgression."

Old Abraham raised his hand to silence the chieftain. "Aphiah, you shouldn't need a reminder that you aren't part of this court. You're just a witness, and we've already heard your words. I won't hesitate to have the men of Ephraim remove you if you interrupt again."

He stared at Aphiah for a moment, then turned back to Abiasaph. "If you didn't kill the Nubian, then who did?"

"I can't answer that question."

"Oh? Why not? Do you know who killed the Nubian?"

"I don't know all things. However, I know I didn't kill him."

Elishama rubbed his hands together, wondering how to make sense of such replies. "Was there anyone else in the field with you?"

"Yes."

"Well, then, why didn't you say so? Who was it?"

"I can't answer that, either."

"What? How do you know there was someone else in the field if you can't answer me?"

"Because Orusi didn't kill himself, and I didn't kill him, either."

Old Abraham waited. Inwardly, he smiled at Abiasaph's answers. He knew Abiasaph wasn't trying to be rude, but he had an odd way of answering. Elishama wasn't sure that Abiasaph was helping his case.

"Abiasaph, when you left me this morning, it was my conclusion that nothing was more important to you than to relate the old stories to your son. Am I right?"

"Yes."

"Before the Nubian was killed, what was your thinking on that matter?"

"It was the same, Elishama."

"What's your thinking now?"

Abiasaph paused. "Now I feel like something's been cut out of me. I'm anguished, because I can't do what I planned."

"I see. Please sit. You've stood long enough."

Mishael rose to address the chieftain. "Elishama, I don't understand your questions about the stories of old. What do they have to do with this killing?"

"Murder, my friend, is committed with the heart, not the hands. After the heart has made the decision, then the hands carry it out. If the heart hasn't agreed, the hands can do nothing. Of course, I'm speaking of killing done by one who lies in wait.

"That was why I was interested in knowing the intentions of Abiasaph's heart. Unless there are more questions, we'll hear from Caleb, the Judaite."

Mishael sat.

Caleb entered the court soon after the proceedings began. He stood to address them. "Brothers, I was asked by the honored Elishama to investigate this ungodly act. I began by speaking to Aphiah and Joseph. I also investigated their statement and concluded they were speaking the truth as they saw it.

"Then I discovered things that disturbed me. With Oshea's approval, I brought Abiasaph, along with the guards protecting him, to the field of Simeon to find out where he hid while he watched the Nubian. Indeed, there are footprints in that place that match Abiasaph's sandals perfectly.

"Then I went to where Orusi was killed. Directly behind him were footprints where, I believe, the murderer hid. There I found two unusual things. First, the footprints were larger than Abiasaph's sandals, so it's my conclusion that Abiasaph was, indeed, hiding where he said. It is also my conclusion that it wasn't Abiasaph who hid directly behind the Nubian. That was someone with much larger feet.

"I found it would be very difficult, if not impossible, for Abiasaph to have moved from his hiding place in front of and to the left of Orusi to where the murderer obviously hid without having Orusi see him. He would have passed right in front of him. It is my judgment, Elishama, that it's not conclusive that Abiasaph committed this murder."

Mishael stood. "Elishama, Caleb's testimony is interesting, but if Abiasaph murdered Orusi, wouldn't he tell Caleb he hid someplace other than where the murderer hid? There's no law against someone else walking through that field and leaving fresh footprints, either before the killing or afterward.

"There are many in this community who have sandals that are Abiasaph's size. Caleb's information is interesting and important, but it's not conclusive."

The gathering was very quiet as the men of the court reviewed what they'd just heard. Abiasaph sat uncomfortably in their midst. The crime, his arrest, and trial happened so quickly, he had no time to understand it.

*My life is in their hands,* he thought. *There's nothing I can do about it. I can't persuade them of the truth, and, if I tell them every-*

*thing, they wouldn't believe me. Will Caleb's information sway them? What of Caath? What will happen to him? I hope I made him strong enough to go on without me.*

When he realized he would lose his son, he finally understood how much he loved the boy, but it was too late to make amends.

*Is the Almighty One getting vengeance against me for all the years I hated Him? If so, why have the others things happened? I don't understand. Why'd I spend all that time with Old Abraham only to have this happen?*

"Abiasaph, please relate to me what you did leading up to finding the Nubian," Elishama said.

Abiasaph didn't want to but had little choice. He would rather not discuss it and let them do whatever they wished, just to have it over with. Although his mind said no, his mouth opened, and he began to speak.

"I was walking, Elishama. That's all. I saw the guard go into the field. He was looking strangely, as if hiding something. I followed him in, but I don't know why. Later, I found him dead with a knife beside him. I knew I had to run away, or I'd be suspected of killing him."

"That's all?"

"Yes."

Elishama held up his hand, indicating he wanted to think for a moment before speaking. He would have liked things to be clearer, but he had to come to a decision based on what he knew. Still, he had enough. Without spending time with Abiasaph earlier that day, his decision would have been much more difficult. That time allowed him to know Abiasaph better, and that was vital in making the decision he faced.

Finally, he turned to the men of the court. "Men of Israel, I can't judge Abiasaph for this murder. There are no witnesses to the killing. Though it seems that by what we've been told, he must have done this thing, my heart tells a different story. Caleb's testimony has spread a veil of uncertainty over the situation."

"Elishama," Uzza said, standing, "I'm ready for a count."

Old Abraham looked around. No one disagreed. "Men of Israel, if you are convinced that Abiasaph killed the Nubian, then stand."

Aphiah stood immediately. Mishael rose slowly, paused, and then sat back down. Jephunnah began to rise, then sank down, too, shaking his head toward Old Abraham.

"Elishama," Jephunnah said, "I'm not sure. It appears it can't be another man, but my heart won't allow me to judge this man for the killing."

Uzza and Old Abraham remained seated. After a moment, Elishama said, "We can't judge you, Abiasaph, for we are divided in our thoughts. The Lord has judged you innocent of this wrongdoing. The matter will be laid to rest. Let us stand before the Lord."

The court rose, and Old Abraham adjourned with a prayer. "God of Abraham, Isaac, and Jacob, You've made Your wisdom known to us. We honor You. We're grateful, Lord, that You're preserving Your people at this time. You're the Lord of that great promise made to our fathers. We await You joyfully and anxiously. So be it."

He smiled at the startled Levite. "You're free, Abiasaph. Go as you choose."

Abiasaph was stunned. It hadn't sunk in yet that he'd been judged innocent. He'd been ready to accept death. "Elishama, how did you know I wasn't guilty of this crime? I don't understand."

"My friend, after years of waiting, you decided this morning to tell your son of the traditions of our fathers, to tell him of the Lord whom we serve and for whose coming we patiently wait. You planned to tell him this evening, and I don't believe you would have endangered those plans by devising a trap for the Nubian soldier. I can't make those two thoughts agree. I know how strong the first desire in your heart was—and still is.

"Though I was certain of your innocence, it was important that we have solid evidence to back my thoughts. The information Caleb brought made it much easier.

"With that in mind, and with the agreement of other members of this court, I had to consider that to grant death in this matter, we must agree on several things. We had to prove you were lying in wait, having already decided to kill. We had to agree you did it out of enmity or a feeling of strong hate for the man. There had to be two witnesses who saw the killing. Finally, Mishael, our blood avenger, had to agree.

"We couldn't meet those demands. To satisfy your curiosity further, let's ask Mishael how he feels." He turned toward Mishael. "Have you thought further about avenging Orusi's death?"

Mishael walked over to Abiasaph and clasped his shoulder firmly. "No. I didn't think Abiasaph did such a thing, but I was uncertain in my mind because of the story we heard. It didn't look good for you, Abiasaph, but that will be forgotten now. We must learn who killed the Nubian and bring him to justice in our community."

Abiasaph was overwhelmed. He heard it, but he didn't believe it. He'd been positive the judgment would be against him, yet somehow, justice prevailed.

Aphiah wasn't so certain. He stood, indicating a desire to speak. Elishama nodded.

"Brothers, this isn't right," Aphiah said. "We can't pass judgment based on what we think the man may have wanted to do later tonight. What about the facts that were presented? He was seen there and ran away in clear sight. He had already attempted to kill the man once. Should we not discuss it further and make sure we're of one mind?"

"We are of one mind, Aphiah," Elishama said. "The Lord has given us His desire in this matter, and it's closed." He nodded and smiled toward Abiasaph, letting him know nothing had changed.

Oshea appeared and raised his arm to get Elishama's attention. "Grandfather, I just heard that Mosheh and Aaron are on their way to the tent of elders to meet with the chieftains and tribal elders. All our leaders must attend. They have further instructions for us from the Almighty One. If this trial's over, they want us there immediately."

Abiasaph, free to return home, rose from the center of the circle of men. With his eyes, he silently gave his gratitude to each of them, and he walked to Oshea to tell him the result.

"Praise be to God, the Almighty One of Israel!" Oshea grinned. "I knew even as we brought you here that you hadn't done it. The Lord God of Abraham knew, too, and granted wisdom to grandfather. What excellent news! Now hurry home to your son. He may have heard otherwise and might be fearful."

Abiasaph was glad of Oshea's words. The Almighty had granted Old Abraham wisdom so he would know the truth, even though all circumstances seemed against it. He hoped Caath hadn't heard about the trial. Abiasaph wanted him to hear the news directly from him.

He walked away quickly, feeling a heaviness lift from him. Silently, he thanked the Almighty One for his rescue—the same Almighty One he had hated for so long.

# CHAPTER TWENTY-ONE

# HEROES AND CHAMPIONS

The news of Mosheh and Aaron's upcoming meeting with the chieftains circulated rapidly. Reaction in the camp was varied. Most of the men were excited and anxious, awaiting the latest news. Some were upset and blamed Mosheh for their troubles, while others were steeped in confusion. The meeting made little difference to the latter group.

Isus, the son of Jogli, went off in search of someone to talk with. He knew Mosheh's arrival was important. Tension in the camp had been rising over the past three days. Most of the men knew that having three free days in a row was about the limit of their good fortune. The guards would be back soon, and they wouldn't be happy.

That created much fear and confusion. There were many of the Hebrews who attached importance to everything Mosheh said or did. His coming meant something, and that created a different kind of tension. Isus, however, wasn't sure. He couldn't guess what it all meant, so he forced himself to wait and see.

Abiasaph was cleaning his sheepfold when his neighbor brought him the news about Mosheh, which he had already heard. He said nothing to the Gnat, merely listened, thanked him, and continued working. The Gnat left, able to see Abiasaph wouldn't be much help.

Abiasaph walked to the opening in the fold, set down his tools, and leaned against the gate, wondering what news Mosheh brought.

Only a few days earlier, he would have been angry hearing such news. He might even have joined the Behemoth in speaking out against Mosheh and Aaron. Now he felt differently and was interested in whatever Mosheh had to say.

As he thought about the possibilities, he realized he felt excited. He almost couldn't believe the tremendous change that had taken place in him in such a short time. He'd gone from a bitter, depressed man to a hopeful Hebrew, someone who looked for answers from Mosheh. That was amazing, and it happened over a short span of a few days.

He knew that if such a change hadn't come over him, he might have ended up like his father. He wouldn't have seen it happening, but, since he had changed, it was easy now to see the path he'd been on. He was grateful to Oshea, Libni, Hor-em-heb, and Elishama. They'd all had a part in the change within him. For the first time in his life, Abiasaph was excited about the meeting between Mosheh and the elders.

Picking up his cleaning spade, he returned to work with renewed vigor, eagerly awaiting the sons of Zichri to join him.

\* \* \*

The Gnat found Mugolla-sekh-mugolla sitting quietly by himself along the pathway. The dwarf wasn't full of humor and chatter as he usually was. When the Gnat saw him, he spoke eagerly.

"Mugolla-sekh-mugolla, my wise friend, have you heard about Mosheh coming today to speak to the leaders of my people? What do you think? I've been thinking deeply about it."

Little Beer Man, cocking his head, looked at the slight Hebrew with amusement. He was very disturbed at such news, and he replied sharply, but he also spoke deliberately, knowing the Gnat would cling to each word.

"Yes, I've heard. Your people, Isus, are very ignorant. They aren't considering wise solutions to their misfortunes. When the gods of the Two Lands have finished dealing so strongly with the pharaoh, the ruler of all the land, then will they not also deal kindly with him? What will happen to your people then?

"You're openly making a mockery of a serious time in the shaping of the world. Remember, Isus, that regardless of what you see, the gods shine brightly on Ramesses. Hasn't he recently ventured deeper into the world, conquering nations and expanding his kingdom? Would the gods of the Two Lands turn against him now and destroy him? No. It's a simple matter of understanding the gods and their desires. I, the small, wise one from the south, know the gods. Pay heed, Isus.

"Pharaoh Ramesses, the great ruler of Egypt, hasn't paid satisfactory tribute to the gods. Being a god himself, he's built his name to where it's known and feared throughout the world. The ruling gods are jealous, as they should be. This is their just and wholesome discipline against the god king. It will end soon. When it does, the pharaoh, in all his fury, may well destroy the entire Hebrew people, which you call Israel. Will you blame him? Of course you will. You'll be terrified, cursing the greatest king in all the land, but Ramesses will be just in his actions."

He stared coldly at the Gnat, waiting for a reaction, but Isus was frozen in anticipation, ready to hear more.

"What will the gods do to your prince Mosheh when they've finished dealing with Ramesses? They'll crush him, take the blasphemous words he has spoken against the pharaoh, and cause them to plague the ears of you large-nosed people.

"Your Mosheh desires to be a hero and have stories told about him forever. Even your own people are divided concerning him. You have no heroes. I've heard the stories you tell, but there are no champions in them. They talk about Abraham, but he, like Mosheh, was old and dying before he accomplished anything. What did he do? He had a son! What kind of a hero is that?

"You're a lifeless people. You have no past to be proud of, and you have no future. Your people want a hero, so you chose an old man well past his years. He's no champion. You should have become one with the people of the Two Lands. This land is full of great champions. Pharaoh Ramesses is a champion worth more than anyone in your history. Listen and pay heed, Hebrew man.

"As a young man, the great pharaoh Ramesses, who shall live forever, was given command of the army of his father, Pharaoh Seti. He led his army to great victories over enemies large, stronger, and with greater weapons, even as a boy in his teens. His exploits were so immense, the proud king gave him his own harem even at such a tender age. Every child in school learns of the many adventures of the boy king. I could relate them for days without pause, telling the tales and adventures of our beloved pharaoh, creator of magnificent structures. He won more battles than any pharaoh before him, and, like the renowned Sinuhe, many were fought single-handedly.

"Sinuhe? Who's he? I never heard of him."

"Aha! Sinuhe was a champion that every child of Kemet knows. His is one of the great stories in the history of the Two Lands, a great man who became a traitor to his country, but his true valor, which he never lost, allowed him to become a champion even while he sojourned in a strange country. His great deeds and accomplishments were so outstanding, then became known here, and he eventually returned to a welcoming people as a great warrior and champion."

"Tell me of him. I would like to know his story."

"Of course. Open your ears and your mind. You shall learn from a wise teacher of the Two Lands. Many years ago, the illustrious Sinuhe was an official in the court of the royal family and a favorite of King Amenemhet. During that king's reign, the Two Lands became involved in a great and bloody war. Sinuhe was given charge of a major portion of the king's army and led them to many victories. While he was in command, he received word that the king had been assassinated. In the confusion that followed, different factions warred, and Sinuhe knew, as a great warrior who followed the king, that he would be killed.

"Frightened, he deserted his command and fled across the Nile into the red land far beyond our borders. For a good hero, the story would have ended there, as a tragic end to a great man, but a hero's hero is different. He continues being a hero and champion regardless of the circumstances.

"After Sinuhe fled the Two Lands, he ran out of food and water and nearly starved to death on the desert floor. He was found by a tribe of sand crossers. They helped him regain his health, and, in time, his strength. He became a prince in the foreign tribe and was wisely given command of their army. He led them to victory over other tribes and nations.

"It was said he fought a giant who stood twelve feet tall and slew him in a tortuous battle. His fame was renowned. Merchants and traders who came to the Two Lands told the story of the great desert champion.

"In his old age, he returned to the land of pyramids, those magnificent houses of eternity. Sesostris, the king, heard of his accomplishments and restored him to the court and gave him a place of high honor. The entire land bowed before Sinuhe, and his place is carved in the memory of the Two Lands forever.

"That is a champion of the people. He's not like this Mosheh, who is old and hasn't done anything. I know he was a good commander of the king's army when he was a prince of this land, but his fighting days are over. Even your own people disagree about him. No one bows before him. Instead, they spit on him and revile him. He won't lead your people anywhere, but you refuse to admit it. Instead, you're like a chariot on a rainy day, stuck in the mud and mire, unable to get out. Because of that, you'll all perish.

"Isus, while living in the land of Goshen, I've come to know many of you. Some—let it be known by the mercy of the gods that I say this—are people of worth, not to be compared to the great people of Kemet, but nevertheless, there are people of value among you. It will be a shame when you're all destroyed, turned under like the earth at the touch of the plow. That is what the gods will do when they finish disciplining the pharaoh.

"I know Mosheh is calling your princes together to hear his lies, and you ask me what I think. I wonder who will rule over the land of Goshen. Isus, the one called the Gnat, you Hebrews chose this land well, and it has responded to you. But now, this nation of sheep blindly follows an unseen shepherd who is leading them into death and destruction.

289

"Who will be left but I, the small, wise one from the south, along with some other foreigners and a few people of Kemet? I've already lost my land. Although this new one is disliked, I have adopted it. You mad Hebrews will lose this land, too. You're fortunate I've chosen to speak with you. That's how disturbed I am.

"What will you do, Hebrew man? I can tell you. You'll follow the words of whoever speaks into your ears last."

Mugolla stood and waddled toward the community of foreigners where he lived, mumbling as he went.

"Goshen, you have prospered, but your tenants have lost their minds. What will happen to me? Gods of our great pharaoh Ramesses, what will happen to your Little Deer Man?"

The Gnat watched him go, shaking his head and wondering if he'd just heard the words of a wise man, deceiver, fool, or enemy. Whatever they were, those words greatly affected him. He walked off feeling thoroughly confused and ready to listen to anyone else who wanted to talk.

# CHAPTER TWENTY-TWO

# THE PROMISE IS TRUE

The elders and chieftains gathered in the large tent, awaiting the latest news from Mosheh, their leader. Mosheh and Aaron sat in the front of the group, talking quietly with Elishama and Eldad. Some of the others sat patiently, waiting for the next word from their God. Others talked, though their conversations centered on Mosheh and Aaron and the news they brought.

When Mosheh learned that all had arrived, he motioned for quiet. Aaron stood and spoke to the Hebrew leaders.

"Men of Israel, hear me. The Lord God of Israel, the God of Abraham, has again spoken to my brother, Mosheh. He has given us further instructions to prepare us for our deliverance from this land.

"Mosheh has spoken with Pharaoh Ramesses again. The Lord took him through the darkness and into the pharaoh's court. Ramesses has again refused the Lord's instructions, and the Lord, in turn, has given us our final instructions."

There was a loud, excited murmur that swept through the gathering when they heard the word *final*. Many leaned forward to hear more.

"Today, brothers, is to be the final day of thick darkness that hovers over the land of our enemies. That darkness will leave the land tomorrow, but there will not be a work day under the cruel hand of Pharaoh Ramesses and his taskmasters. When the darkness lifts tomorrow morning, here is what you must do.

"Let everyone in your tribes and clans, including women and children, go to their neighbors in the Two Lands, the red people, the people of Kemet, and receive gifts from them. Tell them you're going into the wilderness to sacrifice at the command of your God, and you've been ordered by Him to receive gifts from them at Mosheh's command. Jewels, gold and silver, bronze platters, and wooden vessels—receive anything they give you. The Lord has assured us we'll find favor with the people of Kemet.

"Many of those people now fear us. They've felt the heavy hand of our God upon them, their families, animals, and land. They'll gladly give you what you ask. They're ready to do anything to remove us from their midst. Take that which you receive from them and pack it away to carry in your wagons and on your beasts of burden we'll be taking from this land. Do nothing else. Do not spend or use the gifts. Pack them away. Do nothing more than what the Lord commands."

The elders and leaders exchanged glances at those words. Mosheh had told them something like that would happen. Excitement stirred through the room. Aaron waited until the noise quieted, then spoke again.

"The Lord said to Mosheh that at midnight on a given day a few days hence, He, the Lord, will go out into the land of Kemet and throughout the Two Lands. He will slay the firstborn of every living thing in the land. Yes, that's correct! The Lord will go unto the land and will slay the firstborn of *every* living thing in the land.

"He will slay the firstborn of the priests and officials, those of peasants and slaves, those of guards and soldiers, and those even of the animals. He will even slay the firstborn of Pharaoh Usimare Setpenre Ramesses."

He spoke the pharaoh's full name to draw out the moment, and the rumbling excitement filtering through the room energized the men. The old Levite raised his hand to gain their attention again.

"We'll see the pharaoh one more time and will tell him of the Lord's judgment in this. Ramesses will again close his ears, but it will be for the last time. Our God has spoken to Mosheh that

His great vengeance against our tormentors has come full turn. He will break their spirit. Ramesses will bow down before us and beg Mosheh to take us, the people of Israel, from his land.

"Our time has come, my brothers. Our God has not been idle, asleep, or forgetful. He has been watching, and He is ready to move swiftly against this land and its rulers."

Aaron stopped speaking, and the Hebrew leaders sang praises to God. They stood and raised their arms, hands outstretched, toward the tent roof, their lips uttering sacred words reserved for such moments.

After some time, the men settled upon their mats. Quiet prevailed, but their smiles seemed etched in stone. They had waited so long for that moment, and they enjoyed it immensely.

"The Lord God of Israel has further instructions," Aaron said. "Listen carefully, brothers. Tomorrow is the tenth day of the month. Let each house of your community choose a lamb, or, if necessary, let two houses share one lamb, so that none will be wasted. It must be a lamb without blemish, a male in its first year, a young one of either your sheep or goats, depending on your herd.

"You shall keep this lamb until the fourteenth day of the month, the day of butchering. Each man of the congregation of Israel shall kill his lamb in the evening of that day.

"Then let each man take a bunch of hyssop, dip it in the lamb's blood, and strike the two side posts and upper door posts of each house wherein the lamb shall be eaten. Let those who are in tents do likewise with the side acacia poles and upper pole. Brothers, let no one go out the door of your house once that blood has been struck until the coming morning.

"Let the whole of Israel on that night eat of the lamb that has been roasted in fire and partake of unleavened bread. Let them eat the lamb with herbs, but only chicory and lettuce and the bitter herbs of the field, for this has been a bitter time of our lives. Let all of the meat be roasted. None shall be eaten raw as the people of Kemet have taught us. Let none be soaked in water, and eat all of it. Let none remain until the morning, including the head and legs. If any can't be eaten, burn it.

"You shall eat this meal in the manner I have said. Gird yourselves and be ready to leave this land. Gird not only your loins, but place sandals on your feet and keep your staff in your hand as you eat. Eat quickly, for this will be the night of the Lord's Passover.

"We will call this night Passover, for the Almighty One will slay all the firstborn in the land, man and animal, but He will pass over every house that has fresh blood sprinkled in the way I told you. Yes, men of Israel, the Lord God of Israel, the God of our father Abraham, Isaac, and Jacob, shall march through this land of desolation with His swordsmen at His side. He shall execute the final judgment against this land, its people, and its powerless gods.

"There will be wailing throughout the land that will deafen your ears, but against us, the children of Israel, who have obediently struck our door posts with the blood of the Passover lamb, there shall be no judgment. The Lord shall pass over us and slay all around us.

"The Lord has further told Mosheh that this day shall be remembered forever by His people. It shall be a feast to be celebrated at the same time each year for generations to come. Every year when this is celebrated, every man of Israel shall tell the story of this great feat to his children."

Aaron paused, caught up in the excitement of the moment. He smiled at the others, and continued.

"Brothers, as you pass on these instructions to those of your charge, be not too hasty with those who are against us. Be patient. Give them time to think and realize that we're preparing to finally depart from this place. Everyone must know the promise is true. We've known and waited patiently for it, but there are many who haven't believed what they've heard. They, too, must know the promise is true. Indeed, the promise is true."

Aaron stopped and looked at Mosheh, who nodded. Slowly, he rose and walked, carrying his staff, a few steps into the midst of the elders and chieftains. When he spoke, his voice was strong, deep, and encouraging.

"Chieftains of the children of Israel, I've contemplated all night on the gracious compassion of our Lord and even more whether we deserve such great compassion. Nevertheless, He does what He promises. Has it not always been that way? Very soon, He'll bring about that which he promised to our father Abraham so many years ago.

"Be in a worshipful mood for the rest of this day. Let us prepare to do His bidding. Fear not to take from the people of Kemet that which you've been commanded. They'll gladly give you all you ask. Has the Lord lied to us yet? No. He will never do so. He's commanded us to receive gifts from our neighbors, and that's what we shall do."

Mosheh relaxed his shoulders and smiled at the leaders crowding the tent. "It's been worth waiting for, my brothers. If you're concerned because of the difficulty in your lives, then I pray you, think of those who lived before us. They slaved throughout their lives and died without seeing this promise. Would your sires, your fathers before you, exchange places with you if they could? Be of courageous mind and cheerful face to those in your command. Relate everything my brother has said.

"Be sure that everyone understands the necessity of taking from our enemies. It's been commanded by the Lord. Appoint a few men from each community to count the number in each house and measure it against the size of the lamb. Those appointed will decide which houses will share in this feast of the Lord's Passover.

"Be sure each understands the sprinkling of the blood. If anyone refuses, for any reason, he will lose the life of his firstborn. There is no time for disagreement, brothers. Those days must be past. The future of Israel and ourselves depends on our obedience to the Lord's instructions.

"We'll go see the madman again tomorrow. Our words will fall on deaf ears, for his heart will still be like stone. Not for long, my brothers. Go now in peace. Be joyful, patient, and understanding."

Mosheh stood silently for a few minutes, a half-smile on his face. The rugged, bearded Levite turned and walked to Elishama and clasped his friend's hand. "You, my friend who waited patiently for so long, who has not wavered in your belief, are this day blessed of God. You will, indeed, see that which your heart has longed for."

Elishama looked into Mosheh's face and felt his heart fill with gratitude. He wondered why he'd been chosen to see that great day when so many others hadn't. A single tear fell from his eye and disappeared into the coarse hair of his beard.

"Mosheh, will you and Aaron join me for a meal of vegetables?" he asked. "I would greatly enjoy your company."

Mosheh nodded. The three men left the tent and walked toward the Ephramite community and Elishama's house.

The meeting was over.

# CHAPTER TWENTY-THREE

# MIRED IN THE MUD

The three Simeonite brothers walked to the sheepfold, greeted Abiasaph and Caath, and began work. Shimri went off by himself to work alone. Abiasaph watched him closely. It was easy to see he wasn't his usual boisterous self. Abiasaph motioned Tebaliah to join him working in the fenced area.

"Why's Shimri so quiet?" he asked. "That's not like him."

"I don't know. He's been like this since earlier this morning. He came back to the house from wherever he was and wouldn't talk to anyone. Father is worse, but Shimri hasn't shown much concern about that, either. It's beyond me. I'd like to think it's because of Father's deteriorating state, but I don't think so. This is very unusual. Maybe we'll know soon. He can't stay withdrawn like this for long. It's very unlike him."

"Your brother is strange sometimes. Knowing Shimri, he'll get over it soon, especially if the Little Beer Man shows up. Are you excited by Mosheh's news?"

Tebaliah looked at him strangely. It wasn't like Abiasaph to speak of Mosheh without fire in his eyes. He knew Abiasaph was one like Shimri who cursed Mosheh and Aaron for their interference in the lives of the Hebrews. They were among the first to blame Mosheh for the increased beatings by the taskmasters, yet Abiasaph had just spoken of the man with an entirely different attitude.

Abiasaph saw an answer might not be forthcoming, so he smiled, leaving the young Simeonite alone. He went into the sheepfold and sent Caath and Shobab out to work with Tebaliah so he could be alone with Shimri. They worked together for a while without speaking, and then Abiasaph asked, "Aren't you even going to say hello? If you're angry, it's not with me, is it?"

"No, no. Can't I be quiet if I wish?"

"Yes, you may be quiet, but allow your ears to be awake. I want to speak to you about something. Earlier, I was walking through the community and came to where the Simeon path meets the one from Benjamin. I was thinking about many things, and suddenly, I saw that black Nubian, the one who beat Caath, who we saw yesterday."

Shimri froze and stared at Abiasaph. "Keep talking. I'm listening."

"He didn't see me, so I hid behind some trees and watched him, wondering what he was doing in the field of Simeon. After a few minutes, he looked around and went into the field, then disappeared. I waited a few moments, then I went after him."

"What? Why'd you go in?"

"I'm not sure. It wasn't a wise decision, but I did it. I didn't see him for a few minutes, and then I found him lying dead on the ground. He'd been stabbed with a knife. What do you think of that?"

"What should I think? If he's dead, he's dead. It's better for us. He didn't belong here. Did you tell anyone?"

"I didn't have to. Aphiah, the Ruebenite chieftain, and a young man who was with him, saw me as I left the field, then went in and found the dead man just like I did. Aphiah went immediately to the elders, and they accused me of murdering the Nubian. The elders set up a court against me, to judge me for killing him."

"What? No! You didn't kill him, Abiasaph! They can't judge you for that!"

"That's true. The court has already met and decided, though, that I was telling the truth. With help from Caleb, they determined that I was innocent. I've been judged free, but that still leaves the question of who killed Orusi."

"Why ask me? Ask the court of judges. Who do they say did it, eh? Have they decided?"

"They don't know, though Caleb and the others are continuing their investigation. Who do you think killed him?"

"Why do you ask? Do I look like a judge?"

"I'm asking, my friend, because you were also in the field of Simeon at that time. I saw you before I found the dead man, but I said nothing to the court. You're my one friend, and the dead man wasn't one of us. What happened in there? Why'd you kill him?"

"Why?" Suddenly outraged, Shimri shouted. "Are you my accuser, Abiasaph? You're my only friend, and you accuse me of killing the guard who has probably killed many of our brothers. Have you been drinking too much wine? Have these free days softened your mind?"

Abiasaph's eyes were very gentle as he looked at his friend. "Shimri, no one in Goshen knows you better than I, not even your family. I know your hatred and how you think. I know that you sometimes act without thinking, and I know how much revenge is in your heart. I accuse you, because I know you killed the Nubian guard. My question isn't if you did it, but why."

The large Simeonite sighed. The secret broken, his tension was relieved, and he relaxed after many hours of strain. He leaned against the wooden gate and spoke slowly and softly.

"Abiasaph, as you know, I've been living with hate inside me for a long time. When I saw the black man yesterday, I would've killed him if I could, had they not pulled me away from him. It wasn't because he was Nubian, black, or even a foreigner. It was because he was a guard who lorded over us and beat us, and he enjoyed it. I didn't set out to kill him. I wasn't looking for him. He came to my community. I didn't go into his.

"I watched him walk along the path, and I hid so he wouldn't see me. I wondered what he was doing there. Maybe he was tricking us and was really working for the guards and soldiers. The story he told Oshea and the rest is nothing but lies.

"I went into the field first and hid, watching him from there. When he came in, I moved away and stood there for a long time, but the longer I was there, the angrier I became, and the more reasons I had to kill him. The more I felt the hatred in me, the more I wanted to release it.

299

"Suddenly, I knew I'd kill him. My body shook with the desire. I knew I must kill him or I'd scream out, then he'd find me and kill me. I didn't know if he had any weapons.

"He's an enemy, Abiasaph. People like him beat, torture, torment, and kill us every day. We're supposed to smile at him and say, 'Come, solider of Kemet, live with us and be rescued?' Bah!

"I'm not sorry for what I did, but I would have been very sorry if you had been judged guilty. I would have come forward and told them I did it. You can be sure of that."

Abiasaph believed him. The two men shared a sense of honor. He put his arm around his friend and squeezed tightly.

"It's finished, Shimri. As I said, I've said nothing to anyone about seeing you in the field, and I won't. We've forgotten it. However, I want to hear your response to something else. I visited Old Abraham this morning, before the killing, and we talked for some time."

"What? What has he to do with you? Are you becoming a Mosheh, my friend? Abiasaph, the rescuer! Where's your staff? Can you turn it into a snake?" He laughed.

"I'm serious. I sat and listened to him for hours. He spoke about the promise and the deliverance. I've thought harder about it than ever before."

"You fool. You sound like Tebaliah. What's the matter with you? Are you losing your strength? Don't fall for those lies. You're too smart for that.

"Abiasaph, you're well known throughout the camp as the one man who has slavery mastered. You didn't fall for Mosheh's tricks before. Why fall for them now? What's happening to you? Do I still know you? Are you still Abiasaph, the Levite with a young son?"

"No, no. Stop your foolish chatter. I haven't changed my thinking that much. I'm still Abiasaph, and I'm not Oshea or Libni, but I'm doing a lot more thinking. I didn't understand the promise the way I do now, and I can't shut it from my mind. That wouldn't be wise.

"Shimri, suppose what they say is true. Suppose the Almighty One *is* coming to rescue us, and it happens soon. What will we do if we aren't ready? You must have heard about the latest message from Mosheh and Aaron."

"I don't listen to such things," Shimri said.

"You should. You can't disagree with something you know nothing about. You can only disagree after you understand it. I, too, refused to hear any of that talk because of my bitterness, but I was wrong. I know what the others know now and can make better decisions. I'm more comfortable in my mind. Some of these things I'm still not sure about, but I know I'll make better decisions.

"Think of this, Shimri. Whether you want to hear Mosheh or not, he's saying we'll leave this land in only five days. It's not like he's saying we'll leave soon. This time, they've given us an exact day. It might not be true, but I'd be a fool if I didn't hear them. If we leave this land, I want to go. Are you saying you don't?"

"I say nothing. Mosheh has given us more trouble than help. Why should I heed whatever he says? You've always been the one who was right. Tomorrow, they'll beat and torture us again, but you've lost your ability to think. I haven't. They might beat me badly, but at least I'll know I killed one myself. I'm satisfied."

"No, you're not. You're unhappy, even miserable. Don't I know you better than anyone? You drown your fears in beer. You've been my friend for years, and I don't want you to deceive yourself. Think, Shimri. If the Almighty One told Abraham about the deliverance four hundred years ago, and he said it would happen in four hundred years, that time has come. Then it's possible it just might happen. With all the plagues we've had, it's possible Mosheh's right. Maybe, as he says, he's been speaking with the Almighty One. You know it's possible."

The Behemoth threw down his tool and walked away to lean on the fence. "Abiasaph, why are you doing this to me? Why are you trying to change me? Do you hate me? I thought you were my friend. I'm satisfied with my life. I drink and feel good. I hate and feel good. I even fight and feel good."

"None of that's true," Abiasaph answered. "You're still deceiving yourself. You need to tell the truth, at least to me. Tell me truly about this promise and what you think of it."

The Behemoth rubbed his hands over his coarse face, and his expression softened, as did his voice. "Abiasaph...I know these things are probably true. I convince myself otherwise, because that's my position. I've already hardened myself against the possibility. If it's true, then it's too late for me. If I change now and talk like Oshea and Tebaliah, I'll become the joke of the camp. The Gnat will be thought wiser than me. I'm not totally convinced that the elders are right. What can I do? I can't change. It's too late for me, much too late. I'm afraid changing is impossible."

"Shimri, you're like the swine of Kemet in a muddy basin. You are where you don't want to be, and you refuse to move. You don't need to change anything or tell anyone anything. All you must do is open your mind to the possibility and prepare yourself in case the Almighty One rescues us. Is that so difficult?"

"Abiasaph, you're the thinker. You'll do what is right. I'm no longer a thinker. I've given up, and it's easier. If I try to change, I'll have to experience the hurt all over again, and I'm tired of it. I'm content hating and drinking. When I drink enough, the hate goes away, and I sing my songs. That's where I want to go right now, too. I'm thirsty."

Before he could leave, Shobab ran into the sheepfold. "Shimri, a message just came from our house! We're to return home immediately. Father's failing fast. We must hurry if we wish to see him still alive."

The Behemoth turned to Abiasaph and shrugged. "You see? Even Father chooses to die at the wrong time. Life wasn't meant to be good to me, and it's keeping that promise. You're right. I'm mired in the mud with the swine. Maybe that's where I belong."

# CHAPTER TWENTY-FOUR

# THE HARD-HEARTED ONE

"**H**ave the magicians come yet?"

There was no answer, and he asked louder, accepting the pain of speaking. "Have they come yet? Answer me!"

Ramesses could barely be heard. Three days in the darkness and its effect on his kingdom angered the proud man more than anything that happened before. His unrelenting wrath had been ready to explode for days. He had screamed and shouted into the darkness from the moment it began, and his voice was almost gone.

"Has Menna returned with the magicians?" he called into the darkness.

"No, Honored One, not yet."

Ramesses tried to speak again but couldn't. He'd lost his voice, but his anger remained strong. The magicians were in the temple dungeon. He'd sent for them earlier to rid him of the latest plague, but they failed to remove it. His earlier magicians had been slain for their inability to fight Mosheh's plagues. The newest ones were little better, but they were the last he had. Destroying them would leave him without any magicians.

He dreaded the times when he couldn't perform his duties. He was a man of great power, and he could unleash it at any time, but he was suddenly powerless.

He wished he could see. Then he would strike Mosheh into the ground. He hated the man.

He'd met Mosheh earlier that day, or at least, he talked to someone who claimed to be Mosheh. How could he know in the blackness? It certainly sounded like Mosheh. How had he gotten into the palace when no one else could move? He said his God made a way for him. If that were true, then why couldn't Ramesses' gods make a way for him?

He'd had his fill of the old Hebrew. He didn't want to see him ever again. His body tensed whenever he thought of Mosheh.

"Argh!" He stood, swinging his fists wildly. His hand struck a nearby table, sending the food he'd ordered earlier to the floor and shattering expensive utensils.

He screamed through gritted teeth, stomped his feet on the marble floor, and stepped away from the security of his throne. His fury couldn't be contained. He was a strong and muscular man and he needed to vent. He needed to lash out.

"Where are my magicians?" he shouted as loudly as he could.

"Menna's coming, Famed One. I hear him. He'll be here in a moment."

As promised, Menna soon arrived with the three magicians. He came close enough to touch his king and let him know he was there.

"Great Pharaoh, it is I, Menna, your faithful servant. The magicians you requested are here with me."

Ramesses wasn't relieved. He didn't expect the magicians to be able to accomplish anything, but he had to defeat Mosheh.

"Magicians, listen carefully before your god. When this plague is finished, your lives won't be spared if you can't perform what I ask. My only demand is for light. If you can't eliminate the plague, as you couldn't yesterday, I must have light to see. Are you so powerless that you can't bring forth a little light into this darkness so I might see and think clearly?"

"Oh, great king, may you live forever," the chief magician said. "Please understand and have mercy upon your servants, the magicians. You've seen that not even torches can bring forth light in this darkness. This is a plague from the God of the Hebrews. He has blocked our power as He did before. We can't perform at all, oh great king. We've tried everything we know, but we have no power against this God."

Ramesses sank into a large, cushioned chair, not surprised by the answer. He'd already guessed that was the case. Much gold, silver, and copper had been spent to purchase the majestic items that adorned his famous palace. Rooms gleamed with lapis lazuli and turquoise. Stairways and throne chairs glistened with expensive, polished, inlaid ivory. Multihued tapestries and brightly painted walls screamed in lavish beauty from every room of the grand house.

Ramesses saw only blackness. His great wealth couldn't answer his dilemma, and his magicians made excuses. He blinked and said quietly, "Kill them. I don't need magicians who can't conjure."

A contingent of soldiers led the screaming magicians away through the darkness to carry out the pharaoh's order.

"Where are the men of wisdom?" he asked. "Where is Tupenthal?"

Immediately, his advisors spoke up, letting the pharaoh know they were nearby.

"Have the men returned that we sent to Mi-Sakhme's house? That was two days ago."

"Yes, honored master. Yesterday, we sent four more to Mi-Sakhme in the event that the others hadn't arrived, but we haven't received a reply. No one has returned. We also sent three contingents of soldiers to the city gate to see what was happening. They haven't returned, either. We sent two groups of men into Goshen to see what the Hebrews are doing. No one has returned, wise pharaoh. We know nothing other than what we have seen and felt here."

Ramesses, not satisfied, cursed loudly, hurting his throat, and swung his arms wildly in anger. "Then how did Mosheh get through the darkness when he came here? Is he greater than all our gods? Why can we do nothing? Why can't we move or see when that old, dying Hebrew can? Answer me!"

No one spoke.

Ramesses sat. He had no answer, either. He didn't want to think about his hated adversary. "Tupenthal, how are the people reacting? Can the peasants handle this plague?"

His chief advisor and trusted friend knew his king well. He didn't want to tell the truth, but lying might mean his life. "Yes, oh great king. There have been some misfortunes, but not many. There are some among us who are rising up against us. They've heard about Mosheh, and they want freedom from the plagues."

"Curse the peasants!" Ramesses retorted. "Send a herald throughout the land. Anyone who's heard speaking against the throne will be taken to the dungeon. Anyone who incites others to rise up against the pharaoh or his rulers will be put to death. That will end this rebelliousness. Do it immediately."

"Yes, oh king, as you say, but I pray you, ruler of the Two Lands, that the people are becoming united in their desire to give Mosheh this three-day journey he has asked for so that our land will once again be holy. Mosheh's god has made a mockery of our gods. The people want peace, oh king."

Ramesses, ranting to himself, didn't hear. "We've heard no reports. None of our messengers have returned. Our magicians are powerless, and our wise men have no wisdom. Can no one tell us what's happening?" He slammed his fist against a cedar table. "Where's the officer you said came with a report from the city? Let us hear him now."

The frightened young officer took a few steps toward the king's voice and related the sad situation throughout Avaris, especially the terrible melee among the guards. Ramesses, listening, thought hard.

He knew Mosheh was smart, perhaps the smartest enemy he'd ever faced. Ramesses had never been defeated, and he wouldn't surrender to Mosheh, either. However, it was clever of the man to slowly turn the people against their king. The people, not smart enough to see through such trickery, were falling into a trap. Didn't they realize that their pharaoh was smarter than any adversary? He won every battle in which he fought, regardless of the odds. Where was their faith in their leader, not to mention their support and loyalty?

Ramesses wasn't prepared for his own people's disloyalty, but he would show them. When he proved victorious again, they would flock to him.

He experienced agony waiting for the situation to turn in his favor. Every day, the possibility of defeat loomed larger, so he fought hard to close his mind to such thoughts.

He had little patience and was unaccustomed to waiting. Whatever he wanted, he got. Whatever he commanded, it was done without question. But for the first time in his life, he had no control over his own destiny, and that took its toll. His uncontrollable anger caused the deaths of many servants and officials in the household.

It was because of the darkness. It was worse than any of the other plagues. He couldn't see, gain information, or converse properly. The darkness had completely eliminated one of his greatest assets — his cold, intimidating stare. Though his subjects didn't dare look into his face, everyone knew of his stare, and it usually worked.

The young officer finished his report. Nothing he'd said helped. The darkness struck three days earlier, and no one was able to gather any worthwhile information. Ramesses' chest tightened, and he felt a sudden sharp pain. He clutched his chest, silently cursing that now he had to endure pain on top of all else. Nothing was going his way.

"Aargghh!" he shouted, astonishing the others in the room.

"Honored Master, I have important news," Menna said.

"Speak."

"Dearest Ruler, one of the handmaidens belonging to your queen has arrived with disturbing news. Please sit, Master, and I'll speak to you about this."

"No! Where is my Nefertari? What is this news? Tell me!" His screaming affected his throat so much, he spat blood. Still, he shouted, "Tell me!"

"My honored ruler, greatest pharaoh of all, this isn't good news. It appears, oh king, that one of the guards has attacked your queen and taken advantage of her in her bedchamber. The palace midwife is with her, and the palace physician is on his way. She appears not to have been hurt physically, but she was intruded upon. Her bed has been defiled."

The pharaoh lurched to his feet, shouting, cursing, kicking, and swinging his arms at anything in his way. The officers of his court, Menna, and all others moved away as quickly as they could. They'd seen Ramesses' rages before and wanted no part of it. The darkness forced them to move blindly, so they fell over each other onto tables, chairs, and statues, creating more noise and injury.

Ramesses was completely out of control. He'd gotten hold of Tupenthal, the eldest of his wise men, and choked him, banging his head against a brick wall while screaming and cursing with the last of his voice and spitting blood everywhere. The others didn't know what he was doing. In his rage, he didn't know he was beating and choking a man he truly loved, one he had already killed.

After many minutes, his ire subsided, and he felt his way around the room until he reached his throne. Exhausted, he slumped into it and regained control of his breathing.

"Menna," he whispered, "bring wine for all of us. We must talk. We must defeat Mosheh. Let us think wisely. We'll devise a plan that will work. The gods will be with us. We can be certain of that. Let us relax over some wine. We'll rest, then we'll be ready to think wisely."

"King, pray that you indulge me, Master, but is there any word to send to your queen?"

"My queen? What about her? She's probably asleep in her rooms. Let her rest. I'll send for her later." He sat quietly for a few minutes. "Has Menna gone? Menna? Are you here?"

Once assured Menna had left for wine, he called, "Tupenthal! Send someone to Nefertari and my son. Look after their comfort. I haven't heard from them in hours. Tupenthal? Do you hear me?"

There was no answer.

"Is anyone with me?"

"Yes, Honored One. Many of us are," someone said. "I don't know about Tupenthal. He hasn't answered. I doubt he would have left without telling you."

The men moved about the room, looking for the elderly advisor.

"Great Pharaoh, there's someone here on the floor," a man said. "I can't tell who it is, but he's not moving. I fear he is dead. The face is older. I believe this is Tupenthal, but he's dead. I don't know what happened. He's covered in blood or a liquid of some kind."

"Quiet!" the pharaoh commanded, realizing he must have killed Tupenthal. He vaguely remembered choking and beating someone earlier, but that seemed like a dream rather than a real event. There had been a lot of confusion. Tupenthal could have died by any number of means. Now Ramesses would have to appoint another advisor.

What had happened to his queen? Hadn't someone mentioned her earlier? Then he remembered. Someone had raped her, although Menna said she wasn't injured. The physician was with her. Who could have done it? Had the man been captured?

"Menna!"

"Yes, Master. I'm here. I sent for your wine. How can I be of further service to you, oh great king?"

"Who defiled the bed of my queen? Which soldier committed this dastardly act?"

Menna tried to answer, but he coughed and spat blood. The darkness was causing terrible hardships for all the people. He forced himself to relax. "I'm afraid, Master, we have yet to find out who committed this act. As soon as the physician has finished with the queen, the palace investigators will speak with her and attempt to learn who it was. We'll interview every soldier on the grounds until we know the answer. When the darkness lifts, we'll resolve the issue quickly. Until then, my king, it will be difficult.

"Curse this darkness! Has anyone examined my son? I ordered that, didn't I? Be about it immediately. I'm awaiting a report."

He wondered why his land was filled with such imbeciles. Was he the only one who could stand up to the pressure? What would have happened to the Two Lands without him? The people owed him their lives. He built the land and conquered the invaders. Now those same ingrates were considering rebellion. He wouldn't let it happen.

Finally, the wine arrived. Menna handed the pharaoh his goblet filled with sweet liquid. Ramesses took a long, slow drink and sat back in his chair, thinking about the years of rebuilding that were wasted because of the plagues.

Where was the justice in it? He was nearly finished with his work, and now this happened. There was still a lot to be done. What would happen if he lost the Hebrew slaves? That would set the project back so far it might never recover. He couldn't let that happen. He had to outsmart Mosheh.

"Where are my advisors and priests?" he called.

"We're all here, oh lord."

"Let us think. We must outwit Mosheh. We can't let the Hebrews leave to perform their sacrifice, because they might never return. We can't endure these terrors much longer, either. Give me your thoughts."

The room fell silent. Minutes passed. Mempa, the oldest of the wise men, spoke cautiously, knowing Ramesses' anger.

"Honored one, this is Mempa. Our gods, oh great king, have been silent for a long time. They'll surely awaken and put Mosheh to shame. We can be certain of that. They have always come to our aid, and they will do so again."

"Enough! I'm ready to put all you advisors away. You speak empty words that do no good. Any peasant can walk into this room and speak as wisely as you. Drink your wine. Speak only if the gods have given you wisdom. I'm not feeling tolerant today, so don't challenge me. Menna, bring more wine."

Ramesses, thinking hard, needed an answer. He knew Mosheh would be back, and he felt he could talk the Hebrew into lifting the darkness. He'd made promises he had no intention of keeping before. Mosheh was very trusting. Ramesses could talk him into it. Of course, he had no concrete plan to offer. He just wanted the terrible darkness to end. Maybe he could satisfy his own people and eliminate Mosheh, too.

"Tomorrow," he whispered, his throat very sore, "bring me Mosheh. Send one hundred or one thousand men if necessary, but bring him to me. Tell him I have relented in my anger toward him. Say I have considered his request to take his people into the desert, and I'd like to speak with him about it."

"Honored one," someone asked, "will you allow the Hebrews to have their day of sacrifice? Won't that mean we've lost power over them?"

"Mempa," a younger sage replied sarcastically, "are you implying we have no control over the Hebrews? It can be argued who is controlling whom. They're slaves under our whips, but we're victims of these terrible plagues, and they sit by and watch us suffer."

"Enough of such talk!" Ramesses snapped. "Shall I have your heads, too? What's the value of keeping you to advise me if I must continually decide for myself what to do while you argue among yourselves, accomplishing nothing? Listen to my plan.

"We'll tell Mosheh he may have his wish. He may take his men into the wilderness to sacrifice to his God, but first, he must release the plague of darkness. That will mean we have the advantage again. He may take the Hebrew women but not the children. Those will remain in Goshen."

"Honored One," Mempa said, "I doubt Mosheh will accept your terms. He's too smart for that. He's wise enough not to leave the children here alone. He doesn't trust you. He has shown that before in previous meetings."

He knew that Ramesses had already made such an offer to Mosheh only to be turned down. He hated reminding the pharaoh of that.

"Well, then, if we must, we'll let the children go, too, but only after he begs. We'll relent, letting him think he's won. We retain all their herds and flocks. We lost our cattle to the plagues, and that will allow us to replenish our herds. The Hebrews can go, but, while they're away, we'll take the best animals from their herds and flocks and hide them for ourselves. Tell Mi-Sakhme. He must know of this. Tell him he can rebuild his stables that way, too."

He thought for a moment and nodded. "That's what we'll do. While they're off having their sacrifice, we'll rob their flocks. When they return, I will kill that old troublemaker myself. He's been a snare to us too long. I'll figure out a way. There will be no more trouble from Mosheh."

"Master," a young sage said, "you forget that Mosheh just refused that offer during his last visit. You're tired, great one. Perhaps you should rest and talk with us later."

Ramesses felt his steward tapping his shoulder. "Yes? What is it?"

"Great King, the six men who were sent to Goshen have returned with bad news. They walked through the darkness all day yesterday, frequently becoming lost, and even finding themselves back here at the temple. They say they walked in circles without understanding how or why. They carefully followed the proper course. They are back, but they are fearful and choose not to speak directly with you, since they have nothing to report."

"Nothing to report! Everyone has nothing to report." He fought to control himself. Nothing would be accomplished with yelling and fighting. He'd made his decision, and it would work.

"Then it's done," he said with finality. The plan has been made. "Amenet," he ordered the captain of his palace guard, "early tomorrow, send one hundred men into Goshen. I don't care how they get there, but be sure that they do. You will personally deliver my message to Mosheh.

"Tell him I've had a change of heart and wish to speak with him concerning his wish to journey into the desert for a sacrifice to his god. Be sure that he comes back with you. Whatever you have to say, go ahead, but bring him with you. Then I'll outwit him with my plan.

"Of course, if the gods remove this darkness beforehand, then do nothing until I instruct you. You may choose to alter the plan if that happens.

"The land won't crumble while I'm pharaoh. Be gone. Allow me to be alone. Menna, bring more wine. Send for Nefertari, but be sure many servants are with my son, so he won't be sad or frightened. Tell him his king looks after him."

After dismissing his court, Ramesses slumped into his chair. Having a course of action made him feel better. He relaxed. He wanted Nefertari with him. She, too, had been expressing her disfavor lately. He would soothe her, and everything would be all right. The land was safe with him as pharaoh. There was no cause for fear.

"I've never lost a battle before," he whispered, "and I won't lose one now."

He closed his eyes and desperately tried to rest.

# CHAPTER TWENTY-FIVE

# POOR ISUS

The Gnat walked back to his hut feeling empty. The new instructions at the meeting clashed with what Mugolla-sekh-mugolla told him earlier. He hadn't accepted everything the little man said, knowing the foreigner was against the Hebrews in almost everything.

He didn't agree with everything Mosheh said, either. He certainly made a strong point. The new orders had a tremendous impact on the Gnat. The other men in the clan seemed to feel the same way. He had to decide what to tell Tirzah. She would demand to know all that the elders said and what the people thought. He didn't want to repeat what the Little Beer Man told him, because it was blasphemous. Isus was still a Hebrew, and he couldn't turn against his people or traditions that easily.

As he reached his house, he stood outside to gather his thoughts. What should he tell Tirzah? She would demand an explanation, because she knew where he'd been. He had to say something. Maybe she didn't know he was back.

He moved away from the opening so she couldn't see him. He understood the elders' thinking. Those ideas were fresh in his mind. Many of the men in the community seemed to believe it would happen as Mosheh said. Isus was willing to believe, too. It was what he wanted to believe. He was proud of being a Hebrew, and he felt better when things went well for him and his nation.

Not everyone agreed, including Mugolla-sekh-mugolla. He had many cruel things to say about Mosheh and his words.

As the Gnat stood outside the door, thinking, Tirzah, much to his dismay, suddenly appeared in the doorway.

"Isus, come in here. Something's happening. I can tell. People are talking everywhere, and you have been, too. Come in and tell me the latest talk."

The Gnat turned slowly and entered the hut. "Would you like something to drink, Tirzah?"

"Yes. Bring me milk with honey. I don't feel well. The physician won't see me. It's horrible what I must go through. Milk with honey would be good for me. Use the large cup you made for me. Everyone is so involved with thinking about what to do, no one cares about those of us who are suffering. What will become of us? Who has made plans? Life's cruel, Isus. Only those who rule live in peace.

"What's the news? I've heard people talking. What's causing all this commotion? Why didn't you come in and tell me right away? You know I have to know things immediately. My life is filled with misery. Don't begrudge me news from the encampment. Where's my milk? What's taking you so long? Are you ignoring me?" she shouted.

He walked slowly into her chamber, staring at her with hate in his heart. He handed her a cup of milk and small platter of mild herbs and bread.

"Were you listening to me?" she asked. "You never listen. You don't care how much I suffer, do you? I want to know what's going on. What is everyone so excited about?"

The Gnat, sitting against the hut wall, pulled his knees to his chin, then wrapped his arms around them and sighed. He hoped he could answer her without creating more confusion in his own mind. "Mosheh brought new instructions to the chieftains. His word is that tomorrow, we must go to our Kemet friends and receive from them all they are willing to give in silver, gold, and precious stones. We're to take them and keep them for the time of our deliverance."

"What? Do they think we're fools? How will you see tomorrow in Kemet to ask anyone anything? It's still black, isn't it?"

"Yes, it is."

"Then how will you see to go into the land? You've heard the stories. People have died from that blackness. Do the elders think we're equally foolish? Are we to go to those who have become our enemies and demand they give us their possessions? The elders must be drunk. Have they spent their free time drinking? Didn't you or anyone else ask about this? How can we go into the land when it's all black?"

"Tirzah, the elders said the darkness will be gone by morning. We'll be able to see throughout the land again. The Almighty One will remove the darkness, and the sun will warm the land. In the light of day, we're supposed to approach our neighbors. That's what they said. I don't know any more, but, if the darkness is gone, we can certainly see our neighbors."

"Isus, Isus, who are the men who decided the darkness will lift tomorrow? Can they force the hand of the gods? If Mosheh is so powerful, why didn't he remove it before? I don't understand. Is there anyone who is wise you talked to? I don't trust our leaders. Look where they led us, into slavery, torment, and misery all our lives. Are we to follow their instructions? What do the people of Kemet say? Have you spoken to any of them?"

The Gnat sighed. He didn't want to relate what Mugolla-sekh-mugolla told him, but he had little choice. He wiped his hand across his face, laid his arms in his lap, and spoke slowly.

"Yes, Tirzah. I spoke to the little exile, the one called Little Beer Man. I'm afraid he has a very bitter attitude. I'm not sure his words were filled with their usual wisdom."

"Well, what did he say? Who are you to decide if his words are wise?"

"He spoke with much anger. We weren't discussing the instructions from Mosheh, however. We didn't know about that when I saw him. He knew Mosheh was back to speak with the elders, and that didn't please him. He knows his lot has been cast with ours, and he feels that when the darkness lifts, Ramesses will come here to destroy us completely for Mosheh's boldness and unwillingness to honor the gods of the land."

315

"He might be right, Isus. This isn't our land. It's the people's land. It's not ours to take from them or even attempt it. We don't have any men who can fight. We have no land. Our fathers had none. We're doomed.

"I said before that if we were willing to peacefully accept whatever the pharaoh and the gods have for us, there would be no killings or beatings. The people haven't treated us so badly. We have plenty to eat and much freedom. We could accept our place here and live honorably, but the Hebrew people, with their foolish leader, won't accept what's best. They constantly fight and argue and are never satisfied. Is it no wonder that our friends in Kemet don't trust us? That's why they kill us.

"How many times have I said we should always be alert for the chance to join with the people and world of Kemet? They live in peace while we suffer."

"Tirzah, there's no peace in Kemet. Their land has been destroyed. Even today, as we enjoy a free day, they're trapped in darkness."

"But what will happen when the darkness leaves? Who has power then? Not us. Pharaoh and his people have power. Don't you think they'll use it?

"Isus, the darkness is temporary, just like all the other plagues. As before, when it passes, our neighbors will be even angrier with us, because we sit here and mock them. They'll kill us. There's no hope with leaders like we have now."

The Gnat realized his wife thought like Abiasaph. "Tirzah, there's more. The elders have proclaimed a feast day on the fourteenth day of the month. We should prepare for it. On that day, we're to take blood from a fresh kill and put it on the doorposts of our houses as a sign. An angel of death is coming from the Almighty One to slay all the people of the land. Only those with the blood on their houses will survive. Then the people of Israel will leave this land and find a new one."

He stood and stretched his arms toward her, palms open. "I'm amazed by such an order. It makes no sense, but most of the men agreed. They believe the Almighty One will deliver us now. That's what they said."

"Isus, Isus." Tirzah shook her head sadly. "I never heard such a ridiculous story. It sounds like something to lull a child to sleep.

"Think for a moment. Suppose we have rain, and the blood is washed away? What would the angel do, kill everyone? The men who tell such stories are mad. Mosheh is a dreamer. I don't trust him. Will the pharaoh allow us to have such a feast? Never. He will probably kill many of our people when the darkness lifts. I can't tell what to do. We need to know what's safest for us. We need to be protected, though we don't know from whom or what."

What could Isus say or do? How could he convince her? She had no loyalty toward her people. All she wanted was her own comfort. The Gnat wasn't like that. He was a Hebrew and proud of it.

He knew, deep in his heart, he would probably do whatever the men did. They would follow Mosheh's instructions, and so would he. However, he would be alert to whatever else was being said or done. Anything could happen. He had to be prepared.

"Tirzah, not only the elders, but most of the men believe the Almighty One will come to rescue us this time. The elders have proclaimed that the time is near. That's why they commanded us to gather gold and silver from our neighbors.

"I've decided to keep a careful eye on everything that's happening in the camp. We want to be one with our tribe and people, so we should follow the instructions, especially if the darkness lifts tomorrow. That would show that the elders' words are true.

"As for the feast, it's still early. We don't need to decide that right now."

Tirzah was deep in thought. Isus knew, however, that he had scored a point. Her silence proved it. The more he thought about it, the more he agreed with himself. That was the best course of action. He would go with the men to gather riches from the neighbors, assuming all would go together.

He felt good about his decision, but his good feelings ended when Tirzah spoke. "No, Isus. We won't go to our neighbors and take goods from them. We might need to be friends with them later. That's a very foolish idea. Let the others go. Who will know if we don't go with them? They'll probably have to turn over all they receive to the elders, anyway."

"Tirzah, the instructions were for us to keep it. What will they say when the time comes, and we have nothing to show?"

"Don't be a fool. Simply say no one gave you anything. Do you really think the people of Kemet will part with their possessions just because we ask? They hate us. We need not participate in that. Let's be wise and stay friends with them. We don't know what tomorrow might bring. The time may come when we have no choice but to remain with our Kemet neighbors, even as servants. That would be better than staying here as slaves."

The Gnat was torn. He didn't know what to do. He didn't want Tirzah upset, but he also feared to separate himself from the rest of the community.

"Tirzah, let's think it over as we sleep. In the morning, we'll see the situation more clearly. Then we can decide. There's plenty of time. We'll do what's best for us and, especially, for you."

He walked to the hut door, wondering if the elders might be right. He looked at the doorposts and tried to envision them covered in blood while an angel with a sword ran through camp, stopping to check each door.

It didn't seem possible. What if it rained as Tirzah said? The blood would be washed off. Once again, it seemed she was right. He wished someone at the meeting had thought of that idea.

He hoped someone would have an answer in the next few days. Then he'd know what to do. In the meantime, he had a lot to worry about. What would he do in the morning? Could he go with the others and not tell Tirzah? What would happen to them if he didn't go? He dreaded that thought.

Of course, if the blackness were still there in the morning, he wouldn't have to worry about going into Kemet. If they went, suppose no one offered them anything? He shook his head. It was painful to be so confused. Why did life have to be so difficult? Why couldn't everyone agree? That would be much easier.

His head hurt, and he wanted to stop thinking. Was there any way to avoid it? He hated the confusion in his mind. It felt like a large bird flying around, looking for someone to attack with its sharp beak. The problem was, he was the only one it attacked.

He walked down the path toward Shimri's house, wanting to sit with him or Little Beer Man and drink beer like they did. That would be a new experience, but he suddenly wanted it very badly.

He would have to listen to them talk, and he wasn't sure he wanted that, because it would bring more confusion. Still, he would like some beer. It would help him forget. He needed to sit, relax, and let his mind be free for a few hours.

The Gnat hadn't drunk beer like others in his community. He had a few sips, but he knew it was a good way to take one's mind off things. That was what he needed. He wanted to sit and drink and not have to think about anything, to have his confusion recede for a while.

That would be good medicine. He promised himself he wouldn't become as drunk as Shimri. Having never been drunk before, he wondered what it was like.

He walked on, rubbing his hands in anticipation, looking forward to getting drink. As he walked, he smiled.

# CHAPTER TWENTY-SIX

# THE FINAL BLESSING

The three brothers sat in the small room, waiting anxiously. Shobab was restless, pacing the dirt floor. Zichri was near death. He'd been dying for months, but the end was near. Mishma, the elder of the clan, was with the old man in his room.

There was so much trouble in the family. Shobab wanted his father to die simply, but it wasn't to be. Even close to death, Zichri was aware of the problems his sons faced. Shimri and Tebaliah had many differences, but the main one was talk of deliverance. Like Tebaliah, Shobab was excited by the recent news. He wasn't sure what to believe, but if it turned out to be true, it would be the most wonderful thing he'd ever experienced. It would be great to leave the land and know he never had to return or be a slave under the pharaoh's whip again. The idea was like a dream. He hoped it was true, but he didn't have Tebaliah's faith.

Shimri was the opposite. His manner had become exceedingly cruel recently even toward members of his family. Many of the older men in camp avoided him, because Shimri always seemed to bring trouble with him. He hated Tebaliah, which saddened Shobab. It hurt him to see such bitterness between brothers. Tebaliah wasn't bitter in return, though. He just ignored Shimri.

As Zichri lay in bed, gasping his last breaths, his sons disagreed about the blessing.

Shimri wanted to forego it. "Let the old man die. Who cares?"

Shobab didn't like seeing his brother like that. He knew Shimri would feel differently if he were sober. To be honest, Shimri didn't really feel that way, but he'd been negative for so long, he couldn't stop himself.

Shobab wanted the bickering to end and have the three brothers live together without fighting. Perhaps that would happen when their father died, but with Shimri's temper and moods, unity might never come.

"Sit down, Shobab!" the Behemoth said loudly. "You'll wear a rut in the floor. Let the old man die and be done with. He doesn't need us in there. He can't see and can barely hear. Let it be over. He has no blessing for us."

The young Simeonite usually listened to his older brother, but Shimri was wrong this time. All Hebrew men eagerly awaited their father's final blessing. Shimri probably didn't want it just because his two brothers did. He was bitter about everything. All he cared about was hoping his father wouldn't realize he was drunk again.

Tebaliah sat quietly in one corner, sad that his father wouldn't live to see the deliverance. He didn't know if his father even believed in it. No one had been able to speak with him for two days. There was nothing he could do about it. His father was as stubborn in death as in life. He wouldn't change at the last minute, even if he knew about the new instructions. That saddened Tebaliah. The man was his father, after all, and he loved him.

Mishma finally emerged from Zichri's room and motioned the sons in quietly. "Your father will speak to you. Come kneel beside his bed."

Suddenly, the Behemoth changed his attitude and was first into the room, eagerly moving to his father's bedside.

The other two sons walked to where their father lay very still on the woven mat. Zichri reached out a hand to touch his sons and ran his fingers over Shimri's face to see who it was. Assured his eldest son was there, Zichri spoke in a voice that was stronger than they'd heard in month, but it was filled with dejection.

"My sons, my time is at hand. My life is finished. It's been hard and cruel, and, even at the end, it has the taste of a bitter, unrefreshing drink. I've earned no more than that. I lived as I lived, and I shall also die that way—in bitterness.

"Tebaliah? Where are you?"

His second son moved closer so Zichri could feel his face. The dying man wanted to make sure his sons sat in the proper order."

"I'm not the first of Simeon's children to die in hatred, nor will I be the last, but I've been to you not a father at all. I could have lived my life better than I did, being a better father to each of you, but I've been what I've been. My life is finished. It's up to you to continue life, but your lives are pitiful, too. We Hebrews are the damned of the earth."

He coughed, and Mishma went to him and laid his hand on the old man's head to calm him. Zichri wasn't to be denied his final words of hatred, though. His coughing subsided, and he took a deep breath.

"My sons, take from this life what you can. At death is nothing but bitterness. A life of slavery leaves no fond memories. Build an army if you can and fight the cursed red men. To slave for the pharaoh every day and sleep with bitterness each night has no gain or worth. What is there to life anymore? Will it be any different for you?"

"Father!" Tebaliah shouted to the nearly deaf man, "we're ready to leave this land in five days. It has been ordered by the Almighty One, and it shall be so. Can you hear me, Father? This is wonderful news."

"Zichri, my father," Shimri said, "you talk like a madman. Tebaliah, you listen like one, too. We must slave under the pharaoh or be killed. We have no choice. We can't raise an army to fight him. We have no weapons. We would all end up dead. You're speaking nonsense. You hate what the Black Land has done to us, and so do I.

"But we can forget, and I enjoy doing that. While Tebaliah deludes himself, believing dreams never end, the rest of us have built a fine, small herd. You can die, Father, knowing that I, your eldest, have done well."

The room was silent. Shobab was startled by his brother's boldness. Tebaliah was merely saddened by the outburst. Zichri slowly raised his arm to get their attention again. He gave no indication he'd heard either of his sons speak.

"I have things yet to say, my sons. Pay heed. I'm filled with anger at the life we live, and I'm also angry with myself. I hate, but I've been wrong. Tebaliah, my son, you might be closer to the truth than any of us."

"Nonsense!" Shimri snapped. "You're not thinking clearly, Father. Tebaliah is weak like a woman and dreams things that will never be. Listen to me. I'm your eldest son. I've seen more things than the other two. Give me your blessing, Father, before you run out of time. I'm the leader of this family. Give me your blessing!"

Zichri raised his arm again but with more difficulty. "I have but little time remaining. I must speak over each of you. Come closer."

"Father," Shimri said more gently, "If you have little time left, give me your blessing that I mighty carry it as your heir."

To their surprise, Zichri seemed to have heard. "No, Shimri, my son. What blessing can I give you? You haven't been a blessing to the others nor to me. My mind sees no good in you and no good for our people. I see only constant slavery under the pharaoh. I have no blessing to give. That would be empty words. There are, however, words I must speak from deep within me. I have words for each of you that aren't mine. Come, that you may hear me. Shimri, let me touch you."

The Behemoth, filled with indignation, reached his hand to his father. Zichri placed it under his thigh, and he spoke with boldness and power, though he had little time left. Mishma and Tebaliah recognized that Zichri was under a power much greater than himself.

"Shimri, son of trouble, you were properly named. You have spit into the eye of the very God Who breathed life into your once-still body. You won't hearken to the voice of those who would lead you into righteousness. You've given up your right to this family, and you and your family will suffer from your indignation.

"Therefore, you and your sons will be swallowed up by the very earth upon which you walk. Your sons after you will die with you because of the rebellious spirit you have planted in them. Your seed will die and be buried in the earth, nevermore to be heard from."

Shimri, yanking his hand from his father's leg, jumped to his feet. "You're an old man, Zichri, my father. You speak without thinking. By the gods, I won't accept this curse!"

He shoved Shobab aside so hard he fell, then Shimri looked at the others, hurt and fear showing on his face. He bolted through the doorway into the cool night air.

Zichri continued as if not noticing the outburst. He raised his arm and called Tebaliah to his side. The crippled Simeonite immediately went to his father and took his hand.

"Here I am, father."

Zichri placed his right hand on Tebaliah's head. "Tebaliah, dipped of the Almighty One. You were named by your mother. She looked into the future and knew how you would believe. You've been immersed in the bowl of righteousness. It will be counted as a blessing to your inheritance. Yea, though your life be short, your seed shall live on and prosper in a new land. Look after my Shobab as if he were your own. I give him to you."

Tebaliah sat motionless, tears streaming down his face. His deepest and most private desire had been heard by the Lord—he would marry and produce a son. He was very grateful, and he wasn't concerned about the prediction of an early death. Due to his worsening condition, he'd already assumed that. Because of that condition, he had also felt he'd never have an heir. He was overcome with joy.

He embraced his father. "Father," he said, emotion showing in his speech, "we were told today that our time of deliverance is nigh. In a few days, we leave this land to receive the inheritance of Abraham. It's coming true as I always said."

Zichri didn't reply and stared at his son. Tebaliah realized the old man couldn't see or hear, and he was so close to death, every second could be his last. He motioned for Shobab.

Mishma helped Tebaliah to his feet. Zichri's coughing worsened. Finally, he controlled himself, although he was very short of breath. Shobab touched his father to let him know he was there. Zichri took his son's hand and followed it to his shoulder and face, running his fingers lightly across the young man's face and head. He placed his hand upon his son's head.

"Shobab," he said with difficulty, "like the leaves that fall from the tree, you move in the direction of the wind. Likewise, my son ..."

He coughed uncontrollably. Mishma and Tebaliah came to his aid but could do little. Zichri paused, then tried to continue. He opened his mouth, only no words came, and he slowly closed his eyes.

The three men looked at each other. Zichri was dead.

Shobab was distraught and lost control. He shook his father's shoulder. "Father! You can't die without completing my blessing. What of my seed?"

He turned and looked pleadingly at Tebaliah. His father was dead, and there would be no blessing. Shobab tried to regain his composure, but he still gripped his father's shoulder tightly without realizing it. Mishma gently pulled him away from the dead man.

"What of my seed?" he asked Tebaliah. "How will I know my blessing?"

"I can't answer you," his brother said, putting his arm around Shobab and holding him tightly. "Father said his words weren't his own. Only the Lord knows what remains for you. Take comfort that at least it wasn't a curse. You face the same situation as many of our people whose fathers died at an early age and couldn't give a blessing to their sons. The Almighty One won't alter His plan concerning you because of this. You know from father's words that even he saw the error of his life.

"Shobab, you must no longer listen to Shimri. He'll lead you into the same pit he has dug for himself. You heard our father's words. If I'm too weak for you to listen to, consult Mishma or Libni. You always liked him.

"Father is dead, and we can do no more for him. Let us tear our clothes and mourn. We must prepare him for burial. We'll mourn the rest of the night. Tomorrow, however, we must follow Mosheh's instructions. Come. We'll be all right."

They walked out of the room arm in arm. Shobab knew he would be safe with Tebaliah. With his father gone, he no longer felt forced to live under Shimri's direction. He didn't know why, but he no longer feared his older brother.

He held onto Tebaliah tightly as they walked, realizing how much he needed that good brother.

*  *  *

Knocking people down as he went, Shimri stormed through the community, searching for the Little Beer Man. He found him near the well of Benjamin, relaxing against a sycamore tree, drinking from his specially designed cup.

"There you are, dwarf! I've come to drink a large quantity of your Black Land beer. I'm feeling mean and angry so don't play word games with me. Speak only if I ask you a question. I just want to sit and drink."

"It's the luck of the gods that you've brought," the little man said. "I planned to come here with only a cup of beer to enjoy alone, but, as I left, I changed my mind and brought two jugs. The beer is excellent today. You will enjoy it."

The Behemoth sat beside Mugolla-sekh-mugolla and took a long drink of the freshly brewed beer. He began to feel lightheaded, and his tense muscles relaxed. He took another long drink and knew everything would be all right.

"Well, little frog, you're right. Today, your beer is excellent. I shall drink much of it, as I have much to forget. This has already eased my pain."

He took another long drink, draining his cup. His companion refilled it and smiled. He thought the two of them were alike. Both were lonely men, able to find solace only in drinking.

"Speak to me now, Little Beer Man. Tell a story of humor that I might drink and laugh and be entertained. Don't spare this evil people of Israel, either. I, too, am tired of them. I only wish I were a foreigner that I might have nothing to do with either the red people or the Hebrews. Curse them all, little frog."

He took another long drink, belched, and said, "Be at it, funny man. Speak of your many gods with their funny names. Tell me a story of your great thievery, filled with your ridiculous lies. It's pleasant to the ears. Be at it. Tell me of your pet hippopotamus or whatever you like, but entertain me. I'm too sad."

He gave a forced laugh, spilling beer down his hairy chest. Rising to the occasion, Mugolla-sekh-mugolla began telling stories of his exploits with the harem women in Mi-Sakhme's house.

# CHAPTER TWENTY-SEVEN

# TEARS OF LOVE

Evening's light stole away. The night sky was in place, creating a stark contrast to the blackness still invading the pharaoh's land. Throughout the camp at Goshen, men prepared for the morning. The thick black curtain over the land would be lifted the following day. Most of the men of Israel didn't know what would happen next.

Many prepared for another day of rebuilding Avaris under the whips of the angry guards and soldiers, who would certainly be more brutal than usual. Those who feared what was to come weren't very happy and didn't rejoice in the news from the elders. They were more concerned with their safety. Like the rest of Goshen, they hoped Mosheh was right, and they'd soon leave for a new land. Recent history, however, indicated that wouldn't happen. If the latest news turned out to be false, too, the situation for the Hebrews would be much worse.

Most Hebrews, however, held onto their hope and leaned toward what the elders said, that there would be no work day in the morning. Instead, they were to go to their closest neighbors in Kemet and be given jewels and other goods. Most of them were apprehensive about it, wondering how it would happen. Many had ideas and plans, and excitement moved through the camp.

If Mosheh's announcement were true, it would be the greatest moment in their lives. The prospect of being lifted from slavery and unhappiness was more than most could comprehend. Much of their conversation revolved around that topic. Excitement and tension ran high.

It was a busy night. Every emotion appeared in the camp that night. Though excitement prevailed, there was also anger, confusion, and apathy. Many arguments came and went. The Hebrew leaders were very busy trying to keep their communities calm, encouraged, and prepared.

* * *

Mugolla-sekh-mugolla reached his square, reed-and-mud house at the edge of the foreigners' community. He went in, sighed, and sat on the cold, damp floor for many minutes, reflecting on the events of the past few days.

All the Hebrew leaders were running around excitedly, actually believing the stupid talk of deliverance. Even those who disagreed with them were affected by it. Only Shimri ignored them.

He looked around the room and saw his brewing utensils sitting idly against the far wall. They were an important part of his life, yet they lay idle and lifeless.

"If the Hebrews leave," he whispered, "you won't be much use to me any longer."

The former Kemet steward poured another cup of the thick beer. He'd already had quite a bit but still felt disenchanted. Beer would help him see the situation more clearly—or help him not care.

Nothing was working to his advantage recently. No one wanted to listen to him. The Hebrews wanted only to discuss Mosheh's ridiculous ideas.

They were being deceived. Nothing Mosheh had said or done could bring them deliverance from their status as slaves. The most recent event wouldn't do it, either, but those dumb sheep couldn't see it. They put all their energy into a false hope.

He couldn't really blame them. They had to have something to look forward to, something he didn't have. He was alone, a foreigner even to other foreigners. He disliked being alone, even though he'd been solitary most of his life. Being a lonely person surrounded by others was different than just being lonely with no one around. He doubted anyone else had ever experienced that.

He knew his beer making and storytelling brought him companionship, but was it really companionship? Did anyone really like him? Did they want to be with him because of who he was, or was it just to drink and be entertained?

What difference did it make? That was his life, a man destined to be one with the Two Lands and a steward in a grand house. Then destiny took a strange turn and made him a foreigner, the lowest of the low, living with the pharaoh's slaves. He couldn't change that, could he? Beer making and storytelling brought companionship, but there was no friendship. Beer making was important to him. That was his way of becoming accepted by the Hebrews. He was good at it, and they knew it.

They also believed they were leaving the land and leaving him behind.

They would miss him. Wherever they went, as soon as they chose to relax and drink beer, they'd miss him, his beer, and his excellent entertainment. Maybe they'd invite him to come.

He shook his head. They wouldn't do that. They were too excited. If it happened the way they were told, they wouldn't even think about him. Where did that leave him?

He wasn't a Hebrew and didn't want to go anywhere with them. He believed in the gods of Kemet and the magic of the sorcerers, but he was no longer part of Kemet, and he would soon no longer be part of Goshen, either.

He was an outcast. He had no family and couldn't remember if he ever had. He supposed he'd have to start all over, but who would remain if the Hebrews left the land? Would any of the foreigners go with them?

He didn't want that. He badly wanted the stories of Mosheh to be lies. He didn't want anyone to leave. Goshen was important to the overall success of the Two Lands. Surely, no one could work that land as well as the Hebrews.

He stood and waddled to the corner of his hut to pick up a long, silver-handled knife before returning to his mat. He turned it over in his hand, set it down, and refilled his cup.

When he was first exiled to Goshen over one year earlier, he almost used that knife to kill himself. He'd been very depressed, but he chose to give himself another chance. He would live with those strange people, who had been his enemies before that.

It was obvious he had accomplished his goal to some degree, but he'd never really been happy in Goshen. He lived best where excitement abounded, so he could use his crafty mind. The Hebrews were nothing but slaves, and they might soon be gone.

He turned the knife over in his hands, looking at it longingly. "Will I ever use you, my friend?" he muttered. "I almost did once. Beer is the answer to loneliness, but you're the answer to sadness."

He patted it like a close friend before setting it aside. "I'll wait until tomorrow. Who knows what tomorrow might bring?"

He shook his large head as he pondered that question. "Will I be here alone? Will I sit with Shimri, drinking beer and telling stories, or will the Hebrews be marched back to the workyards, leaving me alone? If that happens, I know what to do. I'll brew all day and have plenty of beer for the Hebrews when they return.

"Will I awaken and find Goshen empty? Will there be no braying of animals, talking among men and women, and no children running around?"

He picked up the sharp, silver-handled knife and kissed it gently. "Or will you, my gleaming friend, send me off to a land from which I will never return? Will I finally meet the many gods I have believed in? We'll see, my friend."

* * *

Libni and Hor-em-heb walked through the barley fields that hadn't yet been harvested. They were prepared for the coming day and had been ready throughout the time of the plagues. They needed only wait and follow the Lord's instructions through their elders.

They were on their way back to their house to begin a small celebration. Hor-em-heb had announced his desire to be circumcised so he could be a true Hebrew.

"I just had a strange thought," Libni said. "It's a sad one, too. This grain will never be harvested. The people of Kemet, after this great judgment by our God, will be left in confusion for some time. What will become of our fields and gardens? Will the Lord allow this fruit to go to our enemies, or will He destroy it?"

Hor-em-heb pulled off an ear of grain and crunched it between his fingers. "Libni, my dear friend," he said sadly, "my feelings are twofold as I think of going out with my new people. You've been forced to live in this land under bondage, waiting and hoping for the wonderful intervention we're having. I, however, have lived in this land as part of it, freely and without challenge. When I left the glory of the house of Ptah and entered a house with no floor, it was because I wanted to, not because I was forced.

"I'm a Hebrew now, at least in my thoughts. You're my new people, the people of Israel. This has been of my own choosing, something I wanted to do. I won't miss the people of Kemet, the royal house, or the gods. I won't even miss the pharaoh or my siblings. I've turned my back on them to become one of the children of Israel."

He stopped walking, broke off an ear of grain, and stared at it longingly. "But I'll miss this land, Libni. It's part of me, and I'm part of it." He shrugged, forcing a smile for his compassionate friend. "God is giving us a new land, filled with all good things. And that will be my new land, too, Libni."

Libni placed his hand on his friend's shoulder and nodded, then they walked together, filled with thoughts of joy.

\* \* \*

The Behemoth sat against the sheep gate. His legs stretched out in front of him, and his head hung against his chest. He sat that way for a long time, then he suddenly jerked his arm up, knocking over the goatskin half-filled with beer. He sadly watched the beer disappear into the ground.

He wanted to pick up the goatskin, but that was too difficult. He watched beer run over the ground until the goatskin was empty. As he slid onto his back, he called out to the beer.

"Stop!" He knew it would do no good. He waved toward the empty goatskin, showing his disgust at its inability to remain filled, then he slowly pulled himself to more of a sitting position, although it did no good.

He was too drunk to stay seated. He smiled at himself as he slowly slid to a prone position again. He needed something to drink, but his goatskin was empty. He would have to wait for Mugolla-sekh-mugolla.

"Hurry up, dwarf. I'm busy." He thought how funny it was he couldn't sit up, and then he laughed for a long time. He'd never been so drunk.

A few feet away, a still figure lay stretched on the ground, resembling a large cross placed in the middle of the pathway. The Gnat's head lay in a puddle of his own vomit. The smell bothered him, but he couldn't do anything about it. He was startled by the Behemoth's sudden laughter. His eyelids fluttered occasionally, but he couldn't move. That didn't bother him. He could always move in the morning.

He would have preferred a blanket against the cold air. Since he wasn't sure where he was, he didn't know how far away his blanket was. He didn't know how to get it. He could call for Tirzah, but that didn't seem like a good idea. He decided to follow his inner feelings and leave her alone.

He wouldn't worry. In the morning, he would be better and could get his blanket then.

He wondered if he were paralyzed. He couldn't move at all—his legs, arms, or head. He didn't seem to care. His head was dizzy, but he didn't have the pain he usually had. He felt as if he were someone else, looking at himself lying there, except he couldn't see himself. That couldn't be true, anyway. It was confusing. He'd been drinking beer, but he didn't know how much.

Somewhere in the back of his mind was the thought of going on a trip. He couldn't sort it out. His head didn't hurt, although his stomach did. It was hard to think, because he'd been sick most of the time. His stomach churned again.

"Oh, please," he mumbled. "Not again. Please?"

It was too late. As he writhed in pain, the sound of retching reached the Behemoth's ears. Within moments, he was sick, too.

Two young men from the tribe of Benjamin came along. The remark the older one made summed up the situation perfectly.

"What a waste."

*   *   *

Abiasaph purposely waited for that late hour to talk to Caath. The meal was finished and chores were done, so the time was perfect. Caath put Idbash to bed, petting and talking to her. Abiasaph noticed how close his son was to the small animal. That was good for both of them.

Caath sat beside his father, who smiled.

"Caath, today, as you know, Mosheh came to the elders with more instructions for our people. He promised that the darkness over Avaris and the Black Land will be gone by morning. He says we won't go back to the city to work. The Almighty One has told Mosheh that He will deliver the encampment from the land in five days. If only it's true!

"Before we go, we'll have a celebration, a feast. We'll kill a lamb and take the blood and sprinkle it above and beside the door. That's a sign for the Almighty One. While we sleep, He will come through the land and kill the firstborn of anyone whose door isn't sprinkled with lamb's blood—people and animals. Can you imagine what that will be like? I wouldn't want to be near the city when that happens.

"In the morning, we leave with our flocks and possessions to go to a land the Almighty One has prepared for us."

Caath was stunned. That was his father, the man who'd always been against the Almighty One, talking about Him happily and excitedly. Caath's jaw dropped as he stared. His father had changed. He knew about the death of the Nubian guard and how his father was almost judged guilty. Could that have made such a change in him?

"What else, Papa?" he asked.

"Tomorrow morning, we go to our neighbors of Kemet and take from them gold, silver, wood, jewels, or other precious things. We'll take them with us when we leave.

335

"It's said we'll no longer have to be slaves. We're going to a new land, to become a new nation. If it's true, then it truly is a time for celebration."

"Papa, do you really believe those things? Do you believe the Almighty One will take us from the land in five days, and we won't have to work in the city anymore?"

Abiasaph smiled warmly at his son. He'd come too close to losing him, and he had finally realized how important the boy was to him and how he cared for him. He touched Caath's hand, and then slowly returned his hand to his side.

"Caath, I'm trying very hard to do something new. Truthfully, if we awake tomorrow morning and see the darkness is gone, I'll probably expect soldiers to show up. I'm prepared for that. You must be prepared, too, but I hope very much I'm wrong. I want to be wrong this time. If I am, we'll go with the others and gather spoils from the people of Kemet, then we'll prepare the feast the way we were told. We'll eat it girded and ready to leave. Blood will be sprinkled on our doorposts.

"I haven't believed this way before, Caath, but I'm not a fool. The elders and Mosheh are serious about these things. I know they believe.

"So to answer you, no, I can't say I fully believe it'll happen this way. I want to, though. Certainly, I believe now more than ever before. Every day, it seems I come a little closer to believing like Oshea and Elishama. Maybe this time, son, they're right. If so, I will gladly admit I was wrong."

Caath heard the words he'd been longing to hear, but he still couldn't believe it. His own papa? It was too good to be true, but he saw the joy on his father's face.

He didn't know what to do. He sat and stared at Abiasaph, but he felt something dancing inside him. He was excited, happy, and very glad.

"Come, Caath. Let's walk together."

He immediately jumped to his feet. The two Levites went out the doorway, and Caath stopped to look at the doorposts, almost picturing the lamb's blood on them. It was very exciting. He wasn't sure what his father believed, but Caath believed like Oshea. He expected the prophecies to come true just like the elders said. He hoped his father believed that way, too.

They walked down the path to the edge of the community, where the fields began. As they walked side by side, Caath looked up into his father's face and saw things he'd never seen there before.

His father had been bitter and filled with hatred, but he'd been lonely, too. He tried to hide it from others, but Caath knew. Lately, as his understanding matured, Caath felt sorry for his father. In the last few days, he'd finally seen how wrong his father had been.

Then suddenly, everything changed. Caath hoped it was right. It was the first time he'd allowed himself to hope. He hoped with all his might that his father was changing the way he seemed.

"Papa, where are we going?"

Abiasaph slowed his pace and took Caath's hand. He smiled warmly at his son. "I thought we'd go out into the fields and sit awhile. I'd like to tell you some of the old stories about Abraham, Jacob, and Levi, our own father."

Caath stopped in shock. "Papa?" He looked at him but couldn't speak. "Oh, Papa!" Tears poured from his eyes. The young boy had just broken his vow never to cry, but he couldn't help it. He didn't know how his father would react, but he was too overcome with emotion. It was the best day of his whole life.

Abiasaph released Caath's hand and put an arm around his shoulder to pull him close. "It's all right, Caath. You may cry. I think I understand, and my thinking has changed, I guess."

That made Caath cry even harder.

"Come." His father smiled down at him.

They walked farther into the field, Abiasaph holding his son's hand again. Caath felt his father's warmth and strength through the fingers that had molded bricks and built temples against his will for years. His hands had always been strong, but that night, Caath felt a new kind of strength in them.

Caath looked into his father's face. He was older than his years, but he had wisdom, too. There was strength and gentleness in a face that had previously never been gentle. Caath wanted to reach up and kiss that wonderful face.

Suddenly, he realized that the new hope he felt, the wonderful feeling that made him want to jump and shout, the new way his father looked at him, and the way he felt in return, was more than he had ever expected out of life.

He continued crying, tears rolling down his cheeks. He didn't want to talk or do anything else except cry. He thought about Tola, his best friend, and his new lamb, Idbash. As much as he cared about them, he was glad they weren't with them. He wanted it to be just like it was, him and his new papa.

From deep inside Caath came the gentle word *love*. As that wonderful word danced in his mind, he squeezed his father's hand and looked into his face. Abiasaph ran his fingers across the boy's cheeks and felt wet tears of joy.

"I love you, Papa." The sweet word rolled easily from his lips. He looked straight into his father's face and saw in shock as tears formed in his father's eyes.

Abiasaph gripped his son's shoulder gently but firmly as tears rolled down his face to disappear into his stubby beard. "Caath, I love you, too. I love you, too, my son."

All the years of frustration and bitterness broke and dissipated in Abiasaph's heart, and tears poured forth from his eyes. The man and his son held each other and wept unabashedly, releasing each other from a greater bondage than the slavery they'd been in.

After many minutes, Caath lifted his head from Abiasaph's broad chest. "Papa, I'm ready to hear the stories of old."

Abiasaph smiled. The two Levites continued walking just as the setting sun broke through a final cloud and beamed an approving smile onto the land of Goshen.

# Other books by Peter Hess

The Gohan Thriller Series:
Book I – Invisible Hero
Book II – International Intrigue
Book III – Samson and the Banditos

CPSIA information can be obtained at www.ICGtesting.com
Printed in the USA
LVOW052007260612

287753LV00002B/163/A